Nalini Sin

"Breathtaking blend of passion, adventure, and the paranormal."
—Gena Showalter, *New York Times* bestselling author

"A must read for all of my fans. Nalini Singh is a major new talent."
—Christine Feehan, #1 *New York Times* bestselling author

Ilona Andrews

"Splendid . . . Edgy dark fantasy touched with just the right amount of humor." —Patricia Briggs, #1 *New York Times* bestselling author

"Recommend[ed] . . . to fans of Charlaine Harris and Patricia Briggs, and to anyone who enjoys a romantic fairy tale." —*Dear Author*

Sharon Shinn

"Provocative." —Anne McCaffrey

"The most promising and original writer of fantasy to come along since Robin McKinley." —Peter Beagle

Meljean Brook

"I can't resist a book by Meljean Brook!"
—Gena Showalter, *New York Times* bestselling author

"Brilliant, heartbreaking, genre-bending—even, I dare say, epic."
—Marjorie M. Liu, *New York Times* bestselling author

Angels of Darkness

NALINI SINGH

ILONA ANDREWS

SHARON SHINN

MELJEAN BROOK

BERKLEY SENSATION, NEW YORK

THE BERKLEY PUBLISHING GROUP
Published by the Penguin Group
Penguin Group (USA) Inc.
375 Hudson Street, New York, New York 10014, USA
Penguin Group (Canada), 90 Eglinton Avenue East, Suite 700, Toronto, Ontario M4P 2Y3, Canada
(a division of Pearson Penguin Canada Inc.)
Penguin Books Ltd., 80 Strand, London WC2R 0RL, England
Penguin Group Ireland, 25 St. Stephen's Green, Dublin 2, Ireland (a division of Penguin Books Ltd.)
Penguin Group (Australia), 250 Camberwell Road, Camberwell, Victoria 3124, Australia
(a division of Pearson Australia Group Pty. Ltd.)
Penguin Books India Pvt. Ltd., 11 Community Centre, Panchsheel Park, New Delhi—110 017, India
Penguin Group (NZ), 67 Apollo Drive, Rosedale, Auckland 0632, New Zealand
(a division of Pearson New Zealand Ltd.)
Penguin Books (South Africa) (Pty.) Ltd., 24 Sturdee Avenue, Rosebank, Johannesburg 2196,
South Africa

Penguin Books Ltd., Registered Offices: 80 Strand, London WC2R 0RL, England

This book is an original publication of The Berkley Publishing Group.

These stories are works of fiction. Names, characters, places, and incidents either are the product of the authors' imaginations or are used fictitiously, and any resemblance to actual persons, living or dead, business establishments, events, or locales is entirely coincidental. The publisher does not have any control over and does not assume any responsibility for authors or third-party websites or their content.

PRINTING HISTORY
Berkley Sensation trade paperback edition / October 2011

Library of Congress Cataloging-in-Publication Data

Angels of darkness / Nalini Singh . . . [et al.].
    p.   cm.
  ISBN 978-0-425-24312-1
  1. Paranormal romance stories, American.   2. Fantasy fiction, American.   I. Singh, Nalini, 1977–
PS648.F3A66 2011
813'.087660806—dc23

2011024566

PRINTED IN THE UNITED STATES OF AMERICA

10 9 8 7 6 5 4 3 2 1

CONTENTS

Angel's Wolf

Nalini Singh

CHAPTER 1

Noel had been given a promotion in being assigned to the lush green state of Louisiana, but the position was a double-edged sword. Though the area was part of Raphael's territory, the archangel had assigned the day-to-day ruling of it to Nimra, an angel who had lived six hundred years. Nowhere close to Raphael in age, but old enough—even if age alone was not the arbiter of power when it came to the immortal race.

Nimra had more strength in her fine bones than angels twice her age and had ruled this region for eighty years; she'd been considered a power when most of her peers were still working in the courts of their seniors. Hardly surprising when it was said that she had a will of iron and a capacity for cruelty untempered by mercy.

He was no fool. He knew this "promotion" was in truth a silent, cutting statement that he was no longer the man he'd once been— and no longer of use. His hand fisted. The torn and bloodied flesh, the broken bones, the glass that had been driven into his wounds by the servants of a crazed angel, it was all gone courtesy of his vampirism. The only things that remained were the nightmares . . . and the damage within.

Noel didn't see the same man he always had when he looked in the mirror. He saw a victim, someone who had been beaten to a pulp and left to die. They'd taken his eyes, shattered his legs, crushed his fingers until the pieces were pebbles in a sack of flesh. The recovery process had been brutal, had taken every ounce of his will. But if this insulting position was to be his fate, it would've been better not to survive. Before the attack, he'd been on the short list for a senior position in the Tower from which Raphael ruled North America. Now he was a second-tier guard in one of the darkest of courts.

At its center stood Nimra.

Only five feet tall, she had the most delicate of builds. But the angel was no girlish-appearing waif. No, Nimra had curves that had probably led more than one man to his ruin. She also had skin the shade of melted toffee, a glowing complement to the luxuriant warmth of this region she called her own, and tumbling curls that gleamed blue-black against the dark jade of her gown. Those heavy curls cascaded down her back with a playfulness that suited neither her reputation nor the cold heart that had to beat beneath a chest that spoke of sin and seduction, her breasts ripe and almost too full for her frame.

Her eyes slammed into his at that moment, as if she'd sensed his scrutiny. Those eyes, a deep topaz painted with shimmering streaks of amber, were sharp and incisive. And right now, they were focused on him as she walked across the large room she used as her audience chamber, the only sounds the rustle of her wings, the soft caress of her gown against her skin.

She dressed like an angel of old, the quiet elegance of her clothing reminiscent of ancient Greece. He hadn't been born then, but he'd seen the paintings kept in the angelic stronghold that was the Refuge, seen, too, other angels who continued to dress in a way they considered far more regal than the clothing of modern times. None had looked like this—with her gown held up by simple clasps of gold at the shoulders and a thin braided rope of the same color around her waist, Nimra could've been some ancient goddess.

Beautiful.

Powerful.

Lethal.

"Noel," she said and the sound of his name was touched with the whisper of an accent that was of this region, and yet held echoes of other places, other times. "You will attend me." With that, she swept out of the room, her wings a rich, deep brown shot with glittering streaks that echoed the color of her eyes. Arching over her shoulders and stroking down to caress the gleaming wood of the floor, those wings were the only things in his vision as he turned to follow.

The exquisite shade of her wings spoke not of the cold viciousness of a dark court, but of the solid calm of the earth and the trees. That much, at least, wasn't false advertising. Nimra's home was not what he'd been expecting. A sprawling and graceful old lady with soaring ceilings situated on an extensive estate about an hour out of New Orleans, it had a multitude of windows as well as balconies ringing every level. Most had no railing—as befitted the home of a being with wings. The roof, too, had been built with an angel in mind. It sloped, but not at an acute angle, not enough to make it dangerous for landings.

However, notwithstanding the beauty of the house, it was the gardens that made the place. Cascading with blooms both exotic and ordinary, and full of trees gnarled with age alongside newly budding plants, those gardens whispered of peace . . . the kind of place where a broken man might sit, try to find himself again. Except, Noel thought as he followed Nimra up a flight of stairs, he was fairly certain that what he'd lost when he'd been ambushed and then debased until his face was unrecognizable, his body so much meat, was gone forever.

Nimra halted in front of a pair of large wooden doors carved with a filigree of jasmine in bloom, shooting him an expectant look over her shoulder when he stopped behind her. "The doors," she said with what he was certain was a thread of amusement in that voice kissed by the music of the bayou.

Taking care not to brush her wings, he walked around to pull one open. "I apologize." The words came out harsh, his throat unaccustomed to speech these days. "I'm not used to being a—" He cut himself off in midsentence, having no idea what to call himself.

"Come." Nimra continued to walk down the corridor lined with windows that bathed the varnished floors in the molten, languid sunlight of this place that held both the bold, brazen beauty of New Orleans as well as an older, quieter elegance. Each windowsill was set with earth-toned pots that overflowed with the most cheerful, unexpected bursts of color—pansies and wildflowers, daisies and chrysanthemums.

Noel found himself fighting the desire to stroke their petals, feel the velvet softness against his skin. It was an unexpected urge, and it made him pull back, tug his shields even tighter around himself. He couldn't afford to be vulnerable here, in this court where he'd been sent to rot—it wasn't a stretch to believe that everyone was waiting for him to give up on life and complete what his attackers had begun.

His jaw set in a brutal line just as Nimra spoke again. While her tone was rough silk—the kind that spoke of secrets in the bedroom and pleasure that could turn to pain—her words were pragmatic. "We will talk in my chambers."

Those chambers lay beyond another set of wooden doors, these painted with images of exotic birds flitting through blossom-heavy trees. Feminine and pretty, there was nothing in the images that spoke of the hardness that was part of Nimra's reputation, but if Noel knew one thing after his more than two centuries of existence, it was that any being who had lived over half a millennium had long learned to hide what she didn't wish to show.

His guard up, he walked in behind her, closing the painted doors quietly at his back. He didn't know what he'd expected, but it wasn't the graceful white furniture scattered with jewel-toned cushions, the liquid sunlight pouring in through the open French doors, the well-read books set on an end table. The plants, however, were no longer a surprise, and they gave him a sense of freedom even as he stood stifled and imprisoned by his broken self, his pledge of service to Raphael, and thus to Nimra.

Walking to the French doors, Nimra closed them, shutting out the world before she turned to face him once more. "We will speak in privacy."

Noel gave a stiff nod, another thought cutting through his mind with punishing suddenness. Some of the angelic race, old and jaded, found pleasure in taking lovers they could control, treating those lovers like . . . fresh meat, to be used and then discarded. He would never be that, and if Nimra expected it of him . . .

He was a vampire, an almost-immortal who'd had over two hundred years to grow into his power. She might kill him, but he'd draw blood before it was over. "What would you have of me?"

Nimra heard the menace beneath the outwardly polite question and wondered who exactly Raphael had sent her. She'd made some quiet inquiries of a scholar she knew in the Refuge, had learned of the horrific assault Noel had survived, but the man himself remained a mystery. When she'd asked Raphael to tell her more than the bare facts about the vampire he was assigning to her court, he'd said only, "He is loyal and highly capable. He is what you need."

What the archangel had not said was that Noel had eyes of a piercing ice blue filled with so many shadows she could almost touch them, and a face that was hewn out of roughest stone. Not a beautiful man—no, he was too harshly put together for that, but one who would never want for female attention, he was so very, very *male*. From the hard set of his jaw to the deep brown of his hair, to the muscular strength of his body, he drew the eye . . . much as a mountain lion did.

Dressed in blue jeans and a white T-shirt, utterly unlike the formal clothing favored by the other men in her court, he'd nonetheless overshadowed them with the silent intensity of his presence.

Now, he threatened to take over her rooms, his masculine energy a stark counterpoint to the femininity of the furnishings.

It annoyed her that this vampire of not much more than two hundred could inspire such feelings in her, an angel who demanded respect from those twice her age and who had the trust of an archangel. Which was why she said, "Would you give me anything I asked?" in a tone laced with power.

White lines bracketed his lips. "I'll be no one's slave."

Nimra blinked, realization swift and dark. It did her vanity no good to see that he believed she had to force her lovers, but she knew enough of her own kind to understand the thought wasn't unwarranted. However, the fact that it had been the first one in his mind . . . No, she thought, surely Raphael would have warned her if Noel had been misused in that way. Then again, the archangel who held enough power in his body to level cities and burn empires was a law unto himself. She could assume nothing.

"Slavery," she said, turning to another set of doors, "offers no challenges. I have never understood the allure."

As he followed at her back, she had the sense of having a great beast on a leash—and that beast wasn't at all happy with the situation. Intriguing, even if it did prick at her temper that there was so much power in him, this vampire Raphael had sent in response to her request. That, of course, was the crux of it—Noel was Raphael's man, and Raphael did not suffer the weak.

Once inside the chamber, she nodded at him to close the door behind himself. She wouldn't have thought to take such measures even a month ago, she'd had such trust in her people. Now . . . The pain was one she'd had to live with for the past fourteen days, and it had become no easier to bear in that time.

Walking past the smooth and well-loved wooden desk situated beside the large window, a place where she often sat to write her personal correspondence, she lifted her hands to unlock the upper doors of the armoire against the wall. The curling tendrils of a fine fern brushed the backs of her hands, a whispered caress as she revealed—set into the back wall of the armoire—the door to what appeared to be a simple safe, but one no burglar would ever be able to crack.

Retrieving a tiny vial half-filled with a luminescent fluid from within, she turned and said, "Do you know what this is?" to the man who stood immobile as stone several feet from her.

A shuttered expression but there was no discounting the intelligence in that penetrating gaze. "I haven't seen anything like it before."

So beautiful, she thought, watching the colors tumble and foam within the vial when she tilted it to the light, the crystal itself etched only with a simple sigil, signifying her name, and thin decorative lines in fine gold. "That is because this fluid is beyond rare," she murmured, "created from the extract of a plant found in the deepest, most impenetrable part of Borneo's rain forests." Closing the distance between them, she held it out toward him.

The vial looked ridiculously small in his big hand, a toy stolen from a crying child. Lifting it to his eyes, he tilted it with care. The fluid spread on the crystal, making the surface glow. "What is it?"

"Midnight." Taking the vial when he returned it, she placed it on her writing desk. "A hint of it will kill a human, a fraction more will place a vampire into a coma, and a quarter of an ounce is enough to ensure most angels of less than eight hundred will not wake for ten long hours."

Noel's gaze crashed into hers. "So your intended victim doesn't stand the smallest chance."

She was unsurprised by his conclusion—it was nothing less than could be expected, given her reputation. "I have had this for three hundred years. It was gifted to me by a friend who thought I might one day have need of it." Her lips lifted at the corners at the thought of the angel who had given her this most lethal of weapons—as a human older brother might give his sister a knife or a gun. "He has ever seen me as fragile."

* * *

Noel thought this friend couldn't know her well. Nimra might look as if she'd break under the slightest pressure, but she didn't hold Louisiana against all the other powers in the wider region, including the brutal Nazarach, by being a wilting lily. Not being as blind, he never took his eyes off her, even when she picked up the vial and returned it to the safe, her wings so exquisite and inviting in front of him.

Their tactile beauty was a trap, a lure to the unwary to drop their guard. Noel had never been that innocent—and after the events in the Refuge . . . If there had been any innocence left in him, it was long dead.

"Two weeks ago," Nimra murmured, closing the armoire doors and turning to face him once more, "someone attempted to use Midnight on me."

CHAPTER 2

Noel sucked in a breath. "Did they succeed?"

The relief that rushed through him when she shook her head was a ravaging storm. He'd been helpless in the Refuge, bound and trapped as pieces of glass and metal were shoved into his very flesh until that flesh grew over it, trapping the excruciating shards of pain—and though he had no loyalty to Nimra except through his ties to Raphael, he didn't want to think of her with her spirit broken and her wings crumpled. "How did you escape?"

"The poison was placed into a glass of iced tea," she said, shifting to touch her finger to the glossy leaf of a plant by the writing desk. "It is tasteless and colorless once blended with any other liquid, so I wouldn't have noticed it, had no reason to consider that anything in my home might be unsafe for me. But I had a cat, Queen." Her breath caught for a fragment of a second, sharp and brittle. "She jumped up onto the table when I wasn't watching and sipped at the drink. She was dead before I even had a chance to scold her for her misbehavior."

Noel knew the sorrow that marked Nimra's face was, in all probability, an attempt to manipulate his emotions, but still he found himself liking her better for being saddened by the death of her pet. "I'm sorry."

A slight incline of her head, a regal acknowledgment. "I had the tea tested without alerting anyone in this court, discovered it held Midnight." Smooth honey brown skin stretched tight over the line of her jaw. "If the assassin had succeeded, I would have been insensible for hours—and those who knew of my incapacitated state could have come in and ensured full death."

Angels were as close to immortal as was possible in this world. The only beings more powerful were the Cadre of Ten, the archangels who ruled the world. Unless they pissed off one of the Cadre, death wasn't something angels had to worry about except in very limited circumstances—depending on the years they'd lived and their inherent power.

Noel didn't know Nimra's level of power but he knew that if someone were to decapitate a strong angel, remove his or her organs, including the brain, then burn everything, it was unlikely the angel would survive. Unlikely but not impossible. Noel had no way of knowing the truth of it, but it was said angels of a certain age and strength could regenerate from the ashes of a normal fire.

"Or worse," he added softly, because while death might be the ultimate goal, many of the oldest immortals lived only for the pain and suffering of others, as if their capacity for gentler emotions had been corroded away long ago. He could well imagine what someone like Nazarach would do to Nimra if he had her alone and vulnerable.

"Yes." She turned to the windows beyond that little writing desk—formed with a daintiness that would crumble under one of Noel's fists—her gaze on the wild beauty of the gardens below. "Only those who are trusted enough to be in my inner court, and carefully vetted servants, are ever anywhere near my food."

"Because of this act of treachery, I can no longer trust men and women who have been with me for decades, if not centuries." Calm, tempered words sliced with anger. "Midnight is near impossible to acquire, even for angels—which means the one who betrayed me is working in the service of someone who holds considerable power."

Noel felt a spark within him, one he'd thought had been extinguished in that blood-soaked room where his abductors had brutalized him for no reason except that it gave them a twisted kind of pleasure. They might have justified the act by calling it a political ploy, but he'd heard their laughter, felt the black that stained their souls. "Why are you telling me this?"

An arch look over her shoulder. "I do not need a slave, Noel"—his name carried a slight French emphasis that turned it into something exotic—"but I do need someone whose loyalty is beyond question. Raphael says you are that man."

He had not been cast aside after all.

It was a shock to the system, a jolt that brought him to life when he'd been the walking dead for so long. "You're certain it's one of your people?" he asked, his blood pumping in hard pulses through his veins.

Her answer was oblique and it held a quiet, thrumming anger. "There were no strangers in my home the day the Midnight was used." Her wings flared out, blocking the light as she continued to focus beyond the windows. "They are mine, but one has been tainted."

"You're six hundred years old," Noel said, knowing she saw nothing of the gardens at that instant. "You can force them to speak the truth."

"I cannot bend wills," she said, surprising him with the straight answer. "That has never been one of my gifts—and torturing my entire court to unearth one traitor seems a trifle extreme."

He thought he heard a dark amusement beneath the anger, but with her face turned to the window, her profile shadowed by the tumble of those blue-black curls, he couldn't tell for sure. "Do they know why I'm here?"

Shaking her head, Nimra turned to him once more, her expression betraying nothing, the flawless mask of an immortal. "It is probable they believe the very thing you did—that Raphael has sent you to me because you are broken and I need a toy." A lifted eyebrow.

He felt as if he'd been called to the carpet. "My apologies, Lady Nimra."

"Do attempt to sound a fraction more sincere"—a cool order—"or this deception will fail miserably."

"I'm afraid I'll never be able to pull off being a poodle."

To his shock, she laughed, the sound a husky feminine stroke across his senses. "Very well," she said, eyes glittering with gemstone brightness in the sunlight. "You may be a wolf on a long leash."

Noel was startled to feel a different kind of heat within him, a slow-burning ember, dark and potent. Since waking in the Medica, his body destroyed, he'd felt no desire, had thought that part of him dead. But Nimra's laugh made his body stir enough that he noticed. It was tempting to follow that flicker of heat, to hold the ember up to the light of day, but he didn't allow her laugh or the exquisite caress of her femininity to wipe the truth from his mind—that the angel with the jewel-dusted wings was deadly. And that while she might be in the right in this particular game, she was no innocent.

He heard screams that night. The nightmare always surprised him, though he'd been having it since he opened his eyes in the Medica after the assault. Because the fact was, he'd lost the ability to scream several hours into the torture, remaining conscious only because his attackers had made it a point to never cross that fine line. Broken bones, torn flesh, excruciating burns—vampires could take a lot of damage without the escape of the cold dark of unconsciousness.

He didn't remember screaming even at the start, determined not to give in, but he must have—for the echo of it haunted his dreams. Or perhaps the screams rang inside his mind because that was the sole place he'd had that had been his own, his strength, his dignity stripped from him with malicious force.

Throwing off the sweat-soaked sheets as he shoved away the memories, he got out of bed and walked to the window he'd left open to the honeysuckle-scented air. The heavy warmth of it stroked over his cheeks, fingered its way through his hair, but did nothing to cool his overheated flesh. Still, he lingered, staring out into the inky dark of the night and the slumbering silhouettes of the gardens and trees that sprawled out in every direction.

It was perhaps twenty minutes later, right when he was about to turn away, that he glimpsed wings. They weren't Nimra's. Frowning, he angled himself so as to be invisible from the ground and watched. The angel appeared out of the shadows a minute later and stopped, his face lifted up toward Nimra's window—a long, motionless moment—before he carried on.

Interesting.

Pushing away from the window when there was no further movement, Noel walked into the shower, realizing he'd glimpsed the tall male in the audience chamber earlier. The angel had stood on Nimra's right as she dealt with a number of important petitions, so there was no doubting the fact that he was one of her inner circle. Noel intended to find out everything else about him later today.

It was still dark when he walked out of the shower, but he knew there was no point in attempting to sleep now—and as a vampire, he could go without sleep for long periods. Part of him didn't know why he even tried to find such rest. Even on the nights when he didn't hear the screams, he heard the laughter.

Nimra walked out into the gardens the next morning to find that Noel had beaten her to the dawn. He sat on a wrought-iron bench beneath the branches of an old cypress, his eyes on the clear waters of the stream that snaked through her lands before joining a wider tributary that led into the bayou. He was so motionless, he appeared carved from the same stone as the silken moss-covered rocks that guarded the waterway.

She stepped quietly, intending to take the path that would skirt away from him, for she understood the value of silence, but he lifted his head at that instant. Even with the distance between them, she was caught by the wintry blue of those eyes—eyes she knew had been destroyed in the attack at the Refuge, his face beaten in with such viciousness he'd only been recognized because of a ring worn on a shattered finger.

Anger, cold and dangerous, slid through her veins, but she kept her tone easy. "*Bonjour,* Noel." Her wings brushed the curling white and pink flowers of the wild azalea bushes on either side of her, and the dew showered a welcome caress on her feathers.

He rose to his feet, a big man who moved with predatory grace. "You wake early, Lady Nimra."

And you, Nimra thought, *do not sleep.* "Walk with me."

"A command?"

Definitely a wolf. "A request."

He fell into step beside her, and they walked in silence through the rows of flowers nodding sleepily in the hazy early morning light, their petals seeking the red-orange rays of the rising sun. It was her habit to spread her wings when she was outdoors thus, but she kept them folded today, maintaining a small distance between her and this vampire who was so very contained, she couldn't help but wonder what lay beneath the surface.

A plaintive meow had her bending to look under the hedgerow. "There you are, Mimosa." She plucked the elderly cat out from under the dark green shade of a plant dotted with bursts of tiny yellow flowers. "What are you doing awake and about so very early?" The gray cat, her fur sprinkled with white, nuzzled at her chin before settling down in her arms for another nap.

She was aware of Noel glancing at her as she stroked her hand over Mimosa's fur, but said nothing. Like a wounded animal, he would not react well to pressure. He would have to come to her—if he ever did—in his own time, at his own pace.

"Those tufted ears," he said at last, looking at the comical puffs that tipped Mimosa's otherwise neat head. "That's why you call her Mimosa."

It made her smile that he'd guessed. "Yes—and because the first time I saw her, she was standing near a mimosa plant, snapping her paw out at the leaves, then jumping back as they closed." In the process, she'd managed to get several of the fluffy dandelion-like flowers on her head, a tiny crown.

"How many pets do you have?"

She rubbed Mimosa's back, felt the old cat purr against her ribs. "Just Mimosa now. She misses Queen, though Queen used to tire her out with her antics, she was so young."

Noel wasn't used to seeing angels acting in any way human. Yet Nimra, her arms full of that ancient feline, appeared very much so. "Would you like me to hold her?"

"No. Mimosa weighs far less than she should—it's only her fur that makes her appear so." Her face was solemn in the hushed secrecy of dawn. "Grief has put her off her food, and she has lived so many years already . . ."

It was instinct to reach out, to rub his finger along the top of the cat's head. "She's been with you a long time."

"Two decades," Nimra said. "I don't know where she came from. She looked up from her game with the mimosa plant that day and decided I was hers." A slow smile that blew the embers within him to darker, hotter life. "She has ever accompanied me on my morning walks since then, though now the cold bothers her."

The gentle care in those words went against everything he'd heard of Nimra. She was feared by vampires and angels across the country. Even the most aggressive angels stayed clear of Nimra's territory— when to all outward appearances, her powers were nothing compared to many of theirs. Which made Noel wonder exactly how much of what he saw before him was the truth, and how much a well-practiced illusion.

She lifted her head at that moment and the soft gold of the rising sun touched her face, lit up those topaz eyes, so bright and luminous. "This is my favorite time of day, when everything is still full of promise."

Around him, the gardens began to stir to life as the sky became ablaze with streaks of deep orange and a pink so dark it was almost crimson, and in front of him stood a beautiful woman with wings of jewel-dusted brown. A man could surrender to such a moment . . . but the very strength of that allure made him take a step back, remind himself of the cold, hard facts behind his presence here. "Is there anyone you suspect of being the traitor?"

Nimra didn't protest the sudden change in the direction of the conversation. "I cannot bring myself to suspect any of my own of such an act." Her hand moved over the slumbering cat in her arms, slow and with an endless patience. "It is worse than a knife in the dark, for at least then I would have a shadow to focus on. This . . . I do not like it, Noel."

Something about the way she said his name curled around him, a subtle magic that had his shields slamming shut. Perhaps this was Nimra's power—the ability to entice people into believing whatever she wished them to believe. The idea of it made his jaw go tight, every cell in his body on alert for the danger he was certain lurked behind the delicate bones of that exquisite face.

As if she'd heard his thoughts, she shook her head. "Such mistrust." It was a murmur. "Such age in your eyes, as if you have lived far more centuries than I know you to have done."

Noel said nothing.

Soft ebony curls glimmered with deepest blue in the dawn sunlight as she continued to pet Mimosa. "I will formally introduce you to my people this—"

"I'd prefer to meet them on my own."

One eyebrow rose at the interruption, the first hint of true arrogance he'd seen. It was strangely comforting. Angels of Nimra's age and strength were used to power, used to being in control. He'd have

been more suspicious if she'd taken the interruption and disagree-
ment with the unruffled tranquillity she'd shown to date.

"Why?" The demand of an immortal who held a territory in an
iron grip.

But Noel had found his way again after months in the impenetrable darkness, would allow no one to push him off course. "If there
is a traitor, it makes no sense to alienate your entire court," he
reminded her. "Which will happen very quickly if you make it a
point to introduce your new . . . amusement to them all."

She continued to watch him with eyes full of power.

Perhaps other men might've been intimidated, but, illusion or
truth, Noel was fascinated by the layers of her. "Are your people truly
dim enough," he said, "to accept that story once you make it clear I
have value to you?"

Nimra's hand stilled on her pet's fur. "Take care, Noel," she said
in a quiet voice that hummed with the reality of the strength contained within her small frame. "I have not held this land by allowing anyone to walk over me."

"That," he said, holding a gaze gone stormy with warning, "is
not something I ever doubted." Never did he forget that behind her
delicate build and feminine beauty lay an immortal who was said
to be so cruel that she caused bone-chilling terror in even those of
her own kind.

CHAPTER 3

The first person Noel met when he stepped into the huge room at the front of the house was a tall, dark-eyed, dark-haired angel who had the look of arrogance Noel associated with angels beyond a certain level of power—but with an edge of condescension thrown in for flavor. "Christian," the angel said, his wings a soft white with a few sharp threads of black . . . the same wings Noel had seen from his bedroom window earlier that morning.

Nodding, he said, "Noel," and held out his hand.

Christian ignored it. "You're new to the court." A smile as serrated as a saw blade. "I hear you come to us from the Refuge."

Noel didn't miss the unspoken message—Christian knew what had been done to him, and the angel would use that knowledge to twist the knife deeper when he wished. "Yes." He smiled, as if he hadn't caught either the warning, or the implicit threat. "Nimra's court isn't what I expected." There was no overt opulence, no miasma of fear.

"Don't be taken in," Christian said, his eyes as hard as diamonds though his facade of arctic politeness never slipped. "There is a reason the others fear her teeth."

Noel rocked back lazily on his heels. "Been bitten?"

The angel's wings spread a fraction, then snapped tight. "Insolence will only be tolerated so long as you warm her bed."

"Then I better warm it for a long time." Noel shot him a cocky grin, figuring he might as well play the part to the hilt.

"Is Christian giving you a hard time?" The question came from a long-legged female dressed in a tight black knee-length skirt and white shirt that flattered a slender figure with graceful curves. Paired with those legs and uptilted eyes of a deep impossible turquoise against sun-golden skin, it made her a stunner. Not an angel, but a vampire old enough that immortality had worked its magic on what had surely been a spectacular canvas to begin with.

Noel deepened his smile in response to her flirtatious wink. "I think I can handle Christian," he said, holding out his hand once again. "I'm Noel."

"Asirani." Her fingers closed over his own. He allowed it but he felt nothing. He'd felt nothing ever since he'd been taken . . . except for that odd, unexpected ember of sensation stirred awake by Nimra's laugh.

Releasing Asirani's hand, he looked from the vampire to the angel. "So, tell me about this court."

Christian ignored him, while Asirani twined an arm through his own and led him across the huge central room that appeared to function as the audience chamber when necessary, but was otherwise the center of the court. "Have you eaten?" Thick black lashes lifted, turquoise eyes looking meaningfully into his.

"I'm afraid Lady Nimra doesn't like to share," he murmured, thinking of the sealed bags of blood that had been left in the small fridge in his room. "I thank you for the offer." Whatever her motive, it had been a considerate question.

Fact was, taking blood from a human or vampiric donor wasn't something he'd had any inclination to do since waking from the assault. The head healer at the Medica, Keir, had been very good about providing him with stored blood without question. Maybe

Nimra's courtesy, too, was as a result of Keir's influence. The healer seemed to command a great deal of respect from angelkind—even the archangels themselves.

"Hmm." Asirani squeezed his arm, her fingers brushing his biceps. "You are a surprising choice."

"Am I?"

A throaty laugh. "Ah, cleverer than you look, aren't you?" Eyes dancing, she stopped beside a window, her face to the room. "Nimra," she said in a low tone, "has not taken a lover for many years. Christian always believed that when she chose to break her fast, it would be with him."

Noel glanced over at the angel, who was now talking to an older human male, and found himself wondering why Nimra hadn't invited Christian to her bed. In spite of the appearance he gave of being a stuffy aristocrat, the man was clearly sharply intelligent, and he moved in a way that said he'd had training in how to fight. No useless fop, but an asset.

As Asirani was no vacant hanger-on.

"Do you all live here?" he asked her, intrigued that this court appeared to be made up of the strong.

"Some of us have rooms here, but Nimra maintains a wing that is hers alone." Leading him to the long table set with food to the side of the room, she released his arm to pluck a plump grape from an assortment of fruit and pop it into her mouth. Though vampires couldn't gain the nourishment they needed from food, they could digest and appreciate the taste—Asirani's hum of pleasure made it plain she enjoyed utilizing every one of her senses.

Noel had no interest in such sensuality, but he was moving to pick up a couple of blueberries so as not to stand out, when the hairs rose on the back of his neck. Not fear, but an instinctive, primal awareness. He wasn't the least surprised to turn around to discover that Nimra had entered the room. The others receded from his consciousness, his eyes locking with the power and intensity of her own.

"Excuse me," he murmured to Asirani, crossing the gleaming wood of the floor to come to a halt in front of the angel who was proving to be an irresistible enigma. "My lady."

Her gaze was impenetrable. "I see you have met Asirani."

"And Christian."

A slight tightening of her mouth. "I do not think you have met Fen. Come."

She led him toward the elderly human man Noel had seen with Christian. He sat surrounded by papers at a desk in a sun-drenched corner of the room. As they neared him, it became clear the man was even older than Noel had first guessed, his nut-brown skin lined with countless wrinkles. Yet his eyes were dark little pebbles, shiny with life, his lips mobile. They lifted in a smile as Nimra got closer, and Noel realized the man's eyesight was deteriorating in spite of the flashing brightness of his gaze.

Nimra stopped him with a hand on his shoulder when he began to struggle to his feet. "How many times must I tell you, Fen? You've earned the right to sit in my presence." A smile so vibrant, it cut at Noel's heart. "In fact, you've earned the right to dance naked in my presence should you so wish."

The old man laughed, his voice cracked with age. "That would be a sight, eh, my lady?" Squeezing her hand, he looked up at Noel. "Have you let a man make an honest woman of you at last?"

Leaning forward, Nimra kissed Fen on both cheeks, her wings brushing inadvertently against Noel. "You are my only love, you know that."

Fen's laughter segued into a deep smile, his fingers lighting on Nimra's cheek before dropping to the desk once more. "I am a blessed man indeed."

Noel could almost feel the history that ran between the two of them, but no matter their words, there was nothing loverlike in that richness of memory. There was instead an almost father-daughter element to it, in spite of the fact that Nimra remained immortally young, while the march of time had caught up with Fen.

Rising to her full height, Nimra said, "This is Noel," before returning her attention to Fen. "He is my guest."

"Is that what they're calling it these days?" Twinkling eyes shifted to give Noel a closer inspection. "He isn't as pretty as Christian."

"Somehow," Noel muttered, "I think I'll survive."

The riposte caused Fen to laugh in that hacking old-man way. "I like this one, Nimra. You should keep him."

"We shall see," Nimra said, a tart bite to her words. "As we both know, people are not always who they appear to be."

Something unseen passed between the angel and the aged human at that instant, with Fen raising Nimra's hand to his lips and pressing a kiss to the back. "Sometimes, they are more." Fen's eyes lifted for a bare instant to snap across Noel's and he had the feeling the words were meant for him rather than the angel whose hand Fen still held.

Then Asirani click-clacked into his vision on sky-high heels and the moment broke. "My lady," the vampire said to Nimra, "Augustus is here and insisting he speak with you."

Nimra's expression turned dark. "He's beginning to try my patience." Folding back her wings tight to her spine, she nodded good-bye to Fen and strode off without a word to Noel, Asirani by her side.

Fen nudged at Noel with a cane he hadn't seen until that moment. "Perhaps not quite what you expected, eh?"

Noel raised an eyebrow. "If you mean the arrogance, I'm well versed in it. I worked with Raphael's Seven." The vampires and angels in service to the archangel were powerful immortals in their own right. Dmitri, the leader of the Seven, was stronger than a large number of angels; he could take and hold a territory if he so chose.

"But," Fen insisted, lips curved in a shrewd smile, "have you experienced it in a woman? In a lover?"

"Blindness has never been one of my faults." The bitter irony of his words made him laugh within. After the assault, he hadn't even had eyes for the days it had taken his flesh to regenerate. "It's not yours, either, though it looks to me as if you prefer to give the appearance of it." He'd seen the way the old man's gaze had turned dull when Asirani neared.

"Smart, too." Fen waved him to a chair across from his own. Taking it, Noel braced his forearm on the gleaming cherrywood of the desk and looked out at the vast main area. Christian was deep in conversation with another woman, a curvaceous beauty with long, straight hair to the base of her spine and the most guileless face Noel had ever seen. "Who's that?" he asked, having guessed what role Fen played in Nimra's court.

The old man's expression softened to utter tenderness. "My daughter, Amariyah." Smiling at her when she turned to wave at him, he sighed. "She was Made at twenty-seven. It does my heart good to know that she'll live on long after I'm gone."

Vampirism did turn humans into almost-immortals, but the life was hardly an easy one, especially the first hundred years after the Making, when the vampire was in service to an angel. The century-long Contract was the price the angels demanded for the gift of being able to live long past the span of a mortal life. "How much of her Contract remains?"

"None," Fen said, to Noel's surprise.

"Unless you had her before you were born," Noel said, continuing to watch Amariyah and Christian, "that's impossible."

"Even I'm not that efficient." A phlegmy laugh. "I've been in service to Nimra since I was a lad of but twenty. Mariyah was born a year later. Been some sixty-five years that I've served my lady—the Contract was written to take that into account."

Noel had never heard of such a concession. That the angel who ruled New Orleans and its surrounds had done this said a great deal about both Fen's worth to her, and her own capacity for loyalty. It wasn't a trait he'd expected to find in an angel known far and wide for the harshness of her punishments. "Your daughter is beautiful," he said, but his mind was on another woman, one with wings that had lain so warm and heavy against him for a fleeting moment earlier.

Fen sighed. "Yes, too beautiful. And too sweet a soul. I wouldn't have permitted her to be Made if Nimra hadn't vowed to care for her."

Amariyah broke off her conversation at that instant to walk over. "Papa," she said and, unlike the echoes of another continent that flavored her father's speech, the bayou ran dark and languid in her voice, "you did not eat your breakfast today. Do you think you can fool your Amariyah?"

"Ach, girl. You're embarrassing me in front of my new friend."

Amariyah held out her hand. "Good morning, Noel. You are quite the topic of conversation in this court."

Shaking that hand, with its skin several shades lighter than her father's, Noel gave what he hoped was an easy smile. "All good, I'm sure."

Fen's daughter shook her head, the dimples that dented her cheeks making her appear even more innocent. "I'm afraid not. Christian is, as my grandmother would've said, 'very put out.' Excuse me a moment." Bustling over to the sideboard, she filled a plate before returning. "You will eat, Papa, or I will tell Lady Nimra."

Fen grumbled but Noel could see he was pleased at the attention. Rising, Noel waved a hand at his seat. "I think your father would prefer your company to mine."

Amariyah dimpled again. "Thank you, Noel. If you need anything in the court, let me know." Walking with him a few steps, she smiled again, and this time there was nothing guileless about it. "My father likes to see me as an innocent," she murmured in a low voice, "and so I am one for him. But I am a woman grown." With that unsubtle message, she was gone.

Frowning, Noel went to leave the audience chamber, skirting a young maid walking in with a fresh carafe of coffee. Then again . . . Turning, he walked back to snag a cup off a small side table. "May I beg a cup?" he asked, making sure to keep his voice gentle.

Her cheeks colored a pretty red, but she poured for him with steady hands.

"Thank you."

Nodding, she dropped her head and headed to the main table, placing the carafe on the surface. No one paid her any mind, and—their potential complicity in the attempted assassination aside—it made Noel wonder just how much the servants heard, how much they remembered.

Nimra stared at Augustus across the length of the small formal library where she handled her day-to-day affairs. "You know I won't change my mind," she said, "and still you insist."

The big man, his skin a gleaming dark mahogany, snapped out wings of a deep russet streaked with white, his arms folded across his massive chest. "You are a woman, Nimra," he boomed. "It's unnatural that you should be this alone."

Other female angels would've done something nasty to Augustus by now. Theirs was not a society where men alone held power. The most powerful of the archangels was Lijuan, and she was very much a woman. Or had been. No one knew what she'd become since her "evolution."

It was Nimra's cross to bear that Augustus was a childhood friend, less than two decades older than her. Nothing in the scheme of things, given the length of angelic lives. "Friendship," she said to Augustus, "will only get you so far."

The idiot male smiled that huge smile that always made her feel as if the sun had come out. "I would treat you as a queen." Dropping his arms and folding back his wings, he moved across the room. "You know I am no Eitriel."

Her heart pulsed into a hard knot of pain at the sound of that name. So many years now, and yet the bruise remained. She no longer missed Eitriel, but she missed what he'd stolen from her, hated the scars he'd left behind. "Be that as it may," she said, stepping nimbly to the side when Augustus would have taken her into his arms, "my mind is made up. I have no wish to tie my life to a man's again."

"Then what am I?" came a rough male voice from the doorway. "A meaningless diversion?"

CHAPTER 4

Startled, Nimra looked up to meet the frigid blue gaze of a vampire who shouldn't have been there.

"Who," Augustus roared at the same time, "is he?!"

"The man Nimra has chosen," Noel said with what she knew was deliberate disrespect in his tone.

Augustus's massive hands fisted. "I'm going to break your scrawny neck, bloodsucker."

"Make sure you rip it off or I'll regenerate," Noel drawled back, settling his body into a combative stance.

"Enough." Nimra had no idea what Noel thought he was doing, but they'd deal with that after she sorted out the problem of Augustus. "Noel is my guest," she said to the other angel, "and so are you. If you can't behave like a civilized being, the door is right there."

Augustus actually growled at her, betraying the years he'd spent as a warrior in Titus's court, conquering and pillaging. "I waited for you, and you throw me over for a pretty-boy vampire?"

Nimra knew she should have been angered but all she felt was an exasperated affection. "Do you really think I don't know about the harem of dancing girls you keep in that castle of yours?"

He had the grace to bow his head a fraction. "None of them are you."

"The past is past," she whispered, placing a hand on his chest and rising up on tiptoe to press a kiss to his jaw. "Eitriel was a friend to us both, and he betrayed us both. You do not have to pay the penance."

His arms came around her, solid and strong. "You are not penance, Nimra."

"But I am not your lodestar, either." She brushed a hand down the primaries of his right wing. It was a familiar caress, but not an intimate one. "Go home, Augustus. Your women will be pining for you."

Grumbling, he glared at Noel. "Put a bruise on her heart and I'll turn your entire body into a bruise." With that, he was gone.

Noel stared after the angel until he disappeared from sight. "Who is Eitriel?"

Nimra's gaze glittered with anger when it slammed into his. "That is none of your concern." The door to the library banged shut in a display of cold temper. "You are here for one purpose only."

Very carefully worded, Noel thought, watching as she walked to the sliding doors that led out into the gardens and pushed them open. Anyone listening would come to the obvious conclusion.

"As I said, Noel," Nimra continued, "take care you do not go too far. I am not a maiden for you to protect."

Stepping out into the gardens with her, he said nothing until they came to the edge of the stream that ran through her land, the water cool and clear. "No," he agreed, knowing he'd crossed a line. Yet he couldn't form an apology—because he wasn't sorry he'd intervened. "You have an interesting court," he said instead when he was certain they were alone, the scent of honeysuckle heavy in the air, though he couldn't see any evidence of the vine.

"Do I?" Tone still touched with the frost of power, Nimra sat down on the same wrought-iron bench he'd used earlier, her wings spread out behind her, strands of topaz shimmering in the sunlight.

"Fen is your eyes and ears and has been for a long time," he said, "while Amariyah was only Made because it soothes his heart to know that she'll live even after he is gone."

Nimra's response had nothing to do with his conclusions. "Noel. Understand this. I can never appear weak."

"Understood." Weakness could get her killed. "However, there's no weakness in having a wolf by your side."

"So long as that wolf does not aspire to seize the reins."

"This wolf has no such desire." Going down on his haunches, he played a river-smoothed pebble over and through his fingers as he returned to the topic of Fen and Amariyah. "Are you always so kind to your court?"

"Fen has earned far more than he has ever asked," Nimra said, wondering if Noel was truly capable of being her wolf without grasping for power. "I will miss him terribly when he is gone." She could see she'd surprised Noel with her confession. Angels, especially those old and powerful enough to hold territories, were not meant to be creatures of emotion, of heart.

"Who will you miss when they are gone?" she asked, deeply curious about what lay behind the hard shield of his personality. "Do you have human acquaintances and friends?" She didn't expect him to answer, so when he did, she had to hide her own surprise. Only decades of experience made that possible—Eitriel had left her with that, if nothing else.

"I was born on an English moor," he said, his voice shifting to betray the faintest trace of an accent from times long gone.

She found it fascinating. "When were you Made?" she asked. "You were older." Vampires did age, but so slowly that the changes were imperceptible. The lines of maturity on Noel's face came from his human lifetime.

"Thirty-two," he said, his eyes on a plump bumblebee as it buzzed over to the dewberry shrub heavy with fruit on Nimra's right. "I thought I had another life in front of me, but when I found that road cut off, I decided what the hell, I might as well attempt to become a Candidate. I never expected to be chosen on the first attempt."

Nimra angled her head, conscious that angels would've fought to claim him for their courts, this male with both strength and intelligence. "This other life, did it involve a woman?"

"Doesn't it always?" There was no bitterness in his words. "She chose another, and I wanted no one else. After I was Made, I watched over her and her children and somewhere along the way, I became a friend rather than a former lover. Her descendants call me Uncle. I mourn them when they pass."

Nimra thought of the wild windswept beauty of the land where he'd been born, found it fit him to perfection. "Do they still live on the moors?"

A nod, his hair shining in the sunlight. "They are a proud lot, prouder yet of the land they call their own."

"And you?"

"The moor takes ahold of your soul," he said, the rhythms of his homeland dark and rich in his voice. "I return when it calls to me."

Compelled by the glimpse into his past, this complex man, she found her wings unfolding even farther, the Louisiana sun a warm caress across her feathers. "Why does your accent disappear in normal conversation?"

A shrug. "I've spent many, many years away from the moors, but for visits here and there." Dropping the stone, he rose to his feet, six feet plus of tall, muscled male with an expression that was suddenly all business. "Fen, Asirani, Christian, and Amariyah," he said. "Are they the only ones who have access to you on that intimate a level?"

"There is one other," she said, aware the moment was over. "Exeter is an angel who has been with me for over a century. He prefers to spend his time in his room in the western wing, going over his scholarly books."

"Will he be at dinner?"

"I'll ask him to attend." It was difficult to think of sweet, absentminded Exeter wanting to cause her harm. "I cannot suspect him, but then, I cannot suspect any of them."

"At present, there's nothing that points to any one of them beyond the others, so no one can be eliminated." Arms folded, he turned to face her. "Augustus—tell me about him."

"There's nothing to tell." Snapping her wings shut, she rose to her feet. "He is a friend who thinks he needs to be more, that I need him to be more. It has been handled."

Noel could see that Nimra wasn't used to being questioned or pushed. "I don't think Augustus believes it has been handled."

A cold-eyed smile. "As we discussed earlier," she said, "such things are not in your purview."

"On the contrary." Closing the distance between them, he braced his hands on his hips. "Frustrated men do stupid and sometimes deadly things."

A hint of a frown as she reached up to brush away a tiny white blossom that had fallen on her shoulder. "Not Augustus. He has always been a friend first."

"No matter what you choose to believe, his feelings aren't those of a friend." Noel had glimpsed untrammeled rage on the big angel's face when Augustus had first realized what Noel apparently was to Nimra.

White lines bracketed Nimra's mouth. "The point is moot. Augustus visits, but he wasn't here when the Midnight was put into my tea."

"You said certain servants are trusted with your food," Noel pointed out, an exquisite, enticing scent twining through his veins, one that had nothing to do with the gardens. "Yet your focus is clearly on your inner court in the hunt for the traitor. Why?"

"The servants are human. Why would they chance the lethal punishment?" she asked with what appeared to be genuine puzzlement. "Their lives are already so short."

"You'd be surprised what mortals will chance." He thrust a hand through his hair to quell the urge to reach out, twist a blue-black curl around his finger. It continued to disquiet him, how easily she drew him when nothing had penetrated the numbness inside him for months—especially when he had yet to glimpse the nature of the power that was at the root of her reputation. "How many servants do I have to take into account?"

"Three," Nimra informed him. "Violet, Sammi, and Richard."

He made a mental note of the names, then asked, "What will you do today?"

Obviously still annoyed at him for daring to disagree with her, she shot him a look that was pure regal arrogance. "Again, it's nothing you need to know."

He was "only" two hundred and twenty-one years old, but he'd spent that time in the ranks of an archangel's men, the past hundred years in the guard just below the Seven. He had his own arrogance. "It might not be," he said, stepping close enough that she had to tip back her head to meet his gaze, something he knew she would not appreciate, "but I was being polite and civilized, trying to make conversation."

Nimra's eyes narrowed a fraction. "I think you have never been polite and civilized. Stop making the effort—it's ridiculous."

The statement startled a laugh out of him, the sound rough and unused, his chest muscles stretching in a way they hadn't done for a long time.

Nimra found herself taken aback by the impact of Noel's laugh, by the way it transformed his face, lit up the blue of his eyes. It was a glimpse of who he'd been before the events at the Refuge—a man with a hint of wicked in his eyes and the ability to laugh at himself. So when he angled an elbow in invitation, she slipped her hand into the crook of it.

His body heat seeped through the thin fabric of the shirt he wore rolled up to his elbows, to touch her skin, his muscles fluid under her fingers as they walked. For a moment, she forgot that she was an angel four hundred years his senior, an angel someone wanted dead, and simply became a woman taking a walk with a handsome man who was beginning to fascinate her, rough edges and all.

Three days later, Noel had a very good idea of how the court functioned. Nimra was its undisputed center, but she was no prima donna. The word "court" was in fact a misnomer. This was no extravagant place with formal dinners every night and courtiers dressed up to impress, their primary tasks being to look pretty and kiss ass.

Nimra's court was a highly functional unit, the capable skill of her men and women evident. Christian—who showed no sign of thawing to Noel's presence—handled the day-to-day business affairs, including managing the investments that kept the court wealthy. He was assisted in certain tasks by Fen, though from what Noel had seen, it was more of a mentor-mentee relationship. Fen was passing the torch to Christian, who might've been older in years, but was younger in experience.

Asirani, by contrast, was Nimra's social secretary. "She rejects the majority of the invitations," the frustrated vampire said to him on the second day, "which makes my job very challenging." However, the invitations—from other angels, high-level vampires, and humans eager to make contact with the ruling angel—continued to pour in, which meant Asirani was kept busy.

Exeter, the scholar, lived up to his reputation. An eccentric-appearing individual with tufts of dusty gray hair that stuck out in all directions and wings of an astonishing deep yellow stroked with copper, he seemed to spend his time with his head in the clouds. However, a closer look proved him to be a source of both advice and information for Nimra when it came to angelic politics. Fen, by contrast, had his finger on the pulse when it came to the vampiric and human populations.

It was only Amariyah who seemed to have no real position, aside from her care of her father. "Do you remain in this court because of Fen?" he asked her that night after a rare formal dinner, as they stood on the balcony under the silver light of a half-moon, the humid air tangled with the sounds of insects going about their business and a lush dark that was the bayou.

The other vampire sipped from a wineglass of bloodred liquid that sang to Noel's own senses. But he'd fed earlier, and so the hunger was nothing urgent, simply a humming awareness of the potent taste of iron. Before, he would've ignored the glass in her hand to focus on the pulse in her neck, on her wrist, but the idea of putting his mouth to her skin, anyone's skin, of having someone that close—it made his entire body burn cold, the hunger shutting down with harsh finality.

"No," she said at last, flicking out her tongue to collect a drop of blood on her plump lower lip. "I owe Nimra my allegiance for the way I was Made, and while I have nothing to compare it to, the others say this is a good territory. I've heard stories of other courts that make the hairs rise on my arms."

Noel knew those stories were more apt to be true than not. Many immortals were so inhuman that they considered humans and vampires nothing but toys for their amusement, ruling through a mix of bone-deep terror and sadistic pain. In contrast, while Nimra's servants and courtiers treated her with utmost respect, there was no acrid touch of fear, no skittering nervousness.

And yet . . . No ruler who had even a vein of kindness within her could've held off challengers as brutal as Nazarach. It made him question the truth of everything he'd seen to date, wonder if he was being played by the most skillful of adversaries, an angel who'd had six centuries to learn her craft.

Amariyah took a step closer, too close. "You sense it, too, don't you? The lies here." A whisper. "The hints of truth concealed." Her scent was deep and luxuriant, hotly sensual with no subtle undertones.

The bold scent suited the truth of her nature—all color and sex and beauty with no thought to future consequences. Young. He felt ancient in comparison. "I'm new to this court," he said, though he was disturbed by her question, her implication. "I'm very aware of what I don't know."

A curve to her lips that held a vicious edge. "And you must of course please your mistress. Without her, you have no place here."

"I'm no cipher," Noel said, knowing that everyone here had to have investigated his background by now. Christian clearly had, though Noel didn't think the angel would've shared what he'd dug up—there was a stiff kind of pride to Christian that said he was above gossip—but he wasn't the only one with connections. The safest course would be to assume the entire inner court knew of his past—the good, and the ugly. "I can always return to my service in Raphael's guard."

Fingers brushing his jaw, warm and caressing. "Why did you leave it?"

He took a discreet step back, recoiling inwardly from the uninvited touch. "I completed my Contract over a century ago, but remained with Raphael because working for an archangel is exhilarating." He'd seen and done incredible things, used every bit of his skill and intelligence to complete the tasks he'd been set. "But Nimra is . . . unique." That, too, was true.

Amariyah's tone tried for a false lightness but her bitterness was too deep to be hidden. "She's an angel. Vampires are no match for their beauty and grace."

"It depends on the vampire," Noel said, turning to face the open balcony doors. His gaze caught on the tableau inside the main room—Asirani touching Christian's arm in an invitation that was unmistakable. Dressed in a cheongsam of deepest indigo bordered with gold, her hair swept off her face, her vibrant beauty was a stunning counterpoint to Christian's almost acetic elegance.

The angelic male leaned down to hear what it was she had to say, but he held himself with a severity that was unnatural, his mouth set in an unsmiling line.

"Look at them," Amariyah murmured, and he realized she'd followed his line of sight. "Asirani has ever tried to gain Christian's affections, but she falls a poor second in comparison to Nimra." Again, the words held hidden blades.

"Asirani is a stunning woman in her own right." Noel watched as Christian tugged off the vampire's hands with implacable gentleness and walked away. Asirani's expression shut down, her spine a rod of steel.

Amariyah shrugged. "Shall we walk back inside?"

Noel had the feeling she'd expected far more support for her views than she'd received from him. "I think I'll stay awhile longer."

She left without a word, stalking into the main room in a flash of brilliant red that was the tight silk of her ankle-length dress, the fall of her coal black hair stroking over the lush curves of her body. He watched her walk up to Asirani, lay her hand on the other woman's shoulder, squeeze. As she dipped her head to speak to the vampire, he sensed another feminine presence, this one a complex, mysterious orchid to Amariyah's showy rose.

CHAPTER 5

When he glanced over the balcony, it was to see Nimra walking arm in arm with Fen along an avenue of night-blooming flowers, the elderly man's steps slow and awkward in comparison to her grace, his hand trembling on the cane. Yet the way Nimra compensated for his age and speed told Noel that this was something they did often, the angel with her wings of jewel-dusted brown, and the human man in the twilight of his life.

Compelled by the puzzle of her, Noel found himself walking down the steps to the garden to follow in their wake. An unexpected meow had him stopping on the last step and looking down into the dark, his vision more acute than a mortal's. Mimosa lay under a bush full of tiny starlike flowers closed up for the night, her body quivering.

The intrepid cat hadn't come to Noel in the days he'd been here, but tonight she stayed in place as he bent down and picked her up, holding her close to the warmth of his chest. "Are you cold, old girl?" he murmured, stroking her with one hand. When she continued to shiver, he opened up the buttons of his formal black shirt and put her against his skin. Dropping her head, she curled into him, her shivers starting to fade. "There you go."

He continued to stroke her as he walked the way Fen and Nimra
had disappeared. Mimosa was fragile under his hand, as fine boned
as her mistress. It was strangely soothing to hold her, and for the first
time in a long while, Noel thought back to the boy he'd been. He'd
had a pet, too, a great old mutt who had followed Noel around with
utter faithfulness until his body gave out. Noel had buried him on
the moor, steeped the ground in his tears where no one could see him.

Mimosa stirred against his chest as he turned the corner, catching the scent of her mistress. Nimra was on the other side of the
moon-silvered pond in front of him, her wings sweeping over the
grass as she bent to check some drowsy blooms, the lazy wind shap-
ing the dark blue of her gown to her body with a lover's attention.
Fen sat on a stone bench on this side, and the quiet patience with
which he watched her held complete devotion.

Not Fen, Noel decided. The old man had always been an unlikely
conspirator in the plot to disable or kill Nimra, but the expression
on his face this night destroyed even the faintest glimmer of suspicion. No man could look at a woman in such a way and then watch
the light fade forever from her eyes. "Strength and heart and courage," Fen said without turning around. "There is no other like her."

"Yes." Walking closer, Noel took a seat beside Fen, Mimosa purring against his skin. "I think," he said, his gaze on the angel who
even now tugged at things deep inside of him, "you need to send
Amariyah from this court."

A quiet sigh, a weathered hand clenching on the cane. "She has
ever had a jealousy toward angels that I've never understood. She is
a beautiful woman, a near-immortal, and yet all she sees are the
things she can't have, can't do."

Noel said nothing, because Fen spoke the truth. Amariyah might
see herself as an adult, but she was a spoiled child in many ways.

"I sometimes think," Fen continued, "I did her a disfavor by asking Nimra to take my years of service into account as part of my
daughter's Contract. A century of service might have taught her to
value what she is—for the angels value it."

Noel wasn't so sure. He'd seen Amariyah hold up a cup of coffee in front of Violet only the day before, tell the little maid that it was cold, then pour the liquid very deliberately onto the floor. There had been other acts when she thought herself unseen, and then the conversation tonight. The selfishness in her nature seemed innate, as immutable as stone. But whether it had turned deadly remained to be seen.

"Yours was a gift of love," he said to Fen as Nimra rose from her investigation of the plants, looked over her shoulder.

It was familiar now, the way his skin went tense in a waiting kind of expectation at the touch of her gaze. They hadn't made physical contact again since that walk in the garden, but Noel was discovering that, doubts about her true nature or not, his body was no longer averse to the idea of intimacy. Not when it came to this one woman.

He'd never had an angelic lover before. He wasn't pretty enough to be pursued by those angels who kept harems of men, and he was glad for it. On the flip side, most angels were far too inhuman for the raw sexuality of his nature. Nimra, however, was like no other angel he'd ever met, a mystery within an enigma.

He'd seen her in the gardens more than once, her fingers literally in the earth. Once or twice, when he'd muttered something less than sophisticated under his breath, her eyes had sparkled not with rebuke, but with humor. And now, as she circled the pond to come to stand with her hand on Fen's shoulder, her hair tumbling around her in soft curls, her expression was curious in a way he found unexpected in an angel of her age and strength.

"Are you seducing my cat, Noel?"

He stroked his palm over Mimosa's slumbering body. "It is I who have been seduced."

"Indeed." A single word twined with power. "I see the women of the court are quite taken with you. Even shy Violet blushes when you are near."

The little maidservant had proven to be a fount of information about the court when Noel tracked her down in the kitchens and charmed her into speaking with him. He'd already pushed the other two servants down the list of suspects after a subtle investigation— utilizing his access to Tower resources—had revealed no weak points in their lives that could make Sammi or Richard vulnerable to being turned, or signs of any sudden wealth. And after his discussion with Violet, he was certain beyond any doubt that she'd had nothing to do with the attempted assassination, either. Unlike Amariyah's faux guilelessness, Violet's was very much real—in spite of the ugliness of her past.

A runaway from a stepfather who had looked at her with far too much interest, Violet had collapsed half-starved on the edge of Nimra's estate. The angel had been flying over her lands, seen the girl, carried her home in her own arms. She'd nursed Violet back to health and, when the teenager shied at the thought of school, hired a tutor for her. Though Nimra expected no service from one so young, the proud girl insisted on "earning her way" with her duties in the mornings, the afternoons being set aside for her studies.

"I adore her," Violet had told Noel with fierce loyalty. "There isn't anything I wouldn't do for Lady Nimra. Anything."

Now, Noel looked up. "Violet is more apt to ambush me on a dark night, if she considers me a threat to you, than flirt with me."

Fen cackled. "He has the right of it. That child worships the ground you walk on."

"We are not gods, to be worshipped," Nimra said, a troubled look on her face. "I would not wish it of her—she needs to spread her wings, live her own life."

"She's like a rescued pup," Fen said, coughing into a trembling fist. "Even if you cast her out, send her into the world, she'll return most stubbornly to your side. You may as well let her be—she'll find her own happiness faster if she's able to do what she can to ensure yours."

"So wise." Nimra made no effort to assist the old man as Fen struggled to get to his feet.

Help, Noel understood as he rose as well, would neither be welcomed nor accepted.

The walk back was slow and quiet, Nimra's wings brushing the grass in front of him as she walked arm in arm with Fen. Strolling along behind them, Noel felt content in a way that was difficult to describe. The humid Louisiana night, the air filled with the sounds of frogs croaking and leaves rustling, Nimra's soft voice as she spoke with Fen, it was a lush sea that embraced him, blunting the raw edges within, the parts yet broken.

"Good night, my lady," Fen said when they reached the small, freestanding cottage that he shared with Amariyah. To Noel, he said, "I'll think on what you said. But I'm an old man—she'll go when I am no longer here in any case."

Nimra's wings made a rustling sound as she resettled them before joining Noel to return to the house. Skirting the main rooms in unspoken agreement, they turned toward her personal wing—Noel's room was next to her own, the area private. "Amariyah may have her faults," Nimra said at last, holding out her arms when Mimosa stirred again, "but she does love Fen."

Noel passed the cat over with care.

Purring happily in her mistress's embrace, Mimosa returned to her slumber. Noel did up a couple of the buttons on his shirt but left the rest undone, the night breeze languid against his skin. "Did you know that Asirani is in love with Christian?"

A sigh. "I was hoping it was an infatuation, would pass." She shook her head. "Christian is very rigid in his views—he believes angels should mate only among our own kind."

"Ah." That explained the intensity of the angel's response to Noel. "It's not a common view." Especially when it came to the most powerful vampires.

"Christian thinks angel-vampire pairings are undesirable, as such a pairing cannot create a child—and we have so few children already."

Noel thought of the angelic children at the Refuge, so vulnerable

with their unwieldy wings and plump childish legs, their trilling
laughter a constant music. "Children are a gift," he agreed. "Is it
something you—" He stopped speaking as Mimosa made a tiny
sound of distress.

"My apologies, little one," Nimra said, petting the cat until it laid
its head back down. "I will not squeeze you so tight again."

A chill speared through Noel's veins. When Nimra didn't say
anything else, he thought about letting it go, but the slowly reawak-
ening part of him insisted on engaging with her, on discovering her
secrets. "You lost a child."

It was the gentleness in Noel's voice that tore the wound wide open.
"He didn't have the chance to become a child," Nimra said, the
words shards of glass in her throat, the blood pooling in her chest as
it once had at her feet. "My womb couldn't carry him, and so I lost
him before he was truly formed." She hadn't spoken of her lost babe
since that terrible night when the storm had crashed against the
house with unrelenting fury. Fen had been the one who'd found her,
the only one who knew what had happened. Eitriel had left a month
prior, after stabbing a knife straight into her heart.

"I'm sorry." Noel's hand on the back of her head, strong and masculine as he stroked her in much the same way he'd stroked Mimosa
moments before. But he didn't stop with her hair, moving his hand
down to her lower back, careful not to touch the inner surfaces of
her wings—that was an intimacy to be given, not taken.

He pressed against the base of her spine. She jerked up her head,
startled. Instead of backing away, he curved his body toward her
own, Mimosa slumbering in between them. He had no right to hold
her in such a familiar way, no right to touch an angel of her power . . .
but she didn't stop him. Didn't want to stop him.

It had been a long time since she'd been held.

Laying her head against his chest, the beat of his heart strong and
steady, she lifted her eyes to the silver light of the half-moon. "The

moon was dark that night," she said, the memory imprinted into her very cells, to be carried through all eternity, "the air torn with the scream of a storm that felled trees and lifted roofs. I didn't want my babe to leave me in the dark, but there was nothing I could do."

He held her tighter, his arm brushing against her wing. Still he didn't withdraw, though all vampires were trained to know that angels did not like their wings touched except by those they considered their intimates. Part of her, the part that held the arrogance of a race that ruled the world, was affronted. But most of her was quietly pleased by Noel's refusal to follow the rules in a situation that wouldn't be served by them.

"I had no children as a mortal," he murmured, his free hand moving over her hair, "and I know it's unlikely I'll ever have them now."

"Unlikely, but not impossible." Vampires had a window of opportunity of roughly two hundred years after their Making to sire children, those offspring being mortal. Noel had been Made two hundred and twenty-one years ago. She'd heard of one or two children being conceived after that period of time. "Do you wish to sire a child?"

"Only if that child is created in love." His hand fisted in her hair. "And I do have children I consider family."

"Yes." The thought of children's laughter dancing over the moors eased the ache in her heart. "I think I should like to spend time with them."

"I'll take you if you want," he offered with a laugh. "But I warn you—they're a wild, wild lot. The babes are likely to pull at your wings and expect to be cuddled on the slightest pretext."

"True torture."

Another laugh, his chest vibrating under her cheek.

"You do not sleep, Noel," she said to him after long, quiet moments held against the steady beat of his heart, that big body warm around her own. "I hear you walking in the hall."

The first night, she'd wondered why he didn't leave the wing and head out into the gardens. Only later had she understood that he was acting as what she'd named him—her wolf. Any assassin would have to go through Noel to get to her. Though she was the more powerful, his act had left her with a sense of trust that the Midnight had stolen from her.

"Vampires need little sleep," he said, his voice distant, though he continued to hold her.

She knew that wasn't the reason he stalked the corridors like a beast caged, but decided to keep her silence. Too many lines had already been crossed this night, and there would be consequences, things neither one of them was yet ready to face.

It was the next day that Nimra's heart broke all over again. She was in the library, working through her contacts for hints about who in her court might have links to someone who could access Midnight—a fact she'd checked earlier without result, but that Noel had requested she recheck, in case anything new had floated up— when Violet ran into the room. Tears streaked the girl's face. "My lady, Mimosa—"

Nimra was running around the desk before Violet finished speaking. "Where?"

"The garden, by the balcony."

It was a favorite sunning spot for the aged cat. Sweeping through the hallways, Nimra ran out onto the balcony to find both Noel and Christian crouching at the bottom of the steps. Noel had his arms full of something, and Nimra's heart clenched at the realization of his burden, her sorrow tempered only by the knowledge that Mimosa had lived a full and happy life.

Then Christian saw her and rose into the air to land on the balcony in front of her. "My lady, it's better if you don't—"

Nimra was already rising over him, her wings spread wide, her sorrow transmuting into a strange kind of panic at his attempt to stop her from going to Mimosa. When she landed opposite Noel, the first thing she saw was the limp gray tail hanging over his arm. "I am too late . . ."

A weak meow had her jumping forward to take Mimosa from his arms. He passed the cat over without a word. Mimosa seemed to settle as soon as she was in her mistress's arms, her head lying heavily against Nimra's breast as Nimra hummed to her. Five quiet minutes later, and her beloved companion of many years was gone.

Fighting tears, for an angel of her power and responsibility could not be seen to break, Nimra raised her head, met blue eyes gone flinty with anger. "What do I need to know?"

CHAPTER 6

He nodded at a piece of meat sitting on the ground beside where Mimosa had liked to soak up the sun. "It'll have to be tested, but I believe it was poisoned." He brought her attention to where poor Mimosa had thrown up after chewing on the meat. "Violet."

The maid ran down with a plastic bag. Taking it, Noel bagged the meat. "I'll handle it," he said to Violet when she went to take it from him.

Nodding, the maid hesitated, then ran back up the steps. "I'll make my lady some tea."

No tea would calm the rage in Nimra's heart, but she wouldn't taint Mimosa's spirit with it. Holding her dear old pet, she turned to walk in the direction of the southern gardens, a wild wonderland that had been Mimosa's favorite playground before age clipped her wings. She was aware of two deep male voices behind her, knew Noel had won whatever argument had taken place, for he appeared at her side.

He didn't say a word until Christian landed beside him with a small shovel in hand. Grasping it, she heard him murmur something to the angel before Christian left in a rustle of wings. She didn't make any effort to listen to their conversation, her attention on cradling

Mimosa as gently as possible. "You were a faithful companion," she told the cat, her throat catching. "I shall miss you." Some—mortals and immortals alike—would call her stupid for bestowing so much love on a creature with such an ephemeral life span, but they did not understand.

"Immortals," she said to Noel as they neared the southern gardens, "live so long that we become jaded, our hearts hardened. For some, cruelty and pain are the only things that engender an emotion." Nazarach, ruler of Atlanta and adjacent areas, was one such angel, his home saturated with screams.

"An animal is innocent," Noel said, "without guile or hidden motivation. To love one is to nurture softness within your own heart."

It didn't surprise her that he comprehended that quiet truth. "She taught me so much." Nimra stepped through the curved stone archway that led into the concealed gardens Mimosa had adored. She heard Noel suck in a breath when he glimpsed the tangle of roses and wildflowers, sweet pecan and other trees heavy with fruit, pathways overgrown until they were near impassable.

"I didn't know this existed." He reached out to touch an extravagant white rose.

She knew he felt not shock, but wonder. Like the young kitten Mimosa had once been, Noel carried a touch of wildness within him. "She will enjoy being a part of this garden, I think." Her throat felt raw, lined with sandpaper.

Noel followed her in silence as she walked through the tangled pathways to a spot under the sheltering arms of a magnolia that had stood through storm and wind and time. When she stopped, he hefted the shovel and began to dig. It didn't take long to dig deep enough for Mimosa's body, but instead of nodding at her to lay her pet down, Noel went to the closest bush heavy with blooms. Plucking off handfuls of color, he walked back and lined the bottom of the tiny grave.

Nimra couldn't hold back the tears any longer. They rolled down her face in silence as Noel went back two more times. When he was done, the grave held a velvet carpet of pink, white, and yellow petals, soft as fresh-fallen snow. Going to her knees, Nimra brushed a kiss to her pet's head and laid her down.

The petals stroked against the backs of her hands as she lifted them out from under Mimosa. "I should've brought something to wrap her in."

"I think," Noel said, showering more blooms over Mimosa, "she would prefer this. It is a fitting burial for a cat who loved to roam, don't you think?"

She gave a jerky nod and reached back to tug out several of her primary feathers. "When she was a kitten," she told Noel, "Mimosa was fascinated by my feathers. She would attempt to steal them when I wasn't looking."

"Was she ever successful?"

"Once or twice," she said, a watery laugh escaping her. "And then she'd run so fast, it was as if she were the wind itself. I never did find where she hid my feathers." With those words, she placed the primaries beside Mimosa before blanketing her in another layer of petals. "Good-bye, little one."

Noel covered up the grave in quiet, and she placed more blossoms over the top, along with a large stone Noel found in the garden. They stayed for long, still minutes beside the grave, until Nimra felt a caress of wind along her senses, gentle as a sigh. Releasing a silent breath, she turned and began to walk back, Noel by her side.

He touched a hand to her shoulder. "Wait." Propping the shovel against one thigh, he used the thumbs of both hands to wipe away the tears on her face. "There," he whispered, "now you are Nimra again. Strong and cruel and pitiless."

She leaned into the touch, and when he cupped her face, when he touched his lips to her own, she didn't remind him that his role was as her wolf, not her lover. Instead, she let him sip at her mouth, let him warm the cold place in her heart with the rough heat of his masculinity.

When he lifted his mouth, she fisted her hand in his shirt. "More, Noel." Almost an order.

Shaking his head, he brushed back her hair with a tenderness she'd never felt from a lover. "I won't take advantage of you. Today, I'll be your friend."

"Fen has been my friend for decades," she said, sliding her arm into his when he offered it to her. "And he never presumed to put his mouth on mine."

"Obviously I'll be a different kind of friend."

The lighthearted words served to calm her, until by the time they emerged into the main gardens, she was the angel who ruled New Orleans and its surrounds once more—hard and powerful and without vulnerability. "You will discover who hurt Mimosa," she said to Noel, "and you will tell me." There would be no mercy for the perpetrator.

The first thing Noel did after escorting Nimra to her personal study, was to head out to track down Violet. The maid had given him a fleeting but significant look when she'd brought him the plastic bag—the contents of which he'd surrendered to Christian earlier, because he'd needed to be by Nimra's side when she buried Mimosa.

However, he hadn't taken more than three steps out of the private wing when Violet walked into the corridor with a tea tray. "I saw Lady Nimra return," she said, lines of worry around her eyes. "Should I . . . ?"

"I'll take it in," Noel said. "Wait for me here."

The teenager gave a swift bob of her head while Noel ducked inside. Nimra was standing by the window, her back to the door. Leaving the tray on the coffee table, he walked to stand behind her, his hands on her shoulders. "Eat something."

"Not yet, Noel."

Knowing she needed to grieve in private, this strong woman who had the heart to love a creature so very small and defenseless, he left her with a fleeting stroke through her hair.

Violet was half hiding in an alcove, her eyes fearful. "If she sees me, Noel, she'll know."

"Who?" he asked, though he had a very good idea.

"Amariyah." The girl hugged herself tight. "She thought no one was in the kitchens when she came in because I always hide when she's near—she's spiteful." A gulping breath. "I saw her take the meat, and thought it was strange but didn't really worry about it."

"Thank you, Violet," he said, certain she spoke the truth. "No one will know the information came from you."

The maid drew up her shoulders. "If you need me to, I'll swear witness before the whole court. Mimosa dying so soon after Queen, it'll have broken my lady's heart. Some say she doesn't have one, but I know different."

Noel stayed in the corridor for long minutes after Violet left, considering the maid's statement. His faith in her aside, the fact was, it was her word against that of a vampire. A vampire who was the child of the most trusted member of Nimra's court. Amariyah could turn around and accuse Violet of the same act.

It was dusk by the time he decided on a course of action. Heading away from the private wing, he walked down not to the main dining room, but toward Fen's cottage. As he'd expected, Amariyah was at home with her father. Entering at Fen's invitation, Noel sat with the elderly man for a while, talking of nothing and everything.

When the subject of Mimosa came up, he made sure his gaze met Amariyah's. "I have a very good idea of the person behind the cowardly act," he said, making no effort to hide his contempt. "It's just a case of how hard they'll make it."

From the way Amariyah's face drained of blood, it was clear she understood the threat. And if there was one thing in the vampire that was true and good, it was her love for her father. Her eyes beseeched him not to bring up the subject in front of Fen. Since Noel had no desire to hurt the old man—would've never carried through with the unspoken threat—he excused himself after a few more minutes.

"I'll walk with Noel a little, Father," the female vampire said, rising to her feet in a fall of vivid violet fabric that appeared as light and airy as the wind, the simple gown leaving her arms bare and flirting with her ankles.

"Go, go." Fen chuckled. "Just remember, he belongs to an angel. Don't go poaching there."

From the rigidity of Amariyah's smile, she didn't appreciate the reminder of her place in the hierarchy of things. But her tone was light as she said, "Do credit me with a few brain cells."

That elicited a wracking laugh from Fen, his chest rattling in a way that concerned Noel. Amariyah was immediately by his side. "Papa."

Fen waved off the help. "Go on, Mariyah."

"We should call a doctor," Noel said, not liking the strain in Fen's breathing.

Fen's response was a laugh, his dark eyes twinkling. "Ain't nothing a doctor can do about age. I'm an old man with an old man's bones."

When Amariyah hesitated, Fen urged Noel to take her outside. Noel would've insisted on a doctor, but one look at Fen's face told him that would be a lost battle—the elderly man's body might've turned frail, but his will remained strong as steel. Such a will demanded respect.

"Until we next speak," he said to Fen as he left with a nod, taking Amariyah with him.

Fen's daughter was silent as they walked deep into the verdant spread of the gardens, her steps jerky, her spine stiff. "How did you know it was me?" she said the instant they were in a private spot, beneath the arms of a gnarled old tree with bark of darkest brown.

"That doesn't matter. What matters is the why of it."

Her shrug was graceful, her beauty marred by the petulant ugliness of her expression. "What do you care? Her *ladyship* will execute me for putting that horrid old thing out of its misery, and all will be well with her perfect world."

Noel had glimpsed Amariyah's inexplicable animosity toward Nimra soon after their first meeting, but this callousness was something unexpected. "Why, Amariyah?" he asked again, catching a leaf as it floated to the ground.

Hissing out a breath, the vampire pointed a trembling finger at him. "She'll live forever, while I have to watch my father die." A fist slamming into her heart. "He asked to be Made, and she refused him! Now he is an old man taking his last breaths, and hurting every instant."

Noel didn't know how angels picked those who were to be Made, but he'd been part of Raphael's senior guard long enough to understand that there was a level of biological compatibility involved. From everything he'd witnessed of Nimra and Fen's relationship, it was clear the angel would've Made Fen if she'd been able. "Does your father know you feel this way?" he asked, rubbing his thumb over the smooth green surface of the leaf in his hand.

Her face twisted into a mask of rage. "He adores her—as far as he's concerned, the bitch can do no wrong. He doesn't even blame her for the fact that he's dying! He told me that there are things I don't know! That was his justification for her."

It was impossible not to pity the pain that had driven Amariyah to such an abhorrent act, but it didn't in any way lessen her crime or his anger. "And the Midnight?"

"I didn't do anything at midnight." A scathing response. "I gave the cat the meat just after dawn. There, you have your confession. Take me to the one who holds your leash."

The dig had no impact. Unlike Amariyah, Noel knew who he was, and, though Nimra might disagree, he understood that even an angel could not stand alone. Raphael had his Seven. Nimra would have Noel. For, secrets or not, he was becoming ever more convinced that what he saw was the truth, Nimra's cruel reputation the cleverest of illusions.

Instead of taking Fen's daughter to the private wing, he put her in the downstairs library and—seeing Christian—asked him to make sure she remained there.

"Do I look like your servant?" A glacial question.

"Now's not the time, Christian."

The angel's shrewd eyes narrowed before he nodded. "I'll keep watch."

Nimra shook her head in stunned disbelief when Noel told her the identity of the perpetrator. "I knew she was a little resentful, but never would I have believed her capable of such."

"I'm convinced she had nothing to do with the Midnight," Noel continued in a pragmatic tone, but in his eyes she saw the cutting edge of blackest anger. "She seemed genuinely confused when I mentioned it."

Ice, bleak and cold, invaded her veins. "So I have two who hate me in my court—it puts my ability to read my people in the spotlight, does it not?"

"This court has a heart that is missing in most." Fierce words from her wolf. "Don't let those of Amariyah and her ilk steal what you've built here." He held out a hand.

And waited.

I can never appear weak.

Still, she reached out and slid her hand into the rough warmth of his own, wanting to feel "human," if only for a bare few instants, before she had to become a monster. His fingers curled around her own, a small act of possession. She wondered if he sought to press a claim now, when she could not accept it, but he released her hand the instant they hit the hallways where they might encounter others, watching with eyes of keen blue as she became Nimra the ruler once more.

"Does Fen know?" she asked, wanting no such pain for her friend.

"I didn't tell him."

Nimra nodded. "Good."

Neither one of them spoke again until they walked into the library, Christian exchanging a stiff nod with Noel before the other angel left. Closing the doors, Noel stood with his back to them while she walked across the floor to face a sullen Amariyah where she stood in front of the unused fireplace set with pinecones and dried flowers. Violet's hand at work.

The vampire spoke before Nimra could say a word, her tone defiant. "My father had nothing to do with it."

"Your loyalty to Fen does you credit," Nimra said, making sure her voice betrayed nothing, "but this is one act I can't forgive, not even for him." She had no intention of being cruel, but neither could she be merciful. Because a vampire like Amariyah would see in that mercy a weakness, one that would incite her to ever more depraved acts. "You took a life, Amariyah. A small life, a tiny light, but a life nonetheless."

Amariyah's hands fisted in the sides of her diaphanous gown, pulling it tight across her thighs. "Then you can explain my death to him." A bitter laugh. "I'm sure he'll forgive you as he's forgiven the fact that you're the reason for his own death."

Nimra's chest grew stiff with anguish, but she kept those emotions off her face, having had centuries of experience at concealing her true self when necessary. "You won't die," she said in a tone so cold, it came from the dark, powerful heart of her. "Or you shouldn't, unless you've been doing things beyond that which anyone knows."

True fear flickered into Amariyah's eyes for the first time, sweat breaking out along her brow. "What're you going to do to me?" In that question was the sudden knowledge that there was a reason Nimra was feared by even the most brutal.

Crossing the distance between them, Nimra touched her fingers to the vampire's hand with a gentleness that hid a weapon of such viciousness, the merest glimpse of it had left her enemies a trembling wreck. "This."

Though Noel saw nothing, felt nothing, Amariyah began to shudder, then convulse, her body falling to the floor in a wild cacophony of limbs and clashing teeth. When she quietened at last, her eyes remained locked tight, whimpers escaping her mouth as her bones shook, as if from the greatest cold.

"Each time I do this," Nimra said, her gaze haunted as she looked at the fallen woman, "it takes something from me."

Scooping up a violently shivering Amariyah, Noel placed her on the sofa, pulling a cashmere throw off the back to cover her. "She's bleeding a little where she seems to have cut her lip"—he used a tissue from a nearby box to wipe it away—"but otherwise appears fine on a physical level." He felt a glimmer of understanding about the reason behind Nimra's reputation, but it whispered away before he could grasp it.

Nimra said nothing, walking to stand in front of the large windows that looked out over the gardens, those jewel-dusted wings trailing along the gleaming varnish of the wooden floors. Unable, unwilling, to leave her so alone and distant, he walked to join her. But when he put his hand on the side of her neck, urging her to lean on him, she resisted. "This is why Nazarach fears me," she murmured, but said nothing further.

He could've pushed, but he made the choice to stand by her side instead, knowing she would not break, would not soften until this was done. Paying her own penance, he thought, though Amariyah was the one who'd caused irreparable harm.

CHAPTER 7

It took two days for Amariyah to wake. Out of respect for Fen, Nimra had decreed that no word of this would ever reach him, with both Violet and Christian sworn to secrecy. Noel had no fear that either would break their word. Violet was beyond loyal, and Christian, in spite of his jealousy, was honorable to the core. Fen himself had been told that Amariyah had been sent out of state on an errand for Nimra, and would likely be tired when she returned.

Noel was with the vampire when she finally woke, her eyes hollow, her bones cutting against skin gone dull and lifeless. "Any other person who dared such an act," he told her, "would be on the street right now, but because your father doesn't know of what you did, you'll be permitted to remain here.

"But," he added, "step one foot out of line, and I will personally ensure true death." It was a harsh statement, but his own loyalty was to Nimra, and more, he understood the predator that lived beneath the skin of every vampire, had glimpsed a twisted darkness in Amariyah that enjoyed causing pain to those who were helpless to fight back.

Whatever the other vampire heard in his voice—or perhaps it

was the echo of her punishment—had fear creeping across her face. "My father is the only reason I'm still here," she whispered, her voice raw. "I'll be gone from the house of this monster the second he leaves me."

Nimra stood at the window of her private sitting room, watching Amariyah's unsteady progress through the dusk to the cottage. Christian had arranged for Fen to be out, so Amariyah would have time to clean herself up. "Fen is very intelligent," she said to the man who'd entered the room without knocking. "I'm not sure he'll accept the story about a business trip once he sees her gaunt appearance." Blood and sleep would revive Amariyah, but it would take hours.

"Christian just sent me a message to say he engineered a delay from the city—they'll spend the night."

"Good." She kept her back to him, knowing he had questions to which he deserved answers. Not because he was her wolf, but because he was becoming more, becoming something she'd never expected.

Now, he said, "I brought you some food."

Turning as Amariyah disappeared from sight, she met that gaze so startlingly bright in the shadowy light of day fading into night. "Do you think you'll simply wear me down to your way of doing things?"

"Of course." An unexpected smile that burned through the cold that had lingered in her veins ever since the punishment, as her body remembered that she was not only a being of terrible power, but a feminine creature. "I am a man, after all."

Knowing she was being charmed, but unable to resist, she walked with him to the informal dining area—where he'd placed a tray full of fruit, sandwiches, and cookies. "This is no meal fit for an angel," she said when he pulled out a chair.

"I see your smile, my lady Nimra." A kiss pressed to her nape, a hot intimacy she had not given him permission to take.

"You walk a dangerous road, Noel."

He rubbed his thumbs along the tendons that ran down the back of her neck, his touch firm and sure. "I never was one for taking the easy path." His lips against her ear, his body big and solid around her own as he slid his hands down to brace them on the arms of her chair. "But first you must eat."

When he moved to sit beside her, lifting a succulent slice of peach to her lips, she should've reminded him that she was no child. An angel could go without food for long periods and not suffer any ill effects. But the past few days had cut jagged wounds inside her and Noel, with his rough tenderness, spoke to a part of her that had not seen the light since centuries before Eitriel.

Inexplicable that it should be this vampire, damaged on such a deep level, who should have so profound an impact on her . . . or perhaps not. Because beyond the shadows in the blue, she glimpsed the wary hope of a brutalized wolf.

So she allowed him to feed her the peach, then slices of pear, bites of sandwich, followed by a rich chocolate cookie. Somewhere along the way, she ended up sitting with her knees pressed up to his chair, his legs on either side of her own. Her hands spread on his thighs, the rock-solid strength of him flexing taut and beautiful under her touch.

Other parts of him were taut, too.

But though his eyes lingered on her lips, his thumb brushing off crumbs that weren't there, he didn't seek to come to her bed, this wolf who was starting to entangle himself in her life in a way no man had ever dared to attempt.

Noel didn't sleep again that night, his mind full of the echoes of evil, the laughter of those who had debased him until he was less than an animal.

"It is done," Raphael had said to him after it was all over, his face merciless in judgment, his wings glowing with power. "They have been executed."

At the time, Noel had said, "Good," with vicious pleasure, but now he knew vengeance alone would never be enough. His attackers had marked him in ways that might never be erased.

"Noel."

Jerking up his head at that familiar feminine voice, he found Nimra had stepped out into the corridor where he paced in a vain attempt to outrun the laughter. "I woke you." It was well past midnight.

"Sleep is an indulgence for me, not a necessity." Eyes of brilliant topaz glimmering with streaks of amber, vivid against the cream of a fluid gown cinched at both shoulders, she said, "I would walk in the gardens."

He fell into step with her. She said nothing until they reached the beautifully eerie shadows of the woods where the stream originated. "An immortal has many memories." Her voice was an intimate caress in the night, her words poignant with ancient knowledge. "Even the most painful of them fade in time."

"Some memories," he said, "are embedded." As the glass had been embedded in his flesh. As . . . other things, had been embedded in his body. His hand fisted.

Nimra's wing brushed against his arm. "But is it a memory you wish to shine like a jewel, keep always at the forefront?"

"I can't control it," he admitted through a jaw clenched so tight, he could hear his bones grinding against each other, drowning out the whispering secrets of the warm Louisiana night.

An angel's perceptive gaze met his under the silver caress of the moon. "You will learn." There was utmost confidence in her voice.

His laugh was harsh. "Yeah? What makes you so sure?"

"Because that is who you are, Noel." Stepping forward, she raised her hand to touch his cheek, her wings arcing at her back.

When he flinched at the contact, she didn't pull back. "What was done to you," she said, "would've broken other men. It did not break you."

"I'm not who I once was."

"Neither am I." She dropped her hand, and he found he didn't like the kiss of the night against his skin now that he'd felt the softness of her. "Life changes us. To wish otherwise is pointless."

The pragmatic truth of her words affected him more than any gentle reassurances. "Nimra."

She looked at him with those inhuman eyes. "My wolf."

So breathtaking, he thought, so dangerous. "There are other ways to blunt the impact of memory." It was a sudden, primal decision. Too long, he'd been hiding in the dark too long.

Nimra knew what Noel was asking, knew, too, that if she acquiesced, he would be no easy lover—either in the act or in his temperament afterward. "I have not taken a lover," she murmured, her gaze on the rough angles of his face, "for many years."

Noel said nothing.

"Very well."

"So romantic."

There was a black edge to the words, but Nimra didn't take it personally. Like the wolf she called him, he might yet show her his teeth. Trust was a precious commodity, one that took time to develop. Patience was something Nimra had learned long ago. "Romance," she said, turning to head back to the house, "is a matter of interpretation."

Nothing from the man at her side, not until they were behind the closed doors of her suite. "No matter what the interpretation," he warned, his body held with a rigid control that told her he was on the finest of edges, "it's not what I'm going to give you tonight."

Touching her fingers to his jaw, she allowed the desire, so heavy and drugging in her veins, to show on her face. "And it's not what I need." What she'd done to Amariyah had been just, but it had marked her as it always did. Tonight she needed to feel like a woman, not the inhuman monster Amariyah had named her.

A strong hand gripped her wrist. "Sex for sex's sake?"

Noel's anger, his pain, was a raw blade, cutting and tearing, but Nimra was made of sterner stuff. "If I wanted that, I would've accepted Christian into my bed long ago."

Ice blue turned to midnight as his hand tightened. All at once, her pulse was in her mouth, on her skin. "You hunger," she whispered as her blood sang to the haunting kiss of this vampire's touch.

His gaze went to the pulse that thudded in her neck, his thumb rubbing over the beat in her wrist. "I haven't fed from the vein in months." It was a harsh admission. "I would rip out your throat."

"I'm immortal," she reminded him when he released his grip on her wrist to curve his fingers around that throat. "You can't hurt me."

A laugh that sounded like broken glass. "There are ways to hurt a woman that have nothing to do with anything so simple as pain."

And she knew. Understood what she had to do. Pulling away to walk into her dressing room, she returned with a long silk scarf. "Then I," she said, handing him the strip of peacock blue, "will have to trust you." In saying the words, she found her humanity—it was the woman who offered him this, not a being with a terrible gift.

Noel's hand clenched around the soft fabric. It was a symbol, nothing more, Nimra's power more than enough to permit escape should she wish it. But that she'd given it to him meant she'd seen the broken pieces he didn't want anyone to see . . . and still she looked at him with a woman's lingering appreciation. "No bonds," he said, letting the scarf float to the floor in a grace of blue. "Never any bonds."

"As you say, Noel." Holding his gaze with the promise of her own, she reached up to the clasps on her shoulders, flicked them open. Her gown shimmered over her body to pool at her feet, knocking all the air out of him.

She may have been petite, but she was lush curves and feminine invitation, the smooth brown of her skin interrupted only by a triangle of lace at the juncture of her thighs. Her breasts were full and heavy against her slender frame, her nipples dark and, at this moment, furled into tight buds. Spreading her wings in invitation, she waited.

The choice was his.

As you say, Noel.

Such a simple statement. Such a powerful gift.

Reaching out, he cupped the erotic weight of one breast, had the satisfaction of feeling a tremor race across her skin. It awakened the part of him that had gone into numb slumber when his abusers had turned him into a piece of meat, crushed and broken. Tonight, that part, the one that had made him an adventurer who'd conquered mountains, caused women to sigh in pleasure, roared to the surface.

It was instinct to thrust his hand into her hair, to slant his mouth over her own, to demand entrance. She opened to him, dark and hot and sweet, her power a lick against his senses as lusciously female as the body under his touch. Tucking her closer, he slid his hand up from her breast to grip her jaw, holding her in place as he explored every inch of that mouth he'd dreamed of tasting for longer than she knew.

He wanted to move slow, to map every curve and every pleasure point, but her pulse, it beat a seductive tattoo against his senses, inviting him to take that which he hadn't taken for months. Circling his hand around to her neck, he rubbed his thumb over the beating invitation of her. Her hands clenched on his waist, but she made no demur when he began to kiss his way down to the spot that was a siren song to the vampirism that was as much a part of him as his desire for her.

Lips against his ear. "Sip from me, Noel. It is a gift given freely."

He'd never been a man who fed indiscriminately. When he hadn't had a lover, he'd turned to friends, for the feeding didn't need to be a sexual thing. Since the attack, he hadn't been able to stand being that intimate with another being. Even now, with this woman who made him hunger in every way, and though his erection was a hard ridge in his pants, he said, "I can't make it pleasurable." Not because he'd lost the ability, but because he wasn't ready for the connection forged by the sexual ecstasy his kiss could bestow . . . the vulnerability that came with allowing another being any kind of inroad into him.

She arched her neck in silent response.

His blood pounding in time to her own, he slid his arms around her, his fingers brushing her wings as he sucked a kiss over the spot before piercing the delicate skin with his fangs. Her blood was an erotic rush against his senses, the punch of power staggering. The hunger in him, the darkness that had turned into a furious rage during the events at the Refuge, rose to the surface, glorying in the taste of her. She saturated his senses, drowned him in sensation, and in spite of his earlier words, he was male enough to want her to feel the same.

Acting on naked instinct, he pumped pleasure into her system as he took blood from hers, felt her body arch, shudder—he hadn't held anything back, hadn't stopped with simple arousal. She came apart in his arms, her blood earthy with the flavor of her desire. Drugged to raw pleasure, he found he'd thrust his thigh between her own, splayed his hands on her back, his fingers touching the sensitive inner edges of her wings, her breasts crushed against his chest.

But as he halted in his gluttony to lick the small wounds closed, he discovered he didn't flinch at having let her so near—and not only on the physical level. Perhaps it was because she'd ceded him the control he needed . . . or perhaps it was simply because she was Nimra.

Nimra lay boneless in Noel's arms, conscious of him licking at the skin of her neck to heal the marks caused by his fangs. She didn't tell him not to worry—the puncture site would've healed on its own in minutes—because it was an unexpected pleasure to know he wanted to care for her, this man who had left her body quivering in ecstasy unlike any she had ever before felt, even as his own flesh strained hard and unsatiated against her abdomen.

When he nuzzled at her before raising his head, the affection was another act she hadn't expected, a sign of the man hidden beyond the shadows of nightmare. As she luxuriated in the feeling, he stroked one hand down the center of her back, just touching the sensitive edges where her wings grew out of her back. "Does that feel good?" he murmured, a difference to him that made her skin tighten over her flesh, her thighs clench on the rough intrusion of his own.

"Yes." No angel allowed anyone but a trusted lover to caress her in such a fashion. "Are you not afraid?" she asked, echoes of her own past sliding oily and dark through the aftershocks of pleasure. "You saw what I did to Amariyah."

Noel continued with the exquisite delicacy of his caresses. "You did what you did with thought and care. You aren't a capricious woman."

She'd given him her blood, her body, but his words, they were as precious. "I'm pleased you see me in such a way." It was strange to be standing here unclothed, in the arms of a man who continued to wear his armor of cotton and denim—and yet she was, if not content, then oddly at peace.

Then Noel spoke, and his words carried within them the promise of splintering the peace to nothingness. "Will you tell me about your power?"

CHAPTER 8

"What would you say if I told you it was a secret for me to keep?"

No change in his expression. "I'm patient."

Laughing at the arrogance even as something very old in her grew still, quiet, she went to touch her fingers to his face, dropped her hand midway. "I would show you, Noel, but no." It would be a violation for this man who'd had all choice stripped from him by the monsters who had stained the Refuge with their crimes, regardless of the fact that he'd feel no pain, only the same bone-melting pleasure he'd lavished on her. "I give back," she whispered. "I give back what was given unto others."

"Pleasure for pleasure," Noel said, understanding at once. "Pain for pain."

A solemn nod. "It is not the act itself, but the *intent* behind it that determines what someone will feel when I use my power."

It made him change his hold, shift her into the protection of his body. Yes, she was a powerful angel, but whatever it was her gift demanded from her, it haunted her. "That's why Nazarach leaves you alone." The other angel was renowned for his viciousness.

Nimra's voice when it came, was hard. "We had a meeting when

I first took over this territory. He thought to control me. He has never returned to my lands."

Noel felt his lips curve in a feral smile. "Good."

Noel's body continued to hum with the taste of Nimra the next day. Her blood held such power that he knew he wouldn't need to feed again for a week . . . though there were different kinds of need, he thought, as he began to go through the file Nimra had sent him that morning. It was a list of people she knew had had access to Midnight and who might wish her harm.

However, from what Noel understood of the people on the list— and what he was able to learn from Dmitri when he called the leader of Raphael's Seven—none of them would have left anything to chance, especially given how difficult Midnight was to source. The fact that Nimra's cat had died, betraying the game, spoke of an amateur. Of course, there was also the old adage that poison was a woman's weapon.

Amariyah had convinced him with her confusion, and Asirani— no matter her unrequited feelings for Christian—seemed loyal. But Noel wasn't about to write her off without further investigation. Knowing the vampire had a habit of coming in early to the small office she had on the lower floor, he decided to see if he could track her down. He was in the corridor leading to her office when he heard whispering, low and furious. It was instinct to soften his footsteps.

". . . just listen." Soft, feminine. Asirani.

"It will change nothing." Christian's stiff tones. "I don't wish to hurt you, but I have no such feelings for you."

"She's never going to look at you the way you want." Not bitter, almost . . . sad.

"That is none of your concern."

"Of course it is. She might be our lady, but she's also my friend." An exhale that telegraphed frustration. "She plays with Noel, but it's because he's a vampire. There's no chance of a serious relationship."

"I will be here when she is ready for that relationship."

Noel stepped forward until he could see the pair reflected in the antique mirror on the other side of the corridor. Asirani, striking in a sheath of emerald green, her hair swept up off her neck, was shaking her head, her expression solemn, while black-garbed Christian did his impression of a Roman statue. When the female vampire turned, as if to enter her office, Noel retraced his steps away from the couple.

Asirani's view of his relationship with Nimra was hardly news. Many angels took vampiric lovers, but long-term relationships were far rarer. The fact that vampires and angels couldn't have children together was one of the most powerful reasons why. But regardless of what Asirani believed, Nimra didn't play games. For now, she was Noel's. As for the future—his first priority was to ensure her safety.

That thought had him circling back to Asirani.

There had been unhidden care in her tone when she'd spoken of Nimra, a distinct vein of empathy. Disappointment, too, along with a touch of anger—both directed at Christian, but not even an undertone of the kind of resentment she'd need to feel to want Nimra dead. All of which left him with no viable suspects.

Christian could be a prick but he'd swallowed his antagonism and cooperated with Noel when it came to Nimra's interests. Exeter had spent centuries by her side, Fen decades. He couldn't see either man developing such a deep hatred for her without her being aware of the change. As for the two older servants, quite aside from all else, they had proven quietly devoted.

Frowning, he headed out into the breaking day in search of Nimra—because there was one thing they hadn't considered, and it was the very thing that might hold the answer. He half expected to find her beside Mimosa's grave, but midway to the wild gardens where her pet was buried, something made him look up . . . and what he saw stole his breath.

She was stunning against the slate gray sky streaked with the golds, oranges, and pinks of dawn, her wings backlit with soft fire, her body shown to lithe perfection in the layered gown of fine bronze silk that the wind kissed to her skin. Leaning against the smooth trunk of a young magnolia, he indulged in the beauty of her. Seeing her wings spread to their greatest width, her hair whipping off her face as she glided on the air currents reminded him of the Refuge, the remote city that had been his home for so long.

He'd been placed in the angelic stronghold after completing his hundred-year Contract, when he'd chosen to remain in service to Raphael. There, he'd been part of the guard that helped maintain the archangel's holdings in the Refuge, as well as watching over the vulnerable who were the reason for the existence of the hidden mountain city. However, he'd soon been drafted into a roaming squad that took care of tasks all over the world.

New York, where Raphael had his Tower, had been a wonder to a lad who'd come out of the untamed emptiness of the moors. With its soaring buildings and streets buzzing with humanity, he'd been at once overwhelmed and exhilarated. Kinshasa had stirred the explorer's soul that lived within him, the part that had led him to dare the challenge of vampirism in the first place. Paris, Beirut, Liechtenstein, Belize, each place had spoken to him in a different way . . . but none had sung the soft, sultry song that Nimra's territory whispered to his soul.

A caress of jewel-dusted wings against the painted sky, cutting across the air with breathless ease. His heart squeezed, and he wondered if she knew he watched her, if she flew for him. A fraction of an instant later, he caught a glimpse of another set of wings and his mood turned black.

Christian flew to cut under and around Nimra, as if in invitation to dance. His wingspan was larger than hers, his style of flight less graceful, more aggressive. Nimra didn't respond to the invitation, but neither did she land. Instead, as Noel watched, the two angels flew in the same wide sky, cutting across each other's paths on occasion, and sometimes seeming to time their turns and dives to a hairbreadth so as to just miss one another.

Anger simmered through his veins.

It wasn't cold and tight and hard as it had been for so long, but hot, spiked with a raw masculine jealousy. He had no wings, would never be able to follow Nimra onto that playing field. Gritting his teeth, he folded his arms and continued to keep watch. Maybe he couldn't follow, but if Christian thought that gave him the advantage, he didn't know Noel.

Troubled to a depth she hadn't been for decades, since the day she learned of Eitriel's betrayal, Nimra had come to seek solace in the skies. She'd found no answers in the endless sweep of dawn, and now discovered she was being watched by the very same eyes that had caused her disquiet. It was a compulsion to fly for him, to show him her power, her strength.

Noel had taken only her blood, not her body, in the dark heat of the night's intimacy, and yet he'd touched her too deep all the same. She'd been ready to offer surcease, find some peace for herself. But somehow, he'd wrapped a wolf-strong tendril around her very heart. Nimra wasn't certain she appreciated the vulnerability. It had nothing to do with the scars left by Eitriel, and everything to do with the strength of the draw she felt toward the vampire coming ever closer as she flew in to land.

"Good morning, Noel," she said, folding back her wings as her feet touched the earth.

In answer, he strode across the ground, his strides eating up the distance. And then he kissed her. Hot and hard and all consuming, his lips a burn against her own, his jaw rough against her skin. "You are mine," he said when he finally allowed her to breathe, his thumbs rubbing over her cheekbones. "I don't share." A possessive statement from the core of the man he was, the veneer of civilization stripped away.

The primal intensity of him was a blaze against her senses, but she coated her voice in ice. "Do you think I would betray you?"

"No, Nimra. But if that popinjay doesn't stop flirting with you, blood will be spilled."

Pushing off his hands, she took a step back. "As the ruler of this territory I must deal with many men." If Noel believed he had the right to put limits on her, then he was not the man she'd thought him to be.

"Most of those men don't want to sleep with you," he said in blunt rebuttal. "I reserve the right to introduce my fist to the faces of the ones who do."

Her lips threatened to tug upward. Raw and open and real, this indication of possession was something she could accept. It spoke not of a grab for power, but a territorial display. And Nimra was old enough not to expect a vampire of Noel's age to act in a more modern fashion. "No bloodshed," she said, leaning forward to cup his cheek, claim his mouth with a soft kiss. "Christian is a useful member of my court."

Twenty minutes later, Noel leaned back against the wall beside Nimra's writing desk and watched her walk to the armoire where she kept the Midnight. Her wings were an exotic temptation, reaching out to touch them an impulse he only resisted because neither of them was in the mood for play.

Less than half a minute later, she turned, the vial of Midnight delicate even in her fine-boned hands. Walking to the window, she held it up to the light. Darkness crawled a stealthy shadow across her face. "Yes," she murmured at last, "you are right. There is not as much Midnight as there should be."

He hadn't wanted to be right. "You're certain?"

A nod that sent liquid sunlight gleaming over the blue-black tumble of her hair. "The vial is ringed with circles of gold." She ran her fingers over and along those thin lines. "It is no more than an aesthetic design, but I remember looking at the bottle when it was first given to me and thinking of what some would do for this infinitesimal quantity of Midnight—it just reached over the third line of gold."

Noel crouched down by the window as she held the vial level on the sill. It took a bare few moments for the viscous fluid to settle. When it did, it became apparent that it now hovered *between* the second and third line. He blew out a breath.

"I would that you were wrong, Noel." Leaving the Midnight in his hands, Nimra walked across the room, her wings trailing on the amber-swirled blue of the carpet. "The fact that the assassin came into my chambers and took this means two things."

"The first," Noel said, placing the vial inside the safe and locking it shut, "is that he or she knew it was here."

"Yes—I can count those who have that knowledge on the fingers of one hand, and not use up my fingers." A desolate sadness in every word. "The second is that it means no other powerful angel was involved in this. The hatred is theirs alone."

Noel didn't attempt to comfort her, knowing there could be no comfort—not until the truth was unearthed, the would-be murderer's motives exposed to the light of day. "We need to get an evidence tech in here to see if there are any prints on the vial or the safe that shouldn't be there."

Nimra looked at him as if he were speaking a foreign language. "An evidence tech?"

"It *is* the twenty-first century," he said in a gentle tease, his chest aching at the hurt she would soon have to hide, becoming once more the angel who ruled this territory, ruthless and inhuman. "Such things are possible."

Her eyes narrowed. "Laugh at me at your peril." But she didn't resist when he tugged her into his arms.

He ran his hand down her back, over the heavy warmth of her wings. "I can get hold of someone we can trust."

"To have such a person come into my home—it's not something I welcome." She raised her head, those amazing eyes steely with determination. "But it must be done and soon. Christian has begun to question your presence here beyond that which can be explained by jealousy, and Asirani watches you too closely."

Prick or not, Noel had never discounted Christian's intelligence.

The only surprise was that it had taken the male angel this long to wise up—no doubt his feelings for Nimra had clouded his judgment. As for Nimra's social secretary—"Asirani watches me to make sure I don't hurt you."

Nimra pushed off his chest, her tone remote as she said, "And are you not afraid that I will hurt you?"

Yes. Compelling and dangerous, she'd forced him awake from the numb state he'd been in since the torture. His emotions were raw, new, acutely vulnerable. "I'm your shield," he said, rather than exposing the depth of his susceptibility to her. "If that means taking a hit to protect you, I'll do it without the slightest hesitation." Because Nimra was what angels of her age and power so often weren't—strong, with a heart that still beat, a conscience that still functioned.

She cupped his face, such intensity in her gaze that it was a caress. "I will tell you a secret truth, Noel. No lover has stood for me in all my centuries of existence."

It was a punch to the heart. "What about Eitriel?"

Dropping her hands, she turned her head toward the window. "He is no one." Her words were final, a silent order from an angel used to obedience.

Noel had no intention of allowing her to dictate the bounds of their relationship. "This no one," he said, thrusting his hands into the rich silk of her hair and forcing her to meet his gaze, "walks between us."

Nimra made as if to pull away. He held on. Expression dark with annoyance, she said, "You know I could break your hold."

"Yet here we are."

CHAPTER 9

He was impossible, Nimra thought. Such a man would not be any kind of a manageable companion—no, he would demand and push and take liberties beyond what he should. He would most certainly not treat her with the awe due to her rank and age.

Somewhat to the surprise of the part of her that held centuries of arrogance, the idea enticed rather than repelled. To be challenged, to pit her will against that of this vampire who had been honed in a crucible that would've savaged other men beyond redemption, to dance the most ancient of dances . . . *Yes.*

"Eitriel," she said, "was what a human might call my husband." Angels did not marry as mortals did, did not bind each other with such ties. "We knew one another close to three hundred and forty years."

Noel's scowl was black thunder. "That hardly makes him 'no one.'"

"I was two hundred when we met—"

"A baby," Noel interrupted, hands tightening in her curls. "Angels aren't even allowed to leave the Refuge until reaching a hundred years of age."

She raised an eyebrow. "Do release my hair, Noel."

He unflexed his hands at once. "I'm sorry." Gentle fingers stroking over her scalp. "Bloody uncivilized of me."

Unexpected, that he made her want to smile, when she was about to expose the most horrific period of her life. "We are both aware you will never be Christian."

His eyes gleamed. "Now who's walking a dangerous road?"

Lips curving, she said, "Not a baby, no, but a very young woman." Because of their long life spans, angels matured slower than mortals. However, by two hundred, she'd had the form and face of a woman, had begun to spread her wings, gain a better understanding of who she would one day become.

"Eitriel was my mentor at the start. I studied under him as he taught me what it was to be an angel who might one day rule, though I didn't realize that at the time." It was only later that she'd understood Raphael had seen her burgeoning strength, taken steps to make sure she had the correct training.

Noel's hand curved over her nape, hot and rough. "You fell in love with your teacher."

The memories threatened to roll over her in a crushing wave, but it wasn't the echo of her former lover that caused her chest to fill with such pain as no woman, mortal or immortal, should ever have to experience. "Yes, but not until later, when such a relationship was permissible. I was four hundred and ninety years old.

"For a time, we were happy." But theirs had always been the relationship of teacher to pupil. "Three decades into our relationship, I began to grow exponentially in power and was assigned the territory of Louisiana. It took ten more years for my strength to settle, but when it did, I had long outstripped Eitriel. He was . . . unhappy."

Continuing to caress her nape, Noel snorted. "One of my mortal friends is a psychologist. He would say this Eitriel had inadequacy issues—I'll wager my fangs he had a tiny cock."

Her laugh was shocked out of her. But it faded too soon. "His unhappiness poisoned our relationship," she said, recalling the endless silences that had broken her heart then, but that she'd later recognized as the petulant tantrums of a man who didn't know how to deal with a woman who no longer looked upon his every act with worshipful adoration. "It came as no surprise when he told me he had found another lover." Weaker. Younger. "He said I had become a 'creature' he could no longer bear to touch."

Noel's expression grew dark. "Bastard."

"Yes, he was." She'd accepted that long ago. "We parted then, and I think I would've healed after the hurt had passed. But"—her blood turning to ice—"fate decided to laugh at me. Three days after he left, I discovered I was with child."

In Noel's gaze, she saw the knowledge of the value of that incomparable gift. Angelic births were rare, so rare. Each and every babe was treasured and protected—even by those who would otherwise be enemies. "I would not have kept such a joy from Eitriel, but I needed time to come to terms with it before I told him.

"It never came to that. My babe," she whispered, her hand lying flat over her belly, "was not strong. Keir was often with me that first month after I realized I carried a life in my womb." The healer was the most revered among angelkind. "But he'd been called away the night I began to bleed. Just a little . . . but I knew."

Noel muttered something low and harsh under his breath, spinning away to shove his hands through his hair, before turning in one of those unexpected bursts of movement to tug her into his arms. "Tell me you weren't alone. *Tell me.*"

"Fen," she said, heart heavy at the thought of her old friend grown so very frail, the light of his life beginning to flicker in the slightest wind. "Fen was there. He held me through the terrible dark of that night, until Keir was able to come. If I could Make Fen, I would in a heartbeat, but I cannot." Tears clogged her voice. "He is my dearest friend."

Noel went motionless. "He can walk freely into these rooms?"

"Of course." She and Fen had never again been lady and liege after that stormy night as her babe bled out of her. "We speak here so we will not be interrupted."

Noel's hands clenched on her arms. Frowning, she went to press him for his thoughts when the import of his question hit her. "Not Fen." She wrenched out of his embrace. "He would no more harm me than he would murder Amariyah."

"I," Noel said, "have no idea of how that safe works, much less the combination. I wouldn't even know where to begin. But Fen . . . he knows so many things about you. Such as the date you lost your babe, or the day your child would've been born."

The gentle words were a dagger in her soul. Because he was right. Five decades ago, she'd changed the combination to what would have been her lost babe's birthing day. It hadn't been a conscious choice as such—the date was the first that had come into her mind, embedded into her consciousness. "I will not believe it." Frost in her voice as she fought the anguish that threatened to shatter her. "And I will not allow this evidence technician to come here."

"Nimra."

She cut him off when he would've continued. "I will speak to Fen. Alone." If her old friend had done this, she had to know why. If he had not—and she couldn't bring herself to believe him capable of such treachery—then there was no cause for him to be hurt by the ugliness of suspicion. "Unless you think he'll rise up to stab me while I sit across from him?"

Noel made no effort to hide his irritation, but neither did he stop her as she headed for the door. Exeter was waiting to speak to her at the bottom of the staircase, as was Asirani, but she jerked her head in a sharp negative, not trusting herself to speak. Nothing would be right in her world until she'd unearthed the truth, however terrible it might be.

Fen wasn't at home, but she knew his favorite places, as he knew hers.

"Ah," he said when she tracked him down at the sun-drenched stone bench on the edge of the lily pond, his near-black eyes solemn. "Sadness sits on your shoulders again. I thought the vampire made you happy."

Noel had dropped back as soon as Fen came into sight, giving her the privacy she needed. Heartsick, she took a seat beside her old friend, her wings draping on the grass behind them. "I have kept a secret from you, Fen," she said, eyes on a dragonfly buzzing over the lilies. "Queen died not because her heart failed, but because she drank poison intended for me."

Fen didn't reply for a long moment undisturbed by the wind, the pond smooth glass under the wide green lily pads. "You were so sad," he said at last. "So very, very sad deep inside, where almost no one could see it. But I knew. Even as you smiled, as you ruled, you mourned. So many years you mourned."

Tears burned at the backs of her eyes as his wrinkled hand closed over her own where it lay on the bench between them. "I worried who would watch over you when I was gone." His voice was whispery with age, his fingers containing a tremor that made her heart clench. "I thought the sadness might drown you, leaving you easy prey for the scavengers."

A single tear streaked down her face.

"I wanted only to give you peace." He tried to squeeze her hand, but his strength was not what it had been when he first strode into her court, a man with an endless store of energy. "It broke my heart to see you haunting the gardens as everyone slept, so much pain trapped inside of you. It is arrogant of me to make such a claim, ridiculous, too, but . . . you are my daughter as much as Mariyah."

She turned up her hand, curling her fingers around his own. "Do you think me so fragile, Fen?"

He sighed. "I fear I learned the wrong lessons from my other daughter. She is not strong. We both know it."

"There would've been no one left to protect her after I was gone."

"No. Yet still I could not bear your sadness." Shaking his head, he turned to face her. "I knew I'd made a terrible mistake the very next day, when you faced the world with strength and courage once more, but by then, Queen was dead." Regret put a heavy weight on every word. "I am sorry, my lady. I will take whatever punishment you deem fit."

She squeezed his hand, emotion choking up her throat. "How can

I punish you for loving me, Fen?" The idea of hurting him was anathema to her. He was no assassin, simply old and afraid for the daughters he'd leave behind. "I will not let Amariyah drown," she promised. "As long as I draw breath, I will watch over her."

"Your heart has always been too generous for a woman who wields so much power." Making a clucking sound with his tongue, he waggled an arthritic finger. "It is good your vampire is hewn of harder wood."

This time it was Nimra who shook her head. "Such mortal thoughts," she said, her soul aching with the knowledge of a loss that came ever nearer with each heartbeat. "I do not need a man."

"No, but perhaps you should." A smile so familiar, it would savage her when she could no longer see it. "You can't have failed to notice that those angels who retain their . . . humanity through the ages are the ones who have mates or lovers who stand by them."

It was an astute statement. "Do not die, Fen," she whispered, unable to contain her sorrow. "You were meant to live forever." She'd had his blood tested three years after he'd first come into her court, already aware that this was a man she could trust not to betray her through the ages. But the results had come back negative—Fen's body would reject the process that turned mortal to vampire, reject it with such violence that he'd either die or go incurably insane.

Fen laughed, his skin papery under her own. "I'm rather looking forward to death," he said with a chuckle that made his eyes twinkle. "Finally, I'll know something you never have and maybe never will."

It made her own lips curve. And as the sun moved across the lazy blue of the sky, as the sweet scent of jasmine lingered in the air, she sat with the man who would've been her murderer, and she mourned the day when he would no longer sit with her beside the lily pond as the dragonflies buzzed.

That day came far sooner than she could've ever expected. Fen simply didn't awaken the next morning, passing into death with a peaceful smile on his face. She had him buried with the highest honors, in a grave beside that of his beloved wife. Even Amariyah put aside their enmity for that day, behaving with utmost grace though her face was ravaged by grief.

"Good-bye," she said to Nimra after Christian, his voice pure and beautiful, had sung a heartfelt farewell to a mortal who had been a friend to angels.

Nimra met the vampire's eyes, so akin to her father's and so very dissimilar. "If you ever need anything, you know you have but to call."

Amariyah gave her a tight smile. "There's no need to pretend. He was the only link between us. He's gone now." With that, she turned and walked away, and Nimra knew this was the last time she'd see Fen's daughter. It didn't matter. She had put things in place—Amariyah wouldn't ever be friendless or helpless if in need. This, Nimra would do for Fen . . . for the friend who would never again counsel her with a wisdom no mortal was supposed to possess.

A big hand sliding into hers, his skin rougher than her own. "Come," Noel said. "It's time to go."

It was only when he wiped his thumb across her cheek that she realized she was crying, the tears having come after everyone else had left the graveside. "I will miss him, Noel."

"I know." Sliding his hand up her arm, he placed it around her shoulders and held her close, his body providing a safe haven for the sorrow that poured out of her in an anguished torrent.

In the days after Fen's death, Noel began to discover exactly how much the old man had done for Nimra. From watching over her interests when it came to Louisiana's vampiric residents to ensuring the court remained in balance, Fen had been the center even as he positioned himself on the edges. With his loss came a time of some confusion, as everyone tried to figure out their place in the scheme of things.

Christian, of course, tried to take over, but it was clear from the start that he had too much arrogance to play the subtle political games Fen had managed with such ease . . . and that Noel quietly began to handle. Politician he wasn't, but he had no trouble putting any idea of rank aside to get things done. As for his right to be in the court at all, he hadn't asked Nimra's permission to remain, hadn't asked anyone's permission.

He'd simply called Dmitri and said, "I'm staying."

The vampire, who held more power than any other vamp Noel knew, hadn't been pleased. "You're slated to be stationed in the Tower."

"Unslate me."

Silence, then a dark amusement. "If Nimra ever decides you're too much trouble, I'll have a place waiting for you."

"Thanks, but it won't be needed." Even if Nimra did attempt to throw him out, Noel was having none of it. She was painfully vulnerable right now, and without Fen here to guard her secrets from those who would use her grief to cause her harm, someone had to watch her back. Mind set, he began to do precisely that, using the members of the court, senior and junior, to Nimra's advantage.

Sharp, loyal Asirani was the first to catch on. "I always knew we hadn't seen the real Noel," she said, a glint in her eye, then passed him a small file. "You need to handle this."

It turned out to be a report about a group of young vampires in New Orleans who were acting out, having caught wind of Nimra's grieving distraction. Noel was in the city by nightfall. All under a hundred, the vampires were no match for him—even together. He wasn't only older, he was incredibly strong for his age. As with the angels, some vampires gained power with age, while others reached a static point and remained there.

Noel had grown ever stronger since he was Made, part of the reason he'd been pulled into the guard directly below Raphael's Seven. When the vampires proved stupid enough to think they could take him on, he expended his pent-up energy, his protective fury at being unable to shield Nimra from the pain of Fen's loss, on the idiots.

After they lay bleeding and defeated in front of him in a crumbling alleyway barely lit by the faint wash of yellow from a nearby streetlight, he folded his arms and raised an eyebrow. "Did you think no one was watching?"

The leader of the little pack groaned, his eye turning a beautiful purple. "Fuck, nobody said anything about a fucking enforcer."

"Watch your mouth." Noel had the satisfaction of seeing the man pale. "This was a warning. Next time, I won't hold back. Understood?"

A sea of nods.

Returning to his own room in the early morning hours, while the world was still dark, Noel showered, hitched a towel around his hips, and headed into his bedroom with the intention of grabbing some clothes. What he really wanted to do was go to Nimra. She hadn't slept since Fen's death, would be in the gardens, but the fading bruise on his cheek where one of the vamps had managed to whack him with an elbow, might alert her as to what he'd been up to. He wanted a little more time to settle into this new role before—"Nimra."

Seated on the edge of his bed, her wings spread behind her and her body clad in a long, flowing gown of deepest blue, she looked more like the angel who ruled a territory than she had in days. "Where have you been, Noel?"

CHAPTER 10

N ew Orleans." He would not lie to her.
A wrinkling of her brow. "I see."

"Do you want the details?"

"No, not tonight." Her gaze lingered on the damp lines of his body before she rose from the bed, her wings sweeping across the sheets. *"Bonne nuit."*

He hadn't touched her intimately since the night he'd fed from her, so hot and sweet, but now he crossed the room to stop her with his hands on the silken heat of her upper arms, his chest pressed to her back . . . to her wings. "Nimra." When she stilled, he swept aside the curling ebony of her hair to press his lips to her pulse.

Reaching back, she touched her fingers to his face. "Do you hunger?"

A simple question that staggered him with its generosity, but no longer surprised. Not now that he understood the truth of the woman in his arms. "Stay." Kiss after kiss along the slender line of her neck, a delicate pleasure that made his skin go tight, his own pulse accelerate. "Let me hold you tonight."

A moment's pause and he knew she was weighing up whether or

not to trust him with the depth of her vulnerability. When she shifted to face him, when she allowed him to take her into his arms, to take her to his bed, it turned a key in a dark, hidden corner of his soul, a part that had not seen the light of day since the events that had almost broken him. But they hadn't. And now, he was awake.

Nimra's need for Noel was a deep, unrelenting ache, but she fought the urge to take, to demand from this captivating male with wounds that would take a long time to truly heal. Then his eyes met her own as he braced himself above her, his fingers stroking the sensitive arch of her wing, and there was an intensity to them she'd never before seen. "Put your hands on me, Nimra." A command.

One she was happy to accept. Running her foot over the back of his calf, her gown sliding down her leg, she began to explore the ridges and valleys of his body, so hard, so very masculine. He shuddered under her touch, his breath hot against her jaw as he grazed her with his teeth, his cock pressing in blatant demand against her abdomen.

No civilized lover this.

"You are a beautiful man," she whispered as she closed her fingers over the rigid evidence of his need.

Color darkened his cheekbones. "Uh, whatever you say."

"Such compliance, Noel?" She squeezed him, luxuriating in the velvet-soft skin covering such powerful steel. "I am not sure I believe you."

A groan. "You have your hand on my cock. If you called me an ugly git, I'd agree with you. Just. *Don't. Stop.*"

His unashamed pleasure made her entire body melt. Not only did she continue in her intimate caresses, she began to suck and kiss at his neck until he slammed his mouth down on her own, tender control transforming into untamed sexuality. Demanding and aggressive, he thrust his cock into her grip in time with the thrust of his tongue into her mouth.

His hand fisted in her gown at the same instant, pulling up the material until it bunched at her waist. His fingers were underneath the lace that protected her an instant later, making her arch, cry out into his kiss. Taking that cry as his due, he tore away the lace to stroke her to quivering readiness even as he pulled her hand off him. "Enough." A ragged word against her lips, heavy hair-roughened thighs nudging her own apart.

She wrapped her legs around his hips as he flexed forward and claimed her with a single primal move. Spine bowing, she clung to him, her nails digging into the sweat-slick muscle of his back. When she felt his mouth settle on the pulse in her neck, it made a tremor shake her frame, the spot unbearably sensitive. *Yes.* She fisted one hand in his hair, held him to her. "Now, Noel."

His lips curved against her skin. "Yes, my lady Nimra."

A piercing pleasure radiated out from the point where he drank from her, while his body, his hands, shoved her ever closer to the precipice. Then the two streams of pleasure collided and Nimra flew apart . . . to come to in the arms of a man who looked at her with a furious tenderness that threatened to make her believe in an eternity that did not have to be drenched in loneliness.

T hree days later, she found herself frowning at Asirani. "And there have been no other problems?" While she could believe her fellow angels wouldn't have paid heed to the passing of a mortal, the vampires in the region had long dealt with Fen, understood the role he'd played. It defied belief that they hadn't attempted anything while she'd been wracked by grief.

Asirani avoided her eyes. "You couldn't quite say that."

Nimra waited.

And waited.

"Asirani."

A put-upon sigh. "You're talking to the wrong vampire."

Rather than chasing down the right one, Nimra decided to do her

own probing. What she discovered was that "someone" had negoti-
ated Fen's passing with such skill that any ripples had been few and
handled in a matter of hours. As far as the outside world was concerned, Fen's decades of service had been forgotten as soon as he was
gone, his death a mere inconvenience rather than a splintering pain
that had ripped apart her chest, filled her eyes.

Later that day, she discovered that her reputation as an angel not
to be crossed had in fact *grown* in the time she'd spent mourning her
friend. "Why do I have a letter of apology from the leader of the vampires in New Orleans?" she asked Christian. "He seems to believe I'm
an inch away from executing his entire kiss in a very nasty way."

"His vampires misbehaved," was the response. "It was taken care
of." His face, acetic and closed, told her that was all she'd get.

Intrigued at both the defiance and the realization that Noel and
Christian appeared to have reached some kind of an understanding,
she finally cornered the man responsible for a political game that
had, from all indications, been played with none of Fen's subtlety—
and yet garnered excellent results. "How," she said to Noel when she
discovered him in the wild southern gardens, "did you acquire the
title of my enforcer?"

He jumped up from his kneeling position with a distinctly
guilty—and young—look on his face. "It sounded good."

When she tried to look around him, and to whatever it was that
he was hiding under the shade of a bush laden with tiny blossoms of
pink and white, he shifted to block her view. Scowling, she tapped
the letter of apology against her legs. "What did you do in New
Orleans?"

"The vampires didn't learn their lesson the first time." Cool eyes.
"I had to get creative."

"Explain."

"Heard of the word 'delegation'?" An unflinching stare.

Her lips curved, the ruler in her recognizing strength of a kind
that was rare . . . and that any woman would want by her side. "How
are my stocks doing?"

"Ask Christian. He has a computer for a brain—and I had to give him something to do."

Unexpected, that he'd shared power after taking it with such speed and without bloodshed. "Is there anything I need to know?"

"Nazarach's hounds were nosing around about a week ago, but seems like they had to return home." A shrug as if he'd had nothing to do with it.

"I see." And what she saw was a wonder. This strong male, who was very much a leader, had put himself in her service. Unlike Fen, Noel had intimate access to her, and yet even when she'd been at her most vulnerable, there had been no sly whispers in the sinuous dark, only a luxuriant pleasure that muted the jagged edge of loss.

Before she could form words from the fierce cascade of emotion in her heart, she heard a distinct and inquisitive "meow." Heart tumbling, she tried to see around those big shoulders once more, but he turned to block her view as he crouched down. "You were supposed to stay quiet," he murmured as he rose back up and turned to face her.

The two tiny balls of fur in his arms—comically colored in a patchwork of black and white—butted their heads against his chest, obviously aware this wolf was all bark when it came to the innocent.

"Oh!" She reached out to scratch one tiny head and found the kittens being poured into her arms. Squirming and twisting, they made themselves comfortable against her. "Noel, they're gorgeous."

He snorted. "They're mutts from the local shelter." But his voice held tender amusement. "I figured you wouldn't mind two more strays."

She rubbed her cheek against one kitten, laughed at the jealous grizzling of the second. Such tiny, fragile lives that could give so much joy. "Are they mine?"

"Do I look like a cat man?" Pure masculine affront, arms folded across his chest. "I'm getting a dog—a really big dog. With sharp teeth."

Laughing, she blew him a kiss, feeling younger than she had in centuries. "Thank you."

His scowl faded. "Even Mr. Popinjay cracked a grin when one of them tried to claw off his shoe."

"Oh, they didn't." Christian was so vain about those gleaming boots. "Terrible creatures." They butted up against her chin, wanting to play. "It'll be good to have pets around again," she said, thinking of Mimosa when she'd been young, of Queen. The memories were bittersweet, but they were precious.

Noel walked closer, reaching out to rub the back of the kitten with one black ear and one white. The other, she saw, had two white ones tipped with black. "I'm afraid there's a condition attached to this gift."

Hearing the somber note in his voice, she put the kittens on the ground, knowing they wouldn't wander too far from the cardboard box where they'd evidently been napping. "Tell me," she whispered, looking into that harsh masculine face.

"I'm afraid," he said, opening his fist to reveal a sun-gold ring with a heart of amber, "the archaic human part of me requires this one bond after all."

Amber was often worn by those mortals and vampires who were entangled in a relationship. Nimra had never worn amber for any man. But now, she raised her hand, let him slide the ring onto her finger. It was a slight weight, and it was everything. "I do hope you bought a matching set," she murmured, for it seemed she, too, was not quite civilized enough to require no bonds at all.

Not when it came to Noel.

His smile was a little crooked as he reached into his pocket to pull out a thicker, more masculine ring set with a rough chunk of amber where hers was a delicate filigree with a polished stone. "Perfect."

"We won't be able to have children." He spoke the solemn words as she slid the ring onto his finger with a happiness that went soul deep. "I'm sorry."

A poignant emotion touched her senses, but there was no sorrow. Not with an eternity colored by wild translucent blue. "There will always be those like Violet who need a home," she said, rubbing her thumb over his ring. "Blood of my blood they might not be, but heart of my heart they will be."

Eliminating the small distance between their bodies, Noel stroked his fingers down her left wing, a slow glide that whispered of possession. As did the arms she slid up his chest to curve over his shoulders. There were no words, but none were needed, the metal of his ring warm against her cheek when he cupped her face.

Her wolf. Her Noel.

Alphas: Origins

Ilona Andrews

CHAPTER 1

Karina Tucker took a deep breath. "Jacob, do *not* hit Emily again. Emily, let go of his hair. Don't make me stop this car!"

Her daughter's face swung into the rearview mirror, outraged as only a six-year-old could be. "Mom, he started it!"

"I don't care who started it. If you don't be quiet right now, things will happen!"

"What things?" Melissa whined. Megan, her twin, stuck her tongue out.

Karina furrowed her eyebrows, trying to look mean in the rearview mirror. "Horrible things."

The four children quieted in the back of the van, trying to figure out what "horrible things" meant. The quiet wouldn't last. Karina drove on. The next time Jill called to ask her if she would chaperone a gaggle of first graders for a school field trip, she would claim to have the bubonic plague instead.

The trip itself wasn't that awful. The sun shone bright, and the drive down to the old-timey village, forty-five minutes from Chikasha, was downright pleasant. Nothing but clear sky and flat Oklahoma fields with an occasional thin line of forest between them to break the wind. But now, after a day of hayrides and watching butter being churned and iron nails being hammered, the kids were tired and cranky. They'd been on the road for twenty minutes and the lot of them had already engaged in a World War III–scale conflict three times. She imagined the other parents hadn't fared any better. As the six cars made their way up the rural road, Karina could almost hear the whining emanating from the vehicles ahead of her.

They should have just gotten a school bus. But Jill had panicked half of the parents over the bus not having seat belts. In retrospect, the whole thing seemed silly. Thousands of children rode school buses every day with no problems, seat belts or not. Unfortunately, creating panic was one of her best friend's talents. Jill meant well, but her life was a string of self-created emergencies, which she then cheerfully overcame. Usually Karina pulled her off the edge of the cliff, but with Emily involved, it was hard to maintain perspective.

This pointless worry really had to stop. Emily wasn't made of glass. Eventually Karina would have to let her go on a trip or to a sleepover without her mommy. The thought made Karina squirm. After Jonathan died, she'd taken Emily to a grief counselor, who offered to work with her as well. Karina had turned it down. She'd already been through it, when her parents passed away, and it hadn't made things any easier.

Her cell beeped. Karina pushed the button on her hands-free set. "Yes?"

"How are you holding up?" Jill's voice chirped.

"Fantastic." Would be even better if she didn't have to talk on the phone while driving. "You?"

"I need to go potty!" Jacob announced from the back.

"Robert called Savannah a B word. Other than that we're good," Jill reported.

"I really need to go. Or I'll poop in my pants. And then there'll be a big stain . . ."

"Listen, Jacob needs to go potty." She caught sight of a dark blue sign rising above the trees. "I'm going to pull over at the motel ahead of you."

"What motel?"

"The one on the right. With the big blue sign, says Motel Sunrise?"

"Where?" Jill's voice came through tinted with static. "I don't see it."

"I don't see a motel," Megan reported.

"Look at the blue sign." Emily pointed at the window.

"Well, I don't see it," Jacob declared.

"That's because you're a doofus," Emily said.

"You suck!"

"Quiet!" Karina barked.

The exit rolled up on her right. Karina angled the car into it. "I'm taking this exit," she said to the cell phone. "I'll catch up with you in a minute."

"What exit? Karina, where are you? You were right there and now you're gone. I don't see you in my rearview mirror . . ."

"That's because I took the exit."

"What exit?"

Oh, for the love of God. "I'll talk to you later."

The paved road brought them to a two-story building covered with dark gray stucco. Only one car, an old Jeep, sat in the parking lot.

Karina pulled up before the entrance and hesitated. The building, a crude box with small narrow windows, looked like some sort of institutional structure, an office, or even a prison. It certainly didn't look inviting.

"Now I see it," Megan said.

Karina shook her head. You'd think if you owned a motel, you'd want to make it seem hospitable. Plant some flowers, maybe choose a nice color for the walls, something other than battleship gray. It only made good business sense. As it was, the place radiated a grim, almost menacing air. She had a strong urge to just keep on driving.

"I have to go!" Jacob announced and farted.

Karina jumped out of the van and slid the door open. "Out."

Fifteen seconds later, she herded them inside a small lobby. The lone woman standing behind the counter turned her head at their approach. She was skeletally thin, with long red hair dripping down past her shoulders. Karina glanced at her face and almost marched back out. The woman had eyes like a rattlesnake, no compassion, no kindness, no anger. Nothing at all.

"I'm sorry," Karina said. "Could we please use your facilities? The little boy needs to go to the bathroom."

The woman nodded to the archway on Karina's right. Charming. That's okay. They just needed to get in and get out. "Thank you! Come on, kids."

The archway opened into a long hallway. On the left, several doors punctuated the wall, one marked "Bathroom" and another, at the very end, marked "Stairs." On the right an older man stood in the middle of the hallway. Heavily muscled, with a face like a bulldog, he'd planted himself as if he were about to be overrun by rioters. His eyes watched her with open malice. The kids sensed it, too, and clustered around her. Karina didn't blame them.

"Hi!"

The man said nothing.

Okay. She marched to the bathroom and swung the door open. A single-person bathroom, relatively clean. No scary strangers hiding anywhere. "In you go." She ushered Jacob inside and stood guard by the door.

Minutes ticked off, long and viscous. The man hadn't moved. The children kept quiet under his scrutiny, like tiny rabbits sensing a predator.

Karina knocked on the door gently. "Come on, Jacob. Let the other kids have a turn."

"Almost done."

Karina waited. The man kept staring at her. Gradually his face took on a new expression. Instead of staring her down, he was now studying her as if she were some bizarre alien life-form. That was even more disturbing. Karina fought a shiver.

"Jacob, we need to go."

She heard the toilet flush. Finally.

Jacob emerged from the bathroom. "I washed my hands with soap," he informed her. "Do you want to smell them?"

"No. Does anybody else need to go?"

They shook their heads. Emily hugged her leg. "I want to go home, Mom."

"Excellent idea." Karina led them down the hallway.

The man moved to block their way. "Thank you for letting us use the bathroom," Karina said. "We'll be on our way now."

The man leaned forward. His nostrils fluttered. He sucked in the air through his nose and his face split in a grin. He didn't smile; he showed her his teeth: abnormally large and sharp, triangular like shark teeth, and definitely not human.

Ice skittered down Karina's spine.

The man took a step forward. "You ssshmell like a donor." His teeth took up so much space in his mouth, he slurred the words.

Karina backed away, holding her hands out to shield the kids behind her. She wished she had a can of mace or a gun—some weapon in her purse other than Kleenex, her pocketbook, and a cell phone with a dead battery.

"Let us out!"

The man advanced. "Rishe! The woman ishh a donor."

"We'll be leaving now!" Karina put some steel into her voice. Sometimes if you looked like you were ready to fight, people backed down and looked for an easier target.

The man bared his teeth again and she glimpsed what looked like a second row of fangs behind the first in his mouth. "No, you won't," he said.

Time for emergency measures. "Help!" Karina screamed at the top of her lungs. "Help!"

"No help," he assured her.

The kids began to cry.

Maybe this is a nightmare, flashed in her head. Maybe she was dreaming.

"Mom?" Emily clutched at her jeans.

Dream or not, Karina couldn't let him get a hold of her or the kids. She kept backing away to the door behind her, the one labeled "Stairs."

"Let us go!"

He kept coming. "Rishe! Where are you?"

The wall on their right exploded.

Splintered pieces of wood peppered the hallway, knocking the shark-toothed man back and missing Karina by mere inches. Stunned, she glanced into the gap in the wall. The redheaded woman—Rishe?—jumped over the counter and ran directly at Karina and the children, her face twisted into a grotesque mask. The skin on Rishe's neck bulged, rolling up, as if a tennis ball slid up her throat into her mouth.

This is just crazy . . .

The woman spat.

Something dark flickered through the air. Pain stung Karina's left side. A long thin needle, like the quill of a porcupine, sprouted from her stomach, just under the ribs. She yanked it out on pure instinct. She should've been terrified, but there was no time . . .

Something hit the red-haired woman from behind, arresting her in midstep. Rishe's mouth gaped in a terrified silent scream. Huge claws grasped her face, jerked, and her head twisted completely around.

Oh, my God.

Rishe's body fell, and beyond it Karina glimpsed a *thing*. Huge, dark, inhuman, it stared back at her with malevolent eyes. Its very existence was so at odds with everything Karina knew, that her mind simply refused to believe it was real.

An odd odor saturated the air, dry and slightly metallic, like copper warmed by the sun. The thing stepped over the woman, its gaze fixed on her.

"Run!" Karina turned on her heel and dashed down the hallway, herding the children before her.

The man with shark teeth rose slowly, pulled a wooden splinter out of his eye, tossed it aside, and, with a deep bellow, charged into the lobby through the hole in the wall.

A snarl answered him, a promise of pain and death. It whipped Karina into a frenzy. She swiped Jacob off the floor—he was the smallest—and ran faster to the heavy door barring the stairs. She jerked it open. "Up the stairs, go, go!"

They ran up, whimpering and sobbing. The same fear that drove her propelled them up the stairs better than anything she could've screamed.

Karina slammed the door closed, balancing Jacob on one arm, and looked for something to bar it, but the stairway was empty. Her stomach burned, the pain from the needle puncture spreading up and down her body as if her skin had caught on fire. She ran after the kids. The boy in her arms was stone heavy. They reached the top of the staircase and crowded on the landing.

Below something clanged. There it was again, the scent of hot metal burning her lungs.

Karina set Jacob down and wrenched the door open. They burst into the upstairs hallway. She scanned the rows of doors and tried to shove the nearest one open, but it was locked.

Another—locked, too.

Third—locked.

This is a nightmare. It has to be a nightmare.

A vicious snarl chased them. Emily screamed, a high-pitched shriek that could've broken glass. Karina grabbed her daughter by the hand and dragged her down the hall, to the single window. "Follow me!"

Beyond the window a fire escape waited.

Karina grasped the window latch and jerked it up. Stuck.

Her head swam. The air around her had grown scalding hot. Every breath burned her lungs from the inside out. She stumbled, caught herself on the windowsill, and pulled the sash upward with all her strength. The wood groaned and suddenly the frame slid up.

A door thumped. Kids screamed. The terrible dark beast had made it into the hallway.

She grabbed the nearest child and hurled her onto the fire escape, then the next, and the next. Little feet thudded, running down the metal stairs. Emily was last. Karina clutched her daughter to her and climbed out on the fire escape.

A black van waited below. Several men stood by the van. They had the children. They stood there silently, watching her, so calm while the kids screamed, and suddenly she realized that they and the beast inside were allies. They were trapped.

A growl washed over her.

The world gained crystal clarity, everything becoming painfully vivid and sharp. Slowly Karina turned. Her daughter hugged her, her breath a tiny warm cloud on her neck. The metal rail of the fire escape dug into Karina's back. The thudding of her heart sounded so loud, each beat shook her rib cage like a blow from a sledgehammer. Every breath was a gift.

She saw the thing emerge from the darkness. Slowly, it solidified out of the gloom, one gargantuan paw on the windowsill, then another. Enormous claws scratched the wood. It climbed onto the windowsill and perched there, a mere foot from her. Karina stared into its eyes, inhaled its scent, and knew with absolute certainty that she was going to die.

The thing opened its maw, revealing huge fangs. Its deep voice issued forth in a single mangled word. "Donor."

"Are you sure?" asked a male voice from below.

The beast snarled. Karina jerked back, shielding Emily with her hands. Her legs gave out and she fell to her knees.

"My lady?" said the voice from below, closer now.

She barely turned her head, not daring to take her gaze from the monster in the window. A dark-haired man climbed the fire escape toward her. His face was preternaturally beautiful, his eyes a dark, intense blue. "I have a proposition for you, my lady . . ."

His voice faded, replaced by darkness and the feel of cotton against her body.

I agree.

Karina sat up . . . She was in her bed. The room lay dark about her. A nightmare. That was all.

Her heart thudded in her chest. She rubbed her face and her hands came away slick with cold moisture.

I agree. *"I agree" to what?* What did she agree to in her dream?

It didn't matter. It was a nightmare. In the morning, she'd call the grief counselor.

Karina frowned and pushed free of the blankets. She felt a strange sense of wrongness, as if there was something very important she was missing. Something vital. A small lamp waited on the table next to the bed. She flicked it on and a cone of soft electric light illuminated the room.

The bedroom wasn't hers.

For a moment Karina froze, and then fear caught her in its fist and squeezed. "Emily?" she whispered. "Emily?"

No answer.

She was alone in a strange bedroom.

There could be a rational explanation for this. There had to be. She just didn't know what it was.

I agree. An echo of her voice from the dream. She had a terrible suspicion the unfamiliar bedroom and those two words were connected.

Her clothes were gone. She wore only underwear and a giant T-shirt, three sizes too big.

A pair of carefully folded jeans lay on a chair next to the bed. Her jeans, the ones she had worn on the field trip. Karina pulled them on. She had to find Emily.

The door swung open with ease and she found herself in a hallway. To the left, the hallway ended in a stairway leading up. To her right, a pool of electric light brightened the wooden floor and the rust-colored rug. Quiet voices carried on a soft discussion.

She followed the voices and stepped into a kitchen, blinking against the light. Three men sat at the round table in the center. They turned to look at her. The one sitting farthest from her wore the unearthly face of the man from her dream. His name surfaced from the depths of her memory. Arthur.

I agree.

Arthur nodded to her. "Ah. You're up. Why don't you sit down with us? Henry, please get a chair for Lady Karina." His soft, intimate voice caressed her almost like a touch. It should've been soothing. Instead her insides clenched into a tight knot.

A tall man with a shy smile rose and held a chair out for her. So oddly domestic, all three drinking tea. Nobody was startled by her appearance. Clearly she was expected.

Karina sat. "Thank you." The automatic response rolled from her lips before she even realized it.

"You're welcome," Arthur said. He leaned back with a quiet elegance, artfully posed without putting any effort into it. His hair was soft, black, and brushed back from his perfectly sculpted face. His eyebrows were equally black and so were his eyelashes, long and soft like velvet. They framed big eyes, crystalline blue, distant, and cold. Angelic, she thought. He looked like an angel, not a plump cherub, but an angel who roamed freely in the sky, possessed of heart-wrenching beauty and terrible power, an angel who had stared into the bottomless blue for so long that his eyes had absorbed its color.

"Would you like some tea?" Arthur asked.

"Children . . . ?"

"Safe," he said and she believed the sincerity of his words even though she had no reason to do so.

Arthur rose, took a small blue mug from the shelf behind him, and poured steaming tea into it from a large kettle on the stove. He set the cup in front of her. "Please drink. It will steady your nerves."

Karina looked at the cup.

He drank from his own cup and smiled in encouragement.

She picked up the cup and took a sip. Green tea. Odd taste, slightly sour.

Maybe she was still dreaming. The whole scene had that slightly absurd wrongness found only in dreams.

Karina looked about the table. The man who had offered her the chair, Henry, sat to her right. He was tall and whipcord lean. His face, serious with somber intelligence, lacked Arthur's magnetism, but its sharp angles drew her all the same. His tawny hair was cut close to the scalp, but still showed a trace of a curl. His green eyes regarded her and she read pity in their depths.

The man on her left was model pretty. Strong masculine jaw, deep, dark blue eyes, high cheekbones, a mane of golden wavy hair dripping down to below his waist, hiding half of his face . . . His eyes flashed with wild humor. He gave her a wink, grinned, exposing even white teeth, and tossed his hair back. An ugly scar ripped his left cheek, almost as if something had taken a bite out of him and his flesh hadn't healed right. She fought an urge to look away. He reached for her hand . . .

"Daniel." Arthur's voice gained a slight edge. "That's extremely unwise."

Daniel sat back.

"Just because she didn't scream when she saw your face doesn't mean you get to touch." Henry refilled his cup.

"Please forgive Daniel. He doesn't mean to be rude. He's just forbidden to speak for the time being. Your tea is getting cold," Arthur said.

"He tends to cause problems when he speaks," Henry said.

Daniel gave her a smoldering smile.

She faced Arthur. "What did I agree to?"

Arthur sighed. "I see."

Henry leaned forward. "Perhaps we should mend this."

"Yes. The sooner, the better. Lucas might return and that would make things considerably more complicated."

Daniel laughed softly. If wolves could laugh, they would sound just like him.

Henry held out his hand. "It's easier if you hold on to me."

Karina hesitated.

"You do want to remember, don't you?" Arthur asked.

She put her hand into Henry's. His long warm fingers closed about hers. The world tore in two and she was back on the landing of the fire escape at the not-motel, cradling Emily. Her whole body burned with a terrible ache.

Arthur leaned his head to the side, looked at them for a moment, and plucked Emily from her arms.

"No!" Karina struggled to hold on, but her hands had lost all strength.

Emily didn't kick. Didn't scream. Her face was completely blank, as if she had turned into a doll. Arthur turned and handed her to someone behind him on the stairs.

"Emily!" Karina tried to crawl after her but her body refused to obey.

Arthur touched the hem of her black top and edged it upward. His fingers touched her stomach. Pain pierced her and she cried out.

"Ah. Now see, this isn't good." Arthur shook his head mournfully. "All of this must seem terribly confusing to you and our time is short, so I will keep the explanations simple. This is the house where monsters live. We are the killers of monsters. I suppose that also makes us monsters simply by necessity. I don't know why you're here. It's probably a pure coincidence. An unlucky roll of the dice. You and your children were caught in the cross fire. One of the monsters poisoned you with her throat dart. The wound is fatal. You're dying."

Fear shot down Karina's spine in an icy rush. She didn't think she could have gotten more scared, but his tone, that patient, pleasant, even tone, as if he were discussing lunch, terrified her. *It's not a dream,* she realized. *It's happening. It's happening to me right now. God, please let Emily be okay. Please. I'll do anything.*

"I can smell your fear," Arthur said. "It rolls off your skin. A better man would feel discomfort at your pain. But I'm not a good man. I feel nothing for you. We rarely have to deal with innocent bystanders and when we do, we strive to send them back unharmed, not out of some altruistic impulse, but because we dislike attention. If you hadn't been injured, Henry here would wipe your memory and the five of you would go merrily on your way. As it is, however, you will be dead in the next thirty minutes."

The words refused to leave her mouth. Karina strained and forced them out. "Why are you telling me this?"

His ice-cold smile made her heart jump. "I'm talking to you because I'm about to offer you a deal. You have something we want, my lady. Your body has a genetic predisposition toward producing certain hormones one of us desperately needs. Your subspecies isn't unique, but it's rare enough to make you valuable. I suspect that's also how you were able to find this place, and that's why the yadovita, the redheaded woman, took the time to poison you instead of defending herself from us. Listen carefully, my lady, because I won't repeat myself."

She stared at him, committing each word to memory.

"The creature behind you requires your blood. He will feed on you. His venom will counteract the poison that's killing your body. In return, he will consume the chemicals your body will produce. You will give yourself to the House of Daryon. You will let the beast feed on you. You will live in quarters of our choosing. You can never leave. You can have no contact with the outside world. For your agreement to this, we will spare your life and the lives of the children."

The thing on the windowsill let out a low whine of anticipation. That . . . that beast would feed on her. *Forever. Oh, dear God. I can't do it . . . I can't . . .*

Arthur leaned forward, his face showing no emotion beyond the pleasant, calm composure. "Consider carefully before you answer. I don't offer this deal to you because I like you or because I'm moved by some noble emotion. I do it because we need you. What I propose won't be pleasant for you. You won't enjoy it. In fact, many would say you're better off dying now."

Fog gathered on the edge of her mind, threatening to smother her. Karina clawed at reality, trying to remain conscious.

"My daughter . . ."

The beast growled on the windowsill.

"He guarantees her safety," Arthur said.

"The children . . . will be returned to their families?"

"Yes."

"I agree."

A gentle hand seized her mind and pulled her back through time and space to the reality of the round table and the hot tea mug in her hand. She looked at Arthur.

"My daughter, Emily?"

He didn't answer.

"You promised me the children would be returned to their families. Her father is dead. I'm the only family Emily has. Where is she?"

He smiled, a flat curving of lips without any emotion. "She's at the main house for the time being."

No, she wasn't, Karina realized. He was lying. "I want my daughter. We made a deal. Bring me my daughter, or I am leaving."

Daniel rocked back on his chair and laughed.

A door slammed. Footsteps echoed through the house.

"Cooperate with Lucas and your daughter will be brought to you," Arthur said.

A man walked into the kitchen. Tall, corded with muscle that bulged his T-shirt, he dwarfed the doorway. He wasn't just large, he was massive and wrapped in menace, as if he were a whirlwind of violence, barely contained in the shell of his body. Black hair fell on his hard, aggressive face in long strands. He glanced at her, his eyes green and merciless. She met his gaze and gulped. It was like looking into the eyes of a tiger. His stare promised death.

Recognition sparked in his green irises and flared into rage.

He lunged forward, inhumanly quick, and hit the table with his palm. She jerked back.

"Get your hands off of her!" His voice rippled with a snarl.

Henry raised his hands in the air. The man grasped the chair, Henry still on it, and tossed it aside. Steely fingers grabbed her elbow and pulled her up. He swiped her off the floor with ridiculous ease, locking her in the crook of his arm, and snapped like a rabid dog, "Mine!"

"We have no intention of taking her from you." Arthur sipped his tea.

"Don't any of you fuckers touch her!"

She flailed in his arms, trying to break free, but it was like trying to push back a semi.

"You must forgive Lucas," Arthur told her. "He tends to be over-protective of his food."

A familiar scent of heated metal invaded her nostrils. Panic squirmed through her. She fought harder, but her feet kicked only air. He carried her away out of the kitchen back to the bedroom where she had awakened.

CHAPTER 2

Lucas dropped her on the bed and went to lock the door. "Stay away from Arthur. He's a sick fuck."

He turned and strode toward her, enormous, overwhelming in his sheer size. Karina shrank back until her spine hit the wall.

He looked her over, a long, lingering stare that made her want to cover herself, frowned and ducked into a doorway on the left. Water gushed. Lucas reappeared with a tall glass of water and handed it to her. "Drink this. It will help."

She drank.

He sat on a chair across from her and pulled off his socks. Only now she noticed that he wasn't wearing any shoes. He balled the socks into a clump and tossed them into the room where he'd gotten the water, then shrugged off his T-shirt. Karina's breath caught in her throat. Faded ragged scars crisscrossed his massive back. His legs were long, his waist narrow in comparison to his vast shoulders. His lines were almost perfect. As he squared his shoulders, muscles rolled under his skin, forming hard ridges. He didn't move—he stalked and prowled, like a huge predatory animal, menace cascading from him in waves along with his hot metallic scent.

Her memory thrust Jonathan before her. Her husband had been handsome and well built, an average-sized man. Lucas could've snapped him in half and wouldn't have given it a second thought. He'd just toss the broken body aside and continue on his way. She had no chance. In a physical fight, Lucas would destroy her.

"Drink," he said.

Karina forced some more water down. Her throat had gone dry and she drank again. Suddenly Lucas gathered himself. His gaze fixed on the door. His body tensed, his expression alert. His feet gripped the bare floorboards, his legs bent lightly, as he readied to launch himself into a leap. Muscles bunched and knotted across his shoulders and back. His arms lifted slightly, spread wide, the fingers of his big hands like talons, ready to grasp and crush. His eyes ignited with a hot, hungry fire. Poised like this, he was barely human.

Someone's knuckles rapped on the door.

"What?" Lucas growled.

"Do you want the sedative?" Henry's voice asked.

Lucas glanced at her and asked quietly, "Do you want to be drugged?"

"No."

"She said no," he snarled.

The footsteps retreated. Lucas eased, relaxing slowly, muscle by muscle. He glanced at her with his light green eyes and she shrank from his gaze.

"How much did they tell you?" he asked.

"I know what I agreed to." She hesitated. "Are you . . . ?"

"I am."

She tried to reconcile the beast and the man, and couldn't. That dark, grotesque creature was huge, twice as big as Lucas. A horrible meld of ape, dog, bear—Karina struggled for a comparison, a point of reference, and could find none. Her memory was fuzzy. She remembered fangs and baleful eyes, and massive shoulders sheathed in dark fur. How was it possible? Her mind refused to admit that thing existed. But her body felt Lucas near and knew the beast was real.

She had to have an explanation. Anything at all. "Are you a vampire?" she asked.

"No."

"What are you?"

He sighed. "There's no myth or legend or cute explanation. People here call those like me Demons. It's just a name, nothing religious attached to it. You might also hear people call me Subspecies 30. The rest is complicated." He took her half-empty glass and went to top it off. "I don't actually need your blood to sustain me. I require the endocrine hormones your body will secrete in response to my bite."

"For what?"

"To counteract the effects of my venom. It hurts me."

He handed her the full glass, rubbed his hand across the back of his neck, and held the palm to her face. The odor of hot metal hit her nostrils and she drew back.

"That smell means I'm hungry for you."

He was too close. The cup trembled in Karina's fingers. God, she was scared. It took all of her will not to scream and run. "Will it hurt?"

"Yes. It's not like vampire movies, where the vampire bites the woman and she moans softly and comes all over herself. There's no rapture involved. No climax. Just me chewing on you."

He took her by the chin, lifting her face, and peered into her eyes. Karina pulled back. He leaned closer. She tried to scramble away, but he grasped her shoulder, keeping her still. His lips touched her forehead. "Fever." Lucas grimaced. "Your eyes are still bloodshot."

His presence pressed on her like a physical burden. Karina closed her eyes. She sat there, world shut out, and pretended that everything would be okay even if every instinct assured her it wouldn't. She had to survive and adapt. She had to do whatever was necessary to get her daughter back.

When she opened her eyelids, he waited for her with a synthetic cord in his hands. She hadn't heard him move.

"To keep you still." He moved toward her, uncoiling the cord.

No. Lying there tied up and completely helpless while he drank her blood would be too much. "That's okay," she said quickly. "I won't change my mind."

Lucas kept coming.

"I won't change my mind." Desperation put steel into her voice. "I've agreed to this to save my daughter. They'll let me see her after you feed. I won't run or fight."

He halted.

"Arthur said I would stay here for as long as I live. That means you have to feed frequently. Might as well start it right."

Lucas gripped the rope. His biceps bulged. He snapped the rope apart. Karina winced. "If you're trying to intimidate me, it's too late. I'm already as scared as I'm going to get."

"I'm not trying to scare you." He rolled the section of the rope into a tight wad, wrapped the end about it several times, tied it, and dropped it in her lap. "To bite down. In case it gets too rough."

She picked it up.

Lucas sat next to her. "Arthur isn't in charge of your daughter. I am. I guaranteed her safety. Both of you belong to me."

Lucas leaned to look into her face. She expected rage, hunger, some violent emotion, but instead she saw only steady calm.

"I promise you that no matter what happens between you and me, your daughter will be safe. I will never use her against you. Everyone is afraid of me, and she will never be bullied or mistreated."

Karina stared at him in surprise.

"You wanted to start this right," he said. "We can do that. Let's be honest. The bitch in the hotel poisoned you. Technically she infected you with a virus that secretes a toxin into your bloodstream. To counteract the virus, you need my venom. I've already bitten you once but it will take several feedings before you're in the clear."

"You've bitten me?"

"Left thigh," he said. "I was in the attack variant at the time, and biting you anywhere else would've caused too much damage."

She grabbed at her leg, trying to feel the wound through the fabric of the jeans.

"It was a very quick bite," he said. "To keep you from dying. This will be worse."

He was serious. The thought of him feeding on her, chewing on her, was almost too much to contemplate. "Can we do a blood transfusion instead?"

"No. We've tried in the past and failed. There is some sort of relationship between your blood, my venom, and my saliva that we don't understand. I have to feed on you. You need me to survive and I need you to . . ." He paused. "To counteract my venom."

He was holding something back, she could feel it.

Lucas's eyes held no mercy. "I'm a predator and my body knows that you're my prey. Your fear is exciting. Try not to be so scared. Don't struggle. The more you flail about and whimper, the more excited I'll get. If you get me excited enough, I'll chew up your veins and end up fucking you in a puddle of blood. I take it you don't want that."

"No."

"Then stay calm." He nodded at the cord in her lap. "You sure you don't want to be tied?"

"Yes."

Lucas stretched out on the bed, took her by the waist, and pulled her down, flush against him. They lay together, her butt pressed against his groin, her back tight against his chest. Like two lovers. Jonathan and she used to lie like this after sex. The perversity of it made her shiver.

"Lie still." His arms pulled her tighter to him. The hard shaft of his erection dug into her butt. She tried to edge away from it.

"Don't worry. I can't help it, but I won't molest you. Unless you start moaning and rubbing your ass against me."

She stopped moving. The odor of hot copper was overpowering now. Karina cleared her throat. "I feel light-headed."

"You're breathing in my scent. Your body's reacting. It will speed things up."

That explained the shirt coming off. He wanted no fabric barriers between her and that smell, so it could roll off his skin and take her under. "Do I need to do anything?"

"Just lie there and endure. Your body needs my venom. As I said, I've bitten you already to kill the poison, but you got just enough to keep you alive. This will take some time."

She brushed her hair from her neck, exposing skin. No point in drawing this out.

A low laugh answered her. He spoke into her ear, his breath a warm touch on her skin. "You ever watch hockey?"

"No."

"The Buffalo Sabres had a goalie—Clint Malarchuk. Steve Tuttle, a guy on another team, was trying to score a goal, and as he charged at the crease, a defenseman grabbed him from behind and swung him up. Tuttle's skate caught Malarchuk's neck. A shallow cut, only severed the exterior jugular. Blood sprayed like water from a hose. Covered the whole crease in seconds."

For some reason she couldn't understand, his quiet voice steadied her nerves. "Did he survive?"

"He did. Had the skate cut a bit deeper, he would've been dead in about two minutes." He gathered her even tighter against himself. "The neck nuzzling is fun, but the pressure within the jugular would expel your blood so quickly, it would kill you." His finger traced an outline on the vein on her neck, sending electric shivers along her skin. She wished he hadn't done that.

"If not the neck, then where?"

"The arm works well."

"Can you . . . get on with it?"

"Not yet. The longer we wait, the less painful it will be for you."

His body was hot against hers, his heat seeping into her. His scent enveloped her completely now. Her head spun.

"That's it," he prompted. "Go limp. Don't strain."

"I'm scared," she told him.

"I'm sorry." The undercurrent of violence that permeated everything he said muted slightly.

"What will happen after you feed?"

"You'll pass out. It's like giving blood except messier. Your body will go into shock from my venom. If you survive, you'll get used to the feedings."

"I might die?"

"Yes."

"This just gets better and better."

"Life's a bitch."

The room crawled. "I'm not dreaming, am I?"

"If this is your dream, you're seriously fucked up."

"Who are you . . . all of you?"

"You ask too many questions."

He pulled away from her, turned her arm to him, and bit into the soft flesh just above the elbow. Pain lanced through her. Her body tensed in response, but his arms clamped her down and she could barely breathe.

It hurt. It hurt and hurt, but worse than the pain was the awful sensation of his gnawing teeth and the prickly heat squirming its way up her arm. It spread into her shoulder and fanned out, claiming her body. She wanted to break free, to get away, but Lucas held her tight.

"Promise me you will make sure my daughter is safe if I die."

He didn't answer.

"Promise me."

"I promise," he said.

Karina let herself sink into the pain. Gradually it eased into a steady ache. Her limbs relaxed. She tried to think of something else, anything else, of Emily, of their safe little apartment, of being far away in a different place. But the reality refused to recede. And so she lay there and waited it out, her entire body humming with a distinct unusual pain, until her dizziness blotted out the world and she slipped under.

Lucas nuzzled her thin neck. Feverish. Not too bad. She was healthy. And clean. The blood work from the main house had shown no abnormalities aside from the poison. That was what donors were. Resilient; resistant to most disease.

And grounded. She didn't seem like she would snap, but he'd seen enough people break under the weight of the transition to let his guard slip. And then there was her daughter. Children complicated things.

She just lay there and let him feed.

His first donor, Robert Milder, had to be sedated for the feedings. After him, there was Galatea. He had to tie her up. Every time. She had resented her role, loathed being restrained, despised him, and yet pulled him into her bed; and when they fucked, she drained him so completely, he felt blissfully empty, as if he had poured not only his seed, but his pain into her. She took it all and reveled in it, enjoying the power she wielded over him. He wasn't a fool. He knew she was driven by revenge, but he came back to her again and again, an idiot thirsty for a poisoned spring.

And now he had Karina.

A soothing cold spread through his veins, melting the needles of pain that always prickled him in the aftermath of his transformation from the attack variant. Funny. He had survived for six years on injections, shooting himself up every couple of days, but the synthetic hormones failed to soothe the ache. They managed to dull the pain, yet it had still gnawed at him, until he became convinced it would grind him down to nothing. Karina's body had barely had a chance to respond to his poison, yet even this tiny dose of the hormones brought relief to him. He had forgotten what it was like not to hurt.

Lucas breathed in her scent. The memory of the chase through the motel danced through his mind. He wanted to chase her again. He felt drunk.

He slipped the narrow strap of the tank top off Karina's shoulder, baring her left breast. Bigger, fuller, softer than he had expected. He imagined sliding his palm over the mound, brushing the nipple with his thumb. He pictured how her body would tighten in response, how the nipple would feel erect against his fingers.

He slid his fingers under the waistband of her jeans, pulled it up, and looked at the triangle of her white underwear. His cock ached. He wanted to mount her and thrust it inside her.

So what was stopping him?

Lucas slid his hand up, to her slightly rounded stomach, holding her gently, trying to puzzle it out. Had he tied her up before feeding from her, he would've fucked her by now, of that he was certain.

Trust, he realized. She'd held up her part of the deal. It had cost her. She'd cried toward the end, once her grip on consciousness slipped—silent tears that left wet tracks on her cheeks. Her arm would be sore as hell tomorrow. Provided the fever didn't rise, the poison didn't kill her, and there was a tomorrow in her future. He wanted her to live, but he had done all he could to help her.

The feeding had cost her, but she lay there and let him do his thing, as she had promised, and she expected him to hold up his end of the bargain. And the bargain didn't include fucking rights. She'd made that crystal clear.

He tugged her tank top back into place, covering her up, and pulled her to him, sliding his arm over her. She was his. She would take away his pain and he would guard her in return. That was the agreement.

CHAPTER 3

Karina awoke to an empty room. Bright morning light flooded through the open window, drawing a yellow rectangle on the wooden floor. A draft brought an acrid stink of burning bacon.

Emily.

She pushed free of the sheets and almost fell. Her head swam. Slowly, very slowly she slid off the bed and stood upright. Her throat was so dry, it hurt. A full glass of water sat on the bedside table beside a pair of binoculars and a yellow sticky that read "Drink it." She could practically hear Lucas's growl.

The memory of his gnawing teeth squirmed through her, dragging nausea in its wake. Karina bent over, gripped the night table to steady herself, and saw a square bandage on her arm. She tugged at it, sending a jolt of pain through her limb. The bandage remained stuck. Karina pulled harder, trying to rip it away as if she could shed the memory of Lucas with it. She struggled with it for a few seconds, pain pounding up her biceps in hot prickly bursts, and finally tore it free.

A big bruise stained the bend of her arm. Dark purple, it sat there like a brand. Lucas's proof of ownership. Dried blood was caked in the center, where his teeth had mangled her veins.

The price she paid for Emily's life. And her own. The ache in her arm pushed her to scream at the sheer mind-boggling unfairness of it: at being attacked, kidnapped, hurt, held down by brute force, robbed of her daughter, stripped of her freedom . . . At being plucked from her life. Only a day ago, she felt reasonably safe, secure in the knowledge that she could dial 911 at any moment and bring a police cruiser to her door. She had rights. She had protections. She was a person.

She felt the hot wet tears well in her eyes and clenched her teeth. She had to get a grip. Thinking like a victim would get her nowhere. Yes, it was terrifying. Yes, it hurt. But it didn't kill her. She was still alive and as long as she breathed, she had to fight for herself and her child. She had to obey and be sweet. She had to ingratiate herself. That was her only chance at survival and escape. Karina dropped the bandage on the night table and drained the glass. It was time to find her daughter.

A harsh screech made her turn to the window. She walked to it, picking up the binoculars off the night table on the way. A wide green expanse spread before her, a wooded slope gently rolling away and down, toward mountains, brown and rust, fading to blue and eventually gray in the distance. A scrub forest hugged the roots of the mountains, dotting the grassy prairie in clumps of green. The wind fanned her face, bringing moisture and the tart fragrance of some unknown flower.

It was the middle of summer in southern Oklahoma and the prairie she'd seen through her windshield the day before had been a brown sea of dried grass. This, this looked like spring after weeks of rains somewhere in the foothills of rugged mountains.

Where the hell was she? Looked like complete wilderness, probably miles from any road, any people. Any help. If she escaped, crossing across rugged country with a six-year-old would be very difficult. She would have to plan well and bring a lot of water.

The brush quaked. A small brown animal burst from the growth. It resembled a dog, or maybe a coyote. It dashed across the grass, zigzagging in sheer panic. It didn't run like a coyote.

What in the world?

Karina raised the binoculars to her eyes.

The creature wasn't a dog. If anything it looked like a tiny horse, no more than two feet tall.

The brush shivered and spat three gray shapes onto the grass, one large and two others smaller. They ran upright on a pair of massively muscled legs, their bodies sheathed with gray feathers speckled with spots of black. Long, powerful necks supported heads armed with enormous beaks. The binoculars picked up every detail, from the crests of long feathers on their heads to the tiny vicious eyes.

The horse galloped for its life, veering left. The bird closest to it slid and swung toward the house to right itself. A flash of pale red shot through the empty air, as if the bird had run into an invisible net stretched tight, and the pressure of its body caused the threads to glow. The bird screeched and fell, catapulted back. For a moment it lay on the grass stunned, and then it rolled back to its feet and rejoined the chase.

The small horse was getting tired. It slowed. Foam dripped from its mouth.

The largest bird sprinted. The monstrous beak rose, then came down like an ax, chopping at the horse and knocking it off its feet. The horse rolled in the grass and staggered upright. The three birds danced about it, jabbing and pecking. The horse cried out and fell. Bloody beaks rose again and again . . .

Karina lowered the binoculars.

She didn't know much about zoology, but she knew enough. They weren't emus; they weren't ostriches; no, these were something vicious, something ancient, something that should not exist in Texas or the Ozarks. Or the twenty-first century.

Suddenly she was cold, freezing from head to toe.

A triumphant screech rolled up from the plain.

Karina dropped the binoculars on the side table and slammed the window shut.

A cloud of oily smoke greeted Karina in the kitchen. By the stove, Henry cursed, slid several charred pieces of bacon out of a pan with a spatula, and deposited them onto a plate. He saw her and waved the spatula around, flinging hot drops of grease onto the table. "Good morning."

"Good morning," she answered on autopilot. "I saw . . . birds."

"Terror birds." Henry nodded. "Nasty creatures. Don't worry, there is a large fence around the entire hill. We call it the net—it's thin wire with a powerful current running through it. You're completely safe within the vicinity of the house. They won't come close. Besides, they are mostly cowards. An adult human has nothing to worry about."

One of those things would kill a child. A vision of a bloody beak coming down like a hatchet flashed before Karina's eyes. She swallowed. "My daughter?"

The spatula pointed to Henry's right. "Through that doorway."

Karina forced herself not to run. She skirted the table and walked through the doorway into a living room. Her heart pounded.

A small shape was curled on the couch, hidden by a green blanket. Karina pulled back the covers. Emily lay on the pillow. Her mouth was open slightly, her eyes closed, her hair a tangled mess.

Karina knelt and hugged her gently. Emily stirred and she put her face to her daughter's cheek and clenched herself, trying not to cry.

"Daniel brought her early in the morning. Arthur told him he would let him speak in return," Henry said softly from the doorway. "I've wiped her memory of the assault in the motel—it was too traumatic—so she won't recall anything about the place, and that entire day will be dim for her. There are no long-term effects to memory wipes, but there are some short-term consequences: she will sleep a lot more, she will seem confused, and she might have some anxiety. It should last for about a week. Lucas already called the main house. They have a nice room set up for her."

Karina turned. "I want her to stay with me."

Henry looked uncomfortable. "There is a reason why the three of us are separated from the main house."

"Three? I thought Arthur lived here."

Henry shook his head. "Arthur stays at the main compound. Of our entire group, Lucas is the most feared, Daniel is the most despised, and I'm the least trusted." He paused. "This house isn't the best place for a child."

She paused. "Henry, why in the world would anyone not trust you?" Of the four men she'd met so far, Henry seemed the least insane.

He smiled, apologetic, almost vulnerable, and leaned closer. "I can make you forget we ever had this conversation. I can make you forget about Lucas, about the motel, and, if I strain a little, you won't remember you ever had a daughter."

She paused. It seemed insane, but no less insane than the idea of a man who turned into a nightmarish beast. "Can you read thoughts?"

"Nobody can read thoughts." Henry shook his head. "Not even combat-grade operatives like me."

Combat with whom? Why? He was wording his replies very carefully, thinking about them for a moment before answering. If she pushed him too hard, he would stop talking. "I'm not sure I understand. Do you wipe your enemies' memories?"

Henry took his glasses off and cleaned the lenses with the corner of Emily's blanket. Without his glasses, he seemed younger. "The mind doesn't just store memories. It also governs many functions of the body. I can mentally scout the enemy and tell you their numbers. Obviously the more of them there are, the higher the margin of error is, but typically I'm not off by a significant number. I can find your mind in a crowd of people and attack it, so you'll think you're drowning. I can disconnect your brain from the rest of you and starve it of oxygen until you become a vegetable. My subspecies isn't called Memory Wiper. It's called Mind Bender."

For a moment she was more terrified of him than she was of Lucas, and thinking that he might somehow crack her skull open and peer into her brain scared her even more.

Henry glanced at Emily on the couch. "Do you trust me now? Do you want your daughter near me?"

No. She didn't trust any of them. But the main house, whatever it was, would be full of strangers. The thought of someone full of violent rage, like Lucas, or cold like Arthur, being in charge of Emily without her to shield her daughter made her wince.

Karina clenched her hands. Screaming and hysterics would do her no good. She had to reason with them. She had to be smart. Use logic. "Henry, I'd rather take you and Lucas over a house of people I don't know. Emily woke up alone, without me. She must've been frightened. She's my daughter, Henry. She's safest with me, because I'm her mother and I would give my life to keep her from harm."

"Speak to Lucas," Henry suggested. "I'm sure he will permit some sort of visitation."

Lucas. Lucas had said he owned both of them. She had to make him understand. Karina fixed Emily's blanket and rose. "Can I make her breakfast? Or should I ask Lucas's permission?"

Henry stepped aside. "You're welcome to any food we have." He cleared his throat.

The fridge contained eggs, several pounds of bacon, some slimy cold cuts, a hunk of mozzarella cheese—dried, yellow, and brittle—and a pack of green-looking hot dogs. Karina pulled out eggs and bacon. "Flour?"

Henry dug in one of the cabinets, looking lost, frowned, and opened a door, revealing a huge supply room. "I think in here somewhere."

She stepped into the room. Rows and rows of wooden shelves, filled with cans and jars, a huge spice rack, fifty-pound bags of sugar, flour, rice . . . three large freezers filled with meat. Enough food to feed these men for years. "Are you expecting a long siege?"

"You never know," Henry said with a thin smile. "We've had a few."

"You, Daniel, Lucas, me, Emily . . . is anybody else coming?"

"No. Does this mean we're invited to the meal?"

"I'm using your food."

Henry exhaled, picked up the plate of black bacon strips, and dumped them into the trash. "Thank God."

Karina opened the window first, so the kitchen would air out, and set about making breakfast. Henry parked himself by the refrigerator and watched her. There was something disquieting about Henry. When she looked at him, she got an impression of length: long limbs, long frame, long face. Even though she vaguely recalled that he was slightly shorter than Lucas, he appeared taller. He seemed lean, almost thin, but that notion was deceiving—his sweatshirt sleeves were pulled up to his elbows, revealing forearms sculpted with hard muscle. He smiled often, but the curving of his lips lacked emotion. His smile was paper-thin, an automatic, knee-jerk reaction like blinking.

A Mind Bender. If what he said was true, he could kill Emily in front of her, wipe Karina's mind clean, and she would never remember it.

Karina found Granny Smith apples in the bottom of the fridge and checked the drawers. On the third try she hit what looked like a utility drawer: knives, screwdrivers, bottle openers, and wooden spoons. She fished a medium-sized knife from the drawer, peeled the apples, cored and chopped them, and set them to fry slowly, sprinkling them with brown sugar.

"It smells divine," Henry murmured.

"Is there cinnamon?"

"I am sure there is. It's brown powder, right?" Henry stepped into the pantry.

"Yes." She grabbed the knife, pulled the fabric of her jeans away from her hip, and slid the knife into her pocket. The point of the blade cut the lining and she jammed the knife all the way down to the hilt. The blade scraped against her skin. She glanced down. No blood. Karina exhaled. Cutting herself was a calculated risk—she had no other place to hide the knife. Anywhere else it would make a bulge. She pulled her T-shirt down over it.

Henry came out of the pantry. She held her breath. Maybe he could read thoughts. Maybe he would pluck the image of the knife out of her head. She had to stop thinking about it, but she couldn't. The shape of the knife was probably glowing in her brain.

Henry shook a plastic container of cinnamon. "Found it."

She had to say something or he would realize things were wrong. Karina willed her mouth to move. "Thank you." She took the cinnamon and sprinkled it on the apples.

The bacon rack was missing in action, or perhaps they didn't have one. She layered a plate with paper towels, placed the strips on top, and popped it into the microwave.

"You don't cook often?" she asked.

"On the contrary. I cook quite frequently, out of sheer necessity. Unfortunately, most of what I produce is inedible. Daniel's cooking is even worse than mine, if such a thing is possible. Lucas can grill quite well when pushed to it, but in the kitchen his idea of a meal involves a raw piece of meat, burned on the outside. Adrino was our cook."

"Where is he now?"

"Dead. About nine months ago."

She paused to look at him. "I'm sorry."

Henry nodded. "Thank you."

Karina resumed stirring the pancake batter. "How did he die?"

"Lucas bit him in half."

She stopped. "Was he a member of your family?"

"He was. He was Lucas's cousin on his mother's side, and my stepbrother."

Karina found the griddle and set it on the burners to heat up. She stirred the apples with a wooden spoon, then pulled the bacon out of the microwave and peeled it from the paper towels.

"I can do that," Henry offered.

"Thank you." She poured the pancake batter on the griddle in quick drips and watched the first pancake puff and bubble at the edges. "Why did Lucas kill him?"

"Adrino tried to murder Arthur."

"Why?"

Henry smiled, a quick baring of teeth, meaningless and flat like a mask. "Adrino had raped a woman on base. As a punishment, Arthur had him chained for two months."

"Chained?"

"In the courtyard. Eventually Adrino was let off the chain and everything went quite well, until he attempted to solidify Arthur's blood during the last Christmas dinner. In retrospect, we should have expected it. His subspecies is prone to rashness." Henry smiled again. "You will find that we're a violent, vicious lot, Lady Karina. All of us hate Arthur, hate each other, hate who we are, what we are, why we are. This hate is so deep within us, it's in our bones. Lucas hates stronger than most of us for his own reasons. But Lucas is also far more controlled in his rages than he lets on. He recognizes the simple truth: Arthur is the glue that holds us together. Arthur makes mistakes, and he's brutal, but he's also fair. Every tribe must have a leader. Without the leader there is chaos. May I just mention that your pancakes smell delicious? I don't suppose there is any way I could steal one right now, is there?"

Thirty minutes later, the pancakes were done, the bacon was cooked, and Karina crossed the room to her daughter.

"Emily? Wake up . . ."

"Mommy!" Emily clutched Karina around the neck and hung on with surprisingly fierce strength.

Karina scooped her off the couch and held her close, afraid to hug the tiny body too hard. "I'm here, baby. I love you." Emily never said "mommy." It was always "mom."

"You won't leave?"

A hard knot formed in Karina's throat. "Leaving" was Emily's euphemism for dying. Her daughter thought she had died.

"I will try very hard not to," she promised.

Emily hung on, and Karina gently carried her into the kitchen. "I made your favorite apples."

Slowly Emily's hold on her neck eased. A few seconds later she allowed herself to be put into a chair at the table.

Daniel marched into the kitchen. "Food."

Henry nodded. "Yes."

Daniel pulled out a chair, sat, and reached for the pancakes.

"Let's wait for Lucas," Henry said.

"Fuck Lucas."

Karina looked at Daniel. Henry sighed. Daniel looked back at them, glanced at Emily, and shrugged. "They don't like it that I swear. Do you mind if I swear?"

Emily shook her head.

"See, she doesn't mind."

Lucas loomed in the doorway. One moment it was empty and the next he was just there, green eyes watching her every move with a hungry light. Karina took her chair, trying to ignore it, but his gaze clasped her like an invisible chain. She looked back at him. *Yes, I belong to you. You don't have to ram it down my throat.*

Emily's eyes had grown big. She shied a little when Lucas stepped to the table, aware of his movements. Karina read fear in her daughter's face and reached over to hold her hand. He'd given Emily no reason to fear him, yet she was clearly scared, almost as if she sensed on some primal level that he was a threat.

Lucas sat next to Karina, opposite of Daniel, and reached for the pancakes. She watched him load his plate: four pancakes, four links of sausage, six strips of bacon . . . The plate would hold no more. He pondered it, frustrated, then piled the apples atop the pancakes and drenched the whole thing in maple syrup.

It was good that she had made enough for ten people.

Lucas sliced pancakes with his fork, pierced a slice of the apple, and maneuvered the whole thing into his mouth. Karina sat on the edge of her seat, listening to the elevated tempo of her own heartbeat, watching him chew, and waited for him to throw the plate across the table. She wanted them to like the food; no, she desperately needed the three of them to like the food. Her survival depended on it.

Lucas swallowed. "Good," he said and reached for more.

Karina slumped a little in her chair, unable to hide her relief.

"Good? It's fucking divine," Daniel said. "It's the first decent meal we've had in weeks."

Lucas leveled a heavy stare at him but said nothing.

"Mom," Emily said.

"What, baby?"

"I left my backpack at Jill's house. It has my school stuff in it."

The three men ate, watching her.

"That will be okay, baby," Karina said. "You have to change schools anyway."

"Why?"

"Because we live here now and you'll go to a special school." The words came out painfully.

"Do I have to ride the bus?"

Karina swallowed a lump that had formed in her throat. Acknowledging where they were was hard, as if she were driving nails into her own coffin. "No."

"Why do we have to stay here?"

"This is where I work now."

"Your mother is a slave," Daniel said. "Lucas owns her."

If only she could have reached across the table, she would have hit him with a closed fist so it would hurt. Karina forced neutrality into her face, pulling it on like a mask. Show nothing. Betray no weakness.

"Is a slave better than a payroll supervisor?" Emily asked.

"They're not that different," Karina lied. So many times before she had thought she worked like a slave, pulling in long hours, picking up project after project, perpetually behind, trying to get to the bottom of her to-do stack. She thought she had experienced the worst life could throw at her. All of it seemed so pointless now. Her memories belonged to someone else, a happier, flightier, younger person. She had a new life now and new priorities, chief of which was the welfare of her daughter. She had to keep Emily safe.

Emily poked her pancake with a fork. "What about the house? All our stuff is there . . . my Hello Kitty blanket . . ."

"We'll get new things." She cast a quick glance around the table but none of the three men said anything to break down her fragile promises.

"Will I get my own room?"

Karina looked to Lucas. *Please. Don't separate me from my daughter.*

He wiped his mouth with a napkin, his movements unhurried. "You have to stay at the main house. You can come to visit your mother on weekends. We'll set up a room."

"I want to stay with Mom." Emily's voice was tiny.

"You can't," Lucas said.

Emily bit her lip.

"You'll have a good place at the main house. A room you'll share with a nice girl. Toys. Clothes. Everything you need. If anybody tries to be mean to you, tell them you belong to Lucas. Everyone is afraid of me. Nobody will harm you."

"No," Emily said.

Lucas stopped eating. Karina tensed.

"Are you telling me no?" Lucas asked. His voice was calm.

Emily raised her chin with all of the defiance a six-year-old could muster. "I'm tired and I'm scared, and I'm not going. I'm staying with my mom. Are you going to yell at me?"

"No," Lucas said. "I don't need to."

"You're not my dad. My dad left."

Lucas glanced at Karina.

"I'm a widow," she said quietly.

"I'm not your father, but I'm in charge," Lucas said. "You will obey me anyway."

"Why?" Emily asked.

Lucas leaned forward and stared at Emily. "Because I am big, strong, and scary. And you are very small."

"You're not nice." Emily held his gaze, but Karina could tell it wasn't out of courage. Emily had simply frozen like a baby rabbit looking into the eyes of a wolf.

"It's not a nice world and I can't always be nice," Lucas said. "But I will try and I won't be mean to you without a reason."

Karina put her hand on his forearm, trying to tear his attention away from Emily. It worked; he looked at her.

"Please." It took all of her will to keep the tremble out of her voice. "Please let her stay."

"I want to stay," Emily said. "I'll be good. I'll do all my chores."

"I'll think about it," Lucas said.

CHAPTER 4

A half hour later, breakfast was finished. The men rose one by one, rinsed their plates, and loaded the dishes and silverware into the dishwasher with surprising efficiency. Karina put the last of the food away. Henry had stepped out, but Daniel remained in the kitchen, leaning against the counter, watching her. Lucas loomed by the door, watching Daniel.

"Can I go outside?" Emily asked.

Karina paused. "I don't think that is a good idea."

"Why not?" Daniel arched an eyebrow.

"Because there are scary birds out there."

"There are scary birds? What kind of scary birds?"

"It's safe," Lucas said. "The net keeps everything out."

Karina remembered the bird's body hitting the invisible fence. "What if she walks into this net?"

"She'd have to walk a mile and a half down the hill before she reached it," Lucas said.

"I want to see the birds," Emily said. "Please?"

It would get them out of the house, away from the men and out into the open. She could get a better look around. Maybe she would see a road, or a house, some avenue of escape. Karina wiped her hands with a towel and hung it on the back of the chair. "Okay. But we're going to stay by the house."

"I'll come with you," Lucas said.

All she wanted was the illusion of being alone with her daughter. He wouldn't let her have it. Karina clenched her teeth.

"That's right," Daniel said. "Bite your tongue. It will come in handy."

Lucas gave him a flat stare. For a moment they stood still, then Daniel rolled his eyes and casually wandered out of the kitchen into the side hallway. Lucas moved in the opposite direction, through the doorway. Karina took Emily by the hand. "Come on, baby."

The hallway cut through the house, straight to the door. They passed rooms: a library filled with books from floor to ceiling on the right, a large room with a giant flat-screen TV on the left, and then Lucas opened the door and they stepped on the porch into the sunlight. The yard was grass, small scrawny oaks and brush flanking it on both sides. A path led down the hill into the distance. To the left a huge oak out of sync with the rest of the scrub forest and probably planted, spread its branches.

A shaggy brown dog stepped out from behind the oak. As tall as a Great Dane, it trotted forward on massive legs, its long tail held straight behind it. There was something odd in the way it walked, waddling slightly, more like a bear than a dog.

Karina stepped between Emily and the beast.

The animal stopped. Large brown eyes stared at them from a massive head crowned with round ears.

"Don't worry, he's tame," Lucas said behind her.

The meld of dog and bear peered at Lucas and let out a short snort.

"He doesn't like it when I phase into my attack variant," Lucas said. "It weirds him out for a couple of days. Cedric, don't be a dick. Let the kid pet you."

Another snort. She couldn't really blame the dog. Considering how Lucas looked in his "attack variant" it was a wonder the dog stuck around at all.

Cedric pondered them for a long moment and waddled over. Emily stretched out her hand. Karina's insides clenched into a tight knot.

Cedric nudged Emily's hand with his nose, snorted again, and bumped the bulge in the front pocket of her hoodie.

"What do you have in your pocket?" Karina asked.

Emily dug into her pocket and pulled out a half-eaten apple.

Not again. Karina kept her voice gentle. "Emily, you know you're not supposed to have that . . ."

Cedric sniffed at the apple. His mouth gaped open, revealing huge teeth.

"He won't hurt her," Lucas said with absolute certainty in his voice.

Emily held the apple out. Very carefully, almost gently, Cedric swiped it off her hand, sat on his behind, and raised the fruit to his mouth, holding it with long, dark claws. The black nose sniffed the apple, the jaws opened and closed, and the beast bit a small chunk from the fruit and chewed in obvious pleasure.

"He likes it!" Emily announced and jumped down off the steps into the yard. "Come on, Cedric!"

"Where are you going?" Karina took a step to follow.

"Just to the tree."

The oak was barely fifty feet away. Karina bit her lip. Her instincts told her to clutch her child and not let go, but Emily needed to feel normal. She needed to play. Her daughter didn't understand how precarious their situation was, she had no idea how vulnerable they were, and Karina had to keep it that way.

Emily was looking at her. "Can I go?"

"Yes. You can go."

Emily headed toward the tree. Cedric finished his apple in a hurried gulp, rolled to his paws, and followed her to the tree.

Lucas leaned on a porch post next to Karina. She had expected him to somehow shrink in daylight, as if he were some sort of evil creature of the night whose power faded with the sun, but he remained just as big and menacing. If anything, the sun made it worse—she could see every detail of his severe face. Everything about him, the way he leaned against the rail, the way muscle bulged on his arms and chest, the way he surveyed the yard, inspecting his territory, communicated predator.

Lucas raised his face to the sun, closed his eyes, and smiled. The smile lasted only a moment, gone like a leaf blown by the breeze, but she had seen it. He was handsome and the danger he emanated sharpened that beauty to a lethal edge. He was beautiful in the same deadly way a tiger was beautiful, and now she was locked in a cage with him.

If he was on her side, nobody would ever bother them.

At the tree, Emily picked up a twig and tossed it. Cedric looked at the twig and back at her, slightly puzzled.

"What is he?" Karina asked.

"A bear-dog. We played with their genetics a few generations back. He's gentle like a collie with the kids and he's a lot smarter than an average dog. What's the problem with her having an apple?"

Karina sat on the stairs. "She hoards food."

"Why?"

She didn't want to tell him. The less he knew about them, the less information he could use against her. "It makes her feel safe."

By the tree Emily clapped her hands and explained something to Cedric. He sat on his butt again, listening to her.

"Was she adopted?" Lucas asked quietly.

"No." She wouldn't have expected him to know that adoptive children sometimes exhibited food hoarding. Now she had to explain more just to keep him from getting the wrong idea. "It happened after her father's death. It's not an eating disorder. She doesn't want extra food; she's just trying to control her environment. We handled it, but with everything that's happened she might have relapsed. Please don't berate her or yell at her for it. It . . ."

"It makes things worse," he finished for her. "I know."

"Let me have her," she said, suddenly desperate. "Let me have her here with me. I thought I lost her on that fire escape. You have everything else—my freedom, my body, everything—and I just want one thing. Just let me keep my baby."

Lucas frowned. He didn't seem vicious now. "I'm not doing this to be an asshole."

"I'll keep her out of the way . . ."

Cedric snarled at the bushes, baring his teeth, and lunged into the thicket.

Karina jumped to her feet. Before her knees had straightened, Lucas had leaped over the railing and was sprinting to the tree.

Emily stumbled back. Her mouth gaped in a surprised O.

Karina ran but she was so agonizingly slow.

Lucas reached Emily, pushed her back, out of the way, and crashed through the underbrush.

Karina lunged forward. Her hand closed about Emily's shoulder. She grabbed her daughter and backed away, keeping her hand on her pocket, feeling the hard knife handle through the fabric of her jeans.

Lucas jerked something out of the bushes. Long and green and brown, it writhed in his hand, flailing, the elongated olive tail brushing the ground. He roared, a deep growl that nearly made her jump. "Henry!"

The thing jerked, its throat caught in Lucas's hand. He turned and Karina finally saw it: it resembled a freakishly large bearded dragon lizard bristling with inch-long spikes on its cheeks and sides. As the creature twisted, a crest snapped open along its back, the spikes standing up like the razor-sharp fins of some deepwater fish. The lizard creature clawed at Lucas's arm with long black claws. Blood welled in the scratches.

"A monster!" Emily squeaked.

"No, just a big lizard." Karina kept a death grip on Emily.

Behind her the door burst open. Daniel charged onto the porch. His face contorted. Something brushed past Karina like a sudden draft. The beast jerked and hung motionless, its legs abruptly gone limp.

Lucas carried the lizard to the porch. "Henry!"

Henry burst onto the porch.

Lucas slammed the lizard down onto the porch boards. The creature blinked but lay completely still. Henry knelt by the lizard. His hands touched the back of the creature's skull. He closed his eyes, focused for a long moment, and glanced up. "Its mind is inert. It didn't transmit."

Lucas looked at him. "Sure?"

Henry pushed his glasses back up his nose. "Yes. If it transmitted, there would be evidence of a spike in neural activity."

Lucas raised his fist and brought it down like a hammer. She barely had enough warning to spin Emily around before his fist crushed the lizard's skull, flattening it like an empty Coke can.

"Daniel, call the main house." Lucas turned to her. "Take Emily and go to our room. Don't come out until I get you."

Karina didn't ask what was going on. She just picked Emily up, ran inside the house, and didn't stop until the door of Lucas's room closed behind her.

The day burned down to the afternoon. Emily investigated the room, then she whined about being bored, and finally she fell asleep in the overstuffed chair in the corner. At first Karina listened for every noise and creak outside the door. Her nerves were wound so tight, she could barely sit still.

If the creature in the bushes had been just an ordinary lizard, Lucas would've killed it right away. She had no doubt of it. No, this beast had created an emergency. She had no idea why and that somehow made everything so much worse. Eventually her own anxiety wore her out and she sank into a light sleep, a kind of wakeful drowsiness, where every stray noise made her raise her head.

The room was so quiet. Karina closed her eyes for a moment,

opened them, and then Lucas was there, walking across the room. She hadn't heard the door open.

Lucas scooped Emily out of the chair. Karina surged to her feet. "Where are you taking her?"

"To a different room," he said quietly and went out. She followed him down the hallway to a small bedroom. A bed with a red comforter stood against one wall, next to a bookcase filled with children's books. A desk offered a small computer with a flat-screen monitor.

He'd made her a room. He'd changed his mind.

Lucas deposited Emily on the bed and stepped out. Karina pulled the blanket over Emily's shoulders. She was so tiny on the bed. Karina's mind replayed Lucas clenching the lizard's throat. One squeeze and Emily would be dead.

He waited for her now, in the hallway. Karina made herself step away from the bed and walked out. Lucas closed the door, locked it, and handed her the key. "This is for her protection. Our room doesn't have a lock. Daniel is pissed off tonight, and I'm feeling surly, which makes the house a dangerous place to be, so it's best she stays in this room. This is for tonight only. Tomorrow she will go to the main house."

But the room—it was a child's room, made for a little girl. The blankets and the pillowcases looked brand-new and the rug still had the price sticker on it.

So he hadn't changed his mind. She had from now until morning to convince him to let her keep her daughter. Karina opened her mouth and said the only thing she could think of. "Are you hungry?"

Lucas nodded. "I could eat."

"Any preference?"

"Meat would be nice." He turned away.

"Lucas?"

He glanced at her over his shoulder. "Yes?"

"What's going on?" Karina asked him softly. "What was that thing?"

Lucas grimaced. "It's a long explanation."

"Please. I want to know." Whatever he would tell her had to be better than not knowing.

Lucas sighed. "The woman who poisoned you has friends. Her people are looking for our base, so they are sending scouts out. The lizard was one of them. It's basically a walking camera—it records what it sees and then transmits the information to its owners in short bursts. Luckily we caught this one before any transmissions had gone out."

"And if it had sent this transmission?"

"We'd be evacuating," Lucas said. "We still may. We'll know more in the morning."

Karina hugged her shoulders. "Lucas, where are we?"

He was looking directly at her. "We're on base."

"Where is this base? I've seen those birds. There are no birds like that in North America."

Lucas examined her face for a long breath. "You want the truth?"

"Yes."

He grimaced. "You asked for it. As the planet rotates, fluctuations between the forces of gravity and nuclear reactions on the subleptron and subquark level cause a ripple effect in reality, where time and space are not constant but dynamic. Parts of space-time become incompatible with the current reality and are discarded. In essence, Earth continuously sheds chunks of itself. They linger for a time and dissipate, some slower, some faster. We're in one such chunk—we call them fragments. It was shed sometime during the late Pliocene, approximately two and a half million years ago in what is now Texas. This pocket is stable and shouldn't begin to dissipate for another couple thousand years. Can you make cubed steak?"

"What?" Karina stared at him, sure she had misheard.

"I asked if you can cook cubed steak. I just realized I'd really like some."

"Yes, I can. You're not joking?"

"About the steak?"

"About the fragments."

Lucas shook his head.

This was just insane. "So we're in an alternate reality? Like in a parallel dimension? Like in *Star Trek*?"

"No. A mirror dimension is a self-contained, complete reality. We're in a dimensional fragment." Lucas leaned back against the wall. "Okay, think of an onion. The inner layers are white, and the outer layer is brown. Suppose the outer layer rots. The onion makes a replacement layer, identical to this outer one, and sheds the rotten layer in bits and pieces, some big, some tiny. We are in a piece of that rotten layer."

She stared at him. If he wasn't lying, they weren't anywhere near Oklahoma. They weren't even on the same planet. Escape was impossible.

"Don't think about it too much," Lucas said. "Subquantum mechanics will drive you insane."

"Can we get back? To normal Earth?"

"It depends on how close the layer is to its reality. The motel where you were attacked was in a layer that had barely begun to separate, so we could cross in and out easily. But this pocket has peeled much too far away for you and I to exit on our own. We need someone to rip it. To open a gateway." Lucas pushed off from the wall.

"But we *can* go back?" Surely they had to go back occasionally. Their clothes had tags; their plates had Corelle stamped on the back. Microwaves and refrigerators didn't sprout on prehistoric trees, which meant the people of Daryon had to pop back and forth from the normal Earth to here and back on a whim.

Lucas leaned toward her. His gaze fixed on her. Suddenly he was occupying too much space. She took a step back, her spine pressing against the wall.

A slow smile curved Lucas's lips. "Yes. You can go back. But never without me. If you ever try, I will find you and bring you back." His smile grew wider. "And then all bets are off."

He was looking at her with an open sexual hunger, so intense, for a second she didn't think it could be sincere. She froze, terrified. And then a small part of her responded to it. For a second, Karina wondered what it would be like to cross the distance between them, laugh right into that stare, and walk away, leaving him standing there like an idiot. But as long as he controlled Emily, she could do nothing.

He leaned forward a quarter inch, like a predatory cat about to pounce.

In her mind, Karina gulped and fled down the hallway, her heart hammering too fast and too loud. But showing weakness wasn't an option. Lucas had told her before that he was a predator. If she ran, the predator would chase.

She raised her face toward him. "If I do go back without you, don't find me."

He turned his head to the side, like a dog, studying her. "Or?"

"Or I will kill you."

He laughed, a low rich sound that sent shivers of alarm down her spine. "How?"

"I'll think of something."

She turned her back to him and forced herself to walk slowly toward the kitchen.

Lucas tilted his head and watched Karina retreat down the hallway. The look in her eyes, the angle of her face, the way she stood, everything communicated defiance. She challenged him. She had no idea how exciting this made her. He wanted to pin her against the wall, until she acknowledged that he was strong enough and powerful enough for her. He wanted to kiss and taste and grind and own. Different standards, he reminded himself. For him it would be flirting. For her, it would be a prelude to rape.

Lucas looked at the ceiling. He knew exactly where this violent impulse was coming from. It was an evolutionary echo, the same echo that told him to murder every other male in the house and then hunt her until she gave in. He made a choice to reject it daily. Strangely, it wasn't getting any easier.

Henry's light steps approached him. "Physical assault is probably not the best way to go," Henry murmured.

Sometimes Lucas could swear the man could read thoughts, even though every Mind Bender Lucas had ever met maintained it was impossible. "Playing in my head?"

"Of course not." Henry smiled at him. "Your fists are clenched and it's written all over your face."

He'd figured as much. "She's beginning to ask questions."

"That's a little faster than I expected." Henry frowned. "I wiped almost twelve hours of severe pain from her. Usually a wipe of that extent leaves people inert longer. You're pacing the explanations?"

Lucas nodded. "Not my first time."

He'd helped bring people over a few times before. A human mind could only accept so much. If he flooded her with the information contradicting her view of reality, the impact of it, combined with her physical trauma, would cause her to snap under the pressure. Her body was at its limits already, fighting the poison and coping with his venom and its consequences, which would soon follow.

Lucas started down the hallway. He needed a shower and some time away from everyone to soothe the excitement rushing through his veins.

"Lucas?" Henry called.

Lucas turned.

His cousin looked at him for a long moment. "Be kind."

An hour later Karina put the dinner on the table. The encounter in the hallway kept replaying in her head and she couldn't decide if she'd botched it or handled it well. Emily still slept. Henry had said the fatigue was normal, but she worried all the same.

"Cubed steak." Henry slid into his seat. " 'Beef. It's what's for dinner.' "

Karina took her seat. Lucas sat to the right of her. Too close. She should have served the dinner in the dining room instead of the kitchen. The bigger table would've given her more space.

Lucas crowded her, drinking in her anxiety. Karina swallowed, unable to help herself. He was simply too large and he watched her constantly. Even when she couldn't see him, she couldn't get rid of the pressure his gaze brought. He leaned toward her, emanating menace, and she shrank from him out of sheer self-defense.

His lips stretched and Lucas showed her his teeth, large and sharp. "Am I scary?"

She met his stare. "Yes," she said. "But you know that already. Making me admit it makes you cruel. Corn or beans?"

He drew back. His eyes widened and for a moment the burden of his presence eased. "Corn."

She passed the dish of corn to him.

Daniel sauntered into the room. While Henry migrated from place to place and Lucas stalked, his steps soundless and full of fierce grace, Daniel strode as if his feet did the ground a great favor. He didn't walk but floated, devastating in his beauty and perfectly aware of it.

Daniel took a seat directly opposite her. He speared a steak and dropped it on his plate. "Are you going to do this every day? Cook the dinner, be the dinner?"

"Yes," Karina said with a calm she didn't feel.

"Why? Are you totally spineless? What do you think sucking up will earn you? Look at him." Daniel pointed at Lucas. "He doesn't care."

"I'm not doing it for him."

"Then why?"

"Here we go." Henry rolled his eyes.

Daniel pushed off from the table, balancing his chair on its back legs, and crossed his arms. "No, I want her to enlighten me. How deeply has Stockholm syndrome set in?"

Karina put down her fork. Her instinct told her that whatever she said next would define her place in this house. The idea of some flattering subterfuge crossed her mind and died. She wondered if she should say nothing at all. In the end, she decided on honesty.

"I understand that I can die at any moment. Lucas's cousin died at the last Christmas dinner. For all I know, Lucas might die tomorrow, killed by your enemies or by your family members. Without Lucas I have no worth. My daughter is here because of me. If I'm no longer needed, I expect that neither will she be. I've seen enough of your family to realize we won't be allowed to leave. You will dispose of us as if we never existed. I have to find some way to make myself valued beyond Lucas. Then, if he dies, both my daughter and I might survive."

"And you do this by becoming our housekeeper?" Daniel grinned. "Cooking, cleaning up after us? Tell me, how low will you stoop? If I leave some shit in the bathroom for you, will you clean it up?"

"No," Karina said. "You'll clean your own shit. Unless you're sitting in a pile of it right now, you must know how to aim for the toilet and wipe your own ass."

The amusement in Daniel's eyes crystallized into anger. "If you want to ingratiate yourself, there's a much easier way of doing it. You can come over here right now and suck my cock. That will put you into my good graces much faster than scrubbing the sink."

Karina glanced at Lucas. He cut a piece of steak, chewed with obvious pleasure, and threw her a look that said, *Sit tight.*

"She isn't a fool, Daniel." Henry snagged another roll from the bread basket. "These are delicious. She knows that servicing you would put you and Lucas at each other's throats. You're playing this game for your personal gratification, but Lucas depends on her for his survival. She'd have to be mentally deficient to choose you over him."

Daniel shifted to Lucas. "So what does his lordship think of all this? Your snack has you buried already. Are you flattered?"

Lucas cut into his third steak.

"What would you do in her place? Would you mop the floors, O mighty one?"

Lucas thought about it. "In her place I would've killed the two of you already. But I'm not in her place. And I'm not her. I'm not smaller and weaker than everyone around me, nor do I have a child's life in my hands. She's being prudent, given her situation."

Daniel smirked. "Never thought you'd be so agreeable at the idea of your own death."

"We all must come to terms with it one way or another," Lucas said.

"Maybe I'll help you on your way, then, since you're all prepared. Seems a shame to waste the opportunity."

"Think you can?" Lucas asked with genuine interest.

"Careful, Daniel," Henry said. "That kind of talk will end with you breaking a nail or messing up your hair."

Daniel ignored him and glared at Lucas. "Bring it."

Lucas put down his fork, smiled, and shoved the table aside like it weighed nothing. Karina scrambled out of the way. Lucas's huge hand clamped Daniel's throat. Daniel clawed at Lucas's forearm. The bigger man jerked him off his feet, shook him the way a dog shakes a rat, and slammed him down onto the table. Dishes flew. Trapped in a corner between the counter and the stove, Karina threw her hands in front of her face. A ceramic dish shattered next to her, spraying green beans over the counter.

"No," Henry screamed. "Not inside! Not inside!"

Red marks sliced Lucas's forearms. His skin bulged as if his bones were trying to break free.

"Yeah!" he snarled. "Hurt me more. Is that all you got?" His hand still locked on Daniel's throat, he pulled him up and smashed him onto the table again. "Need some more?" Daniel's face had grown bright red. Lucas jerked him up. "Not done yet?" He drove Daniel back down.

With a thunderous snap, the table broke in two. The two halves fell apart and Daniel crashed onto the floor, Lucas atop him, still crushing his windpipe. Daniel's feet drummed the ground. Veins bulged on his face, his skin turning magenta. His eyes rolled back into his skull.

"Here we go." Henry sighed. "We lose all the good dishes this way." He showed Karina the bread basket. "At least I saved the rolls. And don't worry, I'm keeping Emily asleep."

Lucas released Daniel. The blond man lay unmoving. Lucas stepped over him, his eyes blazing with fury. His gaze locked on her. "Bedtime," Lucas growled and lunged at her. An unstoppable force swept Karina off her feet and she found herself slung over Lucas's back.

"Let me go!" She struggled to pull free.

He swung around to face Henry. "Leave the mess for when he wakes up."

"Will do." Henry saluted him with a roll.

Lucas headed out of the kitchen. Karina tried to grab onto the door frame, but her fingers slipped and she was carried through the darkness of the hallway to the bedroom.

CHAPTER 5

The room swung as Lucas slapped the door closed. Karina expected him to hurl her on the bed but he lowered her to the floor. She stumbled, dizzy from being spun back and forth, and scrambled to get away. Steely fingers caught her arm. He held on to her and sniffed at the sleeve of her sweatshirt. "Green beans. You want a shower?"

His tone was calm. She glanced at his face. All of the rage had gone out of him. He looked worn out, his fury muted to mere smoldering coals.

"Yes." She hesitated. "I don't have any clean clothes."

"That's a problem," Lucas agreed. "I'm sorry about the dinner."

"That's okay." His sudden calm threw her off balance. She stood still, expecting him to swing at her or maybe roar into her face.

Lucas reached into the dresser and pulled out a white T-shirt. "That's the best I can do for now. I'll have something sent up from the main house in the morning."

She took the T-shirt. He didn't offer her any underwear. She would be naked under it.

"Come on." Lucas pulled off his shirt and dropped it on the floor.

Carved muscle bunched on his back. Nude, clothed—he could rape her at any point. Clothes wouldn't provide much of a defense.

He paused, his hand on the door of the bathroom. "Are you coming?"

Not if I can help it. "I'll wait until you're done."

"I'll be in here for hours," he said. "The shower stall is enclosed. You can take your clothes off and I'll see nothing."

For hours . . . Why would he be in the bathroom for hours? "I thought you needed to feed."

"I do, but I won't be feeding for a while."

She followed him, despite knowing better, eager for any crumb of information. "How long is a while?"

"Couple of weeks. Maybe longer. Depends on how quickly you deal with my venom."

"Why?"

"Because too much of my toxin at once will kill you."

She remembered his explanation from the night before. "You said your venom hurts you. Does it hurt now?"

He nodded.

"Always?"

Lucas looked at her. "Always. Worse after I am injured and much worse after I phase out of the attack variant. Sometimes I have seizures after phasing out."

If he hurt always, he would have to feed always . . . "How often do you . . ."

As if reading her thoughts, he shrugged. "Once the optimal ratio of my venom to your hormones is reached in my blood, I'll need to feed every three weeks to maintain it. I won't be drinking as much as the last time. Come on. You need a shower and I need to sit down."

He stepped out of her way. During the day she had used the bathroom in the hallway, near the kitchen. She had assumed this one would be the same.

A room almost as big as the bedroom itself greeted her. A dark green hot tub was sunk into the sealed wooden floor. Beyond it a shower stall stretched the entire length of the wall. Its frame matched the hot tub, but the stall itself consisted of wide, dark green panels, either glass or plastic, thick and frosted from the inside. Lucas hadn't lied—he might be able to discern her shadow, but that was about it. To the right was another stall, which she assumed hid the toilet, next to a large sink. ·

Lucas flipped a switch on the wall and the hot tub jets started, whipping the water into froth.

The shower called to Karina. To go on and disrobe while he was in the tub was insane, but she was covered in food and his scent from the previous night still stained her skin. She could wash him off.

Karina bit her lip and slipped past Lucas to the shower. She closed the door and saw a latch. Relief flooded her. She could lock herself in and for a few minutes pretend she was safe. She slid the latch closed and almost cried.

The shower stall was divided into a dressing area and the shower itself, separated by a curtain. Karina dug into the pocket of her jeans and fished out the knife. The blade seemed so small compared to Lucas. If she stuck it into his back, he might not even notice. She put it on the small metal shelf next to the soap and, pulled off her clothes, dropping them into a rumpled pile on the bench. An array of shampoo bottles and soaps waited her selection. She took the bottle with the picture of a green apple on the side, picked up a bar of soap at random, and stepped into the shower. Jets surrounded her on three sides. She turned the big wheel of the faucet and a wide sheet of water spilled on her from above in a warm, soothing waterfall. She dropped the shampoo and the soap. All around her water sprayed and cascaded, drenching her, washing away the scent of warm copper. She stepped into the deluge, closed her eyes, and swayed.

Lucas slid into the hot water. He liked it near scalding. It wasn't quite hot enough, but it was getting there. The currents pummeled his body. He switched the two nearest jets off. The sharp claws of pain that scraped his ribs dulled to a low ache as he healed. His right arm still throbbed. Daniel was getting stronger.

One day one of them would get careless and they might finish each other off. Lucas closed his eyes and submerged. There were worse ways to go than being killed by your brother.

The rage that had driven him these past few days was gone, burned out in an adrenaline rush of violence.

He came up for air and settled with his head on the ledge, positioned in the dip of the shelf, the only place he could sit with the water lapping at his neck.

So tired . . .

The healing was draining his inner resources and he felt thin and weak, as if all of his muscles were a threadbare shirt hanging off his bones. From here he could see the door and the shower stall. She was in there. Naked. Wet. A fruity synthetic scent teased him—she was washing her hair. He pictured her body under the water, her hands sliding over her breasts and down . . .

A dull thud made him lift his head. In the shower, a dark shadow slumped, pressed against the glass.

It had hit her finally. He'd waited the whole day for it.

Lucas climbed out of the hot tub. The shower-stall door was locked. He hit it with his palm and the lock popped open. Karina lay curled in a corner of the shower, a small wet clump. Her legs shivered. Her skin had gained a pale, almost gray tint. He scooped her off the floor.

"No," she stuttered. Her lips had turned blue. Not a good sign.

He bent down. She lashed out. He caught a glint of metal and pulled back, letting the knife blade miss him. Where had she even gotten one? Ah, yes. The kitchen. He plucked the knife out of her fingers and picked her up off the floor.

"No." She pushed against his chest.

"Shhh," he told her. "I'm not going to hurt you."

He carried her out. Her wet skin was ice-cold against his.

She fought him even as he climbed into the tub and lowered her onto the shelf, sinking her up to her chin in the hot water. "Let me go . . ."

Afraid to agitate her any further, he put the full width of the tub between them, giving her room. No need to strain her. If she passed out, the chances of her survival would drop to almost nothing.

It took a full three minutes before her teeth stopped chattering. She looked at him. "Everything hurts."

"Your body is reacting to the venom," he said. "Hot water will help. It soothes the muscles. It's normal." Technically everything he said was true. He just didn't go into the rest of the details. Not yet.

A short bitter laugh slipped from her lips. "Normal? Nothing about this is normal."

True. Not for her anyway. For him, it was business as usual. "Thirsty?"

"Yes."

He waded through the tub, reached for the small fridge beside it, and extracted a bottle of water.

She took the bottle, clamped the plastic cap in her teeth, twisted it off, and drank, draining nearly a third in a single long draft. *That's it . . . Drink, Karina.*

He recalled Galatea's first time. She'd known exactly what would happen. She had been raised for precisely this purpose: to support him. And she loathed him for it. Hate would've been too personal of a word; he didn't rank that high in her mental roster. Galatea hated the family; she hated Arthur because he was in charge; but Lucas she merely despised, disgusted by his touch. The older he got, the more he realized that sex with him was her way of revenge. In feeding he dominated her and she had no choice but to submit. In bed, for a few fleeting moments Galatea dominated him. That first time, when she cried and screamed as her body struggled with its initial dose of his venom, he had tried to hold her. She was so pretty, so fragile . . . He didn't want to break her. She had sensed that small spark of compassion in him, clutched on to it, and twisted it, used it against him again and again, until finally he could stand it no longer.

Living with Galatea meant fighting a constant war. Living with Karina so far was like sparring with an honest fighter. She defied him, but she would never stick a knife in his back. She would try to stab him in plain view.

Lucas sank down into the water and closed his eyes. Thinking about Galatea left a foul taste in his mind. His ribs ached again. Drowsiness came, threatening to smother his mind like a heavy blanket.

Karina's voice tugged on him before he passed out. "Why are you being nice to me?"

"'Nice' isn't in my vocabulary. I'm just tired."

"Your ribs are bruised."

"Daniel."

"I didn't see him hit you."

"He doesn't have to. I'm a Demon, and he's an Acoustic. He can mimic voices and wrench the bones from my body with a focused sound wave." He raised his arms and stood up, showing her the long angry welts outlining his ribs. "If he really pushed, you'd see bone shards puncturing the skin."

She stared at him in horrified silence. He sank back down and closed his eyes.

"Why do you fight like that?" she asked.

"There's no single reason. Sometimes he doesn't like something I've done. Sometimes I do it because he annoys me."

"What about today?"

Lucas sighed. She wouldn't let him be. "Today we fought because Daniel argued with Arthur. Daniel wants to evacuate. Arthur doesn't. Daniel insisted and Arthur bruised his pride. I took Arthur's side. Evacuating the base is costly. One scout isn't reason enough to do it. It's a bad sign—we had seen scouts before in the neighboring fragments, but never this close. But we can't just run at the first hint of trouble."

She frowned. "So twisting bones out of your sockets is the way he demonstrates his displeasure at being pushed around?"

"Pretty much. Daniel wants to be taken seriously. So I treated him as a serious threat and made a big production of it. I was a substitute fight. What he really wanted was a shot at Arthur, which I can't let him take, because Arthur will kill him." Lucas thought of leaving it at that, but something nagged him to explain. "It's complicated. We live by different rules. In your other life, people undergo strict social conditioning that evolved over hundreds of years. They grow up in relative safety and under constant supervision. Parents, schools, peers—all of their interactions fine-tune their behavior until they are . . ."

"Safe?" she suggested.

"Socialized. But Daniel and I grew up as outcasts, with only the extremes of our behavior corrected—so we don't murder someone whenever the urge strikes us. Our interactions are simpler than yours, less layered and closer to . . ." Lucas grappled for the right word. When it came to him, he didn't like it. "Animals. Both of us reached sexual maturity a while ago. We have a strong urge to mate and have our own territory, our own families, and separate lives. Instead we're stuck with each other, in this house, with an illusion of privacy and an excess of aggression. And now there is you. Daniel doesn't really want you for your own sake. He wants you because he views me as competition and now I have something he doesn't. I am the only consequence he fears. He's hostile and defensive, and Arthur made him sit down and shut up today. Daniel had to vent and I'm the only one who would put up with it."

"Why?" she asked softly.

"Because he is my brother."

There was a tiny pause. "But he is not a Demon like you."

"Different fathers," he told her. "All of us within the House of Daryon carry genes from many different subspecies. Our mother was a Demon. My father was a normal human. Daniel's father was a powerful Acoustic. We both played the genetic lottery and got different prizes."

He left out rape, imprisonment, and murder. It sounded much better this way.

"Did Daniel hoard food as a child?"

She was perceptive. He would have to remember that. "Yes."

"And you took care of him?"

"Yes." Because nobody else would.

"Why doesn't he just leave?" she asked. "Why don't you? You don't seem to like living here."

"Because we have a job to do. We guard you from genocide." The mission overrode everything. A logical part of him assured Lucas that life outside of the original mandate existed. He just couldn't picture himself living it. "As long as we exist, you survive."

"I don't understand."

He sighed. This was another long explanation and he had no energy for it today. Nor did he want to shock her again. She'd been through enough. "Monsters exist. They call themselves Ordinators. They want to kill people like you. Normal ordinary people. We exist to keep them from succeeding. That's all there is to it."

"But what do they want?"

"They want you to die."

"Why do they hate us so much?"

He sighed. "They don't hate you. They simply want you not to be. It's a genetic cleansing, a mass extermination. They view the current situation as a mistake, which they're trying to correct. They feel that they are ordained to take your place. Subspecies 61, the 'normal' human, has no value to them, except maybe as an occasional food source in a pinch."

"They're cannibals?" Her voice spiked a little.

"Only some of them. I meant a food resource for their war animals. Do you know what a daeodon is?"

"No."

"It's a nasty breed of entelodon, a prehistoric boar. Picture a predatory pig, twelve feet long, seven feet tall at the shoulder, jaws like a crocodile. It eats anything, and once you mess with its genetics, it gets smart and breeds fast. They need a lot of meat."

When he opened his eyes, he found her looking at him. Karina sat submerged so deeply, only her face floated above the water. Warm color had returned to her cheeks. Her hair, slicked by the shower, swirled in the roiling water.

Mmmmm. Mine.

Lucas could reach out and pull her to him and run his hands up and down her body, to feel the heavy fullness of her breasts, the curve of her ass . . . If it wasn't for fatigue, and the fact that she trusted him, anchoring him to the spot, he might have done it.

His thoughts must've reflected on his face, because she pulled as far from him as the tub would allow. A haunted look claimed her face, sharpening her features. Like a stray dog, he thought, shivering, scared, and ready to bite. He held the key to her: turn it one way and break her; turn it the other and the pressure would ease. He'd been just like that a few years ago. The memory of being scared of everyone was still fresh.

"You know I can't stop you. What consequences do you fear?" Karina asked.

"Right now I just don't want to fight with you," Lucas said. "I fight with Arthur, with Daniel, with Henry. I'm tired." And he wanted her to stop jerking back every time he looked at her. It made him feel like he was a monster and he had enough help with that already.

"If you want peace, let me have Emily."

"No."

She clenched her teeth.

"Maybe later. Down the road."

"Why not now?"

Irritation flared in him. "Because I can't watch the two of you every moment of every day and you are stealing knives."

"The knife was for protection. I won't take another one. I won't try to stab you again . . ."

"It's not me I'm worried about."

She became utterly still. "Oh, my God." Her eyes widened. "You think I would hurt my own daughter?"

"You wouldn't be the first one." Not by a long shot. "Shock is a bitch. Especially when mixed with venom fucking with your hormones."

"She is everything I have."

She looked on the verge of tears. He forced himself to sound calmer. "And that's why you could slit her throat the second I gave her to you. You're both my responsibility. I said I would keep you safe. I don't want you to hurt her or yourself."

"I had the knife since breakfast," she told him. "You sent me into the room with Emily. I didn't kill her. If I'd tried, you couldn't have stopped me . . ."

"Henry was monitoring your mind. Had your stress level spiked, he would've shut you down."

"Then ask him if I tried to kill her or myself. I had the opportunity. I got the knife so I could hurt you. Not myself."

Lucas rose and crossed the tub, pinning her between his body and the tub wall. The feel of her body against his shoved him right to the edge. In his mind all the leashes he put on himself were snapping one by one. Karina turned to the side, trying to hide from him.

"Look at me."

Karina looked at him. Lucas peered into her eyes, looking for some sort of indicator of sanity. "If you had a loaded gun in your hand, would you shoot me?"

"No. If I killed you, I would be next. Either Daniel, Henry, or Arthur would murder me, and Emily would have nobody."

An honest rational answer. "Do you want to die?" He wanted her. He wanted to crush her in his arms and see her want him.

"No." She shook her head.

"What do you want?" He knew what he wanted. She was right there, caught against his chest. His heart was beating too fast.

"I want to escape," she told him. "I want to go back to my life."

She was sane and stable, or as sane as he could expect. Lucas released her and Karina scrambled away from him.

"What would you do if I let you have your daughter, Karina?"

She stopped. He read the answer on her face. *Anything.* She would do anything. She would let *him* do anything, and if he demanded, she would pretend to like it.

It was the answer his mother would've given.

"What do you want?" she asked hoarsely. He felt the tension hidden in her words, as if she stood on the edge of a chasm, waiting for him to push her in.

"Can you bake a chocolate cake?"

There was a tiny pause before she answered. "Yes."

"Make one. For Daniel. It's his favorite."

She waited. When he didn't say anything, she finally asked, "That's it?"

"Yes."

Lucas waited for relief on her face, but she just sat there, clenched up. Still looking for the catch, he realized.

"You'll really let me have her?" He barely heard her voice. "No conditions?"

"Yes." And the more fool he for it. Nothing good would come of it, not with the way they fought. Henry would think him insane. But Lucas felt weary. He didn't have the strength to fight yet another war. And he didn't want her to be miserable. "Make a list of what you both will need, and I'll send it to the main house tomorrow. Last time I checked, you could buy Hello Kitty blankets in any department store . . ."

Karina covered her face and cried.

He sat there and watched her shudder and sob, not knowing what to do with himself. Uncomfortable, as if he were intruding on something private. Guilt rose in him and he wasn't sure where it came from.

"Stop," Lucas growled finally.

"I can't."

Her sobs died gradually. She splashed some water on her face. "Can I stay with her in her room?"

"No. You'll stay with me."

"Can I sleep on the floor?"

"No. You'll sleep in my bed, just like last night."

"Why?"

Because you're mine. And because he would know if she got up in the middle of the night. "Because I want it that way."

"I could—"

He closed his eyes and leaned his head back. "Quiet. No more talking."

"Thank you," she said softly.

"You're welcome."

CHAPTER 6

Karina awoke alone. She dimly recalled seeing Lucas get out of the water, his huge muscled body wet, and feeling a sharp inner clench, the same clench that gripped her when he'd caught her in the tub. She would've liked to pretend it was fear or anxiety, but that would mean lying to herself. When he rose to show her the bruises Daniel had made, she stared at him for a moment too long and it wasn't to study his injured ribs.

Lucas had brought her a towel and when he turned away, giving her a fragile illusion of privacy, she'd draped it around herself and escaped into the bedroom. He didn't follow her. She toweled off, slipped on the giant T-shirt he'd given her, and slid into bed, curling under the blanket into a worried ball. Her nervousness should've kept her awake, but her body simply gave out. Lucas took his time getting to bed and by the time he lay down on the other side, she was half asleep. He asked her something, but her feverish haze mugged her and dragged her under into a dreamless sleep.

Karina struggled to sit up. She felt the steady heat of her slowly burning, low fever. At least she was alive. She forced herself all the way up. Her head swam and the dizziness nearly took her back down.

Up. Up, come on, you can do it.

And now she was talking to herself. Outstanding.

Karina walked to the shower, swaying on wobbling feet. She'd rinsed her underwear last night, and it still hung on the towel hook where she'd left it. Karina touched it. Dry. She slipped the panties on and went to use the bathroom.

A couple of minutes later she made it to the sink. A new toothbrush, still in its case, waited for her. Karina stared at it.

Lucas hadn't kidnapped her. He hadn't forced her into human slavery at gunpoint. She'd been attacked by Rishe and the shark-toothed man, and she'd been given a choice: to die or to live on Lucas's terms. She was a victim of circumstance. That didn't change the fact that Lucas owned her now.

The House of Daryon had stripped every shred of independence from her. She depended on Lucas for everything: her food, her safety, her clothes, the safety and survival of her daughter. He had the power to tell her when to go to bed, where to sleep, when to shower . . . He was protecting her and Emily from some sort of terrible enemy she couldn't understand and he could kill them both at a moment's notice. Any relaxation of the rules became a kindness on his part. A small thing, like a toothbrush, seemed like some great favor. But it wasn't, she told herself. It wasn't. It was a basic necessity for any human being.

Then again, she could've been a slave without any freedom at all. She could've lost her daughter. She could've been raped. All he had to do was say, "I'll give you your daughter," and she would've done anything. The very fact that he thought to leave her a toothbrush was a small miracle.

Her own drive to survive was interfering with her sense of reality. Her instincts drove her to forge an emotional bond. The more Lucas liked her, the less likely he was to murder her or Emily. The more she liked him . . .

Karina took a deep breath. Lucas was physically overwhelming.

The memory of his arms around her flashed before her. Lucas was . . .
He was . . .

She stared at herself in the bathroom mirror. *Just say it. Say it,
acknowledge it, and walk away from it.*

Seductive. Desirable. Shocking. He was masculine in the way
women fantasized men to be: powerful, strong, dangerous. If she had
met him at a party or in a professional setting, when he wore a suit
and she wore something other than his T-shirt and a pair of underwear she'd washed in the shower, she would've sought him out. If he
had spoken to her, she would've been flattered.

For a while, after Jonathan's death, she was so wrapped up in
guilt, and in Emily's well-being, she forgot men existed. It took
almost a year before she became aware of them again: a man with
a nice smile in the checkout line, a random stranger in good shape
stepping out of the car in the parking spot next to her. A small part
of her wanted to be noticed again and checked to see if she was. She
was vulnerable and the way Lucas looked at her left her no doubt
that if she gave him the tiniest indication that she wanted him, he
would rush to oblige and mow down whatever stood in his way.

There was an odd desperation in Lucas under all that violence.
Karina sensed a deep overpowering need to be . . . not accepted
exactly, but to be liked. If she were ruthless, she would seduce him
to make sure he would become dependent on her, but that kind of
manipulation was beyond her. She couldn't bring herself to do it.

Karina looked at her reflection. She could practically see him in
the mirror next to her. She could recall him with crystal clarity:
every powerful line of his body; the promise of raw violence in the
way he moved; the precise curve of his mouth, almost sardonic; the
look in his eyes, the wild, unfiltered look of pure male lust. No, more
than lust. Need.

Thinking of him was like playing with fire.

She had been married; she knew very well that a healthy relationship hinged on respect and constant compromise. With Lucas there

could be no respect and no compromise, because they were not equals. He owned her. She was his property and once she opened the door to a relationship, he wouldn't let her close it.

Karina shut her eyes. She could picture herself wrapped in those powerful arms. It would feel safe, so safe. Her life was broken like a mirror and the shards kept cutting her fingers. She was desperate to forget that she was little more than a slave. She craved that illusion of safety as if it were a drug and she had to score a hit. She wanted to feel the heat of his strong body warming her skin. And she wanted to see him bend, to find out what it would be like to see the vulnerability of intimacy in those hard eyes. She was completely powerless and she needed to feel powerful, as a woman does who is wanted so badly by a man, he would do anything for her.

There it was. All of it, out in the open.

You're sick, she told her reflection.

Well, now it was out. She owned all of it.

She had to keep things in perspective. He was strong and she was weak and vulnerable and not in her right mind. She would take it one day at a time, wait until the last of the poison cleared out of her system, and when a chance to escape presented itself, she would take it—and they would never find her and Emily again. And if she let herself buy into her own lies, she would never wonder what it would have been like to feel him inside her . . . She cut off that thought. The less she imagined it, the better.

Karina opened the toothbrush. She would brush her teeth, locate her jeans, and check on her daughter. And then she would go out there and make a chocolate cake.

Emily seemed to have no memory of Lucas and Daniel's fight the previous night. She slept well and when Karina had come to get her, she got a hug. The violent episode had passed her daughter by completely. Karina held her for a long time, breathing in the scent of her hair. They were both alive. She would get to keep Emily with her. It would be okay. It would be hard and painful, but it would be okay.

Karina took Emily to the kitchen. Sunlight poured in through the open window. Nobody waited for her. Nobody demanded breakfast. The house was quiet and serene. Karina exhaled her tension, pulled the ingredients from the pantry, and started mixing the cake batter.

Henry walked into the kitchen, looking a bit lost. "Good morning!"

"Good morning!" Emily chirped.

"I have something for you." Henry put a drawing pad and a set of watercolor pencils on the table.

"For me?"

"For you."

Emily pried at the pencil case.

"What do you say?" Karina murmured on autopilot.

"Thank you!"

"You're welcome." Henry offered her a small smile.

"Where is everyone?"

"They've gone to check the perimeter net. What is it you're making?"

Karina glanced at him. "A chocolate cake. Did they go to check for signs of those people who sent the lizards to spy on us?"

Henry nodded.

"Lucas called them Ordinators. Henry, who are they? Who are you?"

Henry smiled again and slid his glasses up his nose. "It's a long and complicated explanation. It's better to wait a couple of days. Too much new information too fast will only make things worse."

"I'd like to know."

He shook his head. "You've been through a great deal of violence in the past two days and you've been exposed to things that conflict with your worldview. I don't want to be the one to add to it."

"Henry, not knowing is worse. All I'm asking is that you don't treat me like a slave who is told where to be and what to do and isn't owed any explanation."

"No," he said quietly.

They looked at each other over the table. Karina held his gaze. It might not have been wise, but she wouldn't back down now.

"Look, Mom, I drew Cedric!"

Karina looked down at the ball of brown fluff that looked like a sheep with a sabertooth's fangs. "That's looks very nice, Emily."

When she looked up, the kitchen was empty. Henry had escaped.

The cake smelled of chocolate and vanilla. When Karina took the two round pans out of the oven and set them out to cool, the familiar scents floated through the kitchen, so reminiscent of home and happy times, she almost cried.

A door banged. She looked up just in time to see Lucas loom in the doorway. His face was grim. He glanced at the cake, then at her. She stared back, suddenly terrified that all her thoughts would pour out through her eyes.

He didn't seem to notice. "Would you like new clothes?"

"Yes." Oh, God, yes.

He jerked his head toward the door. "They have some things prepared for you at the main house. I didn't know what size, so you have to come and try them on. Come on, I'll walk with you."

"Can I come?" Emily slid off the chair.

"Yes," Lucas said. "They have clothes for you, too."

"And Cedric?"

"Cedric doesn't need clothes," Lucas said.

"Can he come with us?" Karina asked.

"Sure."

Karina washed her hands, wiped them on a towel, and followed Lucas out. The sun shone bright. Cedric already waited for them at the foot of the stairs. Emily stepped down and the bear-dog rolled to his feet and trotted next to her, nearly as tall as she was.

Lucas led them out of the yard and down a dirt path. It wound around the hill, flanked on the left by stunted oaks and shrubs climbing up the slope and rolling off to the prairie on the right. Cedric and Emily pulled ahead a couple dozen yards. Karina watched them, aware of Lucas striding next to her, like some tiger who had learned to walk upright. The air was dry, and the heat beat down on them from the pale, burned-out sky, painting the path in stripes of bright yellow sunshine.

"We're in a fragment of reality," Karina said.

"Yes," Lucas said.

"Why is the sun shining? Why is there air?"

"Because the fluctuation occurs on the universal level," Lucas said.

"So it's a duplicate sun?"

"No, it's the same sun the Earth has. We just get access to it on a different level. Think of a house with many rooms. We walked out of the main room into a smaller side bedroom, but we're still under the same roof."

Karina sighed. "It makes my head hurt."

"Don't talk about dimensions to any Rippers, then," Lucas said.

"Rippers?"

"They make inter-dimensional rents that let people like you and me travel back and forth. You get one of them started on the subject and the insanity pours out until you want to stick your head in a bucket of water just to wash it out of your mind. When a man has to continuously cut himself, because pain helps him punch through dimensions, you can't expect him to be lucid anyway."

Karina glanced at him. "You seem irritated."

Lucas's thick black eyebrows knitted together. "We found out how the lizard got through the net. It tunneled under it. A long, deep tunnel, almost twenty-five meters."

"And?"

"There was more than one tunnel," Lucas said.

More than one tunnel meant other lizards. "Did you track them down?"

Lucas nodded.

"Did they transmit what they saw?"

Another nod.

"So the enemy knows where we are?"

Lucas grimaced. "Difficult to say. The Rippers are saying there was too much inter-dimensional interference for the transmission to have gone through fully. But it's possible." He clenched his teeth, pondering something, and said, "We had perimeter alarms, infrared, microwave, and frequency sensors. The sensors are very specific: if you look on Cedric's collar, you'll see a transmitter. The transmitter broadcasts a code. The sensors check this code against the database and if the code is active, the sensors don't register an alarm. For some reason someone loaded an old set of codes into the system. The lizards came through fitted with transmitters of their own and when they broadcast the outdated set of codes, the system didn't flag them."

"How did they know which codes to load?"

Lucas's eyes turned darker. "There was a woman. Galatea. She was a donor like you."

He said her name like she was a plague. "Was she your donor?"

"Yes. She defected."

He'd clenched his teeth again. There was more to this story. "Were you lovers?"

Lucas stopped and for a moment she thought she might have pushed him too far. "We fucked," he said.

Aha. She kept pushing. "For how long?"

There was a short pause before he answered. "For four years."

"That's some long fucking," Karina said. He'd loved Galatea. He was in love, and she betrayed him, and now he wanted to kill her. Any woman past the age of fifteen would've connected these dots. He must've been young—it had obviously left a deep scar. "What was she like?"

Lucas took a step toward her. A wild thing looked back at her from his eyes, the thing full of lust and aggression. She realized that in his mind he was peeling off her clothes and thinking of what it would be like, and suddenly she was back in the tub, naked, sitting two feet away from him and afraid he would cross the distance.

He stared at her. "Would you like me to tell you about it?"

She squared her shoulders. "No."

"Are you sure?"

"Yes."

"Okay, then."

He turned and they sped up to narrow the gap between themselves and Emily. Karina kept the pace, exhaling quietly. He had no brakes, at least not the ones she was used to as a woman. Ordinary men didn't end dinners by breaking the table with their brother's spine, they didn't kill lizards by caving their heads in, they didn't turn into monsters, and they didn't feed on women. Ordinary men didn't behave like this outside of movie screens and when they did it on the screen, other men ridiculed them for it. This was a game she couldn't afford to play, because he held the best cards. She had to survive this.

Karina chanced a glance at him. The wild, hungry thing in his eyes was still there. "Since someone had to have uploaded this old code, someone on the inside is helping Galatea," she said, trying to steer him away from whatever he was thinking.

"Looks that way. And when I find them, they'll wish they were never born." His voice contained so much malice, the hairs on the back of her neck stood up.

If this enemy was coming, Emily would be in danger. "Should we evacuate?"

"That's up to Arthur."

"Do you think we should?"

Lucas glanced at her. "It depends on how many people they bring to the fight. This is an old base, and we are actively mining this fragment for aluminum and beryllium. If the Ordinators are coming, they're coming fast. So even if we begin full base evacuation now, we'll take a hit in equipment. The base is run by means of a fiber network. It's a sophisticated computer system that coordinates mining operations, bio-support, communications, and so on. It also has the locations of the nearest bases. If the Ordinators gain access to it, a lot of us will die, which is why the network must be destroyed before the evacuation is complete. Detonating it will make this base uninhabitable. Fragments like this, with a stable climate and ecosystem, are rare. Most fragments we find are dead: no plants, no animals, often no atmosphere. You have to wear a suit and live in a hermetically sealed bunker. And popping back and forth through dimensions leaves a trail. If the Ordinators don't know where we are, they will once we start ripping."

The path ended, joining a larger road that rolled down the hill toward the prairie. In the distance a group of small horses galloped across the grass, ducking in and out of the brush. The vast prairie rolled to the towering mountain ridge, savage and ancient and somehow so much bigger than the modern landscape, that for a moment Karina stopped and simply stared, caught by the natural majesty of it.

"This is paradise compared to some of the fragments I've seen," Lucas said. "If we have a chance, we'll fight for it. Come on."

He turned and strode up the hill. She sped up to keep pace, Emily and Cedric in tow.

They rounded a bend and suddenly before them stood two tall white columns marking an entrance. Thrusting twenty feet up, they curved like the ribs of some prehistoric giant. An intricate network of designs covered the columns, etched into their surface. It drew the eye, hypnotic in its complexity. Once you looked, your gaze just kept sliding and sliding, up along the grooves and curved lines . . .

A hand rested on her shoulder. Karina turned, saw Lucas's fingers on her shoulder, and jerked away. He held his hand in empty air for a second and lowered it.

Karina turned to Emily. Her daughter stood next to her, staring at the column, her expression blank.

"Come," Lucas said.

Karina bent down and took Emily's hand. "Come on, baby."

Emily blinked, as if waking up from a deep sleep, and walked with her. They passed through the arches and Karina stopped again.

Pale buildings with curved roofs spread before her. On second thought, the complex was all one huge building in the shape of a horseshoe, rising three stories high. A beautiful garden lay in the crook of the horseshoe, crisscrossed by covered passageways, stone-lined paths, and lush flowerbeds, artfully bordering artificial ponds. Picturesque shrubs spread their branches. Flowers bloomed, blue, orange, yellow . . . The wind brought the by-now-familiar tart flower scent.

A large white sign stood next to the wide path leading into the garden, its smooth surface marked with an odd script. It had to be writing of some sort—groups of symbols separated by spaces—but it wasn't any language Karina was familiar with.

"What does it say?"

A string of odd words spilled from Lucas's lips, lyrical and surprisingly familiar. She waited for the meaning.

"It says 'The Mandate is everything.' "

"What is the Mandate?"

"The Original Mandate. It's hard to explain in English. There is a word in the primary language, *ile*. It means 'we,' 'us,' but it also means civilization, the best of us, the best of our kind. The mandate is '*Ile* must survive.' "

That explained nothing. "That's it?"

"That's it. On this world, under this set of circumstances, the people among whom you lived are *ile*. We exist to make sure they survive. When we're no longer needed, we'll die out like many other subspecies before us."

The more he explained things, the more confused she became. For now she had to just gather the crumbs of information and hope all would make sense sooner or later.

Lucas walked on, down the wide path of smooth stones. Karina scrambled to follow. They walked side by side along the path and over a bridge. The gardens burrowed into nooks in the buildings here and there, forming small sitting areas. To the left two women sat on a bench, discussing something. They looked so normal. Both wore jeans; the older of the pair had on a flowered top, white on blue; the younger woman wore a familiar yellow blouse—Karina had looked at it in J. C. Penney last week.

Last week. A lifetime ago.

The women saw Lucas. Their faces took on a certain tightness, as if they were straining to keep calm. They looked her over next. Karina met their gaze and saw pity in their eyes. Suddenly it made her furious. If Lucas grabbed her throat right now, they wouldn't lift a finger to help her. They would just sit there and watch him choke her to death and feel sorry for her. She raised her chin and stared at Lucas's back. No, thank you. She didn't need anyone's pity.

Henry's words came back to her. *Lucas is the most feared.* "They're afraid of you," she said.

"I'm the security specialist here; I have the right of judgment," he said. "I can kill anyone on base at any point without any retribution."

"You protect them, and all you get in return is fear. Why do you keep doing this?"

Lucas kept walking. "Because everyone must have a purpose. The Mandate tells me what I am doing is right and must be done and because I'm the biggest and the strongest it's my duty to put myself between my people and danger. I would do it for you."

He would. She believed him. "Lucas . . ."

"Yes?"

She wanted to tell him that if he ever shielded her or Emily, she wouldn't be afraid of him. She wanted to tell him that he didn't have to put up with people shrinking away from him, but inside a cold rational voice warned her that she was losing her grip on reality. The plan had to be to escape. The plan couldn't be to fall for Lucas and be that one sole person who comforted him.

He was looking at her.

"I'm really confused right now," she told him. "So this actually doesn't mean anything."

He nodded. "Okay."

"Bend your arm at the elbow."

He did. Karina reached out. *What am I doing?* She put her hand on his forearm and raised her chin. The two women on the bench stared at them, openmouthed.

"Now we walk," she murmured, avoiding looking at him.

"We can do that," he agreed. They started down the walkway. His arm was rock-steady under her fingers. A few moments, and the dense greenery of rhododendron shrubs hid the women from their view.

"Why?" he asked.

Because she lost it, that's why. "Would you hurt those two women?"

"Not unless they tried to hurt someone else first."

"Then they're in no danger and they know it, but they still make a big production out of you walking by, minding your own business."

"That still doesn't answer my question," he said.

"Can we stop talking about this?"

He didn't say anything. They simply kept walking. It was surreal, Karina reflected. Beautiful flowers, Emily and a tame bear-dog, and she and Lucas striding side by side.

"I'm tired," Emily said.

Karina bent down and picked her up. The effort nearly made her lose her balance. Apparently she was weaker than she thought.

Cedric sniffed at her feet.

"Let her ride him," Lucas offered.

"What?"

"Let her ride him. He doesn't mind."

"I want to ride!" Emily squirmed in her arms.

Karina surveyed the bear-dog. He was almost as big as a pony. Gingerly she lowered Emily on his back.

"Hold on to his fur," Lucas said. Emily dug her fingers into Cedric's brown mane and they were off again.

They emerged from the stand of rhododendrons. Lucas stepped aside, revealing a round plaza paved with dark red stone. A bronze statue rose in the center, a nude man, muscled with crisp precision. Enormous wings thrust from his shoulders. An angel, but not a garden cupid or some mournful cemetery statue. The angel leaned forward, one arm stretched out, his muscles knotted on his frame. The wings thrust up and out, featherless, as if made of sharp bone. The angel's perfect face stared into the distance, its gaze focused. Everything about it communicated fury and power. This was a predatory being about to kill its victim. Metal letters beveled on the side of the statue read "A. Rodin."

Karina glanced at Lucas. "A. Rodin? The sculptor who created *The Thinker*?"

Lucas shrugged. "He says so, but I wouldn't put it past him to have the name slapped on there over the actual sculptor's signature. He is vain enough."

What? He who? She scrutinized the statue.

Oh, God.

The angel wore Arthur's face. It had to be figurative—she hadn't seen any wings on Arthur's back when he offered her tea.

"But Rodin died in the beginning of the last century."

Lucas circled the statue and kept walking.

"Lucas!"

He turned and looked at her over his shoulder, light eyes under black eyebrows like two chunks of ice. "Arthur is a Wither. Subspecies 21. They live a long time."

"How long?"

"Long enough to have met Rodin. Come."

She wanted to freak out. She wanted to scream and kick her feet in panic, because right here, in cold bronze, was the final proof that this was not a nightmare. Instead Karina waved Cedric ahead of her and they kept going deeper into the garden.

Lucas turned left, down a path leading to a section of the building structured with an almost Japanese flair. Except for the white roof, it could've been part of a teahouse. An older woman waited on the covered porch, a stack of clothes neatly folded next to her.

They were twenty feet away from the porch when the siren ripped the quiet into shreds.

CHAPTER 7

Karina pulled Emily off the bear-dog and into her arms.
"Stay close," Lucas barked as he turned and ran back up
the path. She followed him, trying not to stumble. They pounded
over the bridge they'd crossed on the way in.

"What's happening, Mommy?"

"I don't know, baby. Hold on tight."

Emily was so heavy. Karina never remembered her being that
heavy. It was like all of the strength had somehow gone out of her
arms.

They cleared the garden and burst into the open space between
the two spires, Lucas ahead and she, out of breath, a few dozen yards
behind. A group of people stood by the spires, where the road out of
the settlement rolled down the hill. A familiar face looked at her
with merciless sky eyes. Arthur. Daniel's golden mane swung into
view. He grinned at her, a deranged wild grin that had too much
mirth. On the periphery a few yards away, Henry stood with his eyes
closed, tense, his face raised to the sky. A young girl, barely a teenager, stood next to him in an identical pose. To the right an older,

dark-skinned woman and another man, tall and gaunt, imitated them.

"Good of you to join us," Arthur said.

Lucas walked up to stand next to him.

A huge sound came from the distance, deep, booming, as if someone was playing a foghorn like a trumpet.

The girl at Henry's side inhaled sharply and dropped to her knees, breathing in ragged, painful gasps. Henry's eyes snapped open. He thrust his hand out and clenched it into a fist. "Oh no, you don't."

A desperate scream of pure pain came from the distance.

Henry smiled. His face glowed with vicious joy, so shocking that Karina took a step back. He stared into the distance. "Not as fun to pick on someone your own size?"

The scream kept ringing higher and higher, pausing for the mere fraction of a second that it took the agonized being that was making it to gulp some air.

Behind Henry the fallen girl opened her eyes and rose to her feet. The older couple awakened from their trance.

Henry twisted his fist and jerked it, as if ripping something in half.

The scream died.

"Thank you," the girl said.

"It's all right. Next time remember to cloak." Henry turned to Arthur. "They have two hundred civs, fifty pigs, two heavy field artillery batteries, six squads of twenty-five men each, and seven Mind Benders. Minus one."

He'd killed an enemy Mind Bender, Karina realized. Kind, shy Henry crushed him, but not before he made him suffer.

"Too many," someone muttered.

"It's overkill," Daniel said.

"There is at least one Demon, too," Henry said.

Lucas laughed, a bitter, self-assured chuckle.

They had a Demon like Lucas. Lucas would fight it. She saw it in his face. She didn't want him to die.

Something climbed over the crest of the distant hill, spilling onto the prairie. Karina squinted. What in the world . . .

Arthur's face remained serene. "Begin immediate full base evacuation."

A dark-haired woman on Karina's left held out binoculars to her. "Here. Looks like I won't need them."

"Thank you." Karina lowered Emily to the ground and took the binoculars. "Stay with me, baby."

The woman turned and ran, back toward the garden. A moment later the alarm sounded again, but this time in two short bursts.

People peeled off from the group and headed back, deeper into the base. Now was her chance. If she could slip away and go through the gate, she could get away. Nobody would find her in the confusion . . .

"Lady Karina," Arthur's voice rang out.

She snapped back to look at him.

The gaze of his blue eyes bore into her. "Stay close. We must hold until the evacuation is complete. Lucas may have need of your services."

His voice was soft but his eyes left her no doubt—he knew what she was thinking and escape was futile.

Arthur turned and looked out to the plain. She looked, too, raising the binoculars to her eyes. The mountains swung into view, suddenly clear. She tilted the binoculars lower . . .

People came walking over the hill. To the right a middle-aged man in filthy khakis and a ripped shirt with thin blue stripes climbed over a rock. Next to him two dark-skinned men in jeans helped a third limp forward. On the left a woman in business clothes walked on, stumbling. The binoculars captured her face. Her features, caked with grime and dust, twisted into an expression of abject terror.

Karina inhaled sharply. A red-haired teenage girl followed the woman. Her ruffled black skirt hung limply around her skinny legs in torn stockings. She shuddered as she walked and Karina realized she was sobbing.

Karina jerked the binoculars down. "There are people out there!"

"They are captives," Lucas said. "People the Ordinators snatched up here and there, the missing. The pigs are running them at the net. It's designed to stop high-impact projectiles, but if enough body mass hits it at once, it will overload and collapse."

The memory of the bird shocked by that red glow flashed before her. "They will die!"

"That's the idea," Daniel said. "They're trying to break through before we have a chance to detonate the network."

"Can't they just use a tank or a vehicle?"

"The net would fry it," Lucas said grimly. "Biomass is the best way to go."

The people on the right broke into a run. Karina raised the binoculars.

A creature bounded over the hill. Huge and brown, it looked like a seven-foot-tall boar moving too fast on surprisingly long and skinny legs. The pig paused. Its long crocodilian jaws gaped open, flashing fangs as large as her fingers, wider, wider, until the pig's entire head seemed to split in half. A hoarse roar burst forth. The daeodon.

The people in front of the creature scattered like minnows, sprinting across the rough ground toward the net in a ragged herd, a blond man in a once white tank top leading the run. The daeodon roared again and gave chase.

On the left, a second pig crested the hill, sending another group of prisoners into flight. An older man in a torn flannel shirt stumbled and fell, splaying in the dirt. The pig bore down on him. The long jaws dipped down. A shriek rang out, vibrating with the sheer terror of a man who knew his life was ending, and vanished, cut off in mid-note.

On the right, the blond man ran headfirst into the net and jerked, caught by a deep carmine glow. His body convulsed, his legs and arms flailing, as if he were being shocked by a live wire. The man directly behind him tried to slow down, but his momentum carried him right into the red glow and he shook, caught in a similar seizure.

Karina whipped to Lucas. "Can't you do something? Anything? They're dying!"

"We can give them a quick death once they break through," Lucas said.

"But . . ."

"Lucas is correct," Arthur said. "We will spare them the pain."

The air around Arthur shimmered. People backed away. He bowed his head and stood very still.

On the prairie, the prisoners tried to swerve away from the red glow, but the pigs drove them forward. One by one the bodies crashed into the net. Karina turned Emily around. "Don't look, baby."

"What are they doing?"

Lie, she told herself. *Lie*. But the words spilled out on their own. "They are dying, Emily."

"Why?"

"Because the bad guys are killing them."

"Are the bad guys going to get us?"

"No, little one," Henry said. "Arthur and Lucas will kill them."

The red glow bent forward under the weight of many bodies, and still more people were coming across the prairie, herded by the daeodons like sheep. Arthur didn't move. His eyes stared into the distance, somewhere far away.

"How long till the detonation?" Lucas asked.

Henry closed his eyes and opened them. "Three minutes."

Lucas rolled his head right, then left, cracking his neck.

With a bright flash the net collapsed under the weight of the bodies. People fell into the gap, tumbling over each other, convulsing on the ground. The four huge pigs who'd herded them to the net galloped into the gap, trampling the bodies beneath their hooves. The daeodons charged up the slope.

Lucas grunted. His skin seemed to peel off his bones in thick slabs. Bloody mist filled the air. Karina stared, unable to look away. Bones bent, ligaments twisted, and the beast burst forth. It was bigger than she remembered. In her memory, he had morphed into a dark, featureless shadow, but here, in the light of day, she saw every bulge of terrifying muscle, every fang, every sickle claw, every hair in the black crest of his mane.

Fear washed over her, setting every nerve on fire.

The beast turned his head. Lucas's green eyes looked at her from a horrid face.

Don't flinch, she told herself. He was about to fight for them. He could die in the next few moments. She didn't want him to go into it thinking she was disgusted by what he was. Whatever Lucas's faults were, he was about to put himself between the pigs and her daughter. He deserved better than the blind fear the two women in the garden showed him.

She met his gaze. They looked at each other.

"Good luck," she said.

The daeodons roared, pounding up the slope.

The beast who was Lucas nodded to her, leaped down, and smashed into the first pig. His claws sliced across the daeodon's neck and it went down. Lucas swerved away from the gaping jaws, leaped onto the second daeodon, and thrust his claws through the brown hide and wrenched a bloody shard of its spine out.

The third pig halted, unsure. The fourth veered left, around the carnage, and charged up the hill, digging into the hard dirt with its hooves.

Karina clenched Emily closer. Her instinct told her to run, but around her nobody moved.

Twenty yards. Fifteen. Ten.

Daniel stepped forward and clenched his fist. With a dry crunch, the bones of the pigs' front legs snapped. White bone sliced through the muscles and skin. The pig squealed, crashed on its side, and rolled down the hill. Lucas rose from the body of the third pig, leaped over the fallen daeodon as it tumbled down, and smashed its skull with one brutal punch.

"Are we in a story, Mommy?"

Karina looked down into Emily's big brown eyes. *I wish we were.*

I wish we were dreaming. She reached deep inside herself, through the fear and anxiety and disbelief, and when she spoke, her voice was calm and confident. "It will be okay, baby. We will be just fine."

More daeodons spilled from the prairie, dashing toward the base; so many, she couldn't even count. A huge beast led the charge. He looked just like Lucas, except for the reddish fur. The red beast sprinted, widening the distance between himself and the mass of daeodons, moving in powerful leaps that devoured the prairie.

Lucas backed two steps up the slope and planted his giant feet.

The beast thundered at them, hurtling like a cannonball. It jumped and sailed over the mass of writhing human bodies.

Lucas leaped. The two monsters collided in midair and Karina realized that Lucas was visibly smaller. They rolled down the hill, snarling and tearing at each other like two massive feral cats.

The larger beast raked Lucas's side. Blood wet the dirt in a hot spray.

Karina spun to Daniel. "Help him!"

"I can't," he growled. "I need a clear target."

The beasts brawled and snapped, biting and ripping in a tornado of claws and teeth.

The alarm blared again, this time a single long note followed by a short beep. Daniel whirled to an older woman standing next to him. She was short and plump, with an elaborate knot of tiny braids on her head. Her gray pantsuit was pristine, her makeup flawless. She looked like a secretary or a receptionist for an upscale business firm.

"Rip it," Daniel said. "Now."

The woman pulled a knife out of her pantsuit, jerked the sleeve back, and slashed a gash across her skin. Blood welled. The pain must've been excruciating, because she bent nearly double, cradling her arm.

At the bottom of the hill, the larger beast hurled Lucas aside. He flew, flipped in the air, and landed on all fours. Blood streamed from his flanks. The two creatures squared off and collided again.

The woman straightened. A pale green glow burst from her stomach, twisting into thin strands of light. The strands snapped out, flared, and split the empty air in half. A seven-foot circle appeared, filled with darkness.

So that's what the dimensional rip looks like.

Arthur raised his head.

The ground shook under his feet. Tiny rocks bounced up and down. The vibration pounded the bottoms of Karina's shoes.

"Lucas! End it!" Daniel screamed. "End it now!"

The reddish beast leaped, striking with an enormous paw, claws out like daggers. Lucas spun, rolling to the side, inhumanely fast. The large beast landed in the dirt. The moment his paws touched the ground, Lucas vaulted onto his back. Huge teeth flashed and he clamped onto the rival beast's neck. The creature screamed, kicking and trying to roll. Two beasts plunged down.

Karina held her breath.

The black beast rose, slowly.

She exhaled.

Lucas pondered the body of his fallen opponent as if he wasn't sure where he was or what he was doing there. Behind him, the captives, caught between him and the sea of pigs, scrambled to their feet.

The vibration below the surface increased, hitting Karina's feet like the blow of an underground hammer. Tiny red sparks flickered around Arthur.

"Hurry," Henry whispered next to her. His gaze was fixed on Lucas, his voice an insistent low whisper, almost a command. "Hurry."

Lucas jerked. His head snapped up. He saw them and bounded up the hill.

The sparks around Arthur danced faster. Arthur's feet left the ground. He rose three feet into the air, his body tense, looking down at the prairie stretching before him.

Oh, God.

The beast reached the apex of the hill, crashed down in a sickening revolt of flesh, and rose again, as Lucas, bloody and shaking. He shuddered on his feet, careened, and Karina caught him. For a moment his entire weight rested on her. She looked into his eyes and saw pain. And then Daniel pulled him off her and dragged him forward to the rip.

In the distance the foghorn blared frantically. The daeodons closed in. Karina swept Emily into her arms.

Henry wrapped his arm around her. "We must go. You don't want to see this."

They hurried to the rent. She looked back over her shoulder, as if pulled by some invisible force. The sparks darting around Arthur's shoulders paused. For a fraction of a breath they hung motionless, then blinked, then sparked into brilliant light. Red radiance burst from Arthur's shoulders in twin streams, boiling with flashes of white and orange, unfurling into two enormous wings knitted of lightning.

"Come on." Henry pulled her toward the rip. It loomed before them, lightless and frightening, a hole in reality itself.

The red lightning flashed. The front row of captives fell to their knees. Fire spilled from their eyes and mouths, as if they were being incinerated from the inside out. Their faces turned to ash. The second row followed and on and on and on . . . Jets of flames spurted from the ground. The whole hill quaked as if caught in the grip of a powerful earthquake.

Oh, dear God. So that's what a Wither does . . .

"Now!" Henry barked.

Karina took a deep breath, cradled Emily, and stepped into the darkness.

I t was like being underwater. As if she were walking through a flooded tunnel of crystal-clear liquid filled with sunlight. Her body was very light, almost weightless. It lasted a lifetime or a single moment—Karina couldn't tell—and then she stepped onto beige carpet.

For a second she was afraid to move, afraid to do anything, and then she remembered to breathe. The air tasted sweet.

Emily looked at her, blinking.

"Are you okay?" Karina whispered, her voice strained.

Emily stirred. "I know!"

"Know what, Emily?"

"Mom, I know, I know! I am the Courageous Princess. Like in the comic book."

Karina exhaled and hugged her. For some reason, she wanted to cry.

They stood in a foyer. There were people around her, both men and women. In front of her a glass wall guarded a conference room, a long black table with matching chairs; and beyond that a floor-to-ceiling window offered a view of an evening city from above, lit up with electric lights. They had to be on the twentieth floor.

They had gotten away.

In her mind the bodies still burned, vomiting fire and ashes. What the hell was Arthur? What were all of them?

"We shouldn't be here," Henry said next to her, his voice vibrating with alarm. "This is wrong."

A woman behind her snarled. "The fucking Ripper dropped us into the wrong base."

A soft thud made her turn. Lucas crashed onto the carpet and Daniel tried to pick him up. Lucas's eyes were closed. He looked so pale, his skin had gained an almost greenish tint.

She set Emily down and knelt by him, sliding her hand on his forehead. His skin was cold, almost clammy. Blood clung to his rib cage and a big purple bruise stained the right side of his stomach. He looked like he was dying. The heavy metallic scent rolled off him, so thick she almost choked. He wasn't just hungry for her blood. He was starving for it and he hurt.

"What's wrong?"

"Too much venom," Daniel spat out. "He shouldn't have phased into the attack variant so soon after the last fight."

Arthur stepped onto the carpet out of thin air. "He will be fine."

A grimace skewed Daniel's face, stretching his scar. He looked like a rabid dog. "We should've evacuated yesterday. You overwork him. You know he needs at least two weeks between phasings, but you counted on him to save your ass anyway, because you knew he would do it. Look at him. Look at him, Arthur. He's dying from the venom."

Arthur glanced at the skyline. "Not now, Daniel. Where is the Ripper?"

"You are a fucking asshole!"

Henry closed his eyes and opened them. "She isn't in the building."

"Daniel, stop your hysterics and search the building . . ."

"Fuck you!"

"Will the two of you shut up?" Lucas said. His eyes were still closed. A shudder gripped him. He arched his back, his heels digging into the carpet, his arms rigid, his massive body straining against the pain.

Idiots. Karina wrapped her arms around Lucas, trying to hold him down, but it was like trying to hold down a bull. "We need something for his mouth. He's grinding his teeth."

"Vault, now," Arthur snapped. "Pick him up."

People swarmed Lucas, brushing her away. He lashed out, convulsing, throwing a man aside like a rag doll. They pulled Lucas up and dragged him down the hall.

Arthur bent down, grasped her by the elbow, and pulled her to her feet. "Come with us."

"My daughter . . ."

Arthur's fingers clenched her arm like a vise. He pulled her down the hallway, after the clump of people trying to move the convulsing Lucas forward.

Emily ran after her. "Mommy!"

Karina jerked. "Let go of me! You're scaring her!"

"Do you want your daughter to live?" Arthur asked.

"Yes!" Bastard.

"Then do as you're told."

They were almost to the end of the tunnel. Something swung open with a heavy metallic sound. Karina caught a glimpse of a huge vault door standing ajar. The people carrying Lucas ducked into the round opening and parted, and Karina saw a room beyond the door. It lay empty and the light of the white fluorescent lamps reflected off the metal floor and walls.

They would put her into the vault with him. Lucas hurt so badly, he was convulsing. He required her blood and he'd rip her to pieces to get it. If she crossed that threshold, she would die.

"Mommy!"

She dug her heels in. "Emily!"

Henry picked Emily up. "It's okay, little one."

"You agreed to the contract," Arthur said. "Time to honor it. Get in there and do whatever you have to do to keep him alive."

If she didn't go in, they would throw her in. She heard it in Arthur's voice.

Karina jerked her arm out of his hand. "Take care of my baby, Henry."

"I will," he promised.

Karina took a deep breath and walked inside.

"No sudden movements," Henry called out.

The door behind her clanged shut.

CHAPTER 8

Lucas curled into a ball on the floor. The pain scoured the inside of his spine as if someone were scraping his vertebrae with steel wool. It stretched in tight strings through his ligaments; it pooled in his joints, in his fingertips, under his tongue. He felt it in his teeth. It ground him like a grain of wheat between two millstones.

His ears caught the sound of approaching steps.

He forced his eyes open.

Karina knelt by him. He inhaled her scent and felt it spark a deep, angry hunger inside him. She pulled him like a magnet. His body screamed for her blood and the end of the pain. Tearing into her would be bliss.

She was rolling up her sleeve. Her lips were pinched together.

He had to speak now. It hurt and he was tired, but he managed. "Don't."

"Arthur said you had to feed."

"Arthur is a sick fuck. I told you that."

"I can smell you," she said. "You need to feed."

"If I feed now, you'll die."

"If you don't, you will, and then they'll kill Emily."

Ah. For a second he thought she had felt sorry for him, but no. "Nobody will touch Emily. And I'm not dying. Just hurting."

"You look awful." He heard a soft note in her voice. In spite of everything, she cared a little bit. He would take that. That was more than he usually got from anyone.

She hadn't shied back when he phased. Her knees had trembled but she didn't flinch. For that he was grateful.

Karina brushed the grime off his face, her eyes kind, her voice gentle. "Lucas, don't be an idiot. Feed. It will make you feel better."

"The pain isn't fatal. It will pass. You'll need all of your blood before long."

She pulled back. "What does that mean?"

"Do you have a fever?"

"Yes."

"Tired?"

"Yes. Lucas, what is happening to me?"

He almost told her the truth. "I told you before, you're reacting to the venom."

The ache had burrowed deep into the base of his spine. Lucas forced himself to turn, trying to shift his weight, and it exploded into a blinding white, mind-numbing haze, twisting his limbs. Like being punched in the mouth by a star. He passed out.

When he awoke, her scent was everywhere. The hunger stirred inside him, demanding. Lucas clenched his teeth and felt a light touch on his cheek. His eyes snapped open. She was sitting next to him, her back resting against the wall.

"How long was I out?"

"Maybe a minute or two."

"Try to time the next one. I need to know if they're getting shorter."

"Is there anything else I can do?"

The ache rolled back at him. "Talk to me."

"About what?"

"You never did tell me exactly why Emily hoards food."

She sighed and brushed the brown lock of hair from her face. "It happened after Jonathan died."

"Your husband?"

"Yes. I don't want to talk about it."

"Why?"

She met his gaze. "Because then you will know things about me."

"And that would be bad?" Lucas asked.

"Yes."

Now he wanted to know more.

"Does it hurt to be the beast?" she asked.

"No. Phasing is like being a superhero. I'm faster, stronger. Everything is sharper. There are no consequences. I can let myself off the leash. But my attack variant's venom is toxic to my human phase variant. Turning back into a man is a bitch."

A small tremor shook his legs. Lucas grunted and closed his eyes, trying to will the pain away.

"How long will we be locked in here?"

"Until I pull through. Hours. Arthur is trying to keep me safe. I'm an asset and I'm rare and difficult to replace. We shouldn't have come here, to this building." The words came slowly. "This base is not secure. We rent five floors here. We don't own the buildings and don't control access to it."

Karina bent down, looking closer into his eyes. Tiny red rosettes marked the skin on her cheeks and forehead. Her own transformation was closing in. Shit. He hoped she would have another day. He didn't want her to phase here, in the vault, without medical help, without Henry to keep her calm. She could die and he wanted her to live. He had to heal fast.

Heal, Lucas willed in his mind. *Heal.*

The pain exploded in a white burst and dragged him under.

When the light faded he heard her voice, soothing, calm, warm. Like sitting back in the hot tub, soaking his exhausted body while she floated nearby. ". . . met in college. Jonathan was handsome. Funny. His father was the CFO for Drivers Company. It's a big insurance company in the Southwest. Brian's very driven, very conscious about his appearance. Brooks Brothers suits, expensive watch, a new BMW every couple of years. He and Lynda had Jonathan when they were much older, in their forties. Jonathan could do no wrong. He was their golden child. Good at sports, good at academics. He was easygoing and charming. The perfect son."

She leaned her head against the wall. He moved closer to her and rested the back of his head on her ankle. She let him do it. From here he could see her face. He could touch her hand. Lucas closed his eyes and let himself sink into her voice.

"Things always went Jonathan's way. I used to watch a cartoon when I was younger. Two mice were living in a lab, and one was very smart and the other one was a knucklehead. So every night the knucklehead mouse, Pinky, would ask the smart mouse, 'And what are we going to do today, Brain?' And Brain would say, 'Try to take over the world!' And Pinky would get all excited. See, Brain was serious. He was trying to take over the world. But to Pinky it was all a big game. That's kind of how Jonathan was. The world was his huge playground and every day he'd play at taking it over. Some days he was an athlete; other days he was a student. When we met, he was finishing his MBA and I was getting my bachelor's in accounting. My parents had died in a car accident when I was a senior in high school. I had just turned eighteen when they passed."

"I'm sorry," Lucas said and meant it.

"Thank you. They left me just enough money to get me through college and I had to work to feed myself. Before they died, I wanted to go into art history." She laughed a little, a bitter, quiet sound. "I wanted to be an art appraiser. You know, the person who examines art for auctions and museums to determine if it's authentic. I always thought it would be so neat. But I was on my own then, so I went into accounting instead. It seemed . . . sensible. I was trying to be sensible. To have some structure. And then Jonathan shot into my world like a comet. He could make anything seem exciting. He made things fun. His parents were always very formal with me. I don't think they ever understood why he liked me, but Jonathan picked me and he could do no wrong."

He very badly wanted to murder Jonathan.

"It was great at first. Jonathan's father's connections got him a position in a private equity firm. During the day he got to play a businessman and during the night he got to play a husband. And then Emily was born. Well, you've seen her."

"She is pretty," Lucas said.

"She is. Jonathan loved her. It was yet another new game: being a dad. He used to show her off like a cute purebred puppy." She sighed again. "I should've seen it then. Anyway, everything was great for a few years and then the bottom fell out of the economy. Suddenly it wasn't fun anymore."

"The party was over," Lucas guessed.

"Yes. Jonathan had to start working for his living and buckle down, or the firm would cut him loose. I worked, too, and we were doing okay, but we had to mind our p's and q's and Jonathan didn't want to be bogged down with details. We used to have the stupidest conversations. He couldn't understand why he couldn't drop thirty grand on a membership at a country club. It's like his brain couldn't digest the concept of a budget. I mean, the man had a master's degree in business management, for crying out loud." Her voice rose too high and Karina fell silent.

"What happened?" he prompted.

"Finally he decided he was tired of playing with us. He started sending me these long rambling e-mails about how he felt constrained and unhappy and about the need to find himself. He wanted to live fully, he said. To find the zest in life. At first I was concerned, then I thought he was cheating, but he wasn't. It's not like we were ever on the verge of bankruptcy. We just couldn't do exciting things anymore, like ordering champagne for the entire bar. I offered to move; he didn't want to do it. No solution I suggested was good enough. He tortured me like that for about four months. In the end I didn't even care anymore. I should've fought harder maybe, but I remember one of my friends calling and telling me she saw Jonathan at her office party without me, and you know what I thought?"

She paused. Her dark eyes were huge on her pretty face. "I thought, 'Good. Maybe he'll meet someone and I can divorce him.' That's an awful thing to think about your husband. That's when I knew the marriage was over. We were heading downhill, except there was Emily. How do you explain to a four-year-old that Daddy decided he doesn't want her anymore because he needs to go find himself? So I spoke to his parents. I thought maybe they would talk some sense into him."

Lucas grimaced. "You said he could do no wrong."

"Yes, it was stupid, but I was desperate. They called him over to have a heart-to-heart. Jonathan took me out to dinner at the end of the week. I knew something was up; I could just tell. It wasn't a date. He told me he had filed for divorce. He had no problem paying me alimony, and I could retain all my parental rights."

A shadow passed over her face. She seemed small all of a sudden.

"We were in the car, going to pick up Emily from the sitter's. We were fighting about his generosity in regard to my 'parental rights.'" Her voice dripped with bitterness. "He wanted to leave and stay gone. I insisted that Emily needed a father and he couldn't just take off. He was mad. He told me that everyone had a right to be happy. He wanted to be free of me and Emily but he didn't want to be judged for it. And then, all of a sudden, he lost consciousness. It was like someone had flipped a switch. We shot into the opposing lane. I remember headlights. I woke up in the hospital."

She fell silent. "He had a stroke," Karina said finally in a flat voice. "He had fibromuscular dysplasia. Nobody knew. He was healthy as a horse, played racquetball, and then he just died. It was touch and go for me for a little while but I bounced back. I was in the hospital for two weeks. Emily had to stay with his parents. They didn't feed her."

"What?"

"Brian, Jonathan's father, always eats out. When Jonathan died, he spent all his time at a country club. He said it was his way to cope. Lynda is in her seventies. She has a touch of dementia. All she did was eat candy all day, but she wouldn't give Emily any—it would ruin her teeth. She would forget to give Emily lunch, and when she did remember to feed her, she would either try to cook and burn it or she'd give Emily food that had been in the fridge for so long, it wasn't just moldy, it was blooming."

She was crying, not from pity but from anger. There were no tears, but he heard it in Karina's voice, hidden behind the flat tone.

"They had a bowl of nuts set out and Emily told me she would pretend to fall asleep and then sneak out and steal them. When I got out of the hospital, she was six pounds lighter. She barely weighs anything as it is. So now you know why she hoards food. She was terrified, her father had just died, her mother was in the hospital, and her own grandparents wouldn't feed her. I told Arthur she doesn't have anyone except me. I meant it. We are not welcome at that house. They blame me and Emily for Jonathan's stroke. We made his life so difficult, he died to escape."

The red rosettes on her face were turning darker. Karina touched her hand to her forehead and looked at it. Her eyes widened. She rubbed his forearm.

"This is another reaction to the venom?"

"Mmhh-hhm," Lucas said.

"I told you my story. Tell me yours now. It's fair."

"What do you want to know?" he asked, wondering what she would think if she looked inside his mind and saw him strangling her husband.

"Who are you? All of you. Who are you really? I need to know what's happening to me."

Lucas sighed.

She had told him too much, Karina decided. As much as she wanted for it to be a bribe, a down payment for the information he held, at least in part she told him what she did because he was lying beside her, bruised, beat up, bloody, and hurting. He needed a distraction and she had enough compassion to give him one. But she hadn't meant to pour her heart out. It just happened. He was in pain, and although she had the means to ease his suffering, he refused to feed, because he didn't want to hurt her. He wasn't willing to trade his pain for hers. The least she could do was talk and try to distract him.

Karina reached over and touched his hand. His fingers closed on hers. Lucas glanced at her, surprised. They had that in common now—both of them treated any act of kindness with suspicion. She didn't expect kindness anymore, except from him. But she was an outsider. He wasn't.

"There are no scared women here to watch us," he told her.

"It was never for them. It was for you."

She almost cried and couldn't even understand why. It was the stress, Karina told herself. The trauma of watching hundreds of people die at once. And the fever, which kept rising and rising. Her breath felt hot when she exhaled. Her skin was dry and too tight. And now there were rings of red dots all over her arms.

She had never told the entire story of her marriage to anyone. *It's the fever. Of course it is.*

Lucas was looking at her. Sprawled like that, even battered, he looked enormous. If a week ago someone had told her she would be locked in a vault with a nude, bloody man who was trying his best not to devour her to stop his pain, she would've dialed 911 to report a lunatic running amok.

"I'm going to tell you a story," Lucas said. His voice was laced with fatigue. "You can choose to believe it or not. It can be the truth or just a story. It's your choice."

"Okay."

Lucas closed his eyes. "Suppose there is a civilization. A powerful country. It has taken over all of its available territory, but it knows that it must expand. It must continue to grow outward, or it will rot and collapse. This civilization sends colonists out to explore new territories. They find fertile lands and colonize them. When they succeed, they let the knowledge of the large civilization fade. The small colonies grow and prosper on their own, and when they develop enough, they rediscover their mother civilization and rejuvenate it with their unique achievements."

He glanced at her.

"Okay," Karina said. "I can see how that would happen."

"Suppose a new island was found for colonization. An island with an abundant ecosphere and great resources. The civilization had done this many times before and they had developed a protocol. The colony ships arrived and the colonists created thirteen small settlements, Houses, one for each colony ship.

"Genetically, all the colonists belonged to the Base Strain. It's a very stable breed of human, long-lived, resistant to diseases, armed with superior DNA repair mechanisms to counteract mutation. To successfully colonize a new environment, a species must adapt to it. To facilitate this adaptation, most of the colonists were exposed to an agent inhibiting their cellular and DNA repair and vulnerability to native viruses."

"They deliberately made their people weaker? How does that make sense?"

"They didn't just want a colony," Lucas said. "They wanted a unique colony, perfectly in tune with this new island. That's how the civilization kept itself from stagnation. The colonists wanted an explosion of mutations in the future generations, and they needed a shorter life span and faster sexual maturity to pass the new changes on to their offspring. That's why scientists experiment on mice: they breed quickly and don't live very long. The shorter life span goes hand in hand with faster sexual maturity. But it also brings negative anthropological consequences: immaturity, inability to pass on knowledge, loss of ethics and culture, and so on. These consequences were considered acceptable. The colony had to develop on its own without the knowledge of its origin anyway. The sooner people forgot where they came from, the better. A small group of the colonists remained as Base Strain for control purposes. They lived in the settlements, the Houses, and monitored the whole thing. With me?"

Sort of. "Go on."

"Mutations bloomed. A succession of several dozen subspecies of human followed. Some subspecies developed variations, people with similar powers or physiology. Subspecies 29 showed all of the adaptations necessary for survival, but all eight of its types were plagued by sensitivity to heat and alarmingly low fertility. Subspecies 44, type 3, produced exceptional Mind Benders, who were prone to insanity."

"Is that what Henry is?"

Lucas nodded.

"We're not talking about islands, are we?"

"Some say islands," Lucas said. "Some say planets. It's just a story."

A story, right. "Aliens." She stared at him. "Are you trying to tell me that all of us are aliens?"

Lucas sighed. "You could say that. You could also say that once the planet shaped us and twisted our DNA, we are now just as native as anybody else."

"What about Subspecies 30?" *What about you?*

Lucas's eyes fixed on her. "Subspecies 30, types 1 through 5, otherwise known as Demons. A venomous, carnivorous, predatory variant of human with the ability to drastically alter its morphology. They were powerful, aggressive, territorial, and they dominated their point of origin for a few hundred years, hunting in small packs, but this subspecies was not viable long term. They were crippled because their bodies couldn't produce a set of small molecules necessary for their survival, so they had to cannibalize other humans to get it."

"Cannibalize?"

"At that point the various subspecies of human had only a rudimentary language and no memory of where they came from," Lucas said. "No ethics, no morals, nothing. They were forming fledgling societies and 'might is right' was the law. If I need your blood, and there is nothing in my upbringing or experience that tells me I shouldn't, why wouldn't I kill you and eat your flesh? Being a nice guy is a modern concept."

He was serious. He was actually serious.

"Should I keep going?" he asked.

"Yes."

"This went on for hundreds of years. The small remaining pockets of Base Strain, the original colonists, kept as a control group, meticulously documented all of it from their Houses. They didn't interfere. They just cataloged what occurred.

"Then suddenly Subspecies 48 popped on the scene. The Rippers had a fatal vulnerability to cancers but also the ability to rupture holes in reality, accessing dimensional fragments. This was a new development, unknown to the colonists, and nobody knew what to do about it. Some Houses took Ripper children and raised them within the settlements to study them.

"The mutations bloomed and bloomed, until one subspecies emerged as best adapted. It did well in almost every climate. It reproduced quickly, showed mental agility, and demonstrated decent DNA repair. At approximately six thousand planetary cycles, Subspecies 61 was declared viable. The colonists had done their job: they had created the type of human with the best ability to survive and prosper. Now nature needed to take over. All support for other strains ceased, as dictated by the Original Mandate. *Ile* must survive. Subspecies 61 became *ile*. Everyone else needed to die to make room."

"Subspecies 61. Humans," Karina guessed. "Us."

"No," Lucas said. "Them. Your neighbors, your friends. But not you."

Her fever was now so high, she was freezing and melting at the same time. "You said them, not me. What do you mean, not me?"

"I'm getting to that. Other subspecies were dying out, while Subspecies 61 went on to multiply and claim the island."

"The planet." Karina didn't need him to keep babying her.

"The planet," he agreed. "The colony cities began to gradually phase out their technology. They were letting themselves disappear. But there was a protocol breach at one of the cities, as a result of which Subspecies 29, the one that had trouble with heat, discovered where they came from."

"What do you mean?"

Lucas sighed. "I mean that the scientists at the Mare House fucked up. Subspecies 29 produced several unusually smart children. A sudden explosion of kids with genius-level intelligence was rare and odd, so the idiots thought it would be a good idea to study them further. They extracted these children and raised them within Mare with the full knowledge of their history. Well, the kids grew up and decided they didn't want to go gently into that good night while some other breed of human took over.

"There was a quiet coup. By the time it was discovered, Strain 29 and their captive personnel had genetically corrected their short-comings. Now they had no trouble with heat and they bred like rabbits. They decided that they were more viable than Strain 61. They, not humans, were *ile*. A mistake was made and they decided it had to be corrected. They were ordained to take over the Earth."

Now it made sense. "They became the Ordinators?"

"Yes."

"So this is it? They've been trying to kill us off for thousands of years?"

"More or less. They went to war, using the colonists' original technology. The other cities opposed them, but they were weak by that point and in the process of dissolving themselves, so they plucked people from different strains with combat potential. The Ordinators were broken and would've been wiped out, except they acquired Rippers and began hopping through dimensional fragments. Eventually, so did we.

"Strain 61, the *ile* humans, was reproducing too quickly, and their numbers grew too numerous. They saw us and started forming religions and folklore. We had to disappear."

"So this is how it is," Karina said.

He nodded. "People like me have been keeping the Ordinators at bay for over thirty thousand years. Occasionally they break through with a new weapon. Sometimes it's a virus that kills the food supply. Sometimes it's bubonic plague. Sometimes they find a way to fiddle with the climate. The problem is that the Ordinators breed faster than us, they're better organized, and their job is easier: it's much simpler to destroy something than to protect it.

"There were thirteen Houses, one for each landing site. They have one House, the House of Mare. There are probably between one and two hundred thousand of them. We are the soldiers of the remaining twelve Houses. There are maybe fifty thousand of us. We crossbreed and have children with weird powers instead of dying out the way we should. This is the planet where everything went wrong. As humanity moves closer and closer to interstellar space flight, the Ordinators are getting desperate, because once we reconnect with the root civilization, it's all over for them. They abandoned the original mandate and they will be exterminated. They're attacking with everything they've got and we're losing the fight."

She stared at him. "And where do I fit in?"

He took her hand and squeezed it gently. "You know why my people died out?"

"Because their own venom poisoned them?" Karina said.

"That. But also because the colonists had done some projections. It was decided that if we were allowed to exist, we would destroy the other subspecies and then die out before reaching the level of medical sophistication necessary to fix our defect. They poisoned us, wiped out the entire species almost completely. They were right—even now the synthetic substitutes are just a Band-Aid. See, if we could've overcome this handicap, they would've let us murder everyone else, but the problem is that only one very specific subspecies produces the hormones we need. The Base Strain. The donors. The ones who gave rise to all of us."

She jerked her hand back. "You mean I am a descendant of the original colonists?"

"Yes."

"That's not possible."

"It is. Your type has a remarkably stable genome."

"But my parents were normal people!"

"They may not have known who they were. Maybe only one of them was a donor. A donor and Subspecies 61 will produce donor offspring."

"But what about this?" She held out her arms, speckled with brilliant red. "Explain this!"

Lucas sat up. "When I fed on you, the mutation agent entered your bloodstream. In normal humans the mutation agent has grown weak over the generations. But I am carrying a near-full dose and I gave it to you during the feeding. You are changing."

"Into what?!"

"I don't know. I don't know what's in your DNA besides the donor genes. The mutation agent is an inhibitor. It will release the brakes within your body, short-circuiting your DNA repair, and let you develop into something that's already there in your genotype, acquired over the centuries of crossbreeding with different human subspecies but suppressed. You could become Subspecies 61, but I doubt it. Chances are, it will be one of our subspecies instead."

They had taken her freedom, her home, and her dignity, and now they were taking away her body. "No! No, I am not doing it! I won't! You hear me?" Karina surged to her feet. She managed two steps. Pain shot up through her bones. She cried out. The world went red and she crashed onto the floor.

I t hurt. It hurt more than any pain she could remember. At first she begged, then she prayed, then she screamed and whimpered, squeezing her eyes shut, opening them again, glimpsing Lucas's face against the harsh light of the vault, and then sinking into more pain. If only she could pass out completely and be done with it, but no, every time she tried, he shook her back, into the place of hurt.

"Come on, stay with me. Stay awake. Snap out of it."

"Let me be," she snarled.

"You pass out, you die. Come on. Stay with me."

"I hate you! You did this to me!"

"That's right," Lucas snarled right back. "Hate me. Fight with me. Stay awake. You die, Emily will be alone. You don't want to leave your daughter with an asshole like me."

She just wanted the torture to stop.

Another bout of agony rocked her. When it was over, she was so tired, she could barely breathe.

"The other woman . . ." Karina whispered. Forcing the words out felt like trying to swallow glass. "Did she have to do this?"

"Yes."

"Did you kidnap her, too?"

"No." Lucas gathered her closer, holding her against him. "She was one of us. Her family were donors of Daryon."

"Did she hurt, too?"

"Yes."

Lucas's eyes were so dark, they seemed almost brown.

"Tell me about her." She wasn't sure why she wanted to know, but she did.

"She was very smart. And she looked beautiful. Very graceful, fragile, elegant."

"Not like me, then?" Nobody would call her fragile. Or elegant, for that matter.

"Nothing like you," he told her quietly.

The agony burned through her in a crippling spasm. "Why does it sound like a compliment?"

"Because she only looked beautiful. In our world nobody has the luxury of doing nothing," he said. "Everyone has a function. I protect. Someone else oversees mining. Someone else oversees stocks and finances. Galatea's family had only one function: to provide Base Strain to the House. For that they were sheltered, fed, and protected. Galatea never worked a day in her life."

"Must be nice," Karina whispered.

"She didn't think so. She wanted the mutating agent."

"She wanted this? Why?"

"Power," Lucas said. "She thought she would become something much more prized than a donor and she would be free of me. Her father was my first donor. She wasn't supposed to become one, but he died, and she had to take his place. She thought I was an animal. She was convinced that once I fed, she would become a Ripper and could use it as leverage to be free of me."

"What did she become?"

"An Electric. She senses electric currents. It's not an uncommon subspecies. A lot of technicians come from it."

"Uh-oh," Karina managed. Her lips were so dry, but there was no water. "Let me guess: it was your fault, right?"

He nodded. "It was everyone's fault. She used to scream and throw fits, and then she wanted to fuck and she wanted me to beg for it. I was young and stupid. She was older, smarter, and beautiful."

Karina raised her hand and touched his haggard face. "You loved her."

"Yes. And I was so dumb, I thought it was enough. That's why I let it go that far. She once told me that we, the House, had stolen her life. She wanted to stroll the streets of London, visit the Tate Modern, go to concerts in Royal Albert Hall. I offered to take her. She told me that it wouldn't be the same. My presence would poison London for her."

"She sounds charming," Karina managed.

"I am what I am," Lucas said. "No illusions. Life with me is hard, but she made a personal hell for me and her. I wasn't the one who started sex, but I finished it. I dealt with it for four years and when I turned twenty-two, I decided I was done. I went on synthetics and told Arthur to find her a different place. He transferred her to a technical work crew. She tried to stab me with a knife when she found out. Galatea was never fond of getting her hands dirty. Three months later, during an attack, she disappeared. The next time Henry sensed her presence, we ran into the Ordinators."

"She betrayed you."

"Yes, she did." Lucas shifted her carefully. "And now you know the whole story."

"Do you miss her?" she asked.

He peered at her face. "How did you know?"

"I miss my husband," she whispered. "I don't blame you, you know."

"For what?"

"For any of it. For the motel, for the feeding, for this." Karina tried to swallow the pain away, but it remained. She wouldn't make it. She could feel death crouching just a few feet away. "Lucas, you're not a bad person. You have no idea how scary you are, but you're kind and patient. If things were different . . . It has to start right . . . And we just can't, because I would never be more than a slave and you would always own me. Please take care of Emily for me. Don't let anyone hurt her. She's a great kid."

He didn't answer. He just held her.

Karina awoke slowly. Within her body, the pain subsided, gradually, like a receding tide, fighting for every step of its retreat.

She opened her eyes and saw Lucas's neck. Her face was buried in it.

He was kneeling on the floor, looking up. She was wrapped in his arms.

Her voice shook. "Why are you holding me?"

Lucas turned to look at her. His face was too close to hers. "I didn't want you to die alone on the floor."

She said things. Stupid, stupid things. Maybe it was a dream. His eyes assured her that it wasn't.

"Please put me down."

He let her go slowly. Karina slid down onto her knees and sat clumsily on the floor. Her legs shook a little. She felt light, so light and cold. "Is my change over?"

"Yes," he said.

She had survived. "I don't feel any different."

"The change isn't always obvious. Something will trigger it sooner or later." He was looking up again. She glanced up, too, and saw a monitor in the ceiling. It showed an empty hallway.

A man in dark clothes darted across the hallway, brandishing a machine gun, and hid behind the wall.

"We're being attacked," Lucas said. His voice was calm, almost casual.

"How is that possible?" Emily. Henry had her. If they were being attacked, her daughter would be in danger.

More people flickered past on the screen.

"The Ripper must have been an Ordinator mole," Lucas said. "We should've gone to a ranch in Montana—that's our evacuation route from that base. Instead we're in Detroit. This building is nearly abandoned; only the bottom three floors and the top five—those are ours—are operational. The blocks in a one-mile radius around it are basically deserted. We're sitting ducks here."

"Why didn't Arthur evacuate us?"

"I don't know," Lucas said. "The Ordinators likely blocked the exits. We landed into a trap." His face was dark. "Our best chance is to stay here."

No. No, she had to go and find Emily. "Why?"

"I'm at my limit. Normally I would be drugged and sleeping this off for the next two or three days until my body came to terms with my venom. I could barely hold you. Most likely Arthur has sent for reinforcements. The vault is solid and must be opened from the inside. It will take them several hours to get through the door, so it's likely they won't bother with us right away. By the time they get around to it, we might be reinforced. Our best bet is to stay here and wait it out. We probably die either way, but here we have more of a chance. Especially if we're quiet."

"You have to let me out."

He looked at her, obviously trying to decide if she was crazy. She had to convince him she wasn't.

"Henry has Emily," she said. "She's out there somewhere." Out in an abandoned building full of people with guns and God knows what sort of weird powers.

Lucas looked at her for a long moment.

"I have to find her, Lucas. You don't have to come with me. All I ask is that you help me open the door, because I don't know how. I'll find her myself."

L ucas looked at the door. If they opened the vault, he would walk out of it a dead man. She stood before him, her eyes huge and brimming with worry. She just wanted her little girl back and she didn't understand how far gone he was or how many enemies they would face.

Everyone dies, Lucas reflected. He'd been a selfish bastard all of his life. If he walked out of that door and died helping her find her child, at least he'd die doing something worthwhile, not cowering like a dog in the vault, waiting to be gunned down.

And she couldn't go out there alone. She would be dead in minutes.

He sighed, rose, and stepped to the wall. Karina clenched her hands. She couldn't read his face. He touched it and a section of it slid open, revealing a number keypad and a small speaker. His fingers played with the keys. "Cousin?" Lucas said softly.

A faint hiss of static issued from the wall, then Henry's faint voice came through. "Lucas. Red, gray, seven, pinned."

Lucas grimaced. "Is the little girl with you?"

"Yes. Black."

"How bad?"

"I'll live."

"Don't move. I'm coming to get you."

"That's unwise," Henry said.

Lucas slid the panel back in place. "He is two floors below us. He's been shot. Emily is okay; he is keeping her under. He can't move because it's too dangerous and he is cloaking, which makes him harder to find, but they will locate him eventually. The moment we leave this vault, you and I must fight to survive. Remember how you tried to cut me with your knife?"

"Yes."

"Find that woman and be her."

He had no idea how hard she had worked on hiding that woman and how ready she was to let her out.

"Don't move." Lucas walked over to the vault door, punched in a combination in the small number pad, and turned the wheel in the door's center. Something clanged inside the door. Lucas moved to stand on the side. With a soft hiss, the door swung open and Karina stared straight at a man with a gun.

"Hands up!"

She didn't move.

The barrel of the machine gun glared at her, black and huge, like the mouth of a cannon.

"I said hands up!"

Lucas nodded at her. She raised her hands.

"Subspecies?" the man demanded.

"I'm a donor," she said.

The man's eyes widened. "Get up and walk to me."

Lucas shook his head.

"I can't," Karina said, keeping her voice monotone. "I'm sick. I can't walk."

The man moved into the vault, one step at a time, careful, the gun pointing at her. He took three steps in. Lucas lunged, so quick she barely saw it. His hands closed about the man's neck. Bones crunched, and the man sagged down on the floor, limp.

A week earlier, she would've screamed. Now she just got up and ran over to the body.

Lucas staggered, leaned against the wall, and pushed himself upright. He wasn't joking. He really was at his limit.

She crouched by the body and began going through the man's pockets. "I can do this alone."

"Yeah, yeah." He picked up the man's machine gun and handed it to her. "Safety here." He flipped a small switch. "Point and pull the trigger. Your instinct will tell you to keep clenching it. Don't. Count to three in your head and let go of the trigger. Short bursts."

Karina took the gun and raised it. It was heavy like a cement block. "You do realize that I can kill you with this." She didn't mean to say it. It just came out.

"Yes." He turned his back to her and went out of the vault. A pair of jeans and a sweatshirt lay by the door. Lucas pulled on the clothes and started down the hallway. She followed him. He moved like a cat, soundless on bare feet.

They came to the end of the hallway. Lucas leaned against the wall, glanced around the corner, and looked at her. "Point and pull the trigger," he whispered.

"Count to three," she whispered back.

He nodded.

There were people at the end of that hallway. People she would have to kill. *It's them or us.* Kill or be killed.

She took a deep breath, stepped into the hallway, and pulled the trigger. The gun spat thunder. Bullets ripped into four distant shadows. She thought there would be blood, but no. They just jerked and went down, screaming. She pounded the bullets into the bodies for another long breath and let go. Lucas moved next to her.

It was a test, she realized. He had to know if he could rely on her. Well, he could. She'd kill every one of them to get to Emily.

"What happened to letting go on three?"

"There were four of them," she said. Movies and books told her she should be throwing up now, but she didn't feel queasy. Her mouth was dry. It would probably hit her later, but now only Emily mattered. "I decided to take two extra seconds."

* * *

Karina followed Lucas through the dark passageways as fast as she could. She was squeezing everything she had out of her exhausted body. Now that the first flush of adrenaline had worn off, fatigue set in. She didn't walk, she dragged herself forward, shot when Lucas shot, stopped when he stopped. Only the next step mattered and she gritted her teeth and managed it again and again.

They made it to a small door. Lucas punched a code into the lock, the door snapped open, and they went through onto a concrete landing. Lucas punched the lock and the small square light in its corner turned red.

"We rest," he said. "Two minutes."

Karina sank down to the concrete and he sprawled next to her. The grimy floor was like heaven.

"Why are you helping me?"

His voice was a quiet growl. "Because I like you. And your little girl."

She closed her eyes, feeling the cold concrete under her cheek. That wasn't it. Lucas was making up for his past sins, but that wasn't all of it, either. She knew the true answer. She could read it in his worn-out face. He wanted to save her, because he wanted her to stop flinching when she looked at him.

"Thank you," she told him. "Thank you for helping me."

"Time to get up." He rose.

She cried out as he pulled her off the floor and followed him down the stairs. An odd sensation clenched her, almost like some internal spring had compressed inside her and now begged to be released. She stumbled, and it vanished.

One floor. The landing. They were midway down the next flight of stairs when the door below swung open.

An icy presence clenched her mind in a hard grip. It shut her off, trapping her. She couldn't move; she couldn't speak. Time slowed to a crawl.

The door kept opening, wider and wider. She saw inside it; she saw armed people pour out onto the landing. She knew she had to fire. Instead she just stood there, disconnected from her body.

And then Lucas shoved her down and sprayed the landing with bullets.

The presence gripped her mind and squeezed. She couldn't even scream.

Orange sparks flared on Lucas's gun. It died.

More people spilled into the landing over the bodies. Lucas leaped into the attackers. He smashed one out of the way, cracking the man's skull against concrete like a walnut. The man slid down, leaving a bright red stain on the wall. Lucas ripped a woman's throat out with his hand, backhanded another man down the stairs, and shuddered as a handgun barked. Red spray shot out of Lucas's side. He lunged forward and broke the gunman like a twig and dived into the doorway.

The sound faded. She was completely disconnected from her body now. Only her vision worked.

Lucas emerged from the door, bloody, his eyes furious. He must've jerked her up, because her view changed and suddenly he was directly above her. He barked something, angry. The world shook. He dived down. His lips closed on hers. She felt nothing. He jerked back up and rocked back and forth, screaming again.

Henry, she read his lips calling. *Henry.*

He kissed her again and rocked, his face jerking up and down. His hands pushed on her chest. She saw the muscles on his arms flex, but felt nothing. The red stain on his sweatshirt spread wider. Was he doing CPR? Was she dying?

Henry.

The ice cracked. She heard a distant female scream somewhere impossibly far. Warmth flooded into her. Something popped inside her mind and she saw a radiant light, bright and glorious.

She's gone now, Henry's voice said in her mind. *She won't bother you again. You're free. Breathe, Karina. Breathe.*

The world snapped back to its normal speed, jerking her back into her body. She felt everything at once: pain, the hardness of the stair under her back, and the rhythmic push of Lucas's hands on her chest. She gasped. He pulled her up, into his arms.

"Mind Bender attack," he told her. "Up. Keep moving."

The scent of heated metal rising from Lucas was so thick, she almost choked. He wasn't just hurt. He had to be close to dying. If he died, she would be free, but in this moment she didn't care. She just wanted him to survive. "You've been shot."

"We must move," he told her and pulled her up to her feet. "Faster!"

He drove her down the stairs, through the door, and along the narrow hallway. They dashed past a row of offices. Lucas rammed a door head-on and they burst into a small conference room. Henry lay slumped in the corner, his back pressed against a wall that was mirrored floor to ceiling. His cracked glasses sat slightly askew on his blood-smeared face. Emily was curled in the crook of his arm.

Karina cleared the room in a desperate sprint and dropped to her knees. "Is she okay?"

"She's fine," Henry said softly. "She woke up a little when I had to help you, but now she's sleeping again."

Karina hugged her, cradling Emily's small body. Finally.

Lucas shoved the table against the door and landed next to them.

"I see you're bleeding, too, cousin." Henry smiled. "Nice of you to join me."

"Where are the others?" Lucas growled.

"I don't know. We were hit two minutes after you went into the vault. It was a concentrated assault. They came prepared. The seventeenth floor fell within ten minutes. We were retreating, when I got cut off. I went into cloak almost immediately. Our people may have evacuated."

"Without us?" Karina stared at them.

"Arthur probably thought I fed," Lucas said. "Your blood would give me enough of a boost to either get Henry and me clear or to hide."

"They are surrounding us," Henry said. "What's the plan?"

"You and I go. They stay," Lucas said.

"Ah." Henry nodded. "I thought it might be something like that."

"What are you talking about?" Karina gathered Emily closer.

"We're going to open that door," Lucas said. "Henry and I will take off. Henry will make sure they concentrate on us and I will make sure to keep them busy. They will follow us. You will wait here for three minutes, then you will take Emily, go out into the hallway, and turn right. You will come to an intersection. Turn right again. That will get you to the stairs. Shoot anyone you see. Then you get the hell out. If you make it out of the building, Arthur won't look for you right away, since I'll be dead and he won't need a donor immediately. Don't use credit cards, don't stay twice in the same—"

"They will kill you!" No, that was not how this would go. The spring of tension inside her shivered, compressing.

"It was never about me surviving," Lucas said. "I died when we opened the vault."

"He's right," Henry said.

God, he pissed her off. "No." She shook her head, trying to keep a lid on her anger. "We go to the stairs together and fight our way down. Together."

Lucas grabbed her, jerking her close. "You will do as you're told."

"No," she said into his snarl. "I won't. We go together."

The pressure inside her built.

"This isn't a democracy!"

"Lucas, I can't carry Emily and shoot at the same time. I can barely hold this stupid gun with two hands. Do you think I'm Rambo? It's suicide for me, Emily, *and* you."

"She has a point," Henry said.

"See? They will kill me and your grand sacrifice will be wasted. I don't want you to die for nothing. I don't want you to die at all."

"Why the hell not?"

"Because I care if you live or die! My God, you are a moron! We fight our way to the stairs together. We have a better chance that way."

He shook her. "I'm trying to save your daughter, you idiot! I've been doing this a long time and I am telling you, if we go out there, we'll all die."

"He also has a point," Henry said.

Karina exhaled. Emily's life was all that mattered. "Then drink my blood and get her out of here."

"I would have to drain you dry. I'm barely conscious!"

"Do it." Karina told him, furious. "You have the best chance of getting out of here with Emily alive. Drain me."

"No!" he snarled.

"Do it, Lucas!"

"That's nice," Henry said. "But the Ordinators are coming."

"Drain me or we go to the stairs," Karina said.

"No, we'll do this my way."

"Your way, I die, you die, Emily dies!"

"There is no time," Henry said calmly. "You missed your opportunity. We are all about to die. Don't let them take you alive. You will regret it."

The back wall of the conference room shuddered. Cracks crisscrossed the wood. It shattered and rained down in a waterfall of tiny splinters. People stood behind it, people with automatic weapons and dark helmets shielding their faces. In front of them a tall man with pale hair down to his waist slowly lowered his hand, smiling. She looked into his face and saw her own death there.

It hit her like a punch. Emily, she, Lucas, and Henry—the four of them really were about to die.

For nothing. They would die for nothing.

Lucas surged to his feet, trying to shield her.

No. No, this was not happening. She was tired and scared and pissed off and she was done with this shit.

Fuck them all.

The coiled spring inside her snapped free. Fiery power surged through her in a glorious cascade. It was time to set things right.

The smile slid off the blond Ordinator's face. He opened his mouth.

The power surged from her, up and over her shoulders in twin streams.

She looked right into his eyes and said, "Die!"

His face turned green, as if dusted with emerald powder. He crumpled and fell to the floor. She stared at the men behind him and they collapsed like rag dolls.

Two others burst into her view from the left. She turned and *looked* at them and watched them die in midstep.

"Anybody else?" she called out. Her voice rang through the building. "Does anybody else want some? Because I've got plenty!"

Nobody answered. She marched out into the hallway, turned the corner, and saw a hallway full of people.

Die.

They collapsed as one.

They wanted to exterminate humanity. They had declared a war. Fine. If the Ordinators wanted a war, she would introduce them to one.

Karina turned. Lucas was staring at her, his mouth hanging open. Next to him Henry stood, blinking as if he hoped that one of the times when he reopened his eyes he would see something different.

Karina looked above them and saw her own reflection in the mirror wall. Twin streams of green lightning spread out from her shoulders in two radiant green wings. Like Arthur's red ones.

"A Wither," Henry said in a small voice, still blinking. "She's a Wither."

The memory of burning faces flashed before her and she brushed it aside. Fine. She was a Wither and nobody would ever push her around again.

Lucas closed his mouth. His gaze met hers and she saw pride and defiance in his eyes. "Do it quick," he said.

He expected her to kill him.

After everything she'd said to him, he expected her to kill him.

Karina stepped to him. Her lightning wings burned around them. "Don't worry," she told him. "I'm the biggest and the strongest and I'll protect you. We are walking out of here."

Henry stopped blinking.

It took them forty-five minutes to get down the stairs. Karina inhaled the night air. It smelled of acrid smoke and rotting garbage, but she didn't care.

Behind her the building rose like a grim tower. It now belonged to the dead. She had walked through every hallway and checked every room, while Henry and Lucas sat waiting and bleeding on the stairs. She had no idea how many people she killed, but it had to be dozens. She checked their faces to make sure they were dead. They all looked the same: features sunken in, emerald green tint painting their skin.

And now, finally, she was done.

Her lightning wings had vanished, her power exhausted. Reality returned slowly, in bits and pieces.

Next to her Lucas stirred. "If you want to disappear, now is the time. You killed them because they were caught unaware. The House of Daryon won't be. I don't know what your plan is but I know that once Arthur realizes what you are, he'll do everything he can to keep you within the House. You are too powerful to cut loose. He'll kill you if you refuse, and I don't know if I can stop him."

"He's right," Henry said. "It's alarming how often I keep repeating that. Withers, Subspecies 21, have several types. You're type 4. Arthur is type 7. He is more powerful and he has a lot more experience. At your best you can't take him, and it will take you a long time to build your reserves back up to do anything on a massive scale again. Sometimes it takes years. Not to mention that we will have to fight you if you try to kill Arthur."

Karina looked at Lucas. "If I leave, how will you feed?"

"Synthetics," he said. "They take the edge off."

His entire body was tense, like a string pulled too tight. He didn't want her to go. "Why?" she asked.

"That's what you want," he said. "Freedom. One more day or maybe many. It's yours. Take it."

Henry cleared his throat. "The Ordinators . . ."

Lucas looked at him. Henry closed his mouth with a click.

Karina peered at Lucas's face. "Didn't you promise me you would find me if I escaped?"

"I did. I promise you it will take me a really long time to find you. Go now."

She hesitated. Emily stirred in Lucas's arms, waking up.

Lucas could find her—she saw the certainty of it in his eyes. If he could find her, the Ordinators could find her as well, and they would be much more motivated. And even if she did escape, she would always be living on the run, hiding from everyone and afraid of every shadow. She had no doubt that Emily was a donor. She had a responsibility to her child—she had to teach Emily how to protect herself or when they would be found, Emily would be caught unaware, just like she was.

Karina looked out into the city. That way lay freedom. Even twelve hours before, Karina Tucker would've taken it in a blink. But she was no longer that Karina Tucker. Nothing would ever be the same. There was a chasm between her old self and her new self, and it was filled with Ordinator bodies. Too much had happened. It changed her and there was no going back.

The woman who only days before had driven four children on a school trip was dead. She had been a nice girl, kind and a little naive, because she thought she knew what tragedy was. That woman had a small, secure, cozy life. Karina missed her and she took a moment to mourn her. It hurt to let go of that life. She shed it anyway, but not like a butterfly breaking free of the cocoon. More like a snake leaving its old skin. And this new Karina took risks. She was stronger, harder, and more powerful. There was a war going on and she would take part in it.

And even if she chickened out and tried to walk away, the memory of Lucas would keep her from going too far. She had more in common with a man who turned into a monster than she did with Jill and her endless worry over seat belts. She couldn't leave him behind now, back in the place where everyone was scared of him, where Arthur used him with no regard for Lucas's life, where his brother continuously bickered and fought with him. She had Emily. Lucas had no one and he wanted her so badly. And she wanted him. Right or wrong, she no longer cared. It was her decision and she made it.

"Decide," Lucas told her. "We can't stay out in the open."

Only one question remained. Karina took a deep breath and closed the distance between her and Lucas. She lifted her face and looked into his green eyes and kissed him.

For a moment he stood still and then he kissed her back, his mouth eager and hungry for her. When they broke apart, Henry was staring at them.

"I am confused," Henry said.

"Well, I can't let you go back on your own," Karina said. "All beat up and sad. Arthur might kill you somehow, or Daniel will bring the house down, or Henry, you might poison everyone with your cooking."

Emily opened her eyes. "Mommy!"

"Hi, baby."

"Where are we?"

"In Detroit. We had to make a stop here for a little while, but Lucas and Henry are taking us home with them now."

There had to be words to describe the look on Lucas's face, but she didn't know them. He probably didn't know them, either. He looked like he wasn't sure if he were surprised, relieved, happy, or mad.

"I believe there is a fast-food place three blocks north," Henry said. "We could go there, use their phone, and drink coffee while we wait to get picked up. I could use some coffee."

"Can you make it?" Lucas asked.

"If I faint, just leave me in the street."

Lucas slid his shoulder under Henry's arm.

"Thank you."

They started down the street.

"You don't own me anymore," Karina said quietly.

"Fine," Lucas said.

"And I will have my own room."

"Fine."

"And if you need to feed, you will ask me. Nicely."

He stopped and glared at her.

"Nicely," she told him.

"Fine."

"But all kidding aside, you will still cook, right?" Henry asked. "You said—"

"Yes, I will definitely cook."

"Oh, good," Henry said. "I was afraid you would quit and we would have to eat Lucas's cooking."

"My cooking is fine," Lucas said.

Ahead, the familiar yellow-on-red sign rose on the corner.

"Are we going there, Mommy?" Emily pointed at the sign.

"Yes."

"Do we have money to get ice cream?"

"I have twenty dollars," Henry said. "It's a little bloody, but they will take it."

"They'll take it," Lucas said grimly.

Karina pictured Lucas, a little bloody and a little pissed off, breaking the McDonald's counter in half. Hopefully it wouldn't come to that.

"Don't worry, baby. We'll get you all the ice cream you want." Karina glanced back at the husk of the skyscraper. For a second she thought she saw her own self waving good-bye. Her new self smiled back. People who knew the old Karina would judge her, if they knew, but that didn't matter. She made her own choices now.

She put her hand on Lucas's arm. He bent it at his elbow, letting her fingers rest on his muscled forearm, and they walked side by side into the night.

Nocturne

Sharon Shinn

CHAPTER 1

Because I was the newest cook at the school, they had given me
the least desirable shift, the one from midnight until dawn. It
was my job to wash any of the pots that had been left to soak after
dinner, to sweep up the kitchen, to mix the ingredients for bread and
let the dough go through its first rising. Rhesa, the young woman
who had held this position before me, had gladly given up these tasks;
she now came in with three other women to make the evening meal
for the hundred and fifty souls who lived at the school. I could tell
she both pitied me for being stuck with the night duties and felt a
certain smug satisfaction at finally having someone below her in the
staff hierarchy. She was the kind of person who—if she lasted long
enough to be named head cook—would treat everyone below her
with snobbery and contempt.

But the truth was, I liked the night hours. I liked the solitude,
the quiet, and the autonomy. And I relished the chance to explore.

The Gabriel School was an odd place, no question about it. It was
one of a dozen such institutions established sixty or seventy years
ago by the former Archangel and his wife as places for abandoned
street children to get an education. While a few of these schools could

be found in major cities like Semorrah and Luminaux, ours was located on the very edge of the desert that snugged up against the Caitana Mountains. Not only was it situated between sands to the south, mountains to the west, and ocean to the east, it was served by a single infrequently traveled road. In other words, it offered little chance for anyone who lived there to escape somewhere else.

That choice had been deliberate, I assumed, since most of our students had some experience with crime, and many had not come here of their own free will. The theory was that, if they were forced to stay at the Gabriel School long enough to learn a trade, they would eventually become skilled craftspeople who could be gainfully employed, and everyone would benefit.

The problem was, a small school in an inaccessible location wasn't an easy place for teachers and cooks and housekeepers to leave, either, if they got tired of the hard work, the cramped accommodations, or the lack of excitement. But I didn't mind. I didn't feel trapped. I planned on staying at the Gabriel School for a good long time. For one thing, I was tired of running. For another, I had nowhere else to go.

B y the time I had been at the Gabriel School for a month, I had pretty well established a routine. I would go to bed in the morning and rise early in the afternoon to enjoy a few daylight hours to myself. I joined the cooks in the kitchen just as they finished serving dinner, and I completed the cleaning by myself after they drifted back to their rooms. Then I had a couple hours of freedom before it was time to begin assembling ingredients for the morning bread.

I spent those hours exploring the school. The first few weeks were chilly enough to keep me indoors, investigating locked storerooms (easy enough to break into), musty closets, and stairwells that led to underground rooms that everyone else had forgotten. I found a hidden cache of fine wine, a strongbox of gold, and historical documents about the school that were more interesting than you would have supposed. More than once I happened upon romantic liaisons between workers or a pair of students, though I was stealthy enough that none of these trysting couples ever realized I was there. I only watched long enough to be sure that no one was unwilling, and then I quietly backed away.

The fourth week I was there, the weather decidedly improved, and I ventured outside to look around. The Gabriel School owned about ten acres enclosed by a high wrought-iron fence whose narrow metal bars were so rusted through in spots that they would hardly keep an intruder out or a fugitive in. Of the six main buildings, one housed the workers, two housed the students, and two served as class-rooms, kitchen, dining hall, library, and other public spaces. The last one was a barn/stable/storage facility where we kept barrels of dried fruit, shelves of canned vegetables, three cows, five horses, and two ancient carts. There were all sorts of interesting cubbyholes and bins and haylofts in the barn, and I planned to investigate them all.

But the very first night I spent ghosting around the grounds, it wasn't the barn that captured my attention. It was the tall, narrow building at the top of a small hill on the other side of the fence. The house where the headmistress lived. By day it appeared drab and dispirited, with lugubrious gray drapes visible in the ground-floor windows, black ones on the second story, and weathered old boards covering up the openings on the attic level. By night—especially a night such as this one, with a full moon intermittently obscured by flat, listless clouds—it had a sort of wild, sinister allure. I found myself standing with my back to the workers' dorm, my hands wrapped around two of those iron bars, staring up at its eerie silhouette.

It appeared as if everyone in the place was asleep, for no lights showed on any level. Not that too many people inhabited the Great House, as it was called. The headmistress lived there alone except for a housekeeper and a footman, who rarely mingled with staff at the school. And none of us—not student, not teacher, not cook—was permitted to enter the Great House. If an emergency arose and we needed to summon the headmistress, we would ring a brass bell that hung inside the compound. No such emergency had occurred since I had been on the campus.

The instant I had been told of the prohibition against entering the Great House, I had been seized with a desire to do just that. I knew that the day would come when the headmistress fell sick or had to travel, when her servants were off on errands that could only be entrusted to them. There would come a day when that odd, off-putting, off-limits structure would be safe to roam.

Not tonight, however. I stood there another few moments, tracing the outlines of the house with my gaze. A last ragged wisp of cloud shredded away from the moon, and the whole house was lit with a faint phosphorescence. I stayed another moment just to admire the interaction of moonlight and shadow, wishing I was a skilled enough artist to capture the slant of the roof, the narrow structure of the building, the pool of darkness against the front door.

Suddenly, against the moonlight, a shape on the roof lifted and resettled itself.

Primal terror sent a delicious thrill down my back. I wasn't afraid, just startled, since I had not realized anything else in the world was awake and roaming. Some night creature must have nested on top of the house. An owl, perhaps, although a large one; I was almost certain I had seen the sweep of feathers. I stood utterly still, straining to peer through the dark. Yes—there it was again—the distinctive serrated edge of a spread wing, appearing just above the roofline and then disappearing again.

A *very* large owl. Perhaps it was a falcon, used to hunting in the dark, or some kind of night bird I wasn't familiar with. We were near the Caitanas—the god alone knew what kind of creatures might make their homes in the mountains.

I waited another five minutes, another ten, resisting an inner voice that insisted I must return to the kitchen *now* or be late starting the bread. But no mysterious midnight predator lifted its wing above the roofline again, waking my admiration and my curiosity.

I turned to hurry back toward the kitchen, already thinking up a story to explain my tardiness if the dough wasn't done in time. But a sound behind me spun me around to gape at the Great House, dark and featureless in the cloud-crusted moonlight.

It was a single note, liquid and pure and anguished, like the most gorgeous, the most despairing foghorn lowing off a storm-racked coast. I would have said it was music, except it was weeping; it was a song with a single tone, and that was agony. The sound went on and on, sustained by a solitary breath, and then it abruptly stopped. The rest of the night had fallen deathly silent, as if no bird, no insect, no furtive mouse could move or speak in the presence of such beauty and remorse. The world had been struck dumb.

I stood there, mute and motionless, my whole body clenched with waiting. But though I remained silent and still for another thirty minutes, I never heard another sound, never caught another glimpse of that tortured creature. Finally, shivering and uneasy, I made myself turn away and creep through the compound toward the kitchen. I had to confess that I was wishing it was already dawn.

I have always known how to get information without making anyone wonder why I wanted it. So that evening, when I joined the other workers in the kitchen, I took up a station near the head cook, Deborah. She was a big woman, not especially nice, but talkative; she would gossip about anybody as long as you didn't ask her a question outright. That mistake would cause her to sniff loudly and accuse you of having a nasty mind. She appreciated hard work, so she was inclined to like me, and I was careful not to cross her in even the smallest way.

Today I worked beside her, scraping dried gravy off of a platter, and manufacturing noisy yawns until Deborah finally noticed.

"Jovah's bones, Moriah, you look like you're about to fall over!" she exclaimed. "Didn't you sleep last night?"

"Not very well," I admitted. "I got a scare while I was working down here all alone, and I was so edgy I couldn't close my eyes."

"What scared you?" asked Judith. She was a thin, weary woman in her midthirties who had come to the Gabriel School five years before with a small son in tow. My guess was that Judith had once been an angel-seeker and her son was one of those hundreds of children fathered by an angel but unfortunately mortal. A more unscrupulous woman would have dumped him in the streets of Velora or Cedar Hills—to enter a life of crime and no doubt end up here at the Gabriel School, anyway—but clearly Judith had not been capable of the necessary ruthlessness. We hadn't had more than an hour of conversation together all told, but she was the person I liked best in the entire compound.

I glanced over my shoulder toward the hallway that led to several doors, one of them guarding the root cellar. "Last night. Three times. That door would creak open as if someone was coming upstairs. I kept going over to push it shut, and it would come open again. Then I kept thinking I could feel someone staring at me, but I'd turn around, and no one was there." I offered a small shudder. "It just— made me uncomfortable."

Judith nodded. "That happened to me a couple of times when I worked in the kitchen overnight. I just learned to ignore it."

Rhesa, who was scrubbing spills off the great iron stove, glanced over her shoulder uneasily. "That door never swung open while *I* worked here alone."

"There's plenty of places around this school that give me the shivers," said a heavyset, vacuous man named Elon. He was middle-aged and wholly devoid of personality; I sometimes wondered if he'd arrived as a student when he was sixteen and never had the energy to leave. "I don't like the barn at night. *Or* the library."

Deborah snorted. "Not one of them is as peculiar as the Great House," she said.

I pretended to frown. "Why? What's wrong with the Great House?"

Rhesa grimaced at me. "It's *creepy.*"

"Well, it's old and tumbledown," I said. "And I know none of us is supposed to go over there."

"And haven't you ever wondered why?" muttered Elon.

I shrugged. "I thought Headmistress liked her privacy."

Deborah snorted again. "She likes to keep everyone in the school *safe*," she corrected. "That place is haunted."

I wasn't the only worker who exclaimed aloud at this. *Haunted! You're saying there are ghosts at the Great House? Who are they?*

Deborah waved a hand for silence and we all fell quiet. "I've been here twenty years, and I've never set foot in that building," she said dramatically. "And I heard tales about it from the day I arrived. People would see lights flashing in the upper windows. They'd see shapes moving on the roof. There would be sounds—terrible, groaning sounds—and the noise of glass breaking and voices shouting. But only at night. In the morning, it would all be peaceful again."

She glanced around as if to make sure she had everyone's attention, but we were all rapt. "Of course, you'd think all those disturbances were caused by a ghost, but that's not what people believed. They said there was a live man there—sick—hurt—maybe mad— cared for by the woman who *used* to be headmistress, back when I was a girl. A man everyone would recognize, if they could see his face." She nodded for emphasis.

"Who was it?" Rhesa demanded.

Deborah dropped her voice to a whisper and we all leaned in to hear. "The old Archangel."

"Gabriel?" Elon asked.

Deborah shook her head. "Raphael," she breathed.

She met with stares of disbelief. "That can't be," Judith said. "Raphael died when Mount Galo came down."

"And he was *ancient*," Rhesa added.

Deborah frowned, clearly not liking our skepticism. "Everyone *believed* he died when the god threw the thunderbolt against the mountain," she said in a stronger voice. "But he didn't. He was disfigured and crippled, but he survived. And he was brought here to this remote place to live out his days in obscurity."

"But Rhesa's right," Judith objected. "He was fifty or more when the mountain was destroyed, wasn't he? And that was almost seventy years ago. So even if you came here twenty years ago——"

I could see her struggling with the math, but I had already done the calculations. Twenty years ago, Raphael would have been roughly a hundred years old. And even if he had survived those legendary events, he would have been mightily bruised and broken. Every schoolchild learned the story of the time Jovah smote Mount Galo and almost destroyed the world. As the god required, all the people of Samaria had gathered in the mountain's shadow on the Plain of Sharon, prepared to sing the annual Gloria to prove to the god that they were living in harmony. But Raphael had been unwilling to hand over his title of Archangel to Gabriel. He claimed there was no god. He claimed that Jovah would not, as promised, strike the mountain, and then the river, and then the world, if the Gloria was not sung. But when twilight fell, so did the thunderbolts, and the mountain was blown apart. No one had ever seen Raphael or any of his followers again. Not even, I was pretty certain, the former headmistress.

But it was interesting to contemplate the idea of *some* angel taking refuge in the upper stories of the Great House. That would explain the shape of wings. That would explain the heart-wrenching snatch of music. Angels pray to Jovah through song—they fly into the heavens and plead for him to send rain or sunshine or medicines or grain, whatever is most needed at the moment. All of them possess voices so beautiful you might weep to hear them.

So I was prepared to believe I had spotted an angel on the roof of the Great House. It just wasn't Raphael.

Deborah was trying to convince the doubters. "Angels live a very long time," she said firmly. "A hundred years would be nothing to one of them."

Judith—who I suspected had more experience with angels than Deborah did—said, "Maybe, but I never heard of any of them living a hundred and twenty years. Even if it *was* Raphael there at some point, he can't possibly be there now."

"No, but his spirit is," Deborah snapped, clearly annoyed. "It haunts the place."

"Still?" I asked, trying to sound frightened instead of speculative. "That is—do people still hear voices and—and see shapes?"

"*I* never have," Elon said.

"Me, either," Rhesa added.

I glanced at Judith, and she shook her head. Judith was a thoughtful and observant woman. If *she* hadn't noticed any spirits lurking around, then there hadn't been any on the premises for at least five years.

"Sometimes the spirits lie quiet," Deborah said. "And sometimes they are stirred up again. You should feel grateful that you live at the Gabriel School during a time when no ghosts are walking. And as long as all of us stay behind the fence, the ghosts should remain quiet, and everything will be fine."

Rhesa turned back to the stove, already grumbling. "Well, I don't mind not poking around the Great House, but I'm awfully tired of staying *here* all the time," she said in a voice scarcely better than a whine. "There's nothing to *do*. I want to go to Telford or Stockton, or even Breven, just for a day or two."

"I wouldn't mind a trip to Stockton myself," Judith said. "If I don't get another pair of shoes pretty soon, I might just as well go barefoot."

That quickly turned the conversation from spirits to shopping, but I didn't mind. I had learned what I needed to know.

The Great House—isolated, mysterious, and brooding—served as more than just the lodgings for whoever was current headmistress of the Gabriel School. It was a haven for broken angels who needed somewhere to rest and recover. I strongly doubted that a ruined old Raphael had ever lived in its upper stories, but I was willing to bet that, over the past seventy years, an assortment of angelic occupants had taken refuge there.

And one was living there now.

I wondered if it was one I knew.

I would have to be very, very careful.

For the next three weeks, I was obsessed with watching the Great House, trying to get another glimpse of the angel, while making very sure he did not catch sight of me. I kept up my usual routine, except now instead of using any free hours to explore the rest of the compound, I spent them patrolling the patch of fence that served as a border between the school and the house. We were not quite done with winter, so the weather veered from temperate to frigid and back to mild. Some of the nights were so cold I could only stand to be outside for ten minutes.

Twice during that period, I saw the angel again.

The first time was probably a week after our conversation in the kitchen. The half-moon still produced enough light to see by, and the weather was moderate enough to make a midnight stroll bearable. As before, I came to a standstill and wrapped my fingers around the iron bars, though this time I stood in the shadow thrown by one of the school buildings, so that I would be difficult to see. I stared up at the Great House, willing it to spill its secrets.

And I saw a shape rise up from the rooftop as if conjured by faith and longing. It was an angel, all right—there was no mistaking the silhouette. An angel who stood with his head thrown back and his arms upraised and his wings swept back, in an attitude that could not have more plainly bespoken supplication. He stood that way for five minutes, for ten, and then turned abruptly away with the banked rage of a man who knows his prayers will not be answered. Suddenly he pitched to his knees, tripped up by some obstruction on the roof that he had overlooked in the chancy light.

Or—no. Tripped up by something he had not noticed because he could not *see*. I watched as he rose cautiously to a standing position.

I saw him stretch his arms out, as if seeking a wall or handhold; I saw him glide his right foot forward, as if testing the surface ahead for other hazards he might have missed. The fall seemed to have disrupted his sense of orientation. He tilted his head, as if listening for the way the evening breeze played around the surfaces of the roof, then felt his way slowly toward a specific point. It must have been a door that led to the interior, because almost instantly he dropped out of sight and did not reappear.

The angel was *blind*? Oh, as he had proved so often in the past, Jovah had an interesting sense of humor. No need for me to worry that the angel might recognize me. No need for me to fear him at all.

The thought rekindled my desire to somehow gain access to the Great House, only this time I had a clear goal: I wanted a chance to view the angel from a closer range. I couldn't even explain why I wanted to do it, except that it gave me a tremendous sense of freedom to think I could stand in the same room with an angel and not be afraid for my life. It equalized things somehow; it gave me back a measure of dignity. The balance of the world would be righted, and I could abandon the past.

Probably not; but maybe I could gaze at him in silent mockery and simply feel a sense of triumph and relief.

The next time I glimpsed the angel, I heard him sing.

I had been to all three of the angel holds; I had briefly lived in Luminaux, the Blue City that spills over with music and art. Once I had traveled to the Gloria and heard the sacred mass performed by angel choirs. I knew how easy it was to grow drunk on the music angels can make.

But I had never heard anything to match the sound of that angel's song.

This time there was more than that single sustained cry. This time there was a melody of sorts, bitter and drowned and beautiful, and every separate ravished note struck me like a copper blow. It was like being hammered by mournful metal; I felt his music pock my skin and dimple my bones. I felt it run like scattered silver through my veins.

If there were words, I couldn't distinguish them. I couldn't have said if the angel was singing a line from a traditional requiem or improvising a dirge on the spot. All I knew was that the sound made me want to fall to the ground, weeping. Instead, I turned away and blundered through the yard, back toward the school, back toward the kitchen, back to the safety of silence.

CHAPTER 2

Three days later, I found my way into the Great House. Jovah's hand at work, I almost believed. The god had formed the habit of making my oddest prayers come true. Maybe to make up for the fact that he had once tried to destroy me.

I had been sleeping when the messenger appeared that morning, but Judith told me he arrived on a wheezing horse and carried exciting news. The headmistress's daughter was about to be delivered of a baby, and she desperately wanted her mother on hand. The footman had hitched up the two most reliable horses, and within an hour he was driving her down the rutted road, heading toward a tricky mountain pass and west toward Castelana. There were no easy routes to any of the river cities from this side of the Caitanas, so I had to believe they would be gone at least two weeks.

During that period, there would be only one servant minding the Great House, a middle-aged woman who must surely sleep some of the time. I was not wild about the idea of sneaking through the manor under cover of darkness, to be startled by every creak and groan, but it might be my best option.

But then good fortune struck. Or disaster, depending on your perspective.

I had been awake for a couple of hours and was standing outside in the cold air before heading to the kitchen to help clean up the evening meal. I had taken my usual shaded post beside the fence that overlooked the hill leading to the Great House, and I was scanning its porch and windows. So I happened to be watching when the housekeeper stepped through a side door to shake out a rug. I saw her slip in a patch of mud and tumble to the ground, her hands bracing as her feet went flying. I saw her struggle to stand—almost accomplish the feat—and then drop to the ground again, clearly in pain. I watched as she slowly and with great determination inched back toward the stoop, up the three steps, and across the threshold. She was on her bottom the whole time, pulling herself along with her hands and sheer willpower.

I paused a moment to admire her fortitude. Then I made my plans.

It was necessary first to put in an hour in the kitchen, working beside the other cooks until they had all headed off to their beds. It was close to midnight before I slipped outside, let myself out of the tall gate at the front of the complex, and climbed the path leading up to the manor. I forced myself to remain calm, to breathe evenly, as I crested the hill and headed to the side of the house where I had seen the housekeeper fall.

I stood outside the door, took one more deep breath, then stepped inside as if I belonged.

I was instantly inside the kitchen, a much smaller room than the one at the school, but meticulously maintained. It was blessedly warm after the chill outside, and I could catch the aromatic odors of meat and potatoes warming in the oven. Late as it was, the housekeeper was still awake and trying to cope with her crisis. She was sitting on the floor, her back to a wall, her legs stretched out, and a scatter of cloths all around her. She looked up in astonishment as I strolled in, all brisk confidence and breezy certainty.

"Oh, dear, I thought I saw you fall, but I couldn't get free until just now," I said in a sympathetic tone, dropping to a crouch. "What happened? Did you twist your ankle? Or worse?"

She stared at me, speechless for a moment. I put her at about fifty, with years of hard labor showing in her thin face, but she looked tough enough still to heave a table at me, if only she could get close enough to grab the legs. Her hair was an indeterminate brown and pulled back in an impatient bun; her eyes were a narrowed green, dense with intelligence. I had the strange thought that if she and Deborah were to engage in some kind of head servants' brawl, this woman would win handily.

"Who are you?" she finally demanded. Her hands were bunched up in the cloth on either side of her skirt. I figured they were knotted against pain, but she might easily have a weapon concealed in a pocket. She didn't strike me as the type who often allowed herself to be helpless.

"I'm Moriah. I work down at the school," I explained. Going to my knees, I scooted down toward her feet. "Can I see? I'm not a healer, but I know enough to bind your leg if it's sprained, or set it if it's broken."

"It's not broken," she said sharply. And then, "You're not allowed to be here."

"I'm not," I agreed, pulling up her hem so I could look at the damage. It was instantly clear that her left leg was the one that had given way on her. She'd managed to get her shoe off, but the whole ankle and half the foot were already showing a dark purple bruise, and the skin had puffed out in protest. "*Ouch.* That must hurt."

"It does," she said grimly, then repeated, "You're not allowed to be here."

"But if I leave, no one will wrap this for you, or help you into bed, or make sure you're fed in the morning, and you could fall again and strike your head and die," I answered cheerfully. "So let me just take care of this and get you something to eat and try to make you comfortable, and then I can leave before anyone realizes I'm here."

She was silent a moment, clearly unwilling, but realistic enough to realize she would be in very bad shape without assistance. "Very well," she said. "But you can't tell anyone you've been here."

"I won't," I promised. I glanced over with a smile. "What's your name?"

"Alma," she said reluctantly.

A soft name for such a strong woman! "Well, Alma, I apologize in advance if I hurt you. Now let's get this taken care of."

In less than an hour, I had wrapped her foot, helped her sit at the table long enough to eat a meal, and supported her as she hobbled into a small bedroom that opened off the kitchen. She did most of the work of stripping off her clothes and pulling on a nightshirt, but the exertion cost her a great deal; her face was drawn with pain by the time she lowered herself to the bed.

I glanced around as if looking for any final chores I should take care of. "Now, I'll just bring dinner to the angel and then come down and clean up the dishes," I said in a matter-of-fact voice. "Then tomorrow—"

"What did you say?" she interrupted.

I gave her my most innocent look. "I'll take dinner to the angel—"

For the first time, she looked both nonplussed and alarmed. "How do you know—why do you think—"

"I've seen him. At night, on the roof. Heard him, a couple of times. I don't know what's wrong with him, but I assume he's come here for help or healing. And maybe he can make it down two flights of steps to feed himself dinner and maybe he can't." I tilted my head to one side and watched her, my expression inquiring. *Well? Can he? And if he can't, will you let him go hungry?*

Her green eyes burned as she stared back at me, and I watched her internal struggle play out on her face. Clearly this was not a woman who easily betrayed a trust, but she could not reconcile her two warring mandates: *Take care of the angel* and *Keep the angel's existence a secret.* But, really, she had no choice, and I saw the capitulation in her face a second before she spoke.

"All right. Take a tray of food to him on the third floor. He drinks water with his meal, no wine. Bring down his dirty dishes from breakfast. If he needs something else, he'll ask for it, but don't speak to him first."

I knew the answer already, but I wanted my guess confirmed before I actually risked showing my face to an angel. So I asked, "Won't he wonder why *I'm* bringing him dinner instead of you?"

She shook her head and eased herself back onto her pillows. There were a lot of them. The bed was surprisingly plush, given her situation and the severe plainness of the rest of the room. I liked the thought that she allowed herself a single indulgence. "No," she said, "he's blind."

I had to turn away to hide my smile. "I'll be back in a few moments," I told her as I stepped into the kitchen again. I was so delighted with the way my plan had gone so far that I was almost humming as I fixed up a platter.

It turns out it's not easy to carry a heavy tray up two flights if the stairs are narrow and twisty and the only illumination is a small lamp you added to your tray at the last moment, when you realized the house was too old and remote to run on gaslight. I was a little breathless when I arrived at the attic level and found myself in a narrow corridor that ran along one side of the house. Three doors led off the hallway; the two that were closed I guessed to be a bedroom and a closet. The third one stood open in a rather gloomy invitation into what appeared to be a large sitting room. It seemed to take up most of the top story and to be intended as a public space, so I stepped inside with assumed confidence.

A quick look around showed me shadowy groupings of chairs and small tables, boarded-up windows, and a curving iron staircase that had to lead to the roof. In one corner, a large stringed instrument leaned against a wall. There appeared to be stacks of books and

papers on the floor, though they were disordered, as if no one had
touched them in a long time.

In the center of the room, not quite facing me, was the angel. He
was sprawled in one of those special cutaway chairs designed to accom-
modate angel wings, though he sat in it so carelessly that he appeared
to be in danger of slipping out and crashing to the floor. His head was
flung back to rest on the top of the padded back; his wings puddled on
either side of him like dirty garments he had cast off after a tiring day.
It was hard to tell by lamplight, but the clothes he was actually wearing appeared soiled as well. His white shirt looked wrinkled and
stained, and his dark trousers sported a visible rip all the way down
one seam. He was barefoot.

His face was in profile to me so at first all I could tell about his
features was that his chin was firm, his nose was straight, and his
cheekbone sleekly planed. He must not have liked the feel of whiskers on his face, because he had shaved recently, but his dark hair
was long and disordered, spilling over the back of the chair in tangled
knots.

I stood for a long time, holding the tray, staring at him. It was
rare to see an angel—one of the most haughty, disdainful, unlikable
creatures in all of Samaria—humbled and miserable. I wanted to
enjoy the sight for as long as I could.

Then my hand trembled, or I shifted my weight and the floor
creaked beneath me. At any rate, he suddenly realized I was there.
He didn't lift his head, just turned it enough so that he appeared to
be looking in my direction. It was too dark for me to discern what
the trouble was with his eyes. From here they looked like pools of
shadow fringed with sweeping lashes.

"The breakfast plates are on the table," he said in an indifferent
voice that was still musical enough to make me catch my breath. He
didn't seem to realize or care that I had arrived after midnight with
his evening meal. "You can leave dinner there if you like. I'm not
hungry."

I located the table he meant, but set my tray in a different spot because the breakfast dishes took up all the room. Then I regarded him again for a moment before I asked brightly, "So what exactly happened to *you*?"

T he astonishment on the angel's face was comical. He jerked upright and glared in my direction, his wings quivering in indignation. "Who are you? Where's Alma?" he demanded.

I felt a grudging admiration that he knew the servant's name; so many in his position wouldn't. "She sprained her ankle and can barely make it around the house, let alone up the stairs," I said, still in that cheerful voice. "I volunteered to help her out."

"No one is supposed to enter this house without my approval," he said, frowning heavily. "No one asked me if you could come here."

"Well, the headmistress and the footman are gone, and Alma's laid up downstairs, so no one could really ask about your preferences," I said. "As long as Alma's off her feet, you'll have to accept my help—or feed yourself—or starve."

At my tone, his features gathered in a scowl. "*Who* are you?" he repeated.

"Moriah. I'm a cook at the school."

"You're insolent for a cook."

It was all I could do to keep from replying, *You're pathetic for an angel.* Instead I said, "I suppose you're used to being treated with more deference."

"With *civility*," he shot back. "With the sort of politeness anyone would extend to a stranger."

There was a difference; even I had to acknowledge that. "I'll be nice if you will," I said. "Why don't you eat? That way I can take all the dishes down at once. We don't want rats coming for the scraps."

I could tell by his expression he realized this was sensible, but he said, "I told you. I'm not hungry."

He sounded like a petulant girl who hadn't gotten her way on some trivial matter and was determined to sulk about it until everyone noticed. "Maybe not," I said. "But I'm afraid if you won't eat now, you'll be *very* hungry by the time I can make it back here tomorrow night. You really should eat something."

He hesitated a moment, not done sulking, but gave in. "Oh, very well." I expected to have to guide him toward the table where I'd left the tray, but he came to his feet and headed unerringly in its direction, dragging his chair behind him. His wing tips trailed on the floor, completely unheeded, like the cloth belt from a robe that had fallen open when the sash was untied.

"How did you do that?" I asked when he sat down and began feeling for the silverware. "Find the food?"

"I could smell it," he said. He picked up a fork and took a bite of potatoes.

He had not invited me to join him, but I settled into a chair across the table from him and studied his face. "You must have a keen nose."

He considered that while he chewed and swallowed. "Now, maybe," he said. "It's not something I ever noticed before."

"Now—you mean, since you lost your sight?"

"Yes," he said bitterly, "that's exactly what I mean."

"How did it happen?" I asked. Maybe he decided my tone was curious, rather than rude, because he didn't seem offended, though he finished another mouthful of food before he answered.

"I was blinded," he said, "by a thunderbolt from the god's hand."

My eyes opened wide, because *that* was terribly dramatic. "The god was angry at you? What had you done?"

He shook his head, chewing again. For someone who claimed to have no appetite, he was tearing through dinner at a rapid clip. "Not angry. There was a prayer for lightning, and he responded with lightning." The angel took a drink from his water glass. "And destroyed me."

My brows drew down. That was a pretty sketchy story. "Were you the one praying for lightning?"

He shook his head, his expression bleak. He couldn't see *now*, but it was clear he was watching some internal vision. "A boy. I was teaching him some of the elemental prayers. How to beg Jovah for rain, how to ask him to stop the rain. How to pray for thunderbolts."

I'd never given it any thought, but the entire sky must light up with a dazzling display whenever those particular songs are being taught. "I'm surprised the whole lot of you aren't blind by now," I remarked, "with prayers like that on the loose."

The angel shook his head again. "We know the risks, and we contain them," he said. "We know never to sing the whole melodies all the way through. We teach the first half of the prayer, then we work on different songs, then we go back to the plea for lightning. Everyone is always very careful."

"Then what happened?"

"Aaron was young. And confident and careless and curious. Maybe he didn't believe something as simple as a song could call something as terrible as a thunderbolt. Maybe he was showing off. I don't know. But he didn't end the song where he was supposed to. When I realized he was still singing, I ordered him to stop, but he wouldn't. We were in a small building in Cedar Hills—there were twenty students in the room. I started shouting at all of them to get out, get out, and then I ran back to Aaron, to wrestle him to the ground, to *make* him stop." The angel shrugged. "But the prayer was complete. The lightning bolt came. The building was demolished."

"And you were blinded," I finished. "Did you get injured as well?"

He nodded. "I have burns across my back and one down the side of my ribs. Scars now, but bad ones at the time."

"What about Aaron?" I asked. "Was he blinded, too?"

The angel was silent.

"Dead, then," I said with a sigh. "Well, there was a terrible lesson."

The angel laid down his fork. "The world is full of terrible lessons," he said.

I could hardly argue with that. "When did it happen?"

"Two years ago."

"And you've been here that whole time?"

He shook his head. "No. I stayed in Cedar Hills—oh, six months. It took that long to heal, to learn how to—" He shook his head again. *How to navigate the world as a blind man.* "But I found it too painful to be around other angels. So I have moved from place to place, looking for peace."

I glanced around the room, full of shadows and regret. "And found it *here?*"

He gave a small bark of laughter. "Hardly. This is just a stop. A quiet place where no one will bother me while I try to think of what to do next."

"Well, sitting here in solitude all day, doing nothing except thinking about the past, seems like the worst possible way to find peace," I said.

"You don't know anything about it," he snapped.

"Do you think you're the only one who's ever had grief in his life?" I demanded. "Pick five people at random on any street in Samaria, and you'll find that they've suffered at least as much as you have. And most of *them* are getting on with their lives, not sitting in some dark room and moping."

While he had told his story—and I had listened with a certain sympathy—he had seemed to forget how irritating I was, but he was remembering pretty fast now. He came to his feet in one swift movement, and his wings swept behind him with a kind of grandeur.

"I appreciate your insights," he said in an acid voice. "Some other day, perhaps, we can discuss the tragedies *you* have survived." He gestured toward the door; I was interested to note that he knew precisely where it was. That unwary step that had caused him to trip on the roof must have been a rarity. "But I'm tired. Please take *all* the trays with you as you go."

Just to annoy him, I stacked the dishes as noisily as possible. He'd left half his breakfast untouched, but he'd done a good job on the dinner; maybe a little argument was what he needed to stimulate his appetite. Pausing in the doorway, I said, "I'll be back tomorrow night at about this time. Late. If you get hungry before then, can you make your way downstairs?"

"Yes," he said shortly. Unsaid went the rest of the sentence. *But I don't expect to be hungry. I'm never hungry. I'm too sad to eat.*

"Then I'll see you tomorrow."

I paused long enough to give him time to say *I'd rather starve to death than spend another minute talking to you.* But he didn't. He merely stood there, obviously waiting for me to go. I was sure that, no matter how quietly I moved, he would be able to tell when I had left the room.

Alma was sleeping when I checked on her, which made me realize she must be in even worse shape than I'd thought. Otherwise, she would have managed to stay awake long enough to give me a furious scold for spending so long in the angel's room. There were medicinal herbs in the school's infirmary; I would have to bring her some tomorrow night when I returned to take care of the angel.

When I returned to take care of the angel.

My plan had been to trick my way into his presence so I could prove to myself I had no reason to fear him. Instead it seemed I would be bringing him meals and employing edgy banter to prod him out of his melancholy. The situation was so preposterous that, if I hadn't been worried about waking Alma, I would have laughed out loud. Instead, I washed the dishes as quietly as I could and made sure the fire in the oven was out before I finally left the house for the night.

I slept badly—so busy reviewing my conversation with the angel that I kept fending off sleep—and spent the next day sleepwalking through my chores. I managed a quick unobserved visit to the infirmary, where I secured a container of manna-root salve and a roll of bandages so I could rewrap Alma's ankle. Finally I joined the others in the kitchen as they began cleaning up after the evening meal and scrubbed at the pots as I waited impatiently for all of them to go to bed.

Again, it was close to midnight before I could slip outside and hurry up the hill to the Great House. Alma was waiting for me, seated at a kitchen worktable and facing the door. She was a determined one, I gave her credit for that, for she'd found a way to move around the kitchen well enough to put together a simple meal. There was bread cooling on the table and a covered pan warming on the stove.

"How's your ankle today?" I asked as I stepped inside.

She made a face. "Hurts even worse than yesterday, though I wouldn't have thought it possible."

"Let me look at it before I go upstairs," I said. "I brought some salve and better bandages."

I could tell she didn't like it, but she allowed me to examine her injury again. No wonder she was in so much pain. The great purple bruise had spread down toward her toes and up toward her knee, acquiring some interesting tints of red and yellow. But I didn't think there was a broken bone. I turned it gently and prodded it in the likely spots, and she didn't cry out.

"It's going to be a while before you can put any weight on this," I said. "But maybe the manna root will make you feel better."

It did, almost instantly, as it usually does. I've always thought that manna was the best of the god's tangible gifts. She looked both relieved and grateful as the salve went to work, and I saw her surreptitiously flexing her toes. Hoping that the absence of pain was the same thing as healing. Of course, that's never true, no matter how you're hurting.

"How was the angel when you saw him last night?" she asked.

"Short-tempered and feeling sorry for himself" was my prompt reply.

That widened her green eyes, then narrowed them in consternation. "You talked to him? I told you not to bother him."

I shrugged. "I had to explain who I was. And then we exchanged a few more words. He struck me as a very bitter man."

"Anyone might be, under the same circumstances," she said, but she didn't sound convinced. I was willing to bet that Alma had met her share of adversities and refused to buckle under any of them.

"Maybe," I said. I made a neat pile of the salve and bandages, then stood up and began gathering dinner items. "I'm impressed that you were able to cook a meal," I said, peeking under the lid of the pan. It appeared to be dried meat made tender again by baking in juice and onions, and it smelled delicious.

"It took me the entire day to assemble everything," she said. "And I made the easiest meal I could think of."

"Well, he certainly liked what you cooked yesterday," I said, filling up a plate and adding a good chunk of the bread. "He ate it all."

"He did?" She sounded pleased. "Usually I bring back half of what I take him."

I had picked up the tray, but now I paused with a couple more questions. "How long has he been here?" The angel had not answered when I asked him the same question.

"Six or seven weeks."

"And how does he occupy his time?"

"The headmistress usually spends part of the evening with him, but I don't know what they talk about. And sometimes when he's alone, I hear music."

"Singing?"

"Never. Some kind of stringed instrument, but I don't know what."

"And other than that, he just sits up in that room by himself all day, doing nothing? Sweet Jovah singing, it's a wonder he hasn't thrown himself off the roof by now."

She frowned. "I'm sure he has plenty to occupy his thoughts," she said stiffly.

"*Nobody's* thoughts are that interesting," I said and headed toward the door. Just on the other side of it, I turned back. "What's his name?"

Alma was still frowning. "You may address him as angelo, if you need to speak to him at all."

"Of course," I said smoothly, though I had never used the honorific in any of my infrequent conversations with angels, and I wasn't about to start now. "But what's his name? Just so I know it."

"Corban," she said.

"Very well," I said. "I'll go take Corban his dinner."

CHAPTER 3

L ike Alma, the angel was waiting for me, or so it seemed: He had
turned his chair so it faced the door, and his whole posture was
alert. Even his wings were less dispirited, arching behind his back
as if they had been plumped and groomed. It was obvious he had
heard me climbing the steps and could tell by the cadence of my
footfall exactly when I crossed into the room.

"I'm back. Moriah," I said. "Are you hungry tonight?"

"A little," he said.

"You should try to eat everything, since it cost Alma some effort
to make it for you," I said. "Her ankle is still very painful."

"It smells quite good," he said, shifting his body to track me as I
crossed the room. Still dark and gloomy up here. I would have to
bring up multiple lamps and leave them in strategic spots to brighten
the place up.

"I'll tell her you said so. Here. I've set everything out."

Corban came to his feet and crossed the room, but hesitated before
he sat down. "Will you dine with me?" he asked abruptly. "It feels
very odd to eat while someone watches me."

I was starving, and I'd actually put more food on the plate than it seemed likely he'd finish, with the thought that I could sneak a few bites. I laughed.

"I will," I said, "if you don't mind me eating with my fingers."

He offered a smile—small and twisted, but the first one I'd seen on his face. "I doubt I'll notice."

We took our places on opposite sides of the small table, the plate between us. I had moved the lamp over, as well, and now I studied him by its flickering light. He was a handsome man, or he would be, if his face wasn't so closed and woeful. His features were fine, almost delicate, his cheekbones prominent enough to throw their own shadows. His eyebrows were so feathery they might have been painted on with a light hand, and again, he had found the energy to shave himself. He also appeared to have combed his hair. At any rate, it was not quite the mess it had been the day before.

His eyes were a blank and liquid black that seemed to be swirled with streaks of white. But that might just have been the reflections of the flames dancing on the wick.

"It's impossible to tell just by looking," I said.

He looked startled and then displeased. "What is?" he said, though he clearly knew what I meant.

"Your eyes. They don't look burned. And there's no scarring on your face."

"Jovah spared me disfigurement," he said sardonically. "One of his many kindnesses."

"What about pain?" I said.

"Very little now. At the beginning, when the burns were fresh— that was bad."

I finished up a mouthful of food and greedily took another. Even working with dried meat and limited materials, Alma was a good cook. "So you lost your sight, and you have some scars," I said, when I'd swallowed another bite. "Were you harmed in any other way?"

"Those seem to be sufficient evils."

"So your wings weren't injured. You can still fly."

His expression showed how stupid he thought me, or how cruel.

The wings in question fluttered forward a bit, then back, reminding me of nothing so much as the lashing tale of an unhappy cat. "I can't *see*. Of course I can't fly."

I glanced at him in surprise. "Really? You haven't tried it since you were blinded? You might need one of your angel friends to go aloft with you, talk you through it, but I'd think you could fly if someone acted as your guide."

Corban was silent a moment, his face creased with displeasure. At first I thought he was annoyed at me again, but then I realized he was angry at an old memory. "I did try flying with a guide—once—shortly after the accident," he said at last. "But it was terrifying. I had no sense of direction—I don't just mean north and south, I mean up and down. Once I was high enough, it was hard to tell where the ground might be below me. When the wind blew, even a little, I lost my bearings. It was like being—" He seemed to search for words. "Like being caught in a rockslide when a mountain is falling. I was tumbled in all directions. I couldn't see, I was filled with panic."

"Where was your friend?"

"Nearby, watching me flail, thinking if he remained silent I would be forced to figure out my circumstances, which would help me gain confidence. He did come to my aid when it seemed likely I would crash, and we both walked away from the episode shaken. We have only spoken once or twice since."

"Well, obviously *he* was the wrong one to try that with," I said. "And maybe it was too soon."

"I don't think the fear will leave me no matter how long I wait."

I shook my head. I couldn't seem to break the habit, even though he couldn't see me. "No, I mean—you seem to have keen senses of smell and hearing, and maybe those developed after your accident," I said. "Maybe your other senses have grown more acute as well. Maybe you have a better sense of direction. You seem to walk around the room well enough without running into furniture. Maybe you wouldn't fly into trees, or come up on the ground too fast when you tried to land."

I had surprised him; the expression on his face was considering. "Maybe," he said.

"So you should try to fly again."

A ghost of a smile crossed his lips. "We seem to be missing an essential element," he said. "An angel who can fly beside me and help me find my way."

"Couldn't you invite one of your old friends to visit you here?"

"I could, but I can't think of one I would trust enough to guide me in a flight."

"Why do you consider them your friends, then?"

The question seemed to catch him off guard. "They are—they were—people with whom I shared certain experiences," he said. "Certain attitudes. A position in life. We were all alike. None of us were ever comfortable with—" He struggled to express it. "Weakness. In others. We didn't have weaknesses of our own."

Everything he said just reminded me how much I had disliked all the angels I had ever met. "You're all arrogant bastards who think you rule the world," I said. "You don't have compassion for others because you never needed it for yourselves."

He looked both affronted and rueful. "That's not exactly—but to some extent—perhaps," he said.

"So has adversity made you kinder, do you think?" I asked.

He looked like he'd never thought about that, either. "I don't know," he said stiffly. "In the past two years, I haven't been in many situations where I was asked for kindness."

"No, you've spent all your time sitting here, brooding in the dark."

"Well, it seems pointless to brood in the light," he shot back.

I threw my hands in the air. "What do you *do* all day?" I demanded. "Surely you must do something besides sit here in the dark and feel miserable."

I had annoyed him again, but I wasn't sure that was a bad thing. His face took on more color, his gestures were livelier, when he was arguing with me. That couldn't fail but amuse me somewhat. Never before had my abrasive personality looked to have such a beneficial effect on someone. *Particularly* an angel.

"Some of the time I play music," he said. He gestured to the instrument against the wall. *So he knows where he is and where everything is placed inside this room,* I thought. "Some of the time I write it."

"You're able to put the notes down on paper?"

"I misspoke," he said deliberately. "I compose the music. I hear it in my head, and I practice it on the cello. I also have a flute, though I'm not as adept with it."

"Good. I was afraid you did nothing but mope. I'm glad you've found a distraction."

"Yes, since your own capacity for compassion makes you sympathetic to *all* Samaria's creatures."

It was so unexpected that I laughed out loud. "I have plenty of compassion for people who deserve it," I assured him. "I just don't happen to feel sorry for you."

"I must assume that the individuals you pity are truly wretched."

"You're right," I said cheerfully. "I think most people give up too easily, when—if they showed a little determination—they could improve their circumstances. I'm not saying it's easy. But you almost always end up somewhere better than you started."

"Which makes me—for the first time, I might add—curious about *your* life."

I laughed again, but came to my feet and started gathering the dishes. Every speck of food was gone. I'd eaten some of the meal, but honestly, he'd beaten me to most of it. Sparring with me seemed to be good for his appetite.

"And it's an interesting tale, but there's no time to tell it," I said. "I have to get back to the kitchen and finish my shift."

Corban came to his feet, too, his attitude suggesting he was listening to me arrange the plates and silver. "What do you look like?" he asked abruptly.

"I'm beautiful" was my immediate reply. "My hair is black as night and my eyes are so blue people can see their color from across the room. And I'm tall. And voluptuous," I added for good measure.

His expression was thoughtful; he was assessing my words. "Not tall," he decided. "Maybe——" He held his hand out so it was about level with his chin. "This height."

He had gauged it exactly. "Very good," I said dryly.

"So I suppose the rest of it is a lie as well."

"I can't see that it matters what I look like."

He looked interested. "Are you that hideous?"

"No!" Now I was the irritated one; how had *that* happened? "I'm ordinary. My hair is that dirty brown color that so many people have. My eyes are brown, too. My face is too round. I weigh a little more than I'd like. But I do have a good figure," I couldn't resist tacking on at the end. If he was picturing me from my description, he may as well include the good bits.

"How old are you?"

Old enough to know better than to even remotely consider flirting with an angel. "I'll be thirty-two a couple weeks after the Gloria. How old are *you*?"

It was meant for impudence, but he didn't seem to mind. "Thirty-five. Or a hundred and thirty-five, depending on the day."

That made me laugh. "I don't think I'm ever older than seventy, even during my worst weeks. But sometimes I feel sixteen, so I suppose it evens out."

"How did you end up at the Gabriel School?"

I was done gathering the dishes, and I was certainly done with this conversation. "That's part of the story that's too long to tell," I replied, edging for the door. "I'll be late with my chores if I'm gone much longer."

"Will you be back tomorrow?"

I quashed the desire to say *Do you want me back?* Stupid, to try to make a sad and heartsick angel confess some need for me. Who was the pathetic one now? I made my answer casual to cover up my self-disgust. "As long as Alma's unable to climb steps, I suppose I'll be back," I said. "And since I don't think she'll miraculously heal overnight—yes, I'll be here tomorrow."

He didn't say, *Good*. He didn't say *I'll look forward to talking to you again*. He just said, "Very well," and turned away from me before I was even out the door.

The next day was much the same, except I got to bed earlier, slept better, and rose later. I didn't mind nocturnal hours, but if I was going to fill them with twice the usual activity, I needed to husband my energy. Once again, I made hasty work of my most important chores, then climbed clandestinely to the Great House and spent a little time with Alma. Her ankle was still a swollen purple mess, but the salve had greatly reduced her pain, and she thanked me three times for bringing it.

Tonight's meal smelled just as appetizing, but it made me think. "Do you have enough food on hand to continue like this?" I asked. Usually Alma or the footman came down to the school once or twice a week to take supplies from our storerooms. These were supplemented every week by deliveries from Telford, including a few live pigs and chickens that Deborah and Elon slaughtered and dressed.

"For another week, I do," she said. "And I don't have to worry about water—it's piped into the house and drains into an underground line."

I'd noticed that no one had asked me to run a pump or empty chamber pots, for which I was deeply grateful. We had a good plumbing system at the school, so I'd gotten out of the habit of thinking about how precious water was when it wasn't readily available.

"I don't think I can sneak bags of potatoes and whole chickens up here," I said thoughtfully. "If the headmistress isn't back soon, you might have to let Deborah know you need help."

She nodded. "I already realized that. I can't walk down the hill yet, but I think I can wave from the porch and catch someone's attention."

"Good. I'll be on the lookout in case no one else notices."

I finished assembling the tray, and a few minutes later I was carrying it into Corban's room. "Here's your dinner," I said.

But I was speaking to an empty room.

I looked around harder, just in case he was lurking in a corner, but he was nowhere to be seen. It was late, of course; maybe he had already gone to bed. Or was he simply avoiding me, less entertained by my needling conversation than I had supposed?

But almost immediately I registered the temperature of the room, far chillier than it had been on my earlier visits. I set down the tray and followed the swirls of cold air to the trapdoor above the spiral metal staircase that I assumed led to the roof.

He knew I was coming. He had left the trapdoor open. He must expect me to follow him. I grasped the railing and ran up the curving flight of stairs, into the star-cooled night.

Corban was standing in the far corner, posed as if he were gazing out at the ground below. A quick glance showed me that the whole roof was hemmed in with a half wall, just high enough for a medium-sized person to lean an elbow on. A few knobby pipes poked up from below, and chimneys on two sides added interest to the architecture. Otherwise it was a plain rectangular space, flat as a floor, with little to recommend the view.

By the light of the full moon, I could pick out the curls in Corban's hair and the interlaced quills of his wings. He was facing away from me, and I had an excellent view of the way his wings sprang from his back to make their distinctive bell shape. I could see his hands braced against the half wall. His fingers were balled into fists; there was tension in the line of his shoulders.

I was certain he had heard my arrival, and I was too contrary to speak first. So we waited a few moments in silence while I studied the silhouette of his body and he contemplated some thought too private to share.

When he did speak, he sounded irritated already. "You don't like to make things easy for people, do you?"

That made me grin. "Honestly, I don't," I said.

He pivoted, his wings making a lovely, majestic sweep. "You don't even say hello. You don't even let me know you're here."

"You knew I was here."

"That's not the point."

"You think I'm rude?"

"I think you're—" He searched for the right words. "Deliberately provoking."

I grinned. "That's about as accurate a description as I've heard."

"My question would be, why? Is it your goal to make people dislike you?"

"Do you dislike me?" I responded.

His brows twitched together. "I was talking about other people."

"I can be accommodating when I feel like it," I said. "I can get along with people if I want to."

"So you reserve this provoking behavior for *me*."

"Not just you. I was very insubordinate with the housekeeper at my last job, for instance."

"Ah. So you like to challenge authority—or people who believe their station in life puts them above you."

"Yes, but you can see that I only harm myself by such behavior. I lost that position a couple of months ago. *And* the one before it."

"Yet you don't try to be more submissive. More conformable."

"There is a certain contrariness at the base of my personality," I allowed. "It is so hard for me to act the way people expect me to act, even if it's in my own best interests."

"How, I wonder, would someone come by such a trait?"

Oh, there was a story it would take half the night to tell. "I was born with it, I believe," I said lightly.

"But I don't," he said.

I was lost. "Don't what? Don't believe me?"

"Dislike you," he said. "Most of the time."

"I can try harder to be annoying," I offered.

"I'll let you know if that becomes necessary."

It was peculiar to have an angel tell me he didn't dislike me—though that didn't mean he *liked* me, and, at any rate, it scarcely mattered, since I doubted my future held many more intimate night-time conferences with this one. Because I didn't know how to answer him, I changed the subject. "So why are you out here on the roof?"

"I was thinking about something you said."

"Really? What's that?" I rubbed my arms. It was probably ten degrees above freezing and I'd only worn a light jacket since I hadn't expected to be outside any longer than it took to climb the hill.

"Flying."

"*Really?* You think you might be ready to attempt it again? You think you can sense the buildings and the trees—"

"Not that, not yet," he interrupted. "I don't even know if my wings can support my weight."

"Well, we aren't very far from the ground up here," I said. "Three stories. You could jump off the roof and just try to glide down. You'd be careful because you know the ground isn't very far away."

"That's a possibility," he said gravely. "But I want to try some-thing else first. Coming back to the roof."

"That seems harder," I commented.

"Yes," he replied. "A better test."

"And you're not worried about losing your bearings?"

"You'll have to help me, of course. You'll have to call out to me. I would not get so far from the house I would lose the sound of your voice."

I was washed with a sense of pleasure so irrational that I imme-diately tried to destroy it. "You trust me to do that? What if I decide to remain silent, just to confuse you?"

I had thought to baffle him or enrage him or make him so uneasy that he instantly abandoned his plan. But he was getting as good a measure of my personality as I was of his. "In that case," he replied, "I will come awkwardly to ground—perhaps injure myself—attempt to make my way safely back to the house without your help—and then refuse to see you again. Which would cause you to lose what I have come to believe is your very real pleasure in visiting with me for however long this arrangement lasts."

I was silent for a beat. "That was good," I said. "You thought this through before I even arrived tonight, didn't you?"

He was smiling—a real smile, pleased with himself, a little smug, but I had to admit I liked it. "I did," he said. He had started pacing slowly around the perimeter of the roof, as if trying to get an exact feel for its dimensions. I kept turning slightly to keep him in my sight. "I don't think you would betray me in such a fashion. If I ask for your help, and you promise it, I don't think you'll renege."

Oh, yes, a very good measure of my personality. "What do you want me to do?" I asked.

"Stand in the middle of the roof. Where there are no pipes or poles that will trip me up when I land. They are too small for me to sense, and they have brought me down more than once before this. I will go aloft—I will circle—and then I will come down to the sound of your voice."

"How far out will you be able to go and still hear me?"

He cocked his head, as if listening. "It's a still night," he said. "Sound should carry some distance. When your voice grows faint, I'll circle back."

"So you want me to stand here the whole time you're in the sky, shouting out nonsense like an idiot?"

"That shouldn't be too hard for you," he said.

Before I could respond with indignation, he laid a hand on the half wall and vaulted up to a crouch. I was suddenly flooded with a very real fear. "Corban—" I began, but I couldn't think what to say. *Be careful.* As if this was an enterprise where caution was possible. *Are you sure you're ready?* As if I hadn't been the one pushing him to try this very feat. *Good luck.* As if I was afraid he'd fall. . . .

He straightened in one quick, graceful motion, his wings spread to help him keep his balance. For a moment he stood there motionless, limned against the moonlight, a distinctive shape with such primeval power that I felt my breath catch in my throat.

And then the great wings spiked downward, sending a current of wind billowing over the roof, and Corban was airborne.

My fear mutated to outright terror as he seemed to list and stutter against the faint breeze. I could see his wings beating frantically, his arms chopping through the air as if he was fighting to realign his weight. He made one sloppy circle overhead, dipping dangerously close to the corner of the house, before he was able to gain a little altitude. I saw his body straighten out, his arms stop thrashing—and then it was as if he had it. He remembered the trick. He was flying.

He widened his arc, climbing upward at the same time. From this odd vantage point, directly underneath him at intermittent points, I could see the laboring of his wings, feel the faintest draft from his passage. It was so impossible and yet so beautiful, the sight of an angel in flight. I felt an awe, a sense of wonder, as if the god had stepped down and rested his hand upon my shoulder.

Corban's range expanded to an even greater distance. I had the impression that he had grown giddy with motion and, like a drunk man, lost all fear or capability for rational behavior. "Corban, not so far!" I called out, remembering for the first time that I had a responsibility in this little drama. "Corban, can you still hear me?"

For an answer, he canted his body over so that his wings were almost perpendicular to the ground and made a tight spiral back in my direction. "Corban!" I shouted. "Can you still hear me?"

He passed over my head and waved and kept flying.

I twisted to watch his progress and continued to call his name out at regular intervals, adding the occasional *That's too far* and *Come back this way now*. It's hard to know what words to employ when you're acting as a human foghorn. The part of my brain that wasn't taken up by fear was swamped with embarrassment at being in such a ridiculous position, so I started singing a children's lullaby at the top of my lungs. He might mock me for my untrained voice, but at least I didn't have to think about the lyrics.

For all his seeming rashness, it was clear Corban truly was listening to me. He strayed farther than I liked, but almost immediately came back, as if he had discovered the outer border beyond which my voice would not carry. I wasn't sure I could have heard *him* from the same distance, but I knew his ears were sharper than mine.

The wind picked up force and I was terrified that it would blow him off course, but after a shaky moment, he seemed to remember how to ride the draft. *So all I need to worry about is whether I'm going to freeze to death,* I thought, rubbing my arms again and stamping my feet for warmth. I got tired of the lullaby and switched to a tavern ditty. I wondered if he could catch the words, or only the snatched phrases of my melody. I wondered how long he planned to stay out on his first flight in two years. I wondered if he kept circling the house because he was afraid to try to land.

Almost as soon as I had the thought, I realized that he was flying in a narrower and narrower curve, dropping downward as he closed the distance. I abandoned music and began shouting directions. "Corban! This way! You're about twenty yards up now and twenty yards out. All right—now you're just above the wall, you need to come in closer. That's right—and a little lower—"

He adjusted some angle of his feathers and suddenly went into a whole different mode of travel, hovering instead of flying. His body swung from a horizontal to a vertical position, his legs pointed down as if he were feeling for the surface with his toes. His wings, which had been outstretched and quiescent as he glided, were now beating the air again with great energy, holding him in place just a few feet above the roof. I was so close to him I was buffeted by every stroke; my hair whipped around my face.

"Almost there—drop down a few more inches—"

He put his hands out, as if reaching for me, and I unthinkingly grabbed them. Many things happened at once. His feet hit the roof hard and he stumbled into me, clutching my shoulders for support. His wings lashed around us both, helping *his* balance, maybe, but adding to my clumsiness and confusion. For a moment, the world was a chaotic ball of motion and feathers and unexpected heat as our bodies crushed together and we both staggered and tried not to fall over.

And then the angel came to rest with his arms around me and his wings draped over my shoulders and the moon ladling silver over us both. I could feel his rapid heartbeat, the heavy suck and release of breath as he gasped for air, but for a moment what astonished me most was the sheer radiant warmth of his body. I knew, but I had forgotten, that angels' blood ran at a higher temperature than a mortal's, to keep them warm when they flew at high altitudes. I was so cold that I wanted to burrow in, practically dig for shelter against his skin.

Instead I waited another heartbeat, until I was steady on my own feet, and then stepped back just enough to free myself from his arms. His wings still lingered on my shoulder blades, the feathers tickling my throat.

"You did it!" I exclaimed. "Were you scared? Are you excited? What did it feel like?"

"Terrifying. Exhilarating. I thought I would fall—there at the beginning—I couldn't get the height, I thought I would crash down, but I *didn't*. I caught the updraft, and then I remembered, I remembered all of it, as if it had only been a day since the last time I flew—"

"You went pretty far," I said in an encouraging voice. "Maybe a hundred yards out and almost as far up. Could you tell how much distance you were covering?"

"No, but I think with practice I could," he said. "Or maybe I could devise some kind of numerical system—flying at a steady rate for a count of five hundred would mean I had covered a certain set mileage—"

"That sounds like you want to keep trying," I said.

"Yes! There are a lot of things I could experiment with. Pressure, for instance. The air feels different when you reach a certain altitude, so if I make careful assessments of how it feels at different levels, I'll be able to tell how high I am."

I couldn't help laughing. "That's ambitious for someone who hasn't even been aloft for almost two years!"

He grinned. "I know—I must start slowly and build up my strength and gauge how much I really can do. But—I can't describe to you—just the sensation of being in flight—I have missed it so much." He came closer and his voice took a deeper tone. "And I have you to thank for giving me the courage to fly again."

Oh, no, no, no. I could not have gratitude and earnestness from an angel. I was not used to that from *anybody*. "Think how relieved I am that this night went so well," I told him. "If you'd come crashing to the ground and snapped one of your wings—well, that would have been my fault."

"I wouldn't have blamed you," he said, still in that serious manner.

"Are you joking? You'd never have *stopped* blaming me!" I exclaimed. "You'd have spent the rest of your life in some attic, sitting in the dark and cursing my name, hating me even more than that angel who wouldn't help you fly when you first lost your sight."

He took just enough affront to step back a pace; the last feathers of his wing slipped silkily from my shoulder, leaving me even colder than before. "But unlike that old friend, *you* were exceptionally helpful," he said, and his voice had the slightest edge. "I had counted on you to keep calling, but I hadn't expected songs. And such songs! 'The Shy Angel-Seeker of Sweet Semorrah'? The last time I heard *that* piece sung, I was keeping very questionable company."

"You're keeping questionable company now. You just didn't realize it before."

"Oh, I realized it," he replied. "I just haven't had much latitude in my choice of companions."

I snorted in amusement. "Well, I don't mind if you make fun of my song selection," I said. "Just don't make fun of my voice. You can't expect a mortal to sound like an angel."

He looked surprised. "In fact, I was impressed with the quality of your voice," he said. "Am I wrong, or are you an angel's daughter?"

And then I did the stupidest thing. Instead of answering, I caught my breath, as if he had offered me the gravest insult, then turned around and practically ran for the stairwell. I had closed the trapdoor, not wanting the blind angel to put a foot wrong as he tried to land, and now my frozen hands couldn't pry it up fast enough. With a pouncing motion and a swirl of feathers, Corban caught my arm and hauled me to my feet before I could escape.

"Moriah—I'm sorry—I didn't mean to offend you," he said.

"I'm not offended," I grated out through chattering teeth. I tried to jerk free but his hand tightened automatically. High body heat and exceptional strength—oh, angels had far more than their share of advantages. "I'm tired of the conversation."

"You're cold," he said in a wondering voice, suddenly registering the temperature of my skin. He lifted his free hand to wrap around my other arm. "Why didn't you say so before?"

"Well, first, I was watching you fly. Then I was hearing you talk about how much fun it was to fly. Then I was arguing with you. So there hasn't been time."

Unexpectedly, he released me and then drew me against his chest once more. His wings overlapped behind me, a plush cocoon. "We need to get you warmed up."

"We could do that inside," I suggested. It was hard to make that sound convincing when I was snuggled up against him, luxuriating in the heat of his body.

"In a minute," he said. "Why don't you like to talk about the fact that you're an angel's child?"

I had braced myself for the question, and this time I had my armor on. "Why might that be?" I said in a scathing voice. "Oh, maybe because my mother was an angel-seeker. *That's* not something to be proud of. Maybe because I was one of the hundreds of children abandoned every year by women who don't want to be burdened with the care of a mortal child. Maybe because I don't want your pity or your disdain."

He was silent a moment. "And how did you come to be at the Gabriel School?" he asked finally.

I laughed and tugged myself free. Jovah's bones, but it was cold up here once a person stepped outside the protection of an angel's wings. "Only the latest stop in a highly adventurous life," I said. "I'm going downstairs. Your dinner's probably cold by now, but I'd think you'd have built up an appetite."

This time the recalcitrant door opened without a hitch, and I was quickly down the curving staircase into the blessed warmth of the attic. Corban, who had clearly learned to navigate the steps without being able to see them, was right behind me.

"Are you going to stay and eat with me?" he asked.

"No. I've been gone too long as it is."

"Are you coming back tomorrow?"

I wanted to and I didn't want to, and the fact that I wanted to *really* made me not want to. But I hated the idea that someone else might come to the Great House and discover the blind angel. "I suppose," I said ungraciously. "Someone has to look after you."

"Can you come back earlier or stay longer? The more I fly, the more I can build up my strength."

"I don't think so," I said. "I'm just sneaking over here now."

"Sneaking? Why?" he asked.

"Because no one knows there's an injured angel hiding in the Great House," I said tartly. "I thought that was on *your* command. We've all been warned away. People think the place is haunted, so everyone's afraid of the house anyway."

"So why did *you* start coming over?"

I let out my breath on a gusty sigh and offered a partial truth. "Because I'm the kind of person who always goes where I'm not allowed," I said. "I thought you'd have figured that out by now."

He was smiling slightly. "I have. I just wanted to hear you say it."

I made an infuriated sound at the back of my throat. If I was as irksome to others as the angel was to me, I finally understood why some people despised me. "So, yes, I suppose I'll be back," I said as I made my way toward the door.

"And we can practice flying again?" he said.

He sounded so excited, so hopeful, that I couldn't bear to give an equivocal reply. "Yes," I said. "You can practice flying again."

CHAPTER 4

When I entered the kitchen the next evening to help clean up after dinner, everyone fell silent to stare at me. I hid my instinctive apprehension behind a curious expression. "What's wrong?" I asked.

"The housekeeper at the Great House wants to see you," Deborah said, her eyes speculative.

I relaxed a little. Alma must have found a way to signal for help. "She does? Why?"

"She says she knows you," Elon piped up. "You worked together at some shop in Luminaux. She spotted you in the yard the other day and she recognized you."

"Alma's *here*?" I exclaimed. She had made it very easy for me to follow her cues. "I didn't know that! I lost track of her a long time ago."

Deborah said, "She asked if I could spare you for the next few days, since she's had an accident and can't move around too well."

"Oh, no! What happened?"

"Fell and twisted her ankle," Elon said. "And she's all alone in the house, what with the headmistress being gone."

"She hobbled out to the porch and waved a red cloth till someone noticed her," Judith added.

"Everyone was afraid to go up and see what was wrong, of course," Rhesa said. "I mean—the house is haunted! But we sent one of the boys, and she asked for you."

"She wants you to come up every evening and help her make her dinner and keep the house tidy," Deborah said. "You'll have to stay a few hours, I suppose, but you won't need to spend the night."

The words froze me to the spot. Alma probably didn't need me for more than half an hour a day; in fact, as long as she had food in the house, she probably didn't need me at all. Alma was not the one who had requested my presence. . . .

"No, I'd hate to spend the night there," I agreed. "The place is so—spooky." I managed a convincing shiver.

Judith spoke up, her voice deceptively mild. "I suppose someone will have to take over your shift in the kitchen at night," she said. "I don't see how you can do it all."

"Yes, Rhesa will have to go back to night duty for the time being," Deborah agreed.

Judith grinned at me behind Deborah's back—we both hated Rhesa—and Rhesa started whining. "But I *hate* the overnight shift! Isn't it somebody else's turn?"

"Stop complaining!" Deborah said briskly. "It's just for a few days, I'm sure."

I was less sure, but I wasn't about to say so. I was both unnerved and a little excited to think that Corban had gone to such effort to secure my help on a protracted basis. Of course, he really had no one else to ask. It wasn't particularly a compliment to *me* that I was the only one he knew in the entire Gabriel School.

"When should I go up to the Great House? Now? It's so late already."

"She said you should come no matter what time it was, so just head on over."

"It's not fair," Rhesa muttered under her breath, but Deborah gave her a minatory look, and she subsided.

No, it's not fair, I wanted to tell her. *Angels are selfish and high-handed. They don't care who else is inconvenienced as long as their own needs are met. You can't gainsay them, so your only choices are to do what they want or to run away.*

But I found that I didn't want to run away from this particular angel.

Now that I didn't have to creep to the Great House unobserved, I was able to bring fresh supplies to Alma when I climbed up to the house a few minutes later. She was sitting in the kitchen, sipping tea, and I complimented her on her ruse as I put potatoes in the pantry and a crock of butter on the table.

"So what's the name of this place we both worked in Luminaux?" I said. "In case anyone asks me."

"I actually managed a dress shop there, so we might as well claim that," she said. "Have you ever even been to Luminaux?"

I put my hands against my chest in a mock swoon. "The Blue City! The most wonderful place in all of Samaria, as far as I'm concerned." It was an artisans' town, full of musicians and potters and jewelers and painters, and I would live there again in a heartbeat. If I thought I'd be safe.

"So you've moved around a little," she said.

I nodded. "At various times, I've lived in Semorrah and Castelana and Velora. But I was in Monteverde longer than I was anywhere else."

I could tell that caught her attention—most mortal women who spend much time near the holds turn out to be angel-seekers—but she didn't ask any questions.

"Just so you know," she said, "it was the angelo who requested your assistance. I could have gotten along perfectly well on my own."

That made me grin, but I said, "So what did he do? Shout down the stairwell at you?"

She shook her head. She still looked a little unnerved. "He came downstairs, bringing the dinner dishes with him. That's the first time he's been down here since—maybe since he arrived. I was worried he'd bang his head on a door frame or snag one of his wings on a nail, but he managed very well."

"Yes, he's not nearly as helpless as he's let himself believe," I said.

I read agreement in her expression, but she couldn't bring herself to criticize an angel. "Anyway, he said he'd learned you were pulling double duty and he wanted that to stop—but he wanted *you* to keep bringing him his meals." She gave me a shrewd look. "He doesn't like strangers, but I suppose he's gotten used to you."

I suppose he likes your company. What exactly have you been doing to charm the angel out of his misery? "I guess I'd better take him his dinner, then," I said, loading up the tray.

Alma gestured. "I made enough for both of you. I think it makes him more cheerful if he has company while he eats."

Oh, her sharp eyes didn't miss a thing. But all I said was, "Glad to hear it. I'm hungry."

Corban was waiting for me when I made it to the top story—not sitting, as before, but on his feet, as if he had been pacing impatiently until I arrived. "Good, you're here," he said. "Did you remember to bring a coat? It's cold again tonight."

His eagerness made me laugh. "Yes, and a sweater underneath it," I said. "But if you're planning to be outside for a long time, could we eat first? I don't want to starve any more than I want to freeze."

He hesitated, then said, "All right," and moved to the central table. I could almost read the thought in his head. He didn't want to waste the time it would take to consume the meal, but he didn't want to seem indifferent to my needs; he was trying to be considerate of someone else. *Probably for the first time in his life*, I thought as I joined him at the table.

We ate quickly and were back on the roof within twenty minutes. The moon was just past full tonight, and the clouds were thicker; there was a little less light than the night before.

That didn't matter to Corban, of course. He strode straight for the wall on the northern corner and placed his hand on its rough surface. "Just like yesterday," he said and propelled himself up to pose for a moment on its narrow shelf. He shook out his wings as if to shake off water or dust, then pumped them twice.

And then he was flying.

Again, for the first moment or two, I was so enthralled by the sheer impossible gorgeousness of flight that I forgot my own role. I ran to the wall just to watch him swoop and caracole through the air. He didn't seem troubled by the previous night's shakiness; the launch was smooth, the arabesques confident. More quickly than he had the night before, he climbed upward and spiraled outward, and I was seized with fear that he would drift beyond the reach of my voice before I even remembered I was supposed to be singing.

So I drew a hasty breath and offered the first melody I could think of, which happened to be a Manadavvi ballad. I didn't even realize what it was until I was through the first verse, and then I was disgusted with myself. It was sure to elicit even more questions from him than the tavern song, if he recognized it. But maybe he wouldn't. I made myself finish all three verses, just to prove I would, and then picked something as different as I could think of. An Edori love song. Let him comment on my eclectic tastes. That was better than having him ask why I was familiar with Manadavvi customs.

Before the evening ended, I was thinking it was lucky I *did* know such a wide range of songs, because he stayed out more than an hour. I never entirely lost sight of him against the overcast sky, but more than once I was certain he had gone too high or ranged too far to be able to hear me. I guessed that the distance was deliberate. He wanted to prove to himself that he could slip the tether of my voice but still make it back to safety. I hoped he was right. I couldn't imagine what I would do if he disappeared in the night and I had no idea where he had come to ground.

But no such disaster occurred. Just as I was beginning to think my voice would give out completely, I saw his silhouette pass directly over the imperfect circle of the moon and then drop rapidly toward the ground. Too rapidly, it seemed to me—when he was within hailing distance, I abruptly stopped singing and started shouting.

"Corban, slow down! You're too close! You'll crash!" I heard him laugh right before he did something that caused his descent to slow dramatically. Now he was hovering a yard or two above the roof, and the night air was windy with the sweep and drag of his wings.

I took a deep breath. "All right. You're about five feet up. Come down *slowly*. I'm putting up my hands—reach out for me—just a little nearer—"

And *there*. His fingers closed around mine; his body was still so inclined toward flight that he lifted me to my toes, like a boat tugging against its mooring and almost pulling it loose from the pier. Then all at once his feet were solidly on the roof and the sudden cessation of motion caused us to stagger, almost into each other's arms. There was a hectic moment of feathers and body heat and dizziness, and then we both straightened and I stepped away. He let go of my hands.

"That was even better than last night!" he exclaimed. "I *remembered* things—how to bank into a turn, how to slip into a downdraft. It all seems so—so effortless. I can't believe I was afraid before."

I couldn't help laughing. He hardly seemed like the same person I had met a few nights earlier. Maybe it was the moonlight, so enchanted by the sculpture of his wings that it could not resist gilding them with radiance, but he seemed to glow with energy or excitement or hope. Even his skin seemed to hold a faint light. By contrast, I seemed to be hidden in shadows. Even if Corban hadn't lost his sight, I doubted he would have been able to see me.

"Excellent," I said. "The more you practice, the more familiar it will become."

But some of his buoyancy faded as his face showed dissatisfaction. "Well, I can't learn much by flying in circles over the school," he said. "I have to go farther. I have to fly for longer periods."

"Maybe you need to establish routes that you can take from the house to specific destinations," I said. "Routes that have markers that let you know where you are."

He was listening closely. "Yes. For instance, when I fly about ten minutes in that direction"—he pointed straight north—"there's a distinct noise that I catch whenever the wind blows. It sounds like—clattering."

Oddly, I knew exactly the spot he was talking about. I had passed it on my journey to the Gabriel School, and I had convinced the driver to pull over so I could investigate. "It's an abandoned mine," I said. "There are four or five collapsed buildings, and an old windmill that once must have pumped water to the surface. Half of the blades are missing, but when the wind blows, they spin enough to hit one of the old buildings."

"So I know where I am when I'm over *that*," he said. "Then if I can find a landmark that's nearby, I can go out another few miles—"

"And eventually you can fly from point to point to anyplace in Samaria."

But that was going too fast for him. He shook his head. "It just doesn't seem possible," he said. "So many factors would have to be considered. The effect of the wind—the possibility of being blown off course—the fact that any man-made structure could be destroyed at any time and I would lose my point of reference. I could fly for miles in the wrong direction and be completely lost."

I flung my hands in the air. My fingers were practically icicles by now. "Fine! Find reasons it *won't* work instead of trying to find ways it will," I said. "I'm going inside before I freeze to death."

"It's just that there are obstacles," Corban argued, following me to the trapdoor and down the stairs. "I want to fly again, but I have to be careful."

I went straight to the table where our scraps of dinner remained and gulped down a glass of water. The singing and the arguing had left me parched. "Fine," I said again. "I think you're right to take it slowly. But I don't think you should give up."

"I'm not giving up," he said. "I just need more help. You have to come with me."

I almost choked on my last sip of water. "Come with you where?"

"The next time I fly."

I stared at him, unable to answer.

Oh, I'd been carried in an angel's arms before. But not far, and not lately, and not of my own free will. I had no desire to repeat the experience. "No," I said shortly. "But that's the right idea. You can go anywhere you want if you bring someone with you to tell you where you are."

My words had roused his curiosity; he cocked his head. "You're afraid to fly with an angel?" he asked. "You? You're not afraid of anything. And you don't think anyone else should be, either."

"I'm not afraid," I said stiffly. "Just not interested."

"You *sound* afraid."

"Perhaps you're not as good at reading emotions as you like to think."

"Is it the height? Some people are too petrified to even stand on top of a tall building."

"I don't mind reasonable heights. Corban——"

"Have you ever flown before? It's utterly magical. It's not just being in the air, so high above everything, it's the speed and the motion and the sense of——of——limitlessness. It seems like exactly the sort of thing you would love."

I was silent.

He knew precisely where I was, though, because he came a step closer to where I stood by the table. "You *have* flown," he decided. "And you didn't like it. Why not? Some angels are careless about the comfort of their human companions, I know. They go too high—they forget how cold it is for mortal flesh."

"And certainly *you* were never one of those thoughtless angels," I said, hoping my sneering tone would make him drop the topic. "You've always been so considerate."

But he came closer still, brushing aside my words. "That can't be it. I can't see you suffering in silence, even to please an angel. You would have spoken up if the issue was merely discomfort."

I set down my water glass, turned away, and began stacking the dirty dishes on the tray. "I'm going to take these down to the kitchen—"

He caught my arm and turned me back to face him. His darkened eyes were half closed, as if to aid his other senses in picking up information I didn't want to impart. "So you were in an angel's arms, but you didn't want to be," he mused. "Maybe you were embroiled in some kind of legal dispute. Perhaps—were you being brought to an angel hold for a trial? Or even a sentencing?"

Again I refused to answer, but I knew he could feel me trembling. I didn't even bother trying to pull away; his grip was too tight, and I already knew how strong he was.

"An adjudication," he decided. "Your word against someone else's. What was the accusation? And who was your accuser?"

"I'll tell you if you let me go."

He smiled, genuinely amused. "If I let you go, you'll run from the room."

"Corban, this is an old story."

"But one that still haunts you," he said. "I want to hear it." When I still didn't answer, he prompted, "At least tell me where the trial occurred. If an angel was transporting you, you must have gone to one of the holds."

"The Eyrie," I said reluctantly.

His eyebrows rose. "And your case was put before the Archangel?"

"Yes."

"Impressive! Who was your accuser?"

"My employer. A Manadavvi lord who owned property up by Monteverde."

"And what was the crime?"

I took a deep breath. "Attempted murder."

That surprised him so much he actually released me. I almost bolted for the door, but I knew it was pointless. Even if I made good my escape, he would just insist on hearing the tale some other day. He would give me no peace until he knew the details—or until I left him, and the Gabriel School, behind.

I was so tired of running.

"I tried to kill a man," I said in an even voice. "And my only regret is that I was unsuccessful."

Corban nodded and, to my surprise, pulled out one of the narrow-backed chairs. "I think this is a story I have to hear straight through," he said, dropping down and arranging his wings behind him. "So why don't you sit and tell it from the beginning?"

I slowly took a seat across from him. He poured more water, first for himself, then for me, not spilling a drop. It was the first time I'd wished that Alma had included wine with the angel's dinner.

"A few years ago, I got a job working in a Manadavvi household—"

"From the beginning," he interrupted. "Farther back than that."

Sweet Jovah singing, he wanted to trace the entire route of my life. I grimaced, though he couldn't see me, and began speaking with exaggerated patience. "I told you. I was an angel-seeker's daughter, and for years I ran wild on the streets of Monteverde. One day I was begging for bread at a bakery when the owner said she needed extra hands in the kitchen, and if I'd work for my keep she'd train me in a profession. I was smart enough to say yes, and I stayed with her for thirteen years."

I shrugged. Dorothea had been practical, honest, exhausted, and not particularly warm; I'd never come to love her, and she'd never loved me. But I respected her, and I learned a lot from her, and I explored every building and byway in Monteverde when I was making deliveries for her business.

"When she got old enough to retire, she sold the bakery to her nephew and helped me look for another situation. The nephew and I had never gotten along," I added. Not since I'd kneed him in the groin after he tried to slip a hand under my shirt. "I ended up taking a position in the household of a Manadavvi lord—a good job, anyone would have thought."

"But it didn't turn out that way."

"It started out pretty well," I said. "The pay was good, the work was no harder than I was used to, and I got along with most of the other servants." I had become particularly friendly with a woman about my age with antecedents even fuzzier than my own. I always assumed Olive was the bastard child of a Manadavvi landowner and one of his housemaids. She had that Manadavvi look to her, all high cheekbones and flawless skin. All the grooms and footmen were wild for her, but she was good at holding them off. It was going to be marriage or nothing for Olive. She didn't want to go her mother's route, that was plain; she talked about saving enough money to start her own business in Monteverde or one of the river towns. Actually, we talked about pooling our resources and going into business together. It was the first time I could remember having a dream.

"I can guess what happened," Corban said quietly. "The lord took an interest in you, rather forcefully, and you protested."

I made a small snorting sound. "Oh, no, I wasn't built to catch an aristocrat's eye," I said. "And I knew how to dress and how to behave so I didn't get the kind of attention I didn't want. But another girl— Olive. *She* was the one the lord couldn't stop thinking about."

We developed the habit of working in pairs, and I at least always kept a knife concealed under my skirts. But Olive wasn't afraid of him; she didn't seem to realize he was dangerous. She avoided him when she could, but she didn't lie awake at night and worry what he might do to her.

As she should have.

She also didn't spend her free hours sneaking around the ancient, labyrinthine mansion, exploring which stairways led where and which servants' doors opened onto private suites. As I did. There was a day I could have navigated that entire fifty-room house if I had been as blind as Corban. I knew passageways that I swear no one but me remembered. Even the mice had forgotten them.

"What happened to Olive?" Corban prompted when I had been quiet too long.

I didn't want to say the words, didn't want to remember the scene, didn't want in my mind, again, those images of horror. So I spoke as quickly as I could. "He brought her to his room one night against her will. She struggled, he reacted, and by the time I found them, she was no longer breathing." I took a deep breath, because I had somehow run out of air. "By the time I left them, he was bleeding so much that I thought he would surely die."

For a moment, the silence between us was absolute. *Well, there's the worst of it,* I thought. *There's the truth that defines me.* Try to hurt me and I will hurt you back. No matter who you are, no matter how much it costs. And I'm always on guard, waiting for the next blow to fall.

I waited in some defiance for Corban's expressions of disgust and outrage. I realized—much to my fury—that my attitude was tinged with regret. *Now he will order you from the room. Now he will never wish to see you again.* Who cared? He was an angel, self-absorbed and self-righteous and allying himself with power, like all the rest of them. My story would shock him, I was certain, but not because a Manadavvi lord had committed murder in the name of lust. He would be shocked because a servant girl had thought she had the right to fight back.

I couldn't even look at him as I waited for him to denounce me.

His voice, when it came, was threaded with amazement. "That was you?" he demanded. "*You're* the one who cut up Reuel Harth?"

I risked a quick look at him and saw nothing but astonishment on his face. "You know him?"

"Knew him. Everyone did. You'll be happy to know he's dead now."

I took a quick breath. "Did he suffer?"

Corban's mouth opened in a soundless laugh. "Not as much as you'd like, I imagine, but his last three years were unpleasant enough. His face was heavily scarred, you know, from whatever weapon you used. And his reputation was wholly shredded. He was ostracized by Manadavvi and angels alike."

"Because he raped a servant girl?" I said scornfully.

"Because he killed her," Corban corrected me. "I see you have the lowest possible opinion of Samarian justice, but the Archangel has reasonable ethical standards, and she had never liked Reuel to begin with. She was happy to levy a steep fine and censure him in public—she would have liked to do more, but Reuel wouldn't confess to the crime and there was no absolute proof that he'd strangled that poor girl. The servants were mostly afraid to give testimony and his wife wouldn't speak at the trial at all."

"*I* could have told them—" I began in a hot voice, and then abruptly fell silent.

"Exactly. But the woman who had come to her friend's aid so dramatically—and who had been brought to the Eyrie specifically to speak accusations against Reuel Harth—somehow disappeared before the trial began."

I crossed my arms and glared at him, but I felt a gaping hole open in my stomach. The Manadavvi lord escaped some measure of punishment because *I* had run away? Had I been the one to betray Olive after all?

He answered my unspoken wail of remorse. "It wouldn't have made much difference, I expect. The fine might have been heavier—the condemnation more sharply worded. But the end result would have been much the same."

"Thank you," I whispered.

"I always wondered, though," he said. "How did you get out of the Eyrie? There's the new road that lets people go up and down the mountain, but it was still under construction when the trial was going on. I assume you weren't kept under lock and key—but back then, the only way to get off the Eyrie was in an angel's arms. How did you manage to disappear?"

"I went exploring," I said shortly. I was so shaken by the various revelations of the evening that I was having trouble finishing the conversation in a normal tone of voice. "And one day I found this— I can't explain it—this open shaft in the back of the hold. With a contraption that moved up and down from the top of the mountain to the base. I figured out how to use the ropes and pulleys to ride the thing down to the ground."

"Rachel's escape route!" Corban exclaimed. "Of course! She was Gabriel's angelica, you know, and she was afraid of heights, so she didn't like to be flown down from the Eyrie. I'd forgotten that cage-and-pulley system even existed."

"Well, I found it," I said. "And then I hid myself in Velora until everyone stopped looking for me."

I could tell by Corban's expression that he was doing a rough calculation. "But that was—what, three years ago?"

"Four."

"And all this time you've been running? Thinking the angels— or the Manadavvi—were still looking for you?"

"Yes," I said.

"And that's why you're here. At the Gabriel School. Which, as far as I can tell, is at the very edge of civilized existence. You're still running."

"I suppose." I was suddenly so tired I could barely muster the strength to answer.

But Corban was energized. He leaned forward, his face alight. I had the sense he might take my arm again, so I scooted back, out of reach. "Well, you don't have to hide anymore," he said. "Reuel's dead and the angels aren't hunting for you. You can go where you want. Do what you want. Lead a normal life again."

Laughing faintly, I pushed myself to my feet. I figured I'd better leave while I still had the strength to walk home. "I don't know that

I ever led a normal life," I said. "And I'm perfectly happy at the Gabriel School. All I need these days is a place to rest."

He stood up so quickly he almost knocked his chair over. "Wait. I want to ask you—"

I had headed for the door, but now I pivoted back to face him. "We're done talking about my life," I said sharply. "I'll come back tomorrow, and every day after that, but not if you keep asking me questions. Do you understand? I'll help you as long as you need me, but if you don't respect my wishes, I won't work with you anymore. And if you try to make me come to you anyway, I'll leave the school. I'm not afraid to run away. I'm not afraid to start over. I'm not afraid of anything."

I could almost see the words forming on his lips, something like *You're afraid of things in your past that give you pain.* But he didn't say them. His need for my assistance was greater than his desire to pry into my life. "I won't ask any questions," he said quietly.

"Then I'll see you tomorrow," I said.

If I had had the strength, I would have run from the room.

CHAPTER 5

I had to force myself to go back to the Great House the following day. I had tossed and turned all night, torn between hating myself for revealing so much to Corban and experiencing a fierce jubilation at the knowledge that Reuel Harth was dead. I was also haunted by images of Olive's torn and twisted body, images of Reuel Harth's blood seeping into the bedclothes, and other memories that I usually managed to stuff to the very back of my mind.

I closed my eyes against the pictures in my head, turned over on my mattress, and punched my pillow into shape. I vowed never to tell that story again. I was grateful that, when sleep finally arrived, it came unencumbered with dreams.

I yawned through most of the day, but a growing sense of trepidation made me grow more alert as the sun went down. Even if Corban kept his promise, my confession would lie between us like a sucking swamp. One misstep, one incautious word, and either of us could be pulled back in. Our conversations would be awkward, fraught with knowledge, laced with tension.

I shook my head and forced myself to stand straighter. *Not that our conversations have been easy so far,* I reminded myself. He was an angel and I was a servant girl with a violent past. *You're lucky you've been able to manage to exchange any words at all.*

My mouth quirked in a bitter smile. I was certainly right about that.

By nightfall, I was headed back up the hill, bringing a fresh-baked loaf of bread from the school kitchen to spare Alma that task, at least. She was up and hobbling around the kitchen, looking as cheerful as I'd seen her.

"I'm feeling *much* better," she assured me. "I even made it upstairs once, though my ankle hurt for the rest of the day."

I raised my eyebrows. "That's very encouraging! Soon you won't need me here at all!"

She cast me a quick sideways glance while pretending to keep all her attention on the soup she was measuring into two large bowls. "*I* won't, but the angel might," she said. "He was very pleased to see me when I made it to the top of the steps—until he realized I was *me* and not you. Then he managed to be polite, but I could tell he was disappointed."

It was clear she thought there was more to our relationship than there was. "I'm no angel-seeker," I said bluntly. "I'm not trying to seduce him."

Alma was neither shocked nor offended. "I didn't say you were" was her mild response. "Though I'm not sure such a thing would be bad for either of you."

I made a derisive sound. "My life is complicated enough. I don't need to add the indiscretion of falling in love with an angel."

Her smile—so rare and so unexpectedly mischievous—caught me by surprise. "Oh, I don't know. There's nothing quite like taking an angel lover. Some things are worth the inevitable pain."

My eyebrows could hardly go any higher. "Someday we'll have to sit down and talk about *your* interesting past."

Still smiling, she waved a hand to speed me to the door. "Someday," she said. "Right now, you've got more important things to do."

I climbed the stairs and entered Corban's room with a breezy step, determined to pretend as if there had been no wrenching confidences the day before. Evidently he had made the same decision, for he met me at the door with a brisk but friendly greeting.

"Good, you're here," he said, turning immediately toward the central table. "Let's eat quickly so we can go outside."

"This will be a good night for flying," I noted, some of my tension easing at his reasonable tone. I set the tray down and served us both. "The moon's still close to full, there's only a light breeze, and it's a little warmer than it's been the past few nights."

"I hope you brought a jacket, even so," he said, spooning up some soup.

"Yes, thanks so much for your concern."

"Because I want you to come with me when I fly."

I suddenly remembered the part of the previous night's conversation that had led to my emotional confession. I laid down my spoon and said, "I told you, I don't want to do that."

"Yes, I know, you hated it when you tried it, but you have to admit that wasn't a typical incident," he said. He was very carefully not specifying *why* I had been in an angel's arms once before, and I grudgingly gave him credit for that. "Flying is—an indescribable thrill. And so many mortals never get the chance to experience it. Shouldn't you attempt it at least once, with someone you trust—to wipe out that old memory, if nothing else? And maybe to find yourself enthralled and delighted? Moriah, don't you want to go *flying?*"

His voice was so passionate and at the same time so pleading that I had to laugh. The pictures he conjured were sorely tempting, but all I said was, "What makes you think I trust you?"

"Well, I know that I trust *you*," he replied, sounding a little hurt. "I've had to, these past few nights. I would be distressed to learn you didn't feel the same about me."

"Oh, that was very good," I told him. "You practiced that, didn't you?"

He grinned. "Not out loud."

"Corban, I—"

"Will you?" he interrupted. "Please? I have to keep pushing myself, testing myself. Maybe, once I get stronger, I can hire someone to be my guide, but right now I'm not ready to do that. You're the only one who can help me. And I really want to do this."

"You're a manipulative bastard, has anyone ever told you that?" I demanded.

"No, because I never had to manipulate people back when I could *see*," he said. He didn't seem offended at my insult. "I could just do what I wanted without asking for help. But now you're forcing me to beg—to humiliate myself—as a kind woman would not do—"

"You don't sound humiliated. You don't even sound humble."

"But you're kind, aren't you, Moriah?" Now his tone was wheedling.

I exhaled an exaggerated, long-suffering sigh. "Let me finish my meal," I said. "I need to fortify myself against the night air."

"Yesssss!" he exclaimed and slapped a palm to the table. Then, in case that seemed too triumphant, he hastily added, "Thank you most humbly. I hope you will enjoy the experience, but I know you're a little anxious—"

"Just eat," I said. "Let's not waste any more time."

Fifteen minutes later, we were back on the roof. I had buttoned my jacket to my throat and pulled on a pair of gloves Corban lent me, but even so, I wasn't really warm until he picked me up and settled me against his chest. It wasn't just his body temperature that sent a spike of heat through my blood. It was excitement—amazement—nervousness. Attraction. I'd never been this close to a man and not kissed him.

"Put your arms around my neck," he directed. "I'm unlikely to drop you, but that might make you feel more secure."

"Unlikely?" I managed to ask, not sounding too breathless.

I could see his grin in the lavish moonlight. "Well, it's been a while since I've flown with a passenger."

"Jovah's balls," I muttered, then, more urgently, "Corban, if you're not sure you're ready for this——"

"I'm ready," he said and leapt into the air.

I muffled a squeak and tried not to cower in his arms. His whole body was nothing but strain—muscles bunching, wings working, every bone and tendon pulling skyward. I didn't see how he could do it, didn't see how he could possibly lift from a stationary position to an upward arc, carrying a heavy burden, and it was all I could do not to bury my face against his chest so I wouldn't have to watch as we tumbled headlong to the ground. But the powerful wings drove down, sending great gusts of air all around us, and suddenly we were clear of the roof, we were suspended above the dark sprawl of the school, we were high over the narrow snake of the road, we were *flying*.

I wrapped my arms more tightly around Corban's neck and gazed around in rapt astonishment.

The world had never seemed so strange or wondrous. The ground below was a patchwork of variegated textures—corrugated forest, silky sand, a linen weave of grass. Everything was shadowy and mysterious, only half illuminated by the spectral moonlight. It was a landscape from a dream, unreal and beautiful.

"Oh, Corban," I breathed.

"Not so terrifying after all, is it?" he replied.

"It *is* terrifying—but in a wonderful way," I said. "I can't explain it."

"You don't have to," he said. "I know."

He canted to one side, dipping his left wing, and suddenly the winding ribbon of the road disappeared. "Wait," I said, slightly panicked. "I haven't been paying attention. Don't go so far. I have to keep track of where we are."

He leveled out, lower to the ground, and spoke in a soothing voice. "We haven't gone very far yet. Even if we had to land and try to get our bearings, we would only be a mile or so from the house. Do you see anything you recognize?"

"Turn around. Back that way. No, *that* way. If I could find the road—"

In less than a minute, it reappeared and I let out a sharp sigh of relief. "All right, let's go back to the school so I'm *sure* I know where we are. And then we can set out for someplace else. The wreck of the old mine?"

"The ocean?" Corban said.

"Not tonight," I said. "It's too far away, and I'm still getting used to this."

He seemed disappointed. I waited for him to try to cajole me, but he had promised not to disregard my comfort, and so he acquiesced. "Some other night, then," he said. "Where are we now?"

"Back over the school. Turn to your left and you'll be facing straight north. Can you find the mine from here without my assistance?"

"Yes," he said and plunged through the unresisting air.

For this short flight, I didn't need to watch for landmarks. The northbound road stayed always on our left, a comforting and reliable presence. Faster than I would have believed possible, we were close enough to hear the eerie, intermittent sound of the old windmill slapping against the broken roof of the collapsed mine. Corban hovered directly above the wreckage, and I peered down in fascination at the angles and splinters of the abandoned buildings.

"So when you're here, you can still catch my voice from the roof of the Great House?" I said.

"I can't actually hear you this far out," he admitted. "But I know the approximate direction I have to go to return, and once I've flown for about five minutes, I can pick up your voice."

"How do you know which way to come back? I would be wholly turned around if I couldn't see the ground."

I felt his shoulders move in a shrug. "It's automatic, I suppose. I'm always aware of which direction the wind is blowing. If it's at my back when I fly out, I know it needs to be in my face when I return."

"But the wind shifts."

"It does, but the *general* pattern is stable enough to steer by."

"We should put something on the roof of the Great House that makes noise all the time," I said. "Bells, maybe. Chimes. Something that could guide you back if I wasn't there."

"Why wouldn't you be there?"

"I'm just trying to give you more options. Something else to rely on."

He didn't answer, but I could tell he didn't like the idea. It was odd to think he trusted me so much he was not interested in investigating substitutes.

"Show me how well you can get back without any direction from me," I said after a moment of silence. "And let me know when you think we're close to the house. I want to see how accurate your sense of distance is."

"Not yet," he said. "Let's go a little farther out. I want to see if there's another point I can find once I make it this far."

I wasn't positive this was a good idea, but I saw the look of concentration on his face and decided to keep quiet. Corban took a moment to assess something—the feel of the wind, maybe—and then drove his wings down hard enough to gain altitude. I could still see the road from this height, which kept me somewhat relaxed. He leveled out and began flying steadily in a more or less northern direction. I kept my eyes trained on the ground, looking for landmarks, which were mighty sparse in this rocky, sandy, barely habitable stretch of northeastern Samaria. Corban drifted slightly to the west, which was fine by me; we crossed over the northbound road, but it was still visible on my right. I knew that as long as I never lost sight of it, we could always find our way home.

We had been flying for perhaps twenty minutes when Corban began turning his head from side to side like a hunting dog trying to catch an elusive scent. "Something's changed," he said.

I listened as hard as I could, but I couldn't hear anything except the rhythmic sweep and gather of Corban's wings. "You must have the sharpest ears in the country," I commented.

"It's not a sound, it's a—temperature. And a change in air density." He jerked his head toward the left. "What's over there?"

I slewed around in his arms to peer at the western horizon, which was dense with unrelieved night. "Nothing. Just darkness and shadows and—oh! The mountains!" I squirmed, trying to get a better look at the solid blackness. "We're almost at the Caitanas. That's why the air feels different."

"The Caitanas," he repeated, sounding pleased. "I could follow them all the way up to Windy Point. I'd know where I was then."

Windy Point was an old angel hold that Gabriel had destroyed shortly after the god had brought down the mountain. It certainly must have been exciting to live in the days when Gabriel was Archangel. "It doesn't exist anymore. How would that help you?"

"The hold was leveled, but pieces of it remained intact when they were blasted off the mountain," Corban said. "You know why it was called Windy Point, don't you? Because it was this drafty old cave and every time the wind blew, you could hear it moaning through the walls. Even now, if you're right over the peaks where the hold used to be, there's a constant whistling and shrieking. Really spooky the first time you hear it."

"Sounds unnerving," I agreed. "But Corban, it has to be sixty or seventy miles from here. I'm not sure you have the strength to go that far in one trip."

I felt his muscles cord with silent dissent, and then he made a little sigh of agreement. "You're right. It's too far, at least right now. But maybe in a few days—"

"Or a few weeks."

"We can try it."

"It's a good goal," I said. "But I just realized something."

"What's that?" he asked. He had dipped his wing down again and was making a long, lazy loop to turn us back in a southerly direction.

I was impressed; he seemed to have accurately gauged where the mountains were and how to retrace our route.

"You need to live in a place where there's a steady, dependable source of sound so you can always find your way home. Right?"

"Well, I don't want to live in the wreckage of Windy Point, if that's what you're suggesting."

"No. But there *is* a hold in Samaria you could always get back to if all you needed was music."

He was silent a moment. "The Eyrie," he said. "I hadn't thought about that."

I had lived at the hold for nearly a week as I awaited my trial and went exploring its curving gaslit hallways. There was an open central plateau where someone was always performing music—an angel singing a solo, a small choral group offering harmony, a few flautists trying out a requiem someone had written just that morning. Apparently they all signed up for shifts to ensure that there was never a moment of perfect silence at the hold. I had expected to find the incessant music annoying—just another example of angels flaunting their superior talents—but instead I had found it comforting. There were days I had actually wondered what it must be like to live there and feel welcome, from time to time, to join the others in an impromptu concert.

But I hadn't stayed long enough to find out.

"Well, it seems like the perfect place for you," I said. "And you could find some nice young angel-seeker who'd fly with you whenever you wanted to leave."

"That makes it an even more appealing notion," he said dryly. "I'll have to give it some consideration."

I pretended to laugh, but the truth was I felt a little sad. Not that I had ever expected this strange midnight relationship with the blinded angel to last more than week or two, but it was the most interesting, the most enjoyable interlude I had had in years. I would be sorry to see him go. Sorry to see my life return to its usual parameters of drudgery and defensiveness and worry.

Well, at least I could cross *worry* off my list of activities. Among the gifts Corban had bestowed upon me was the knowledge that Reuel Harth was dead and the angels didn't want to apprehend me for crimes against him. I could leave the Gabriel School, if I wanted. I could travel anywhere, look for any kind of work. I could live, as it seemed I had not for so long, in the light. It shouldn't matter that an angel was unlikely to be beside me.

Ridiculous to even entertain those thoughts. I gave my head a tiny shake and concentrated on the landscape below. "Do you know where you are?" I asked Corban.

"I think so. Another few miles and then I turn to my right to find the mine."

"Good. I won't say anything unless you ask for my help."

But he didn't. He made the broad, easterly turn a bit earlier than I would have suggested, but soon enough, the road was within view again, and not long after that, we could hear the familiar clatter of the windmill. Corban spent a few moments circling the mine site, and I realized the percussion of the blades must sound slightly different from different vantage points, because he obviously was trying to orient himself according to their noise. But soon enough he had the cues he wanted, and he set off southward on a course perfectly parallel with the road.

We were within a half mile of the house before he showed indecision. "By this point, I've usually been following your voice for ten minutes, so I haven't needed other markers," he said. "I know I'm close, but I can't find the house without help."

"Still, I'm impressed by how you've managed so far," I told him. "Just keep going in the same direction—drop a little lower—we'll be there in a few moments."

It was clear that he found it much harder to judge his distance to the roof when I was in his arms than when I was on the surface and he was navigating by the sound of my voice. He came down harder than either of us expected, and almost tripped on one of the pipes, so there was a dizzy moment of both of us stumbling and trying to catch our balance before we finally came to a complete halt.

"*Definitely* a good idea to install chimes," I said breathlessly. "Maybe string them around the whole perimeter so you know exactly where you can land."

"Something to work on for another day," he said. "So did you like it? Wasn't it magnificent?"

"It was amazing," I said. "I can't imagine an experience to compare. You must have missed flying very much."

"More than I realized. To think I've gone two years without it—" He shook his head and then spoke in a deeper tone. "And I have you to thank for making it seem possible again."

Oh, no; I still was not interested in the angel's earnest gratitude. *Heartfelt* has always been a word that made me shudder. "And to think, I was only trying to irritate you by insisting you should try to fly," I said lightly. "I wonder if I've done this much good all the other times I was being difficult and annoying."

He laughed, but I could see a look of puzzlement on his face. Or maybe it was speculation. *Why does Moriah always turn the subject when I try to be serious?* "I doubt it," he said. "You're annoying so often. The odds aren't in your favor."

Now it was my turn to laugh. "I'll be back tomorrow—with a compass, if I can find one," I said, heading for the trapdoor. "Then we can go where we like."

"I'll be waiting for you."

I spent the next three nights flying with the angel.

I'll be honest, I could have been dreaming for every minute of those excursions. Who sees the world from such a perspective, barely lit by moonglow, decorated with slabs of stone and stands of miniature trees and the occasional lonely flicker from an isolated homestead? None of it seemed real, not the landscape, not the motion, not the fact that I was held against an angel's heart. And if it was not real, I might as well enjoy it, might as well let my wonder well up unimpeded, my delight spill over without reservation. I might as well drop my usual guards, cast aside cynicism and suspicion. I might as well look around me with a childlike sense of awe.

One night we flew south, above the desert, where the sands unrolled below us as if they stretched, empty and untouched, to the end of the world itself. Once we flew west, above the uneven hump of the Caitanas with their sharp, stark points. Even I could feel the cooler air rising from their stony peaks as if exhaled by the mouth of a chilly god.

Once we flew east, just to the edge of the ocean, where the restless waves rushed back and forth over a narrow stretch of beach, roiling the sand, then smoothing it clean. The wind was stronger here than at any other place during our travels. Corban found it harder to hold to a steady hover; instead, he was pushed in all directions by its mercurial currents. I actually found myself afraid, during a particularly energetic gust, that he would be tossed against one of the rocky overhangs or dashed into the water. I clung to his neck and cried, "Fly back toward land!" He nodded, pushed himself upward to gain altitude, and retreated from the shoreline. We decided there was no need to make that particular journey again.

I had collected a few musical oddments from around the school—ancient, rusted bells from a festive horse bridle; something that looked like a nautical buoy; and a set of glass chimes whose connecting strings had rotted straight through—and I repaired them and set them up around the perimeter of the roof. It didn't take much wind to set any of them in motion, and Corban agreed that these would serve to guide him home if he ever took off without me.

"Though I don't know why I would," he said as we returned from our outing to the sea.

"Well, maybe you'll accidentally drop me some night, and you'll have to make your way back here by yourself," I said.

"I won't accidentally *drop* you," he exclaimed. "And if I did, I'd come down to *find* you instead of returning here."

"Well, that's good to know," I said.

I had opened the trapdoor, and enough light spilled out to let me see him shaking his head. *Why can't Moriah ever be serious?* "Of course, I might *throw* you to the ground some night when you're being particularly exasperating," he said, following me down the stairs.

"Oh, you'd have done that long before now if you were going to," I said cheerfully. "You've gotten used to me by now."

"I don't know   does anyone really get used to you?"

I laughed. "I'll have to think that over."

"So, where shall we go tomorrow night? I think we should head north again—past the mine, toward Windy Point."

"Maybe," I said. "But the moon's already only half full. It's getting smaller and rising later, so it's harder for me to see landmarks. We might have to stay close to home for a while or risk getting lost."

His face showed a quick frown. "If you've got the compass—"

"Which I also can't see in the dark."

"Well, maybe we don't need you to see. If we go to the mine and north from there, I think I can find my way."

"In which case, you don't need me anyway," I said.

His frown deepened. "Of course I need you," he snapped. "I *think* I know where I am, but I could easily miscalculate."

"We'll see," I said. "But we might have to stay close to home and fly for strength, not distance, until the moon starts waxing again."

"Very well," he said reluctantly. "We'll talk about it tomorrow."

But we didn't talk about it the next day, because everything changed; and a few days after that, everything changed again.

CHAPTER 6

Over the past four days, I had continued to spend a few hours in the kitchen, though now I went in early enough to help with the work of preparing dinner. I rarely encountered Rhesa, but I guessed she had complained incessantly to Deborah, because within two days the head cook was asking me when I thought Alma would be well enough for me to resume the overnight shift. I knew Corban was not yet ready to announce his existence to the rest of the world, but pretty soon I would either need to return to my old post or lose my job. Or explain exactly what was taking up all my time at the Great House.

The day after the flight to the ocean, all those options were put on hold. I made my way down to the kitchen in midafternoon to find the place in chaos. Deborah was the only cook in evidence, though she was attended by a small army of students who were rushing between stove and table and pantry, trying to do her bidding.

"No, not the *clotted* cream—sweet Jovah singing, don't you even know what milk looks like? Yes—that jar there. And yes, I meant the potatoes, not the turnips! Moriah! Thank the good god you're here. I was about to send someone to wake you up."

"What's going on? Where are the others?"

"Sick. All of them. With something"—she patted her stomach—"that has made them vomit through the night. *And* about twenty of the students have come down with it as well."

"Oh, no," I said. "I suppose everyone will get it eventually."

"I suppose," she said. "But as long as *we're* healthy, we need to do the work of four. I've already sent a note up to Alma saying that you can't be spared tonight."

I put on an apron. "Obviously not," I said. "Let's get dinner ready."

The illness made its way quickly through the school. About half the students and three-quarters of the staff succumbed over the next few days, though most of them recovered after a couple of bad nights. But two older men, one a teacher and one a handyman, couldn't seem to shake it. They came down with a fever as well as the stomach disorder, and they languished on their beds, refusing to eat or drink.

Judith, who had some healing skills, had turned nurse the minute she recovered enough to get out of bed. I had no interest in tending the patients, but I didn't mind doing the extra laundry and scrubbing down the sickrooms.

"I'm worried about David," Judith told me on the afternoon of the third day. We were folding what seemed like a thousand towels that had just come through the wash. "Jonathan's beginning to improve, but David is getting worse, and I'm almost out of drugs to give him."

"Maybe we should hoist a plague flag," I suggested. People in settlements all over Samaria would catch the attention of angels flying nearby by raising distress signals—called plague flags, though it didn't really matter what disaster they portended. "Ask an angel to pray for more medicine."

"I thought of that," she said. "But I don't know that anyone would see it. We're so remote here—and most of the angels are likely to be headed for the Plain of Sharon."

Startled, I did a quick calculation. Spring had tiptoed to the border of winter while I had not been paying attention, and the equinox
was almost here. "You're right! It's less than a week till the Gloria."

"So I don't think we can expect help from any angels," she ended
with a sigh. "I'll do what I can for him."

I didn't answer as I continued to fold linens. I wondered if Corban
would be willing to sing a prayer to Jovah if the situation was dire.
I didn't know much about it, but I believed angels usually offered
their prayers from a high altitude, and Corban had never gone too
far off the ground since he began flying again. I didn't know if he
was afraid of the winds or the disorientation, but I had to confess I
didn't like the idea of getting way above land, either.

Meanwhile, since that first week when I had spotted him on the
roof of the Great House, I hadn't heard him sing a note. That was
odd, because angels were all steeped in music; they couldn't live
without it, or so it seemed. Corban had told me he composed songs
in his copious free time, but I'd never heard him play, either. I wondered if he had abandoned music in a bitter response to the god he
thought had abandoned him.

But surely if he thought a man's life was at stake . . .

I decided that, if David took a turn for the worse, I would ask
Corban if he was willing to petition the god. And if he said no, I
would mock him and shame him until he agreed. And then he would
fling himself aloft and offer his prayers to Jovah and be successful
and feel proud of himself and fall in love with me because I always
pushed him beyond his fears—or he would be tumbled off course by
a swift, unfriendly wind, and fail to sing a note, and return to land
full of doubt and self-loathing and never wish to speak to me again.

Well, then. Always something to look forward to.

I was still asleep early the next morning when there was a frantic
pounding at my door and the sound of someone calling my name.
My schedule had changed again during this time of illness, so I had

gone to bed around midnight, but I still was not ready to rise with the sun.

"Moriah! Come quickly! He's gone!"

For a moment, I didn't recognize the woman's voice and couldn't think who *he* might be or why I would care if he was missing. But I dragged myself out of bed and opened the door to say *"What?"* in an aggrieved tone.

Alma stared at me, her lined face a study in worry. "Moriah, Corban's not in his room. I don't know where he could be."

Instantly I was wide awake and flooded with fear. "Jovah's balls, he went out on his own," I whispered. "Let me get dressed."

Five minutes later, looking a fright, I brushed past an interested crowd of observers in the hallway and towed Alma down to the ground level of the dorm. I declined to answer the questions tossed out by a handful of students and staff. *What's going on? Who's missing?* I glared at a few people and they eventually stopped trailing behind us as I pulled Alma all the way to the stable. I noticed she walked with a slight limp, but she kept up with me well enough.

Once we were inside the stable, I turned to Alma. I was so full of fear that most of my breath had been squeezed out. It was hard to appear calm, hard to speak, but I focused fiercely on figuring out what I should do. "When did he leave?" I asked.

She looked bewildered. "I don't know. He was there when I brought him dinner last night, but gone when I went up with his breakfast this morning. I didn't even hear him come downstairs."

I shook my head. "He didn't. He's been practicing flying. He left from the roof."

"Flying? But he can't see!"

"He navigates by sound." I paused, pressing my lips together to hold back a whimper of terror. "Or with my help. I suppose he got tired of waiting for me and decided to see how far he could get on his own."

"Dear sweet Jovah," Alma whispered. "He must have gotten lost—and come to ground somewhere—how will we ever find him?"

That was clearly the question. "I think—it seems likeliest—he would try to make it to the place he can always find. The old mine up the road. I'll go there first and then make wider circles around it until I find him."

"I'll come with you," she said.

I hesitated, but if Corban was seriously injured, I'd never be able to get him back here on my own. I was already debating whether I would bring a wagon or merely saddle a horse—it would be easier to cover ground from horseback, but impossible to bring back an injured angel without a wagon.

"All right," I said. "I'll hitch the horses. You get supplies. Food and water and maybe some bandages. Meet me at the gate as soon as you can. Don't tell anyone where we're going."

She paused long enough to give me an incredulous look—*It will be hard to keep the angel a secret once we bring him back in a wag*on— but just nodded and hurried off.

In less than fifteen minutes, we were on our way, heading north on the rutted road. I tried to block from my mind all the horrifying images that clamored to get in, pictures of the angel bruised and broken on the open ground, bloodied and unconscious on a peak in the Caitanas, adrift on the ocean, his great wings spread like seaweed along the surface of the water. How could he have been so reckless, so stupid? *Damn arrogant angels, they think just because they want something, they can reach out their hands and take it,* I thought angrily. *They don't have to wait patiently, like ordinary men, or obey the laws of the physical world.*

But they did. They did.

We were probably still a mile from the mine when I started shouting Corban's name. If he was alive, if he was conscious, he would be able to hear me from a fair distance and call back. When I paused to give my throat a rest, Alma lifted her own voice. "Angelo! Angelo! Where are you?"

About an hour after we set out, we approached the ruins of the mine. I pulled the wagon over so Alma and I could jog over to it through the sandy soil. It was immediately clear how Corban might have lost his bearings here. Sometime in the past week, the elements had wreaked additional damage to the fallen buildings; the windmill had wholly collapsed. There was no longer any rhythmic tapping noise to tell Corban he had arrived at his destination. He must have flown confidently in this direction, been puzzled at the missing sound, wondered if he'd misjudged his route, turned around, tried to get back to the house, felt a rising self-doubt that made him question any choice he made, and ended up thoroughly lost. He could be anywhere within a five-mile radius.

"Corban!" I shouted, but there was no answer.

"Are you sure this is where he came?" Alma asked.

"I'm not sure of anything."

I thought for a moment. It seemed likelier that he had overshot the mark than undershot it—anyway, if he was behind us anywhere along our route, he would have heard us calling. I hoped. "Let's go north," I said. "At least another five miles."

She nodded, and we returned to the wagon. I drove more slowly for the next hour as we peered around, both hoping and fearing to see a crumpled ball of feathers lying along the side of the road. I had given up the notion of shouting his name and now I began singing, hoping the sustained, persistent notes would catch his attention even if he was in a groggy, hallucinatory state. After a few moments, Alma added her voice in a sweet alto harmony. Without conscious thought, I had opened with another Manadavvi ballad, and I raised my eyebrows when it turned out she recognized it. She shrugged and smiled and kept singing.

Just as I was wondering if it was time to widen our search east or west, we heard a voice cry out my name. I jerked on the reins and we both fell abruptly silent, listening hard. There it was again, faint and exhausted. *Moriah!*

My heart leapt. Praise be to Jovah, at least he was alive. "Corban!" I shouted, throwing the reins to Alma, grabbing a flask of water, and jumping out of the wagon. "Keep calling me! I'm on my way!"

His voice came from the eastern side of the road along a stretch that had mostly shaken off the sand of the desert and arrayed itself in stunted trees, prickly bushes, and a hardy vine that covered soil, stone, shrub, or tree with an utter lack of discrimination. Not the worst place for an angel to come down in an uncontrolled fall, though I tripped a half dozen times on a leafy runner or a tree root. "Corban!"

It was five minutes before I found him, huddled in the stippled shade of a squat tree just now unfurling its pale green leaves. His wings drooped behind him, so flat you could mistake them for a cloak thrown behind his shoulders, and his legs were thrust straight out on the grass. Not until I was close enough to see his face could I make out the scratches and bruises on his skin. But I didn't see any gouts of blood, any sticks of bone protruding through the flesh. He'd made a rough landing, maybe, but not a disastrous one.

I skidded to my knees beside him, grabbing his shoulders in a shaking grip. "Corban, are you all right?" I demanded.

His hands came up to lock over my wrists. "Moriah, you found me," he said in a whisper. And then he burst into tears.

I had never in my life seen a man cry.

No one has ever come completely undone in front of me; no one has ever been willing to display, before my cynical eyes, ungovernable weakness or need. I had seen this angel hurt and angry, I had spied on him in his despair, but I had not realized he could be so vulnerable as to weep in my presence.

Without another word, I took him in my arms and drew his head against my breast, comforting him as best I could with the soothing words I had never before had cause to use.

It was a moment before his own words came, halting and disjointed, muffled against my jacket. "—But I couldn't find it—and then the wind came—and I was lost and I didn't *know*—but I thought I could get back—but there was no sound, it was gone. And I was afraid—Moriah, so afraid—"

"Sshhh," I said, patting his head, where the long curls were knotted from a rough wind and a night in the open. "Here. Have some water before you tell the rest."

He took a ragged breath. "I'm so thirsty. Thank you, thank you—"

I didn't speak again until he had practically emptied the flask with quick, greedy swallows. "You must try to compose yourself," I said, my voice more brisk. "Tell me how badly you're hurt. Alma and I came in a wagon and we can—"

"Alma's here?" he demanded, sitting up straighter and actually wiping his sleeve across his nose. I had never seen him make such an inelegant gesture. "Where?"

"I left her with the horses. She's the one who let me know you were missing, so you must be properly grateful to her. But the road is a little distance that way. Can you walk?"

He took another shaky breath. I could see him trying to impose an iron calm. I wondered how much practice he'd had doing that during the darkest days after his blinding, how often he had let himself give in to grief before pulling himself back together. Not often, I guessed. "I don't think anything is broken," he said. "I came down hard, but I didn't crash. But I didn't have any idea where I was—or how to get back—" He pressed his lips together.

"The windmill has fallen over completely—that's why you couldn't hear it," I said. "Even so, you're not too far away. You did a good job navigating with absolutely no clues."

"I didn't think you'd be able to find me."

"Well, I did," I said. He was still holding on to me with one hand, so now I stood and drew him up beside me. He was unsteady for a moment, but didn't cry out in pain and fold back to the ground, which I took as a good sign.

"What about your wings?" I said, for they still hung behind him, limp as laundry. "Were they injured?"

He shook his head and spread them out to their fullest extent. I saw a few bent quills, a couple of patches where the feathers might have been scratched off by an overeager branch, but from what I could tell, he was remarkably unscathed. If he'd been able to figure out which way to go, he could have made his way home.

"We brought the wagon in case you were hurt," I said. "But if you want, we'll just drive it back to the school, singing the whole way. You can take flight and follow us home."

He gathered his wings tightly behind him and shook his head. "I'll ride," he said in a quiet voice. "I'm never flying again."

It was, of course, a cause for goggling eyes and disbelieving cries when Alma and I returned to the Gabriel School with the angel hunched in the back of the wagon. He had accepted the food we'd brought and gratefully finished off a second flask of water, but once we had gotten under way, he had refused to speak in anything but monosyllables. It was a return to the depressed, despairing Corban I had met two weeks before, and I was not sure I would be able to jolt him out of his melancholy a second time.

And obviously, this was not the day to try.

I pulled over when the school was just around the next bend. "It's broad daylight, and people will be watching for our return," I said. "Would you like us to leave you somewhere safe until nightfall, when I'll come back for you?"

His arms rested on his updrawn knees, and his face tilted downward as if he were staring at the floorboards. He shrugged. "I don't care."

I glanced at Alma. "You don't care if everyone sees you being helped from the wagon? If everyone knows that there's an angel living in the Great House, and that he's broken?"

I used the word deliberately, but he barely flinched. "No."

"Corban, are you sure? It's no trouble to come back for you after sundown."

"I'm sure," he said, and slumped back against the side of the wagon. He didn't speak another word for the rest of the drive.

I stopped again at the front of the Great House and let Alma help him up the shallow stairs. I kept my hands lax on the reins and most of my attention on the school grounds, where an afternoon break meant dozens of students and ten or twelve teachers were milling around outside, playing games, enjoying the spring sunshine, and watching the angel stumble into the house. Most of them looked from me to the angel and back at me.

I sighed and tsked at the horses, guiding them downhill toward the stable. I didn't feel up to the exclamations and the demands for information and the repeated protestations of amazement. Despite the fact that I was unspeakably relieved that Corban's adventure had been no worse than it was, I felt as listless and exhausted as the angel himself.

I didn't see Corban for four more days. I did try. I took supplies up to the Great House once a day, paused to speak briefly to Alma, then headed up the stairs to knock on the angel's door. Then I kept knocking, sometimes for ten minutes or more, until he called, "Go away!" By that, and the fact that he continued to swap the breakfast and dinner trays Alma left on a table outside his door, I knew he was still alive.

I had managed to give the thinnest possible explanation to Deborah and my fellow cooks. *I knew there was a sick man in the house, but I didn't know it was an angel. Yes, I suppose he must have been there for weeks. No, I don't know what's wrong with him. No, I don't know what happened when he tried to fly. Yes, it certainly is a tragedy.*

They kept asking questions, but I never volunteered more information. Besides, I didn't see the other workers too often, because I was back on the solitary overnight shift. Most of the staff and students had recovered from the first wave of the stomach sickness, but now the disease was making the rounds for a second time, and Rhesa was among those who succumbed. I didn't mind resuming the night duties while she lay on her bed, fevered and miserable. The schedule suited me well enough—and afforded me the greatest freedom.

On that fourth night, all my chores done and the bread prema-

turely mixed and kneaded, I took off my apron, crept out of the
school, climbed the hill, and quietly let myself into the Great House.
The door to Alma's room was closed, though I wouldn't have put it
past her to be lying awake, listening for my footsteps. *You should
come back some night,* she had said just the day before. *Make him talk
to you.* She hadn't gone so far as to say she would leave the door
unlocked, but she had left the chain off. It had been simple to get
inside.

The harder task would be making it through the door at the top
of the stairs. I knocked for a few minutes, not expecting an answer,
and I didn't get one. So I set the lamp on the table and picked the
lock, which yielded without a fight. Then I retrieved the lamp and
stepped into the room.

Corban stood in the center, his body tense, his wings quivering
behind him in visible indignation. He looked wretched—his clothes
disarrayed, his hair unkempt, even his face unshaven. The room was
a mess, with clothes littered across the floor, a few plates stacked on
a corner table, the cello on its side as if it had been kicked over. All
that was missing was the smell of alcohol and vomit, and he would
have been entirely dissolute.

It was clear he was not going to speak first. I took a moment to
survey the room. "Well," I drawled finally, "I see you managed to
control your frustration with your usual genteel restrain."

His hands balled into fists and he took a step forward. "Yes, your
mockery is all that's been missing during my week of agony."

"It hasn't been a week," I said. "It's been four days. Have you lost
your sense of time along with your pride?"

The anger on his face deepened. I could see he was fighting the
urge to respond. My guess was he had promised himself he wouldn't
speak at all, and he hated me for goading him into one unwary reply
already. Oh, but I had just begun.

"I swear, I've never met anyone worse than you at coping with
adversity," I said. "The slightest setback, and you instantly stop trying."

"The slightest setback?" he demanded. "I *fell* from the *sky!* I could have broken my neck—been paralyzed—even killed! It was *catastrophe,* not—not inconvenience."

"As far as I'm concerned, if you're not dead, you have no excuse for giving up," I said.

"Oh—that's right. I want to take advice about moral courage from the woman who *tried to murder a man* and then spent the next four years running from the crime."

I had expected him to throw that in my face; I was braced for it. So I laughed, which only infuriated him more. "Well, at least my instincts for survival are well honed," I said. "Unlike yours."

"You don't understand—you've never understood," he exclaimed, losing a little more of his self-control. He gestured broadly. "Flying was my *life.* If I cannot fly, I cannot be any of the things I was meant to be! I'm *useless!* I don't care about survival because there's nothing to survive *for.*"

"Well, I've never had much use for angels, but surely you could find some constructive way to pass your time," I said unsympathetically. "There are plenty of blind people who make lace or throw pots or weave fabric or sort objects or do any number of valuable tasks."

He gaped at me as if he could not believe even I could be so insensitive. I grinned and went on. "But surely you have some more specialized skills! You're a musician. Can't you teach singing or playing? There's a whole school of young people just down the hill. Start a class. You might discover a prodigy."

"I have little aptitude for teaching," he ground out.

I remembered that he had been blinded while teaching a young angel how to sing the prayer for thunderbolts, so I abandoned this tack. "Well, then," I said in a considering voice, "what else could you—I know! Aren't angels desperate to populate the world with more little angels? Couldn't you hire yourself out as a sort of stud service?"

It was the most outrageous thing I could think to say. His face went slack with shock, but he was too affronted to answer.

"We could bring girls in from the holds," I said in an inspired tone. "Cedar Hills is the closest, of course, but angel-seekers would come from the Eyrie and Monteverde, too, if they knew they didn't actually have to vie for your attention. You'd just give them each an appointment—an hour, a half hour, whatever you were comfortable with—then send them on their way."

"That's the crudest thing I've ever heard anyone say."

"Really? But it seems so practical! You have a—well, I won't exactly call it a talent—you have a *commodity*, and many people desire it, and you could find some worthwhile purpose in your life by exploiting it. I don't see the drawbacks."

"You're so vulgar," he said and turned away.

I came close enough to put a hand on his arm, but he kept his back to me. "Are you shy? Is that it? Out of practice? There are a couple of workers down at the school who used to be angel-seekers, unless I miss my guess. I'm sure one of them would be glad to help you through the awkward parts."

Now he swung around to face me again. "And who else at the Gabriel School used to be an angel-seeker?" he flung at me. He was angry enough now that he wanted to hit back, and hit back hard. "You? Did you try bedding angels when it turned out your friend was the only one who could catch the attention of a Manadavvi lord?"

I gasped, and then I slapped him so fast I wasn't even aware of forming the intention. He grabbed my wrist before I could strike him a second time. He twisted me closer, my arm bent against his chest so I could not get leverage to punch him with my other hand; his grip was astonishingly strong.

"That's obscene," I panted. "Reuel Harth was a murderer."

"But you don't deny the secondary charge," he purred. "So you *were* an angel-seeker—either before or after you had your adventures at the Manadavvi compound."

"Oh, no, I wasn't," I spat out at him. "I find you all worthless and weak, despite the fact you think you're gifts straight from Jovah's hands. Until I met you, I never wanted to *speak* to one of you, let alone take one as a lover—"

"And now that you've met me?" he whispered. "You want me as a lover?"

"That's *not* what I meant to say—"

But it didn't matter what I meant to say. He jerked me even closer, wrapped his other arm around my shoulders, and covered my mouth with a hard kiss. My skin went up in a blaze of heat; my bones melted against his body. I felt his wings settle around me, caging me, trapping me, exciting me with their delicate, whispering touch. I wrenched my head back to gulp for air, and then lunged forward again, locking my lips to his. Somehow I had gotten my right hand free, or he had released me, because now I had both of my arms around his waist, under his shirt, and I began sliding my palms up and down his hot skin. My fingers reached the ridged, muscular juncture where his wings met his shoulder blades, and I rubbed my thumbs across the roughened skin. He moaned with pleasure and shuddered in my grip.

"If you've never slept with an angel," he murmured, "how did you know to do *that*?"

"Instinct," I laughed against his mouth. "Anything that seems too private to touch—should be touched. In circumstances like this."

He kissed me again. "I thought you didn't come here so you could take me as a lover."

"I came here to drag you out of your bitterness and isolation. If seducing you is the only way to do it, well, I'm prepared to make the sacrifice."

Now he laughed, but the sound was shaky. "I can't—I'm not—I'm not thinking clearly right now and any decisions I make—any choices—might not be rational—"

I deliberately leaned in to rub myself against him. It was immediately clear other parts of his body were also responding to my touch. My fingers tiptoed up his spine again to caress the hard mass of tissue guarding the muscles of his wings. Again he gasped, then he drew me so close that I was lifted off my feet.

"Let's not be rational," I suggested. "Let's do things that will embarrass both of us in the morning."

He did not bother answering that. He merely carried me across the cluttered room to a door that led to an equally messy bedroom, kissing me the entire way.

If you've never made love to an angel, I highly recommend the experience.

There was no light, or only what little seeped in from my lonely lamp, yet that seedy, cramped room seemed lit with fey radiance. I writhed beneath him, my arms twined around his neck, his wings reared up over both our heads like a divine canopy. I felt sheltered, protected, free to open myself to him completely because no danger could make it past the haven of his wings. My hands explored his ribs and hips while his body worked above mine, driving me to frenzy and then to satisfaction. When he cried out and collapsed upon me, gasping for breath, I kissed his cheek and murmured into his hair.

"Oh, I think you've definitely found your purpose in life. No need for all this trauma and despair."

He laughed into my ear. "I don't think you can be sure yet," he whispered. "We'll need to experiment a few more times."

And we did.

CHAPTER 7

When I woke up the next morning, my first thought was that I was glad the angel was blind. Sweet Jovah singing himself into laughing hysteria, I must look like a mad street beggar, my hair in tangles, my lips puffy from too many kisses, my face pale from lack of sleep. But, oh, the angel curled up beside me, his cheek still resting on my naked shoulder—he looked sublimely serene. I could not remember the last time I had seen Corban's face so peaceful. He still bore traces of neglect from four days of wretchedness, but they just served to add a scoundrel's charm to his everyday symmetrical beauty. I felt his whiskers scratch my bare skin, and I couldn't help smiling as I gently combed a finger through his knotted hair.

My second thought was that it wasn't exactly morning.

I frowned as I glanced at the boarded-up window, which nonetheless allowed a few rays of energetic sunlight to muscle in. It had to be well past noon, and it seemed odd that Alma had not come upstairs before this to check on the angel. If she had heard me creep in during the night, she might have realized that I was still on the premises and decided not to intrude on us. But surely she had become alarmed by now and wondered if she might have missed my exit later. She knew how fragile Corban was. She would not leave him alone too long.

No one at the school would expect me to make an appearance for another hour or two; I was safe from inquiry there. But Alma's absence was troubling.

I kissed Corban on the top of his head and gently disentangled myself. After pausing for five minutes to clean myself up, I ran downstairs. I didn't catch the sounds or scents of cooking as I stepped into the kitchen. "Alma? Are you here?"

No—and she hadn't been any time this morning. The room looked exactly as it had the night before when I had paused to light my lamp. There was no pot on the stove, no fire in the oven. The place looked clean, but deserted.

"Alma?" I headed directly to her bedroom, the one that opened off the kitchen, and knocked impatiently on the closed door. "Are you in there?"

I heard a sound—a muffled word, or perhaps a pillow falling to the floor. "I'm coming in," I said and pushed the door open.

Alma lay coiled at the edge of the mattress, one hand trailing over the side to be able to make a quick grab for a bucket nearby. The room smelled of vomit and she looked like death. "Oh, you poor thing," I exclaimed. "You've caught that wretched sickness!"

I took a half hour to clean her up, fetch fresh water, change her nightgown, and try to make her comfortable. She was grateful but listless, and her skin was hotter than an angel's to the touch. My apprehension grew.

"I'm just going to put together a quick meal for Corban, then I'll see if there are any drugs left at the school," I told her. "I'll be back as soon as I can."

She nodded and shut her eyes. I threw together a tray of food and dashed upstairs. Corban was just emerging from the bedroom, his hair wet from a quick cleansing, his face lit with a private smile.

"So you didn't abandon me in the middle of the night," he said. "When I woke up and you were gone, I was afraid you were ashamed or sorry."

I set down the tray and went straight over to put my arms around him, lifting my face for a kiss. He responded with alacrity; apparently he didn't have too many regrets, either. "Not sorry, not for a minute," I said, leaning briefly against him. "But I went downstairs to find Alma, and she's seriously ill, so I've been taking care of her."

He was immediately concerned. "Ill? What's wrong?"

"Same stomach disorder that swept through the school earlier in the week, I think, but it looks like it hit her hard." I hesitated. "I'm not very good in a sickroom. I might need to bring someone else in to nurse her."

He considered for only a moment. "Of course. I suppose everyone already knows—" He gestured. *About me.*

"They know there's an angel here, but they don't know your story." I grinned. "I am very good at *not* sharing information when I want."

He kissed me and pushed me toward the door. "I'm aware. Go take care of Alma."

I lingered a moment, my palm centered on his chest. "I'm sorry for the things I said last night," I said. "Well, the meaner things. But it frightened me to see you so lost. And I sound cruel when I'm afraid."

"Just don't apologize for the kinder things you said—later," he replied. "I like to delude myself that you meant them."

I laughed, pressed my fingers against his lips, and departed.

Downstairs, I checked on Alma again. She was either asleep or in a dead faint; she didn't wake when I shook her. By the time I left the house, I was running.

It was harder than I expected to lure Judith from the school to the Great House. Alma was not the only one who had fallen deathly ill overnight. The old handyman David was comatose, three more teachers had become violently sick, and the effort of caring for them all had left Judith pale and exhausted. And fearful.

"There's nothing I can do for any of them," she told me as we stood outside Alma's room after Judith had made a quick examination. We had roused Alma enough to make her swallow a pill, but it was the last one in the infirmary. "All that's left is broth and kindness."

My own worry was intensifying to the point of panic. "We have to raise a plague flag," I said.

She nodded somberly. "We did that last night. But the Gloria is tomorrow. Angels aren't likely to be flying this way again for another few days."

"So they'll arrive in a day or two and pray for medicine then."

Her face was pinched. "It might be too late. For Alma—for all of them."

I felt as if she'd punched me. *"What?"*

"When fevers run so high, sometimes people don't recover. Or if they do, they're seriously damaged. It's as if such a hot temperature burns the body out and leaves only a shell behind. I've seen it more than once."

I stared at her for a moment, then bolted for the stairs.

Corban was seated in the cutaway chair, his back to the door and the cello between his knees. He was picking at the strings very softly, creating a melody that sounded like raindrops dancing on platters of bronze. It was a merry sound; I took a moment to be surprised that Corban was capable of something so lighthearted. If he was feeling a surge of genuine happiness, might I be in any way responsible?

No time to ask. "Corban," I panted, breathless from my run. "You have to go aloft and pray."

He spun around in his chair, his face registering surprise closely followed by dread. "I can't," he said.

I crossed the room and knelt before him. "You have to. Judith—she's from the school—she says Alma could die. And there are others down at the school. They're all sick. They're all in danger. Their fevers are too high, and their bodies won't recover. And we have no drugs left."

"A plague flag—"

"Tomorrow is the Gloria."

He winced at that, no doubt thinking that if times were different, he would be assembling on the Plain of Sharon with all the other angels. He turned away, carefully leaning the cello against the wall. "I can't do it," he said.

I reached for his nearest hand and cradled it between both of mine. "I'll help you," I whispered. "I know that the best way to catch Jovah's attention is to fly very high, but I'll come with you. I don't care how cold it gets. I don't care how far off the ground it is. I won't make you go alone and I won't let you get lost."

He tore his hand away and jumped to his feet. "It's not just the flying, it's the singing," he said, gesturing in agitation. "I haven't—Moriah, the last time I prayed to the god, he sent a thunderbolt! He blinded me!"

I rose more slowly. "You didn't sing that prayer. It was that boy."

He turned away and began pacing, unerringly avoiding chairs and tables but tripping on discarded shoes and clothes that lay in his path. "Yes, but Jovah sent the thunderbolt anyway! He must have known I was in the room! He could have chosen not to strike me!"

"You think he would send lightning again? Even if you pray for medicines?"

He whirled around in my direction. "I think I cannot bring myself to ask for anything from a god I cannot trust. I cannot pray, I cannot *supplicate*. I am too angry to ask him for anything."

Oh, sweet Jovah, this was not a complication I had anticipated. I had thought I could talk him through his fear, but what he felt was fury for a god who had betrayed him. "I understand, I think," I said, my voice halting. "I don't think it would have mattered who was about to die. I wouldn't have been able to ask Reuel Harth for help to save them."

Corban caught his breath at the comparison, but he didn't speak.

"But Jovah didn't harm me," I went on in a low voice. "Can you teach me the song? Can you carry me up toward the heavens so I can sing it to him? Can you let *me* ask him, if you can't do it yourself?"

It seemed like an hour that we stood there, facing each other, both of us so tense that our hands clenched and our shoulders hunched and our faces were creased with concentration. I didn't know if a mortal could sing the holy songs. I didn't know if I could learn them. I didn't know if Corban could forgive his god even enough to let me try. But I knew I would keep pleading until I heard Judith's weary steps on the stairs as she climbed up to tell us the terrible news.

At last Corban took another shuddering breath and pressed his hand to his forehead, as if pushing all his rioting thoughts back inside. "I won't sing to the god," he said in a quiet voice, "but I'll sing to *you*. Put on a coat. It'll be very cold."

Nothing—not three sweaters, my coat, Alma's coat, and a pair of the headmistress's boots I found in her closet—could keep me warm as Corban hovered so high above the ground that I could no longer make out landmarks below. I felt ice at the edges of my eyes where the tears leaked out. My cheeks felt ready to crack from cold. It wasn't just that the temperature was so bitter, but that the wind was so strong. I couldn't imagine how Corban held himself relatively steady against its incessant buffeting, but in fact, he seemed to be riding the merciless currents without effort; clearly his body remembered this particular skill.

The cold wasn't actually the worst of it. There was no *air* at this altitude, or so it seemed. I found it nearly impossible to inhale. I felt myself gasping and growing light-headed with insufficient oxygen. I couldn't believe that Corban would be able to get enough air to pray.

But he drew an easy breath and began to sing.

This was nothing like that mournful tune I had overheard one night as I spied on the Great House. This was a marching army of a song; this was a piece that burst into houses and ransacked drawers and upended cabinets, searching for treasure. This was a song on a mission.

True to his word, Corban did not lift his voice to the god. He held my body tightly to his and sang the piece to me. I felt the melody surge inside my skull, charge down my spine, bivouac in my elbows and knees. His voice was a confident baritone—foggy on some of the higher notes, from having gone so long unused—but rich and bright and warm. If I had been a god, I would have given him anything he asked for.

He sang the prayer straight through four times, and each complete rendition took about ten minutes. By the end of the second round, I thought my feet had turned to ice and sheared off and plummeted to the ground. By the end of the third one, I thought that the only part of my body still hoarding a small flame of warmth was probably the center of my rib cage. By the time he was almost done with the fourth performance, I was numb all over. I had resigned myself to a frozen death. As if to underscore my fate, the air around us began to coalesce into icy chunks, and slivers of wicked sleet burned my skin as they hissed past my cheeks.

Corban finished the fourth song with a musical flourish, decorating the last note with an unnecessary trill. I waited in desolate silence for him to begin the prayer for a fifth time, but he shouted, "That's done it! We can go back now."

That was when I realized that the hailstorm around me wasn't ice, but pellets of medicine being flung to the ground. Corban might have sung to me, but the god had answered.

It was even harder to explain away the angel's presence once he had stepped forward in such a spectacular fashion. The ground around the school was littered with hard granules; students and teachers spent all day scooping the grains up and racing to carry them back to the infirmary for Judith to dispense. All the patients responded remarkably well to their healing powers, even David recovering quickly enough to sit up in bed two days after he had swallowed the first pill. Alma, too, was soon on her feet, eating and drinking normal food, and apologizing for the inconvenience she had caused.

I was back in the kitchen, fending off more questions, acting as if I was as astonished as everyone else. *It turns out the angel is blind! That's why he's been here all this time. But Judith asked him if he could pray for drugs, and he said he would if someone would go with him. Yes, I was terrified to be so high in the air! And it was so cold! But I would do anything for Alma, you know—and all the others, too, of course.*

Not surprisingly, the other workers—especially the women—began fighting for the chance to visit the Great House, whether to check on Alma or carry up supplies or bring the news that the headmistress was finally returning at the end of the week. The students, even the teachers, looked for excuses to stroll along the line of fencing that overlooked the hill, and one or two enterprising boys actually snuck up to the house and climbed the ivy to reach the roof and wave down at the rest of us.

I tried to convince Corban that he should visit the school and introduce himself to his many admirers—perform a concert some night, perhaps, or at least hold an informal session where students could pepper him with questions. He wasn't ready for the human contact yet, but he was willing to put on a remote show in daylight. He came out to the roof once or twice a day and took off in a low spiral, staying close enough that he could always hear the bells and chimes that would guide him home. The whole school turned out for these maneuvers—classrooms emptied out, dust mops and cook pots were left unattended so that everyone could watch the angel glide and dive through the scented spring air.

I knew it wouldn't be long before these displays no longer satisfied

Corban. He was still distrustful of his god, but he was remembering what it felt like to be an angel in Samaria—a creature of grace and glory and allure. He would figure out soon that he was almost healed; he would realize that there were many other places he would rather be. Places where he could use his gifts and exploit his strengths. Places where he belonged.

Therefore I wasn't surprised, the day before the headmistress's return, to find him pacing on the rooftop, deep in thought. I had continued to visit him every night, and we had shared a great deal of laughter in between the moments we slept and the moments we made love. But I could feel him pulling away, and I knew, when he turned to me so eagerly, what he was about to say.

"Moriah, I have something very important to discuss with you," he said, taking my hands and clasping them against his chest. The gibbous moon made a skewed halo behind his head.

Once again, I was glad he was blind and couldn't read the heartache on my face. Now the trick was to keep it from my voice. "What could it possibly *be*?" I asked in a voice of exaggerated breathlessness.

He laughed. "You think you know, but you don't," he informed me.

"Let me guess. Your triumph a few days ago has led you to realize that even though you can't see, you're still an angel. You can still carry out all the tasks the god set aside for you. And you've realized you can't perform these tasks while you're hiding away in some musty old mansion. You need to return to an angel hold—the Eyrie, at a guess."

"You're wrong," he said, a little smug.

I lifted my eyebrows. "Cedar Hills, then."

He shook his head. "I thought about both of them, but neither one will do. Because you won't come with me if I go to an angel hold."

I stared at him in wordless astonishment.

"See, I did surprise you. You're right that I realize it's time to leave the Gabriel School. But I don't want to go by myself."

"Corban—"

He raised his voice to drown mine out. "And now you're going to tell me that I don't really know what I want. You're going to tell me not to confuse gratitude with love. You're going to say, 'You think you can't function without me, but once you're back in the world you know, you'll find me an inconvenience or an embarrassment. You need to go on to your new life without me.' "

I had nothing to say; he had got it right, almost to the word.

"But I know what I want, and who I want, and what I need to go forward from this point," he said in a persuasive tone. "I know you won't lie to me. I know you won't let me lie to myself. I know you won't fail me, no matter how hard things get. I know I love you." He still had my hands wrapped in his, but now he overlapped his wings behind me and with their insistent pressure drew me closer to his body. "And I believe you love me."

I tried to keep my arms stiff against his chest, resisting as much as I could, though we were only inches apart. "Well, I've *tried* not to love you," I said in a mutinous voice. "*Everybody* falls in love with angels, and I wanted to be different."

"But you didn't succeed."

I sighed and stopped pushing myself away from him. Instantly his wings brought me closer, and he dropped a kiss on my mouth. "I didn't succeed," I admitted.

"And you have no particular reason to stay here at the Gabriel School."

I knew he could feel the movement as I shook my head. "I told myself no more running—I had found a good place here and I should be grateful—but I knew I wouldn't be able to stay once you had gone. It would be too dull. And there would be too many memories."

"So where did you think you might go?" he prompted.

"Someplace I could find work. Maybe start my own business. Now that I know the angels—and the Manadavvi—aren't looking for me, I thought I could go to one of the bigger cities. Semorrah or Castelana."

He shook his head. He was smiling. "That's not where you want to live."

I laughed up at him. When had all the stars come out? The night sky was dense with gaudy sparkles, like a tradesman's wife overdressed for a fine occasion. "What city do *you* think I'd choose?"

"The most beautiful place in all of Samaria," he said. "A city where I can write music—and perform it—a city where every merchant prospers and every artist flourishes. Both of us can do what we like and be happy there."

There was only one place like that. "Luminaux."

"Yes."

"But Corban—"

Again he kissed me, just to make me stop talking, I think. "Yes, I'm sure," he said. "I *don't* want to go back to the holds. I *don't* want to take up that old life. I am not yet ready to forgive Jovah for what he did to me. But I do want to go somewhere an angel is appreciated and where a musician can hone his craft. So the only question I have left is—"

"Will I come with you?" I interjected. If he could speak for me, I could speak for him.

"Yes. Will you?"

It was a risk. He might think he loved me unconditionally, he might believe he would never tire of me, but two people had a tendency to wear on each other, and I was more wearing than most. But I could bear it if he left me, as long as he left me in Luminaux, I thought. And maybe he wouldn't leave me. I guessed I wouldn't know unless I made the experiment.

"Yes," I said. "Just let me get my coat."

Ascension

Meljean Brook

CHAPTER 1

A demon had moved into Riverbend.

Judging by the amount of anger and despair that Marc Revoire could sense ravaging this community, the demon intended to rot the small Illinois town from the inside. A lot of work, a lot of whispers, a lot of doubts to sow. The demon might gain the pleasure of watching a few humans die in the process—but from Marc's vantage point, it seemed easier to wait for a cold snap and watch the male half of Riverbend's teenaged population freeze to death instead.

Though a good four inches of snow had fallen since noon, most of the boys coming out of Riverbend's high school and into the parking lot wore T-shirts and cargo shorts. Some had the sense to pull on a stocking cap and a long-sleeved shirt, but they still shivered and hunched while scraping the snow from their windshields. Apparently, the girls had less to prove. Bundled in coats and scarves, only a few wearing short skirts bared their legs to the cold.

Marc expected the foolish clothing. He also wasn't surprised that they completely ignored his presence, as if a man in a dark suit and with a badge tucked into his belt waited at the building's rear exit every day. After fifty years of watching over the Midwestern states, he'd become accustomed to seeing all kinds of teen behavior, from shy to rebellious, ignorant to insightful, clever to outright stupid.

He was less accustomed to watching a bunch of kids leave school on a Friday afternoon, and not a one of them projecting relief or anticipation for the coming weekend. Instead, Marc sensed resignation, dread. Where those emotions hadn't taken hold, a heavy dose of apathy resided.

Demons usually didn't bother with kids. Teenagers didn't have much power and rarely possessed any money—and though some demons destroyed human souls simply for the pleasure of it, most preferred to gain influence or wealth on the side. If the emotional rot in Riverbend had trickled down to these high schoolers, the bastard had gotten his claws in deep.

As a Guardian, Marc was on a mission to rip those claws out. As a man who'd seen too many lives ruined by too many demons, he'd enjoy every second of it.

One and a half centuries ago, a demon had destroyed the community where he'd lived, too. Sixteen years old and human, Marc hadn't been able to psychically detect the festering seeds the demon had sown, but he hadn't needed to—he'd seen the hate and distrust tearing everyone apart, splitting the community into factions. At the demon's urging, resentment had eventually erupted into violence, and Marc had died after taking a bullet meant for his father. Later, he'd learned that his death had shocked the community so deeply that they'd all taken a step back, tried to untangle all of the lies the demon had been spreading. Not every rift had healed, but they'd begun to move forward again.

Marc had gone on, too. His sacrifice gave him a chance to become a Guardian, a warrior given angelic powers, and it was a chance that he'd taken. After a hundred years of training in Caelum, the Guardians' heavenly city, he'd returned to Earth and begun hunting demons. Some were easier to find than others, their arrogance shin-

ing like a psychic beacon through a town—but this demon was proving to be the clever, hidden variety.

Eventually the demon would reveal itself. They always did, but
Marc didn't plan to wait that long . . . and maybe he wouldn't have to.

One hundred and fifty years of combined training and hunting
demons had taught Marc to listen to his instincts, and right now they
were telling him that something had just changed. Something he
was seeing, hearing, or smelling wasn't as it should be, but his brain
hadn't figured out what his senses had already noted.

Tense now, expectant, he cocked his head. No unusual scents
floated on the air. He could account for every footstep he heard, every
voice, every heartbeat. He glanced up at the roof, the school windows,
scanned the parking lot again. Everything appeared all right, no one
moving too fast and everyone breathing, unlike a demon who might
have forgotten himself. His gaze skimmed the snow, slipping over
the drifts, and stopped.

The play of darkness and light was wrong. Cloud-diffused sunlight cast a faint, long shadow of the school building over the parking
lot, but the long edge didn't match the straight lines of the roof. Marc
looked up.

No one. But now he saw the depression in the snow at the roof's
edge, as if someone had recently crouched there. Perhaps he'd heard
the snow crunch—and even as he watched, the depression deepened
slightly, as if shifting beneath someone's weight.

As if someone was *still* crouching there. Tricky as demons were,
they didn't possess any powers of invisibility, and Marc only knew
of one person who could project such a powerful illusion.

Though that person was also a Guardian, his tension didn't ease.
Of the few people in the world who might seek him out, Radha was
the last woman he expected to see.

Of course, he wasn't *seeing* her yet.

"Your shadow," he said quietly.

A frozen puff of air betrayed her exasperated huff of breath.

When he'd known her, Radha had been frustrated by any holes in her illusions, had constantly striven for perfection. Apparently those small mistakes still irritated her.

Marc knew that if he turned to look now, those shadows would appear exactly as they should. He continued to watch the roof instead. "And you breathed. If I wanted to shoot your head, I'd know exactly where to aim."

"Now you're just rubbing it in," she said, and the illusion concealing her dropped away, revealing her narrowed brown eyes, her wry smile.

He *should* have looked the other way. He should have given himself that break. But it would have only been delaying the inevitable punch to his chest, the sensation of staggering while standing in place. It didn't matter when he saw her, or how often—which *wasn't* often. A few minutes every few years. Never speaking with her, only hearing the lilt in her voice from afar, a lilt that bespoke of English learned over two centuries ago and half a world away.

But she was here now, rising from her crouch at the edge of the roof. Thick black hair tumbled to her waist. The long, curling strands and a few wisps of orange silk formed a scanty covering for her breasts. Scarves knotted at her left hip flirted with her inner thighs, hinting at but never revealing anything other than smooth expanses of skin that she'd dyed indigo.

Behind her, white feathered wings arched over her head. She must have still been concealing herself from everyone else. Even apathetic kids would stop and stare at an almost-nude blue woman with wings standing atop a school building.

He couldn't stop staring, either. Couldn't stop remembering that he'd once unwrapped those scarves. That he'd buried his hands in that impossibly thick hair before burying himself in her body.

She'd left without a word the next day. When he'd tried to discover why, the door he'd knocked on remained closed. The note he'd sent returned unopened.

He hadn't tried again. He'd been young, and damn stupid in those days, but her message had been unmistakable: Leave me alone.

So he had. And afterward, he'd realized that Radha hadn't been the woman who'd gotten away, but the one who should have never been his in the first place. Friends, yes. During those early years of training in Caelum, she'd been a companion he valued and trusted, until he'd given in to lust that he never should have felt. That had been the end. A friendship ruined, and Marc had never been certain whether he'd been blessed for simply having known her or cursed for having lost her.

But he'd done his best to put his feelings away after she'd put him aside, and Radha hadn't spoken to him in almost a hundred and forty years.

Yet now she sought him? Not without reason—and that reason likely had nothing to do with him or one awkward sexual experience when he'd been an overeager virgin.

Spreading her wings, Radha stepped from the roof. She gently glided to his side and landed soundlessly. God, she hadn't been this close to him in so long. He'd almost forgotten how small she was, the top of her head only reaching his shoulder, a waist small enough to span with his hands.

A thin gold chain circled her bare belly instead, with a ruby pendant filling her navel. More gold ringed her slim fingers, and the tip of her right forefinger was capped in a sharp gold claw.

Her gaze lifted to his. Flecks of gold lightened the brown of her eyes, outshining the rows of gold loops in her ears, the small diamond stud piercing her nose.

"Hello, Marc."

"Radha." Putting her aside had also taught him to put everything else away, to focus. "Has something happened?"

"To whom?"

"To anyone that would explain why you're here. Do you have news from Caelum?"

Bad news, probably. It seemed that the only news from Caelum of late had been of that kind, beginning a little over a decade ago when thousands of Guardian warriors had chosen to ascend to the afterlife, leaving far too few of them left to fight demons. Half of the remaining Guardians had been killed by the bloodthirsty nosferatu, and a year later, one of their only remaining healers had been slain after a vampire betrayed another Guardian. To save them all—to save everyone on Earth—the most powerful Guardian, their leader, had sacrificed himself and had been trapped in Hell. There had been victories along the way, too, but nothing seemed to make up for the loss of so many . . . and the bad news just kept on coming.

The last time he'd seen Radha had been a week before, during a gathering in Caelum when they'd all finally seen the crumbling ruin the realm had become in their leader's absence—temples shattered, every dome and spire nothing more than piles of marble rubble. Radha had stood on the opposite side of a broken courtyard, weeping as she'd taken in the devastation.

So different from the first time he'd ever seen her, in another courtyard in another part of the once-beautiful, shining city. Ten years after his transformation, he'd stumbled across a public orgy. The realm was all white marble and the Guardians were of every color—but Radha had been the only blue, and she'd been the first in the mass of bodies that he'd truly seen. Once he had, he couldn't tear his eyes away. With a man's head between her thighs and while kissing another woman's belly, Radha had looked over and spotted Marc watching from the edge of the courtyard. Her gaze had met his, she'd smiled—and crooked her finger.

It had taken all of Marc's strength to walk away. Though many Guardians pursue pleasure, that wasn't a route he planned to take. He'd decided to become a celibate warrior, one of God's chosen, as seemed to befit his transformation and honor the gift of life he'd been given.

So he'd left. He hadn't expected that a curious Radha would follow him—or that she'd so easily accept that he didn't want sex from her.

But he had. God, how he had. The following year was one of torment and bliss, spending hours of each day with a woman who fascinated him in every possible way, who'd quickly become closer to him
than any friend he'd had as human or Guardian, and who he wanted
so desperately. A year of constant trial, every moment a test, reminding himself that a Guardian who fought demons had to learn to resist
temptation, and that a celibate warrior would never touch her.

Then he had. He'd failed the first test he'd given himself, and he'd
paid for it with the end of their friendship.

He'd dedicated himself to his training after that, determined not
to fail again. One hundred and forty years, he'd kept his eyes open,
his mouth shut, and done his job.

But lately that hadn't been enough, and it seemed as if the Guardians were on the losing side, as if everything was crumbling, ending.
The week before, when he'd looked across the ruined courtyard and
witnessed her tears and devastation, he'd wished things were different. He'd wished they were still friends enough that he could hold
her, that he could say something to make her happy—because God
knew, the way things were going, he might not have another chance.

Her friends Rosalia and Mariko had been there instead. Women
who, in their own way, shone as brightly as Radha did.

She hadn't needed him, so he'd remained where he was. It was
easy enough. For a good portion of his life, he'd done nothing but stay
in one place. He didn't do it so much lately, but whenever he saw
Radha, he seemed to recall the skill effortlessly.

"Oh, I see. You think that someone else has died or is trapped in
Hell or that Caelum has been swallowed by the sea." Smiling slightly,
Radha shook her head. A darker blue than her skin, her lips glistened
as if she'd slicked gloss over them. Nothing fragranced, of course.
Nothing that might give her presence away to a demon, nothing that
would give her an odor to conceal. "No one has been hurt, and nothing has happened. I am taking a holiday."

Bullshit. "In southern Illinois?"

"Oh, you say that as if there is nothing to be done or seen here.

You cannot convince me of that, not when this area has been part of your territory for five decades and you have been living here happily for all of it."

Marc wouldn't have said *happily.* He'd had a job. He'd done it. "For a vacation, the Midwest doesn't have anything like your territory does."

Nothing at all like the beaches of Southeast Asia or the mountains of Nepal—or the cities in between.

"That is why I am here. It is not the same at all." Her gaze swept the parking lot. "Look at them. Each with their own vehicle, well fed, clothed."

"If you're hoping to escape to a place without any poverty, it won't be here." And Riverbend was well off, compared to other nearby towns. No open sewers, maybe, but plenty of people were having a rough time.

And desperation of any sort made a demon's job easier.

"That is not what I'm trying to say." With a hint of censure in her voice, she looked to him again. "I have sensed more happiness from those living in slums than I do at this school. Why is that?"

Radha had been a Guardian longer than Marc had—and long enough to know very well why this town felt like this. Was she trying to deflect his questions about this vacation nonsense? He knew she wasn't here for the demon.

"What's going on, Radha? Are you in trouble?"

"If I was, would I need to come to you?"

No, and that was the damn point. He couldn't figure out why she'd come. As a warrior with half a century more experience than Marc, her skills probably exceeded his. With her ability to create illusions, she possessed one of the most powerful Gifts of any Guardian. Marc's own Gift allowed him to haul dirt and stone around, but unless she'd lost something in the mud, there was little he could do that she couldn't do herself.

Not that he'd send her packing. "I hope you know that if you did come to me, I'd do whatever I could to help."

Her lips flattened. She looked away from him before she replied, "Is that so? Thanks so much."

Her doubt struck like a slap. What the hell? Marc stared at her profile, at the sudden rigidity of her posture. She truly didn't know that? Didn't *believe* it?

Did she think he harbored ill will toward her for leaving *one hundred and forty years* ago? What kind of men did she know that held a grudge so long? Hell, he hadn't held a grudge at all. He'd understood that he simply hadn't been what she'd needed—and damn him if he didn't agree with her. He sure as hell hadn't expected her to seek him out now.

He could only think of one reason for it: another Guardian had told Radha that there'd been a threat to his life. Whatever her feelings toward him, whatever doubts, she was a Guardian first.

"Did Khavi use her Gift and foresee something happening to me? Something that you need to stop?"

"No."

"She had a vision of something happening to you, then."

Radha slanted him a sideways glance. "Marc."

He knew that look, that tone. It meant *Don't say stupid things.* When they'd been friends, she'd given him that look rather often.

They weren't friends now, yet she'd still come. With no threat behind it, that left one possibility: she was running from something. Maybe not something dangerous, not something she could fight, but something that had sent her to the least likely place anyone would come looking. Hiding, for some reason.

He'd help her hide, then. If whatever she was running from caught up to her, he'd protect her, give her anything she needed. He'd watch over her until she left again.

"All right," he said. "You're on vacation."

He expected a dazzling grin in response, the one Radha always gave when she got her way. He only got a long, considering look followed by a slow nod, and that hit him harder than her doubt had.

What the hell had he done that laughing, dancing, singing Radha responded to him with such wary reserve?

A familiar pattern of footsteps from inside the school prevented him from asking. He gestured toward the door and said quietly, "Tell me what you sense from these four girls."

Guardians couldn't read thoughts, only detect emotions—and only if the person didn't possess strong psychic shields. Most humans didn't, because they weren't aware of a need to block any mental probes.

These girls had strong enough shields that he couldn't sense anything from them. With enough force, he could break through those shields, but that would bring the demon's attention to the girls, too.

They came through the door, each with a cell phone in hand and a backpack slung over one shoulder. He knew their names by now: Jessica and Lynn in the front, Miklia and Ines in the back. As far as he could tell, Jessica was the leader, but maybe just because she owned the car they all rode in. Focused on their cell phone screens, only Miklia glanced up as she passed Marc. She looked quickly away—but not back at her phone. For a long second, her gaze found Radha, before the girl finally dismissed them both.

Radha's brows lifted as she watched the girls cross the parking lot. "Walking and texting. That takes skill."

"Easier than talking and walking? Half the time, I'm convinced all these kids are just texting the person next to them."

She gave a short laugh, shared her amusement with a glance. Of course she laughed now. He remembered very well that Radha couldn't resist an absurdity. It was probably what had drawn her to him in those early years. Marc could think of few things more absurd than he'd been.

"I thought you'd made yourself invisible," he said. "But Miklia saw you."

"She saw this."

She changed in a smooth, quick transition. No blue skin, just

Radha as she might have looked as a young human woman in Bengal—though she'd certainly never worn a conservative black trouser suit, a badge, or a long wool coat that matched his.

"Everyone who sees me will assume I'm your partner," she said.

"Why didn't I sense your Gift?" A Guardian's power typically felt like a small burst of psychic energy against his mind, and the use of a Gift usually exposed a Guardian's presence to nearby demons. Hers wouldn't—though that hadn't always been so.

When he'd known her, she'd only recently begun using the indigo dye. Her illusions had been strongest when a crack opened in her opponent's psychic shields—and even a demon experienced a moment of surprise when under sudden attack from a blue woman. She'd used that surprise to force her illusions through.

Now, she apparently didn't require a weak spot—Marc knew his shields had remained strong, even though she'd been invisible to him—and she could hide her psychic presence, too.

"It's another illusion, but a psychic one. I just create an illusion of *not* feeling my Gift."

Impressive. "When did you learn to do that?"

"About forty years ago. If I'm fighting, I can't hide it as well, but for work like this, it's easy." She let the illusion fade—but only for him, he realized. Everyone else would still see the federal agent. "I've heard that you finally discovered your Gift when you came back to Earth."

"There was no dirt in Caelum to move around."

No dirt, period. Just a lot of marble, and nothing for his Gift to work with. After he'd left Caelum, though, the pure strength beneath his feet had staggered him. Fifty years on, and his Gift had barely tapped it.

"It fits you. Who has a deeper connection to the earth than a farmer?"

"The dead who are buried in it."

She smiled a little. "Aside from them."

Maybe no one. Even now, though he could plow a field with just a thought, there was almost nothing he liked better than working his hands through the soil—and on any other day, she might have run into him with dirt beneath his fingernails and mud on his boots.

He'd seen Radha come from Earth to Caelum with dust on her bare feet, but it had never seemed to touch her, and it was never what a man noticed. Not when he could remember her dancing, slow and deliberate, her fingers rigid yet as graceful as bird's wings, every movement as precise as a word in a story, every step another tale. Though he couldn't see her feet now in the snow, he knew that instead of mud squishing between her toes, more gold rings circled them.

He'd kissed them once, and all the way up to her smooth, blue thighs. And he'd wondered whether he was blessed or cursed? Looking at her legs now, the answer was obvious. He'd been blessed.

Blissfully, undeservedly blessed.

"So why these girls?"

It was a long story, but he'd try to make it short. "There's a community of about two dozen vampires spread through the towns in this area—a few of them have lived here for almost a hundred years now. They're quiet, take care of themselves, deal with their own problems."

And Marc kept his nose out of their business. As long as vampires weren't feeding from humans or exposing themselves, Guardians left them alone.

"But a couple of months ago, Abram Bronner—the community leader—contacted me for help. There'd been a couple of vampires killed, and except for one, they'd all been exposed to the sun and turned to ash before anyone found them."

Radha nodded, catching on. "A demon?"

"That's what I thought—and in this area, there was one demon, Basriel, who kept giving me the slip. He'd move around, killing other demons, establishing most of the Midwest as his territory."

"And that means taking control of the vampire communities, too. Or crushing them."

"Yes. But a little over a month ago, I caught up to Basriel in Duluth."

"And killed him." It wasn't a question. Of course he had.

"Yes. And I thought that might have been the end of it . . . until I came through the town again a few days ago, and felt this." The anger and rot, spreading from person to person. "I checked in with Bronner, but they haven't had any more trouble, so they hadn't called me in."

"They didn't sense this?"

"They did." Marc shrugged. "From inside, though, it's not as easy to see. There's a plant in the next town that just shut down, people lost their jobs. A big blaze brought down an apartment building—killed half the county fire department—about a month ago. Open up the paper, and all you see is talk of budgets being cut, schools shutting down, unemployment rising, prices going up."

"So with all of those things adding up, there's no reason to assume there's a demon involved. People are understandably stressed and angry."

"Yes. And there might *not* be a demon," Marc said. "I haven't seen evidence of one yet."

"But . . . ?"

"My instincts are telling me otherwise."

"So are mine." Radha glanced toward the parking lot again, where the four girls had packed themselves into Jessica's old Cherokee. "So how are they connected?"

"The little blonde, the one who looked at you—her brother, Jason, was the first vampire killed. Unlike the others, he wasn't ashed. According to Bronner, his parents—who still don't know he was a vampire—found him with a stake through his heart in their home, even though he wasn't living there at the time."

"God," Radha said. "That sounds like something a demon would do. Did you have to come in and cover that up?"

"No. Bronner's got the county coroner in his pocket. I didn't hear about it until later."

"Did the family truly not know he was a vampire?"

"I've spoken to the parents." Using the same line he always did in unsolved cases like these—that the murder resembled a similar one somewhere else, and could he have a moment of their time? "The parents didn't shield their minds and were speaking the truth. But Miklia, she won't talk to me."

"Will the other girls?"

"Not at all."

"And their minds are shielded. So they know something, and they know to hide away what they're feeling."

"Yes. Whether they just know the truth about Jason or saw more than they let on, I'm not sure. But there's something they know, and if it helps me get a bead on the demon, I need to find it."

Radha's crafty, conspiratorial smile appeared. "So, which one do you want to pretend to be? I'll distract the real one while you talk to Miklia."

He had to laugh. "I'm not shape-shifting to look like a girl." Not yet. He would eventually, though, if it became necessary. "Because if there's one thing true about small towns, it's that someone always knows something—even if they don't realize they do."

"What? Riddles aren't any fun, Marc."

"But seeing me as a girl would be?"

She blinked innocently.

Shaking his head, he looked to the school doors again. "One thing that everyone in this town knows is that Miklia didn't always hang out with those girls—and that there'd been a rivalry between them up until Jason was killed."

"So something apparently happened to bring them together."

"I think so, yes."

"Then why aren't we following them? Who are we waiting for?"

We? He didn't question it.

"The former best friend," he said. "The one Miklia left behind."

"Oh." Radha suddenly grinned. "Teen drama. I can't wait."

CHAPTER 2

Radha should have been gone already. Or better yet, she shouldn't have come in the first place. And she definitely shouldn't have cared how he was doing—not Marc Revoire, the bastard who'd once asked God to forgive him for fornicating with her. For a hundred and forty years, she'd determinedly pushed Marc from her heart and thoughts, except for when she wondered how she could have ever fallen for a man who thought of her as something that should be washed off. And she'd done a good job of pushing him from her mind.

Until the week before, when she'd been stupid enough to look his way during the gathering. When she'd been stupid enough to care that he'd seemed so *alone*.

Assholes didn't deserve friends. But still . . . She'd been shocked by the changes in him.

He looked older. Not *old*, but not a youth anymore, either. Physically, he resembled a hardworking human in his midthirties, sun-streaked brown hair, broader through the shoulders than he'd once been, and just as lean through the hips—like the man he might have become if he hadn't sacrificed his life first.

But that wasn't what had surprised her. Many Guardians changed their appearance over time, either to match the demands of their current mission or to blend in with a population. Even Radha had chosen a younger form than the fifty-year-old woman she'd been upon her human death, because after her transformation she'd *felt* younger. Guardians often took a form that reflected what they wanted to be, rather than what they'd once been.

So what the hell had Marc been through that he appeared to bear the weight of the world on his shoulders? Radha didn't know, and she hadn't heard of any terrible loss that he'd suffered, or any soul-breaking trial that a demon might have put him through. And she *would* have heard of it. The Guardians' gossip mill was as strong as any small town's.

Yet it hadn't just been the loneliness or his apparent age. As he'd taken in Caelum's destruction, he hadn't seemed devastated as so many others were. He hadn't seemed afraid. He'd seemed resigned.

As if everything that had happened in the past years had left him little to hope for. As if it had left him little to *live* for. As if he were tired of fighting.

As if he'd lost faith.

She hadn't believed it. Not Marc, not the man determined to be God's chosen warrior at the cost of everything else. But the memory of his weary resignation had nagged at her, and even after the gathering ended, she'd worried for him.

Like an idiot, she'd talked herself into coming here, to watch him in secret and determine whether there was truly anything to worry about. *Not* that she cared. But she was a Guardian, and Guardians took care of their own.

Too bad that she'd forgotten how capable he was of sussing out the holes in her illusions.

So she'd been found out, but Marc seemed all right, anyway. At least, he wasn't flogging himself or crying in a bathroom somewhere. She could have gone.

Except, maybe he *wasn't* all right. He'd always been good at concealing his true feelings from her. After all, she'd spent thousands of hours with him over the course of a single year and never realized that he considered her the biblical equivalent of a diseased whore. So she'd wait a little longer and make certain.

If she helped him track down a demon in the process, all the better. Slaying one was always fun—except for when it was difficult and horrifying. If that happened, it was best that she was here to back him up.

He didn't need the backup yet, though. The kid who came out of the school possessed a wide-open mind, and as soon as he spotted Marc, he trembled with uncertainty and excitement.

So cute. Tall, a bit thin and awkward, with a mop of curly dark hair and determinedly nerdy glasses—but as soon as he grew into his body, Radha suspected the girls in the area would be in trouble.

"Sam Briffee?"

Marc held up his identification, and Radha took a quick look at it. Special Investigations. A legitimate federal law enforcement division, and a legitimate identification, thanks to an arrangement the Guardians had made with the United States government. Radha rarely operated in this country, so she didn't have one.

But then, she didn't really need one. When Marc introduced himself as Special Agent Revoire, she held up a piece of paper. Surrounded by her illusions, the blank paper would feel and look like a real wallet and identification, even if the boy examined it up close. To her disappointment, he didn't—but she had to grin when Marc glanced back at her and paused before saying,

". . . and this is Special Agent Bhattacharyya."

Impressive. He pronounced it correctly. It wasn't really her surname—Radha didn't bother with that ridiculousness—but she liked the rhythm of it.

"I'm Sam." Wary, the boy looked from Radha to Marc. "Why are you looking for me?"

Marc kept his tone even, friendly. "Just to ask a few questions.

Another investigation has opened up new leads in Jason Ward's murder, and so we're looking at a few details. We understand that you're Miklia's friend?"

"Yeah," the boy said. Then more strongly, "Yeah, I am. So his murder is connected to someone else's?"

"That's what we're trying to find out. Do you have a few minutes to talk? Not out here," he added, when the boy hunched in his light jacket and looked up at the sky. "The diner across the street. Our treat."

"Yeah, all right."

Oh, teen boys and their stomachs. Too easy—but it might have been anyway. Curiosity filled him now, and anticipation. Maybe at having a story to tell his peers the next day, or simply at the possibility of learning some grisly detail about the crime.

Maybe she'd show him fake photographs from the fake investigation into that other murder. It would support Marc's cover story and give this boy a little something extra to talk about—and maybe confuse the demon enough that he'd ask questions about the supposed murder, revealing himself.

Though Marc turned and waited, politely gesturing for her to start off first, she shook her head, indicating for him to go on ahead with the boy. This was his show. She'd take up the rear and listen to the other ways the demon revealed himself.

From farther down the street, two people in one of the offices had begun arguing. Only snippets of the fight reached her ears, but it was exactly what she'd have expected.

—*You stood here yesterday and told me that! Are you saying now that you didn't?*—

No. Whatever that person was being accused of lying about, he probably hadn't said it. That was often how a demon worked: shapeshifting to resemble a real person, making promises to loved ones, spreading lies, destroying trust.

And it was what made some demons so difficult to locate. Arrogant and vain, many demons chose to create their own human identity and form, often in the guise of a rich, handsome male, and hunting them was merely a matter of making certain he was a demon and finding an opportunity to slay him. But a demon who made a practice of shape-shifting posed a different challenge: though it often kept a default, day-to-day human identity, the demon could be anyone, at any time, and appearing in the form of a person that the Guardian had already determined *wasn't* a demon. The low-level psychic sweeps Guardians performed wouldn't differentiate human from demon—yet any stronger probes would reveal their own nature, which might send the demon running from Riverbend and starting again elsewhere.

Losing him, unless Marc happened across another town at the right time. They wouldn't want to take that risk.

At the diner's entrance, she vanished her wings rather than trying to maneuver them through the small space. Marc held the door open for her, waiting for her to pass through. Did federal agents bother with such niceties? Radha didn't know. Assholes usually didn't bother, and she wished that it was easier to remember that Marc was one. She wished that it was easier to forget how much she'd loved being with him, the conversations they'd had, and how well they'd fit together. She wished that he didn't look at her now with the quiet concern that she knew had to be false—and she wished that he made his opinion of her overt instead of hiding it behind polite human rituals.

A different sort of illusion, but one she didn't appreciate.

Inside, her own illusion was simple to maintain, creating a lighter echo of Marc's footsteps to cover her lack of shoes. As they crossed to a booth in an empty corner, the wet tracks she left behind on the linoleum had to appear as if they came from leather soles rather than bare feet. The whisper of her scarves became the heavy sound of a wool coat sliding across a vinyl bench seat. Perhaps she missed a few small reflections in the spoons she passed, in the silver carafe of syrup, in the shining wire that made up the baskets holding the jellies, but she altered the reflections in the windows and in the gleaming tabletop.

No one but Marc would look any closer. No one but Marc would *know* to look any closer—and that likely included a demon. If she felt a sudden burst of confusion from one of the people in the diner, she'd know that some part of her illusion needed attention. After she fixed it, humans were usually satisfied, convincing themselves that whatever they'd originally seen had probably been a trick of the light.

Neither Radha nor any other Guardian ignored those feelings. Demons couldn't cast illusions and didn't possess Gifts, but if something *seemed* wrong for any reason, appeared impossible, or just something to dismiss as a trick of the light . . . it probably *was* wrong.

Those little things were often what gave shape-shifting demons away.

Marc slid in next to her, facing the boy. The diner wasn't busy, and the waitress came as soon as they settled. Sam ordered a plate of fries and a soda. Radha liked both and ordered the same, hoping that Marc intended to pay for it. She didn't carry American money, liked her jewelry too much to give it up, and would probably feel a niggle of guilt for passing a piece of blank paper off as a twenty-dollar bill.

Marc requested a black coffee, but let it sit in front of him. He focused on Sam. "How long have you been friends with Miklia?"

"Eighth grade." The kid wriggled out of his backpack, let it flop onto the bench beside him. "Her family moved in from Topeka."

"Almost four years," Marc said. "So you must have met her brother, Jason."

"A few times, yeah. Not at her house, not after he graduated and moved out, but I saw him at the video store some nights. It's not there now, though. They just put in one of those vending machines at the grocery." He shook his head. "No good movies at all."

"I watch mine online," Radha said, though it wasn't at all true. There were few better illusionists than moviemakers, and films were best enjoyed on a large scale. She preferred theaters in the cities, dark and cool, surrounded by a crowd of humans.

"My connection at home sucks, and the library isn't any good for that, not with old Mrs. Carroll always looking over my shoulder or cutting me off after twenty minutes, so . . ." The kid shrugged. "I'm out of luck."

Their sodas arrived, with a paper-wrapped straw dropped next to each glass. Marc thanked the waitress and waited until she'd moved away before asking Sam, "But you're over at Miklia's house often, aren't you? I noticed they have a big collection of DVDs."

"Yeah, they're all movie buffs." Sam stabbed his straw past the cubes of ice. "But I haven't been over there so much lately. It's been a rough time for her. For all of them, I guess. So, you know, I gave her some space."

The resentment suddenly boiling from him didn't echo the concern and support in his voice—and was probably what Marc had been aiming for. People often talked for two reasons: because they wanted to help or because they needed to air a grievance.

Radha hadn't expected this boy's reason would be the second. "I imagine that losing her brother affected her. Any sudden death is a huge change for a family. Did she change, too?"

"Oh, yeah. She started hanging out with Lynn, Ines, Jessica. All of them, they've been in her face since she moved here. We called them the Brainless Bitches. Now she's their BFF." He rolled his eyes. "But she needed space, time to think. She's going through stuff."

And more resentment. Marc obviously didn't miss it, either. "But you'd have given her more support."

"I've been there since eighth grade! I understand her better, could help her out. Instead it's a waste of four years."

Selfish little twit. "Your *friendship* was a waste?"

"What would you call it?"

He probably didn't really want to hear Radha's answer. But since the fries plonked down in front of her, she reached for them instead. Let Marc take this. He glanced at her, tilted a bottle of ketchup her way.

Yuck. "No, thanks."

He looked to Sam. "A waste, then."

"Yeah." The boy shook half a bottle of tomato goop over his fries and dug in. "All these years, I've been waiting for her to see that I'm not like them, not like any jerk. I treat her right—listening to her, being her friend—and she turns to someone else."

"But it should have been you?"

"Yeah. I mean—Whatever. But, yeah. It should count for something."

Maybe Marc agreed with him, maybe not. Radha couldn't tell. But since he hadn't taken a drink of his coffee yet, she floated an eyeball in it.

It was always the little things that gave them away. Not eating or drinking was one of them.

Marc glanced down at his cup. His lips curved a little—*why did that have to be sexy instead of making him look like a smarmy asshole?*— but he took the hint, and took a sip. He didn't choke when she added the sensation of the floating eyeball bumping into his lip, just smiled a bit more, this time directing it at her.

Next time she'd just tell him to take a drink. That wouldn't be any fun, but maybe that was the problem. She remembered all too well how fun he'd been—so unflappable, so solid, no matter what she threw at him. It made her *want* to forget how a few of his words had stabbed through her heart.

She never liked dwelling on anything that had once hurt her. She liked to forget it. With Marc, she *had* to remember, or she'd probably find herself in the same situation again.

When Marc set the cup back down, no eyeball looked up at him. Whether that disappointed him or not, she didn't know. He simply asked Sam, "But you were still close friends when her brother died?"

"Yeah. Well, mostly."

Marc's brows lifted. He hadn't expected that. "Mostly?"

"Not so much. She'd already started hanging out with them."

"But I thought the change came because he'd died."

"Well, yeah. That was after. I mean, it was *really* obvious after that." A flush started up the boy's neck. "Homecoming, right? That's the night he was killed. I remember, because I asked Miklia to go with me. Just as friends, okay? But I thought, maybe if she saw how I treated her well, how I was a great date, something more might finally happen. Four *years*, man. But she said homecoming was silly—and then showed up at the dance with the Brainless Bitches."

"That had to sting," Marc said.

"Yeah. But her brother was killed that night sometime."

"Did she seem upset at the dance?"

Radha shoved another fry into her mouth, reminding herself to keep silent. No doubt this kid had been keeping an eye on Miklia that night. Resenting every second.

"No, she wasn't upset. She just sat at a table with the other three. They left early. I don't know where they went." He shrugged and swiped through a pool of ketchup with his last fry. "Maybe to Perk's Palace. That's where they always seem to be now."

"The coffee shop?"

"Yeah. Because that's where Gregory works."

A little sneer accompanied the name. Marc didn't let it pass by. "Gregory?"

"Yeah. Gregory Jackson. Not Greg, of course. *Gregory.*" Sam shook his head, disgust clear. "New kid this year. He's supposed to be some big shot quarterback from a school in Chicago, right? Except he tore his knee up or something, and they moved here, his mom opened that shop. But he thinks he's better than all of us."

Radha's interest piqued. Marc leaned forward, expression intent. "Better? How so?"

Sam shrugged. "I don't know, it's just an attitude I get from him. Last fall he partnered with Miklia a few times in chemistry, and someone caught them sucking face in the weight room, and that's when she started backing off from me. Like she's comparing us. And I came out on the bad side, even though he's not there half the time now."

"Not there . . . ? Class, or Perk's Palace?"

"Class. And even when he is, he's just half asleep through most of it."

"But does he do well anyway? His grades are all right?"

"I guess so, yeah. He doesn't seem to try hard at anything, but he still gets everything. Even Miklia. And now she's doing the same thing. Her parents never notice anything, so they wouldn't notice that she's skipping half her classes or that she's coming in late to first period—like this morning. She was probably with him all night."

Oh, now that was bitter. Radha hoped he was wrong about Miklia being with him—though not for Sam's sake. A lot of what he'd just described sounded like a scaled-back version of a demon. They didn't usually take a kid's form long term, but a high school quarterback might have just enough influence within the school to be appealing, and it wouldn't be the typical place for a Guardian to look for one.

But in the wake of the kid's rising frustration, Marc returned to their supposed investigation. Good call. They had the info to seek out this Gregory. No need to alienate Sam in the process by forcing him to talk about someone he obviously considered a rival.

"After Jason died, was Miklia the one who told you?"

"No. No, my mom did. I tried to call Miklia right away, to see if she was okay, but I couldn't really get through. And when I finally just went over to her house about a few days later—I thought she might need me, you know?—the Brainless Bitches were in her room with her. It was weird, so I left without really saying anything."

"You didn't see her at school?"

"No, she missed the whole week. And after that, she was just . . . cold." He shook his head. "I don't know, I'm done with her."

Radha couldn't stop herself. "Because you already wasted too much time."

"Yeah. I know, right?" He let out a heavy breath, checked his watch. "Anyway. Anything else? I gotta get home."

"No, thank you." Marc slipped a card across the table. "Call me if you remember something else, any little detail that you think might be relevant. Someone hanging around her house, something that seems out of place."

"Okay. Right. I will." He slid out of the bench, hefted his backpack over his shoulder. "Thanks for the grub."

Marc inclined his head, waited until Sam had walked out of earshot before opening his mouth. Radha beat him to it.

"The quarterback? *Really?*"

His grin eradicated the weariness that seemed to hang over him. Okay, that was proof enough. No matter how resigned and lonely he seemed, he was all right—and she really needed to go soon.

"We'll talk to him next." His gaze lifted to the window. Outside, Sam was walking past, head down and earbuds in. "Do you think he'll grow out of it?"

"Out of being a stalker, pretending to be a girl's best friend for years, just so he can get into her pants?" At least with the more aggressive creeps, a girl knew exactly what they were after. They didn't pretend to care about anything else. Sam was the insidious kind of creep. Could that change? "I don't know. For now, she's well rid of him. *He's* the one who wasted their friendship. Maybe she caught on."

Marc nodded, but she sensed a slight hesitation in him. Now *that* was unexpected. She'd never known him to hesitate over anything.

"What?"

"Is this what you thought I did back then?"

Back then. She knew very well he hadn't. "No. You made it clear that you weren't after sex."

She hadn't been after it, either, not at first. She'd been older, maybe too old for him—living a lifetime as a human, and then the span of another human life as a Guardian by the time she'd met him. But she'd liked him so well, and he'd been so fun. Serious and driven, yet smiling that sexy smile every time she'd gone to visit him, abandoning whatever he was doing to spend time with her.

And before too long, age hadn't seemed to matter. It rarely did with Guardians, not when they could appear however old they wanted to. They were all adults, after all. But maybe, with Marc, their age differences *should* have mattered. She'd known he was still finding his way, adjusting to his new life. But they all had done that. She'd known he'd settle in, eventually, discover who he was, who he wanted to be.

Maybe she'd pushed too hard, though. Maybe he hadn't been old enough—*mature* enough—to resist her when she'd finally given in and kissed him. He certainly hadn't had the experience.

He'd made up for it. All of that seriousness, all of that focus, suddenly turned toward pleasing her. She'd told him what she liked, and he'd applied himself to it very, *very* determinedly—and with an intensity that all but burned her alive.

And for all of her experience, she hadn't known how much she'd wanted that intensity. No surface passion, no going through the motions seeking some fleeting pleasure. With Marc, it had been all fire.

But only because his control had slipped, and he hadn't been able to resist.

He hadn't wanted to be her lover; she'd known that. She didn't know whether he'd pretended to be her friend, though. Maybe he'd just tolerated her. All of those polite human rituals coming to the fore, stopping him from telling her what he really thought of her.

The bastard.

Though Marc nodded in response to her answer, he still had that slightly faraway look, as if trying to work something out without actually asking her. And she realized—his question hadn't been about their friendship. It had been about her *leaving*, about being rid of him.

Did he not know? Did he truly never realize? Disbelieving, she shook her head. "You thought that was why I left? That I thought you'd just been my friend until you got what you wanted? Or maybe—did you think that *I* had gotten what I wanted?"

His jaw tightened, and a slight flush rose beneath his skin. "Or that you realized that I couldn't give it to you."

A hard, bitter laugh shot from her. Oh, God. "Marc, you left me in bed and went to pray. You asked for forgiveness for having sex with me."

"Ah." He closed his eyes as if seeking out the memory, and his uncertainty became chagrin. Mildly embarrassed, but not sorry. The asshole. "I prayed a lot in those days, didn't I? Everything I enjoyed, later I asked forgiveness for. What can I say? I fell in with a bad crowd."

A bad crowd of Guardian religious fanatics. No surprise there. Many Guardians went searching for answers after they were transformed, and those who seemed the most certain and the most vocal about those answers were also the most extreme. Radha had tried out several different belief systems, too, though she was over it by the time she met Marc. And she'd known that he'd been influenced by the fanatics—they'd debated several times. But she'd thought he was still looking for answers, not internalizing the ones that had been given to him.

By calling them a bad crowd, he probably meant for her to laugh, but it still hurt too much. Far too much. And he still didn't get it.

She'd understood him, though. Even back then, she hadn't been surprised that he'd gone to pray. Of *course* he was conflicted. He'd just broken a vow he'd made to himself. She'd understood that perfectly, and she sympathized with it—that was why she'd followed him. She'd intended to lend her support.

Instead, she'd discovered exactly how deeply that bad crowd had gotten to him.

"Marc, you prayed for forgiveness for fornicating with an *unclean* woman."

His big body stilled, his face suddenly rigid as he stared at her. Would he come up with an excuse now? There *was* no excuse. She didn't care what he'd believed. A heathen, an infidel, okay. She absolutely was. *Unclean?* No friend thought that.

"Radha . . ." His voice was hoarse, and his throat worked, as if clearing an obstruction. His gaze searched her face before he closed his eyes. "I *did* say that."

At least he didn't deny it. "I know. I heard."

"So you left."

"My choices were either to cry in front of you, kill you, or leave. I chose the one I could live with."

"God. I can't . . . *God.*" He looked at her again, expression tormented. "I can't take that back. But I'm sorry. I'm damned sorry, Radha. It's not what I think now, and it was unforgivable to say it then."

"Yes." Unforgivable. It didn't matter that his horror and remorse were genuine, that she could feel them pouring from him. It didn't matter that he'd opened his emotions and lowered his shields in the most vulnerable manner a Guardian had, just so that she could see the truth of what he said now.

"It's not enough, but I'm sorry. I had a lot of stupid thoughts then, let a lot of stupid things come out of my mouth, seeing everything as a test of my faith, my dedication—and sex with you as a failure, because I succumbed to temptation. It doesn't justify anything. It doesn't excuse anything. But I'm sorry that my stupidity hurt you, and I hope you know that the thought only came then, when I was hating myself for my weakness and trying to find any reason to punish myself a little more. I never thought it before that moment, or after, and I sure as hell don't think it now."

She knew. With his emotions wide open, she could feel his sincerity. But after what he'd done, what he'd said, it didn't matter that he wasn't that stupid boy now. Did it?

Silent, he waited. Just before he built his psychic shields again, she sensed the pain slipping through the sincerity, the resignation through the remorse, the despair through the horror.

God. What the hell was he carrying around with him? There wasn't anything good in there. No hope, no joy—and he *wasn't* all right. How could he live like this?

But she knew the answer: because he was as solid as the earth, unflappable. Because he'd keep going, even if he ran out of reasons to.

She couldn't read his face or emotions now, but his voice was low and rough.

"Is this what you came for, then? An apology, reparation? To have my head? I'll give it to you."

No, that wasn't why she'd come, though she appreciated the apology. She'd been around long enough to know that it was a rare man who fully accepted responsibility for his actions, who didn't offer any excuses. Marc had apparently become the good man she'd always thought he might be . . . and she should leave now. He *wasn't* all right, but he wouldn't do anything stupid. Not Marc. He wouldn't give up.

But she *couldn't* leave him. Not like this.

"I'm still on vacation," she said. "But I'll take the apology."

He nodded, his gaze holding hers. "I *am* sorry. And if I'd known that I'd hurt you, I'd have apologized long ago."

"It wouldn't have meant anything if you still believed I was unclean." God, even now the word stuck in her throat, made a painful hitch in her chest.

He heard it. His eyes darkened, and his voice thickened, as if he spoke past a constriction in his own throat. "I didn't. And I should have apologized for *thinking* it even for a moment, even not knowing that you'd heard. I've been sorry and ashamed since I realized what a fool I was, believing half the things that I did. But that doesn't even touch how sorry I am, knowing that I hurt you with it."

So he hadn't been an asshole all of this time. "How long ago did you realize you were a fool?"

"About a hundred and forty years ago. About the time that I knocked on your door and you didn't answer—and I thought to myself that you were the best woman I'd ever known, and anyone or anything that tried to convince me differently had to be idiocy. And I realized that I hadn't failed a test of faith when I took you to my bed, but one of arrogance and blindness when I'd asked to be forgiven for it."

"So I'm still just a test, then." Not a woman, but a lesson to be learned.

"Not now," he said. "I stopped believing shit about you and seventy-five percent of the Guardians in Caelum right away. But it took me a little while longer than that to pull my head out of my ass and realize that not everything is about me proving my worthiness as a Guardian, or a trial to pass or fail."

"How many years did that take?"

"About a hundred and thirty." He gave her a crooked grin. "I can be slow."

Not slow. Just immutable. Solid. Good qualities, sometimes. Not always at other times. But it looked as though he'd figured that out. She might have saved herself the hurt if she'd waited, and become friends with *this* man instead of the boy he'd been.

And though she'd been pushing aside and ignoring the hurt his carelessness had caused for so many years, only now could she finally feel it cracking, as if the pain might crumble to dust. It hadn't yet. She could still feel the pain there, right around her heart, but she was suddenly very glad she'd come.

She gave him a smile, and a nudge against his shoulder. "Shall we go find this demon quarterback, then?"

CHAPTER 3

So she was still here. Still hiding from something, obviously, since his apology hadn't been her reason for coming—but he wasn't going to question her about the why. He'd just do what he'd planned to do before, and watch over her until she left.

And in that time, he'd try to repair some of the damage he'd done. Try to rebuild a friendship that he'd always valued over any other, and that he'd had to force himself not to miss after he'd destroyed it. If he couldn't do that, if that was too much to hope for, Marc would just make damn certain he didn't do anything so careless and hurt her again.

Right now, that might just mean catching her if she slipped on the icy sidewalks. A Guardian's feet wouldn't freeze, but he couldn't imagine walking barefoot across the slush and snow as she was.

"It's bothering you," she said.

"What?"

"My feet. You keep looking at them." She wiggled her toes, gold rings winking. "You're not alone. It bothers Mariko, too. She thinks I do it to be like Michael."

The Guardians' leader—who didn't need shoes now anyway, trapped as he was in Hell. "Why do you?"

"Partially because I want to be like Michael." Her grin invited him to laugh with her. Probably every Guardian had admitted such a thing at some point. "But it also helps me build illusions. The better I know how something feels or tastes or looks, the more convincing I can make it. And I like the feeling, too. Cold doesn't hurt us, so why would I protect myself from it?"

"You could cut your feet." God knew how many broken bottles or sharp stones were hidden beneath the snow.

"And heal in less than a minute. You weenie. Afraid of a little blood?"

God, he'd missed her teasing. "Maybe. But you wouldn't like the look of my feet anyway, so I'll spare you the sight of them bare."

"I remember perfectly well how they looked, thank you—and they were nice. Long and lean, just like you. Every part of you was long. That was nice, too."

Was she still teasing him? Probably. But all that he could think was that her feet were just like her, too. Small, delicate, soft—and that when he'd touched them, kissed them, she'd gasped and shivered.

She wasn't shivering now. "Is that the girls' Jeep?"

He forced himself out of that memory, spotted the Cherokee parked in front of the small city library—about a half block down from Perk's Palace.

"That's theirs," he confirmed. "Let's hope we don't have to slay the bastard in front of them."

Radha slanted that *Don't say stupid things* look at him, and he realized that with her Gift, the girls wouldn't see anything that Radha didn't want them to.

But the girls weren't at the coffee shop—and he and Radha wouldn't be slaying Gregory Jackson unless they planned on breaking one of the most important rules that a Guardian had to follow: not to hurt or kill humans. One psychic touch told Marc that the kid behind the cash register was human, through and through. The demon might have taken his shape at some point, but it wasn't here now—and so Gregory Jackson probably wasn't the demon's default identity, the form the demon used when it wasn't shape-shifting and stirring up trouble.

"It figures," Radha murmured. "Finding him after one conversation would have been too easy."

She'd had one conversation since coming to Riverbend. Marc, on the other hand, had talked to about thirty people so far, starting with the county sheriff and his deputies. Still, he had to agree. It would have been too easy.

But it wasn't a wasted trip. Gregory might have seen something that homecoming night, especially if he was with Miklia. He might not know *what* he'd seen, but that was Marc's job—to figure out what fit and what didn't.

On the other hand, he could imagine quite a few places where Gregory Jackson wouldn't fit. Marc wasn't a small man by any measure, and it wasn't often that he had to look up at someone, let alone a seventeen-year-old kid who must have weighed the equivalent of him and Radha put together, all muscle. A small monitor hanging in view of the front counter played a classic football game, and Jackson kept an eye on the television while Marc showed his identification and asked for a few minutes.

"I have a break in five," Jackson said.

Marc glanced at the screen. "The '84 Orange Bowl?"

"Yeah." Jackson flashed a big smile. "Nebraska's about to go for the two-point conversion instead of the tie, and lose it all."

In other words, he'd talk when the game was over. Standing near the glass case of pastries, Radha narrowed her eyes on Marc, but whatever she intended to say had to wait. A black-haired woman in a flour-dusted apron emerged from the back of the store, drying her hands on a towel. No question where Jackson had gotten his height from. Her eyes were level with Marc's.

"Are you here to talk to my son?"

"With your permission," Marc said. "We need to ask him a few questions."

"Is he in any trouble?"

"No, ma'am. We're just gathering information."

"All right, then. And since you're here on the government's dime, you make sure you order something."

Radha tapped her claw-tipped forefinger against the glass case. "I want that."

A four-layer slice of white coconut cake. Jackson's mother retrieved the plate and slid it across the counter. "Forks are at the station by the window. Gregory will bring your coffees out to you."

"In about four minutes," the kid said, watching the game again—but even distracted, he made the correct change.

"Pfft. Worthless boy." She flicked his bottom with the towel, but it was easy to hear the affection in her voice—and easier to feel her pride.

Definitely not a demon, either.

The shop held a mix of mismatched tables and chairs, centered beneath long striped curtains hanging from the middle of the ceiling and drawn back to the corners of the room. A few big pillows and long benches along the walls provided more comfortable seating areas. Pop music piped through the speakers, and Radha danced her way across the floor with small steps and long swings of her hips. With a twirl of blue skin, orange scarves, and black hair, she chose a sturdy square table and sank gracefully into the wooden chair. Less gracefully, Marc sat opposite her, then watched her scrape off half the frosting before digging her fork into the cake.

Before taking a bite, she asked, "You follow American football?"

"This is the Midwest," he said. "I remember that game, and when Nebraska lost. I don't know if a thousand demons descending on a city would have caused the same amount of rage and despair coming from those fans."

"Ah." Radha nodded. "You should visit my territory during the Cricket World Cup."

Maybe he would. "But you follow the matches a bit, don't you? Soccer, too. Because not everyone in your territory follows them—and up north in my territory, it leans toward hockey—but every once in a while, you run across someone who *should* know the language of the sport, but doesn't."

"And it's either a demon or a liar. You're a clever man, Marc."

"Well, I enjoy it, too." He liked the strategy involved, the endless play variations. "And—"

He broke off as, beneath the table, a slight weight fell across his thighs. Radha's icy feet pressed between his legs.

She grinned at him. "I'm trying to warm them up."

God. Her toes wriggled, as if she were snuggling in deeper. Suddenly rock hard, he waited for them to wriggle higher, to torment him a little more. They didn't.

"And what is everyone else seeing?" he asked.

She didn't even glance at the few other people in the coffee shop. "My feet are firmly on the floor. I'm wearing black pumps. *Boring* black pumps. And your muscles are so tense."

Her toes rubbed against his inner thighs. Biting back a groan, Marc caught one of her feet. Still cold, but to a Guardian, that wasn't necessarily unpleasant. Not unpleasant at all.

"What are you doing, Radha?"

Making him pay for that long-ago hurt? A little friendly teasing? Something more?

He'd take anything she dished out, but he damn well wouldn't respond until he knew what she wanted in return.

"I'm having fun."

"Working me up?"

"Am I?" Her eyes began to glow, the gold flecks brightening, casting their own light. Not an illusion at all. A Guardian's eyes did that when they were affected by a deep emotion. "Can a celibate warrior be worked up?"

By Radha? She could probably get a rise out of a stone.

"Marc." It was a soft warning. "I'll cover your eyes."

She drew her foot back. Reluctantly, he let it slip from his grip—realizing that his eyes had begun to glow, too, but that she'd cast an illusion to conceal the green light.

Jackson set two frothy cappuccinos in front of them, swiveled a chair around, and straddled it. "So, agents. It's my turn, huh?"

Word had obviously been getting around. Marc wasn't surprised. But he did wonder what had been spreading. "So you know what we're here for?"

"Somebody died, and you think it's connected to Jason Ward. So you're here hoping that someone remembers some little detail, like a stranger hanging around." He rested his crossed forearms on the table, leaned in. "So, fire away. I can tell you now, I barely knew the guy."

"But you met him a couple of times?"

"Not officially met, but I saw him. He never came in here, at least not while I was working, but he was in the bleachers at a few games. I was benched, so I had time to look at the crowd."

"Was he at the homecoming game?"

Jackson's eyes narrowed, as if looking backward. Slowly, he nodded. "Yeah. I remember him there. But I didn't see him the rest of the night."

"You knew Jason was Miklia's brother?"

"Nah. Not then."

"You knew him from the video store?"

Jackson shook his head. "That was closed by the time we moved here."

Strange. Why recall one stranger in a crowd? "Why did you notice him, then? And remember him?"

As if uncertain, Jackson looked from Radha to Marc, before sighing. "All right. It's not like this is a secret anyway, right? Everyone knows that Ward had those fangs made. Cosmetic dentistry or whatever."

That had been the explanation the coroner had given. "Yes."

"Well, I saw him up in the stands once, cheering. I saw those teeth"—he glanced toward the counter where his mother stood, then leaned in and lowered his voice—"and it creeped me the fuck out. You know what I'm saying? The next game, he wasn't there at first. Then, in the fourth quarter, he suddenly shows up and I thought he was the devil or something. Stupid shit my mom would slap me up the back of the head for. So when I heard about those teeth, that there was a real reason behind them, it was kind of a relief." He sat back again. "I felt sorry for Miklia, though. That was rough for her. A stake through the heart—what is that?"

Probably the least efficient way to kill a vampire, so it was all about setting the scene, and the impact it would have on the family who found him. "That's what we're trying to find out. Did you see Miklia the night of the dance?"

"For homecoming? Yeah. They came in once, wearing those dresses. I think before they went to the dance, because they asked if I'd be there."

"Did you go?"

"Nah. Dances aren't my thing. I worked that night, just so that I had an excuse to get out of it."

So far, then, Sam had been the last to see them. "You were friends with her then?"

"Not really." The kid shrugged, but his emotions skittered about—a little uneasy.

"But you know her well now."

"Nah, I wouldn't say that. I see her a lot—she comes in here practically every night—but we don't talk much."

That uneasiness was still there, but Marc didn't think the boy was lying to him. He glanced at Radha, saw the confusion creasing her brow.

Delicately, she said, "We were told that you were bumping uglies."

"Truth?" Surprise and amusement sent Jackson rocking back with a laugh. "No, nothing like that. I don't have time for that. Moving

here, the injury—it set me back. But I've already got a postgraduate
year at a prep school lined up back East, so I'll have a chance to get
in front of the recruiters again. I don't have time for girls, especially
not ones into the crazy shit they are. Who said that we hooked up?"

Crazy shit? Marc met Radha's eyes. "We can't divulge—"

Jackson waved it off. "Ah, it doesn't matter. Maybe someone saw
us together in the gym last fall, back when she was looking for advice
about getting into fighting shape, building up her endurance."

What the hell? "Fighting shape?"

He nodded. "That's what she said. I was like, whatever. It's all the
same to me."

"Was this before or after her brother died?"

"After," he said immediately. "I mean, that was the only reason I
agreed. I've got work here, correspondence classes, my own workouts,
regular classes . . . I don't have time to be a personal trainer. But she
asked, and her freak brother had just died, so what the hell was I
supposed to say? She and her friends are a little freaky, too, but at least
they aren't going to the dentist for fangs. Oh, bam!—I just got it. Did
this other guy killed have fangs, too? Is that the connection?"

"Yes," Marc said. He'd told the sheriff the same thing, so the lie
would be consistent. But at last they were getting to the reason for
Jackson's uneasiness. "What do you mean, freaky?"

"Not the good kind of freaky, you know what I mean? No, they
bring in all kinds of books, sit around here reading them." He leaned
forward, lowered his voice again. "And I'm not getting into their
business, but after a while, I see a page here, a drawing there. It's all
demon shit. What is it called? *Occult.* Occult shit. They've been coming in for months, reading that stuff."

How many months' worth of reading would the city library have
on their shelves? "All of it from that little library?"

"No, that old librarian there wouldn't carry something like that.
Check this. I went in there once to pick up *The Lightning Thief* for
my little sis, and that old lady told me to be careful, that the Greek

god stuff might lead to practicing voodoo—then she called my mom, in case I didn't pass that warning along. The old lady got an earful then." Jackson laughed, sat back again. "Nah, Miklia and the others have some volunteer thing worked out, and they use the library loan system. She told me that once when I asked how she could stand volunteering for the old bat—it's just so that they have easy access to the books they want."

"Do you overhear what they talk about here?"

"They don't talk. They just text each other."

Marc's gaze shot to Radha's face. Her grin appeared, widening to the edge of a laugh. He could barely stop his own.

"Seriously?" she asked.

"Yeah. I asked her if she thought the music in the shop was too loud for a conversation. She said, 'You never know who is listening'— all serious and shit." He rolled his eyes. "Anyway. If you want to stay and talk to them, they'll probably be here around five thirty, just after the library closes. I should probably get back to work. There's a rush that comes in right at five."

It was almost that now. Marc didn't have anything more for Jackson, not right now. He looked to Radha. She shook her head.

"Thank you, Gregory," Radha told him. "Good luck with the knee and the recruiters next year."

"Thanks. If all goes right, in five years you'll see me throwing in a championship bowl."

"I hope it does." She watched him walk back toward the counter, then looked back to Marc. "Some days, I really like people."

"You don't usually?" Marc didn't believe that.

"Oh, I do. But there are some who make me wonder why the hell we're doing this: always fighting, seeing our friends killed by demons, always seeing so much crap we can't stop—and most of it stuff that humans do to each other. Not to mention outliving every human around us. And then someone comes along and you think: I'm going to get that bastard demon just so he can't touch this one."

"But that's not your only reason."

"It's never my only reason," she said. "But it feels good. Doesn't it?"

Marc glanced at the front counter, where the kid was behind the cash register again, one eye on the television. "It does."

Though she'd gotten her way, once again, she didn't grin as he expected. Instead, her eyes filled.

Crying? Tension and uncertainty took a freezing grip on his gut. "Radha? You all right?"

She shook her head, pressed her lips together, and turned her face away. After a long moment, she looked back to him—tears gone.

Or were they? With her, it was impossible to know.

But her voice was even and light as she said, "So, what next? Do we wait for Miklia and friends to show?"

No point. They weren't more likely to talk now than they had been before. At least, not until he had something concrete to approach them with. "What do you make of the physical training, the books?"

"Probably the same thing that you make of it," she said. "Miklia and her friends saw something the night Jason was killed—they probably saw the demon who killed him. Now they fancy themselves demon hunters. Maybe for revenge, maybe some other reason. So thank goodness for the Rules, yes?"

Yes. Those same rules that forbade Guardians from harming or killing humans also applied to demons, but with harsher consequences. Any Guardian who hurt a human or impeded a human's free will—even with an action as simple as shoving an unwilling human out of danger's path—would have to decide whether to ascend to the afterlife or become human again. A Guardian could break the Rules and live, but every demon would be slain. After a demon broke the Rules, there was no escaping the Guardian Rosalia and the powerful vampire Deacon; psychically bound to the demon from the moment it hurt or killed a human, the pair would find and slay the demon within minutes.

Even in the unlikely event that the girls did track down the demon, it couldn't hurt them. They probably wouldn't be able to hurt it, either, but Marc cared less about the demon's chances of surviving than the girls'.

He checked the sky. Ten minutes of daylight left. The vampires in the area would be waking up at sundown. "Let's talk to Bronner. If these girls looked for information about demons, and if they knew Jason was a part of the community, they might have tried getting it from him or another vampire first."

"And they might have mentioned what they saw."

Marc nodded. "Something sent them looking in the right direction. Maybe it was Jason himself, maybe he mentioned demons or Guardians to them. But if they saw something, the questions they asked might give us an indication of what happened that night."

"How far away is Bronner?"

"Halfway between here and the next town over."

With a grin, Radha formed her wings. They arched behind her, the white tips sweeping the floor. "So we fly?"

He usually waited for dark. "You can cover mine, too?"

Her hand flew to her chest, as if she'd been wounded. "Your doubt kills me. Oh, Marc. I can make you feel like you're wearing wings when you aren't. Of *course* I can cover them."

"All right, then."

He rose from his chair. She did the same, albeit more slowly, and with a glint in her eyes that could have been dangerous or mischievous. She dabbed her forefinger against her cake plate and brought it to her lips, her smile forming beneath the tip.

"You should ask what else I can make you feel."

She didn't give him the chance. Her tongue swept across the pad of her finger—and he felt a warm lick against his. He *tasted* sweet coconut.

Need rushed through him, the ache of arousal. He stared at her, his fingers tightening on the back of the chair, using all of his control not to snap the wood in half—then crash through the table after her.

Her smile widened. "So?"

"It's good cake," he said.

Her laugh was light—and so sweet. He'd suffer through any teasing for it.

"No." She came around the table, letting her fingers trail across the surface, her gold-tipped claw dragging out a long, rough note. "I meant to find out earlier, but we were interrupted. *Can* a celibate warrior be worked up? Now I'm coming over to see whether one can be."

To touch him—in the middle of a busy coffee shop, and yet hidden from them all. His fingers clenched on the wood as she stopped beside him. Her gaze dropped to the front of his pants, and he heard the catch of her breath.

"So. They can."

"I don't know," he said, voice rough.

Glowing again, her gaze lifted to his. He gritted his teeth to stifle his groan when she boldly cupped him through his trousers, then slid her palm up his hardened length.

"This is an illusion, too? I don't think so, Marc."

His head fell forward. Though everything in him strained toward her, he struggled against the urge to thrust into her hand. "No," he managed. "I meant: I'm not a celibate warrior. I gave up that idea a while ago."

Her fingers stilled. Her eyes brightened, shining fiercely gold. "Truly?"

"Yes."

"Good."

With a grin and a sharp rasp of her claw up his rigid length, she turned for the door, orange scarves swirling around her indigo legs. Marc watched her go, hurting in the best—and worst—possible way.

Good. He had no idea what she meant by that.

He hoped to God he'd find out.

Good, because she'd hate to ask him to break his vows again. *If* that was where they were headed.

Radha didn't know if they were, or if she *should*. She wanted to.

But a hundred and forty years had passed, and he was a different man than she'd known. All good, it seemed, but a few hours couldn't really tell her. For all she knew, he might be shacked up with a vampire somewhere. He might be in love with someone. She might get hurt again. Or worse, throw herself at him, and discover that she'd been a fool.

Solid, unflappable—but under it all, he was just a man. And a man's cock hardened when a woman fake-licked coconut icing from his finger. His arousal didn't mean anything except that he was alive and possessed a healthy libido.

And even if he did want sex, that wasn't all *she* wanted. Not anymore. She'd done the pleasure-for-pleasure's-sake thing. It had been fun while it lasted. But she'd changed, too. Now she needed more . . . and it could never be *just* fun with Marc.

So rushing would be idiocy. And they were Guardians; they lived a long time. No need to rush anything.

Unfortunately, Radha knew that she was very, *very* bad at resisting something that she wanted.

At least searching for this demon provided a distraction. Bronner lived along one of the rural roads, and they followed it west, flying under the sliver of a moon. Gently rolling, snow-covered hills passed beneath them. In the distance, the Mississippi snaked southward. Pretty. When the bare trees dressed in their leaves for the summer and green covered the hills, it was probably gorgeous.

Maybe she'd have reason to come back again, and find out.

The vampire's one-level house was situated among a small scattering of homes—mostly humans, Marc told her. Best not to let them see two winged people landing in Bronner's backyard. To conceal their arrival, she concentrated on the illusion of complete invisibility: no sound, no evidence of their footsteps through the snow, no lingering scent of coconut from her mouth.

Another scent hit her almost immediately: blood. Not surprising, given that this was a vampire's home and that they usually fed from each other just after waking—but, given that it smelled like human blood, disturbing.

And a moment later, another scent: human death.

Marc smelled it, too. His jaw tightened, gaze searching the windows of the house. "Can anyone see us?"

"No."

He vanished his wings. A sword appeared in his left hand, called in from his cache of weapons. Radha brought her crossbow in from her own psychic storage. Their tips poisoned with hellhound venom, the crossbow bolts wouldn't badly injure a demon, but the venom would paralyze one. It was a hell of a lot easier to decapitate a demon if it couldn't run away.

They reached the back door. Marc cocked his head, listening for noises from inside.

"I'm concealing our voices, our footsteps," she said. "And I'll conceal the noise when you break open that door."

He nodded, then glanced down at her feet. "Put your shoes on. Something that won't leave a mark."

"What?"

"If a human is dead, I have to call in the sheriff. They'll look for prints. Unless your illusions can cover up real physical evidence, you can't go in with bare feet."

That made sense. In her own territory, she didn't bother—but she also rarely worked with local law enforcement. This was Marc's territory, though, so she'd follow his lead. A pair of flip-flops wouldn't confine her toes. She hated shoes that did.

Marc picked the lock instead of breaking the door down. The scent of death intensified. Quietly, they slipped into a darkened mudroom, then a tiny, bare kitchen. A bucket of cleaning supplies sat on the counter. No plates, pans, or evidence of food. There never was in a vampire's house. Marc's psychic sweep pushed against her shields.

"Do you sense anyone?"

She sent out her own soft probe, searching for any sign of life. "Nothing."

"They sleep in the basement." He entered the hallway leading to the front of the home, passing a bathroom, an empty bedroom. He paused at the edge of the living room, vanished his sword. "God damn it."

Oh. Radha stopped next to him, her breath escaping on a long, heavy sigh. A woman lay between the end of a sofa and the low coffee table, eyes open, her features already locked in the waxy rigidity of death. Middle-aged, dressed in khaki pants, tennis shoes, and yellow latex gloves, she looked like a housewife going about her daily routine. Blood stained the beige carpet beneath her head, a dark pool that must have been congealing for at least a few hours.

As Marc started toward the body, Radha glanced around the room. Nothing broken, nothing disturbed. The front door hadn't been forced. The heavy drapes over the south-facing picture window were wide open. Strange, that. She didn't know any vampires who weren't careful about closing each curtain in the house every morning, even if they slept in a windowless room. Frowning, she walked around the sofa—stopped behind it. Oh, no.

"Marc."

Crouched beside the woman, he looked up. "What did you find?"

"Vampire ash. Two piles, I think. Jewelry." She bent, sifted through the sandy remains, selected a man's signet ring and showed it to him. "Did Bronner wear this?"

Jaw clenching, Marc nodded.

"A woman's ring is here, too. A set of earrings. No clothes." Sick to her stomach, she glanced toward the center of the living room again. Hairs and blood clung to the nearest corner of the coffee table. "What happened here? Did this woman drag them up here into the sun, and then . . . trip? Hit her head?"

"I don't think so." He slid up the woman's short sleeves, revealing the faint discoloration ringing her upper arms. "I think she was grabbed, pushed."

Pushed. Not the most efficient way of killing someone. Her gaze settled on the woman's gloves, and she recalled the cleaning supplies in the kitchen. "Maybe she was here to work and surprised someone.

But when? A demon couldn't have done this to her, not without Deacon and Rosalia being called to slay him—and you'd have sensed them coming."

If not a demon, then a vampire or a human. Vampires didn't *have* to follow the Rules forbidding demons from killing humans, though most knew better than to try. And in many vampire communities, leadership was determined by strength; Guardians didn't interfere with vampire power struggles. If another vampire wanted to take Bronner's place, no Guardian would slay the vampire for killing him. Marc and Radha *would* slay any vampire who killed a human, however.

But if she'd been killed after the sun had risen, a vampire couldn't have done it.

Gently, Marc tested the woman's joints. "She's cold, and almost in full rigor. At least this morning, maybe earlier."

So maybe a vampire, maybe not.

He rose to his feet. "Stay here, make sure no one sees anything through the windows. I'll check out the basement."

It only took him a few moments. Radha had time to vanish all of the ash and jewelry into her psychic storage before he returned, his mouth a tight line of frustration.

"Blood on the bed, the stairs. They were killed down there, dragged up here—the blood trail down the hall was ashed by the sun. The basement door locks from the inside. A reinforced door and lock, but it was bashed down. A human couldn't have done that. Most vampires couldn't. You or I could."

"And a demon could," Radha finished for him. When he nodded, she said, "Do we contact the other vampires in the community, tell them about Bronner?"

"Not yet. You vanished the ash?"

"Yes."

"Good. I left the blood. There's nothing in the DNA that looks different from a human's, and if a human did this, maybe there's a fingerprint, a hair, or something for the courts to nail them with. Did you touch anything?"

She mentally reviewed her steps. "The jewelry, but that's in my cache now."

"All right." He called in a cell phone, began typing out a message. "I'm going through Special Investigations, asking them to leave an anonymous tip for the sheriff. I'll call the county coroner myself. He knew Bronner, knew what he was and was able to keep quiet about it, so I'll let him know I've got the ash, that I need to know the result of the exam as quickly as possible. The sheriff will probably list Bronner and his partner as missing, though."

"You think a human did it," Radha realized. "Despite the bashed-in lock."

"I'm leaning that way. If he was awake, Bronner wouldn't have still been in bed, naked, while someone broke into the basement. But we'll have a better idea whether a vampire *could* have done it if the coroner can give us a time of death. That'll take him a couple of hours tonight, so I'll arrange to meet with him as soon as he's done with the autopsy. The vampire community can wait until then."

"Do you know the coroner?"

"No. But Bronner trusted him."

"Do you?"

"No. I haven't met him. And Bronner said he had the coroner in his pocket. That says 'payout' to me. How many demons with money have you known?"

"All of them," Radha said. "You think they got together and did this?"

"No. But I do wonder about any man that can be bought, even if that money comes from a good man like Bronner." He snapped the phone shut. "Ready? We can't let anyone see us leave."

"I've got that covered. What are we doing until we meet with the coroner?"

"We're going to let the sheriff do his job. My place is a fifteen-minute flight away. We'll wait there. I want to step back for a few hours, do a little research and see if anything anyone told me today doesn't fit. Then take another look at everything, see if there's anything I haven't been seeing."

His gaze fell on the woman's body, her sightless eyes. Finally, shaking his head, he turned away.

"God damn it," he said again.

CHAPTER 4

About a hundred miles north, Marc's modest, cottage-style house sat atop a wooded rise overlooking the river. Though small, the two-level home had more space than many of the apartments Radha had shared with Mariko over the past century, but Marc apparently used it in exactly the same way they used theirs: as a private location where they could be themselves, no illusions or lies needed.

They all had private quarters in Caelum—or they had before the city crumbled—but to Radha, those rooms had never felt like a home, had never felt like *her* space in the way that even a rented apartment on Earth could. Nor did Guardians need the space. They didn't need to sleep, eat, or bathe, and they could carry everything they owned in their cache. Yet Radha liked to shower. She liked to curl up on a comfortable chair that hadn't already been used by half the people in the city. She liked to display little items that she'd collected, rather than hide them away in her cache.

She looked forward to seeing everything that Marc displayed, too.

He vanished his wings immediately after landing on his front porch, then removed his jacket and tie. He led her inside, rolling his white sleeves up his forearms.

"I'll be upstairs at the computer." Though they could see perfectly well in the dark, he switched on a lamp, casting a warm glow over the hardwood floors and sparse furniture. "I'm putting in a few requests for info from Special Investigations. They can access and compile data faster than I can—and I want a transcript of those texts the girls are sending to each other. Is there anything you need?"

For Marc to keep taking off his clothing. That was rushing it, though. She needed to get to know him again first. She needed to learn all the ways he'd changed before she could risk her heart again.

Then he unbuttoned the collar of his shirt, exposing the tanned skin of his throat, and she decided to speed up that learning part a bit.

"I don't need anything," she said. Just a little time to look around.

"All right." He headed for the narrow staircase leading to the second level. "I'll be down soon."

She watched him take the creaking stairs two at a time before making a slow circle of the room. A blue sofa with clean, contemporary lines faced a brick fireplace. On the walls hung a few oil paintings—all pastorals in bold colors. No pastels for Marc.

Radha wasn't fond of them, either.

In the corner, a recessed bookshelf held a mixture of histories and political thrillers in English, a smattering of works in other languages, and a large collection of essays and poetry in French. His native language, she remembered. He'd died in America, but he'd been born in a village in northern France. His family had joined a group of French emigrants who'd settled together in a small farming commune—and she supposed that even in America, French had been the language they'd primarily spoken and read.

A hundred and forty years ago, his accent had still been strong. She barely heard it now and had only just realized that it was all but gone. She'd expected it when he played the federal agent—like the suit, the right accent became part of the role—but even now, while entering his home, his native France played only a faint note in his speech.

Another change, but not a surprising one. How long had he looked over this territory? He would have to adopt a Midwestern accent more often than not. Eventually that would become more natural to him than the only language he'd spoken for sixteen years.

She thumbed through a volume before replacing it. No little keepsakes or baubles cluttered the shelves. On a table at the end of the sofa, a glass bowl held a variety of coins. Odd. Why keep them here? It would be far more useful to keep them in his cache. She had all kinds in hers, in different denominations and currencies—and some old enough to hold more value than they'd started with.

She picked through them. Euros, centavos, reals, rubles, yen, rupees . . . taka. He'd gone to Bangladesh? And recently. With few exceptions, *all* of the dates on the coins were recent. But why have them out? This wasn't the carefully itemized and mounted display of a serious coin collector. Did he just like to look at them? Be reminded of his travels?

If this bowl gave any indication, he'd traveled a lot recently—and he'd traveled widely, including her territory.

And that was fine. It wasn't as if Guardians had to let each other know where they went or ask permission. But he'd been so close . . . and she hadn't known.

Rubbing the coin between her fingers, knowing that he could easily hear her through the ceiling, she said, "When did you go to Bangladesh?"

The tapping of a keyboard stopped. His answer came, as softly spoken as hers. "A year ago."

Why didn't you let me know? But of course he wouldn't have. And she wouldn't have wanted him to. Not then. She'd thought he was still an asshole.

"Were you by yourself?" Such a weenie question. What she really meant was, *Were you* with *someone?*

"I was alone."

Her throat closed. Of course he had been. One look at him a week ago, and she'd known that.

She picked up a handful of coins, let them clink back into the bowl. "All of these places—New Zealand, Russia, the Congo—you went by yourself?"

"Yes." He paused. "Why is my going alone more interesting than where I went? Don't you go anywhere by yourself?"

"Of course." All the time. But when she came back, Radha knew friends would be waiting for her. "But I thought you weren't celibate anymore."

"Ah."

That was all? *Ah?*

"So?" she pressed.

He moved quickly. Across the floor above, down the stairs—within a moment, he stood at the bottom of the steps, regarding her with a penetrating stare. "So?" he repeated. "So . . . what? I don't know what you're getting at. You want the list? It's not long."

Violent rejection speared through her. No, she didn't want a list. She didn't want to know.

"I just don't understand why you're alone *all* the time. Working, okay, we all do that alone. But *here*? When you travel somewhere? Why then?"

"I don't mind my own company."

"That's the point! *Who* would mind it? They'd have to be an idiot."

Some of the stiffness left his shoulders. "And *you* aren't an idiot."

Sometimes. She sighed, lifted her hands. "I just don't understand it."

"And I don't understand who you think I'd be running around with. A human? There's a town up the road where I'll go have a drink sometimes, talk with some of the locals. I'll play a game of pool now and then. But if I plan to stay in this area, and not go around shapeshifted most of the time, I can't show my face too often or people begin to wonder why I'm not aging."

Okay, there was that. She'd had to move several times, too. No one truly minded a blue woman living in their neighborhood, because it wasn't worth getting out the pitchforks and torches for an eccentric who dyed her skin with indigo. But an eternally young one? That would cause more concern. So moving to a new apartment every few decades was preferable to shape-shifting every time she went home.

"And if you mean a woman . . . Hell, I'll just show you why." He crossed the room, pushed open the door separating the living area from the kitchen. At the refrigerator, he pulled a pint of ice cream from the freezer. "I bought this at the grocery a few months ago. There was a long checkout line, and a pretty woman in front of me who let me know she was interested in the dessert. Probably more."

Radha couldn't blame the woman. "Were you?"

"I was tempted. I'd just slain Basriel after chasing him for years, and I didn't have a single person to share that with." He set the ice cream on the table, met her eyes. "But I couldn't share it with that woman. I couldn't tell her anything unless I wanted to lie. So I wasn't all that tempted anymore."

And that was why she didn't want a list, Radha realized. Marc wouldn't be tempted just by sex. There had to be more, and so every woman on that list had meant something more to him.

Starting with her. "So what did you do, instead?"

"I flew east and spent a day walking along the Great Wall."

"That was better than sex?"

"It was better than feeling like shit afterward."

She'd had a few of those. "I suppose I'd rather have spent it walking along the Great Wall, too."

"Then you can go with me next time."

It wasn't really an offer, she recognized. He was just trying to settle this issue, to give a solution to his solo travel that would satisfy her. She knew he didn't expect her to take him up on it.

"That's a good idea." She circled the table, stopped directly in front of him. "Next time, give me a call. I'll join you wherever you decide to go."

Except for a slight clenching of his jaw that betrayed his doubt, he didn't respond—but he didn't back away or laugh in her face, either. In the silence, she reached for the ice-cream pint, pulled in a spoon from her cache, and scraped away the ice crystals that had formed at the top. Vanilla. She wasn't surprised. Simple, not too sweet, with the rich vanilla bean adding such wonderful depth. The perfect flavor for him.

She settled against the table's edge and scooped out a bite. "Why not a Guardian, then?"

He gave a tired laugh, rubbed the back of his neck. Done with this conversation—but she wasn't.

"Well?" she pushed.

Frustration flattened his mouth. "Who? Who's left after the Ascension?"

After thousands of Guardians had gone all at once, choosing to move on to their afterlife? Not many.

So he had a point there, too. "What about before?"

"No. That was about the time I pulled my head out of my ass."

What? She swallowed the ice cream she'd been melting on her tongue. "With the 'God's celibate warrior' thing? Only ten years ago?"

"Yes."

"Was it *because* of the Ascension?"

"Radha—" Now his frustration had an edge to it. "I don't know what you want from me. Are you trying to set me up with another Guardian, couple me off? Because I'm sure as hell not interested in that."

Neither was she. That was the last thing that interested her.

"I'm trying not to rush," she said. "I don't want to be hurt again, and I need to know what kind of man you are now. The problem is, I'm not good at going slow or at resisting something that I want. So I'm trying to find out as much as I can before I jump all over you."

His eyes lit like green flame. With a single step toward her, he leaned forward and flattened his hands on the table on either side of her hips, caging her between his arms.

Bringing his lips within an inch of hers.

The ice cream seemed to evaporate from her tongue. *Oh, yes.* This was what she wanted. This intensity, this focus, this heat—and Marc.

Glowing brilliantly green, his gaze searched hers. "So you want answers first?"

"Yes." Though right now, waiting seemed a more foolish choice than rushing.

"And it's a test to see whether I'm good enough."

Oh. "When you put it that way, it's not what I meant—"

"I know it's not. And I don't want to hurt you, either. I'll do everything I can to keep from doing it again."

And with that simple statement, uncertainty slipped away from her, as easily as a breath. *I don't want to hurt you.* That was all the reassurance she needed, wasn't it? Either she believed that he'd try not to hurt her or she didn't.

She didn't know everything about him yet, but she believed that. Maybe he would hurt her, someday—but if he *tried* not to, if he made the effort, that mattered more.

But he was already straightening, turning away. Fine. She'd lure him back. She reached for the knot tying the scarves at her hip.

"So, you want to know what happened during the Ascension?" He repeated her question before facing her again. "I almost went with them."

Radha froze, her fingers suddenly nerveless with shock and disbelief. *"What?"*

"Yes," he confirmed, smiling slightly.

Maybe he could smile about it. He'd had over a decade to get used to the idea that he'd almost chosen to ascend to the afterlife.

"Why?"

"Well, it was the ultimate test, wasn't it? How much faith do I have?" As if amused by the memory of it now, he shook his head, still smiling. "I wasn't even in Caelum that often, and I saw the Ascension coming. A movement, sweeping through the Guardians—half of them believing that just by existing, they were an insult to God. After all, if He takes care of everything, what does He need Guardians for?"

"*If* He even exists," Radha interrupted. Oh, but she remembered those Guardians. They'd been intolerable. She'd avoided Caelum as much as possible in the year before the Ascension.

The truth was, they just didn't know. Only their leader, Michael, had ever met any angels, when they'd passed on their powers and Caelum to him, along with the responsibility for protecting the Earth. Those powers had enabled him to create the Guardian corps, transforming humans who'd sacrificed themselves. Demons were fallen angels who rebelled against Heaven—but no one she knew had actually seen Heaven. That some power existed was obvious, but the source of it . . . ? Who knew.

Just to piss off some of the more self-righteous Guardians, Radha used to argue that the angels were aliens. She'd almost convinced a few with her illusions, too.

Good riddance to the lot of them.

"We'll debate that later." Marc grinned briefly, as if recalling their old arguments—or looking forward to another. "You know what I think about it. And you know that there were other Guardians saying that the humans needed more faith. That if their belief was strong enough, they'd have enough faith to defeat the demons on their own, that we were getting in the way. That humans didn't need us."

"And *you* believed that?" *She* couldn't believe he had.

"No. That was the problem. I'd seen too much, killed too many demons. I knew humans needed us. But I wondered if I *should* believe it—and I wondered if the reason I'd spent the past forty years being so fucking miserable was just because I didn't believe it enough."

Miserable. Her throat tightened. "Forty years?"

"After I came to Earth and became that celibate warrior I'd

always planned to be. And I did it well, Radha. If I wasn't chasing down a demon then I was searching for another. I never faltered. I never stopped hunting. I never did anything else at all."

How could that be? "Nothing else *at all?*"

"No. And at first it was all right. I had a purpose, I had a mission. I was happy to be carrying it out."

But doing nothing else? She couldn't wrap her mind around it. "Not even stopping for a cup of tea. A biscuit."

"No. I didn't eat or drink."

"Passing a few minutes on a park bench." Or half a day, as Radha sometimes did—especially if there were children about. Using her illusions only as weapons would be such a waste. If demons brought despair, she'd bring a little joy. "Chatting with the old men in a café."

"No."

What would he be unable to resist? Singing, perhaps. He'd sung often in Caelum, and he had a beautiful voice.

"Watching a musician on the street."

He smiled, shaking his head. "No."

"Did *you* sing?"

"No."

She couldn't imagine. Because everything she'd felt in his emotions a few hours before, that loneliness and despair—that was after *ten years* of coming back from that low. Despite every illusion she could cast, every silly thing she thought up, Radha simply couldn't imagine the loneliness and misery that he'd put himself through, the low point he must have reached to even *consider* ascending.

"No wonder Heaven seemed so appealing. If it's not really a space-ship," she said, and his low laugh seemed to break apart the icy pain that clawed at her throat.

"I didn't care about Heaven," he said. "I just wanted to be a Guardian—but I didn't want to live in Hell anymore while being one. And I thought that if I just lacked faith, the Ascension was the perfect way to prove it."

"But?"

"But then I pulled my head out of my ass, as I said. I took a look around Caelum, at all the Guardians there. Not a single one of them was chosen to become a Guardian just because they had faith in something—they had all *done* something. I saved my father. You traded your life for your son's."

And put herself at the mercy of a merciless vampire. Radha grimaced. Though she'd have made the same choice again, a million times over, she could only recall the teeth ripping her throat open, the horrifying pain—and she didn't like to think about it. She rarely spoke of it, and then only briefly.

"You remember that?"

"I haven't forgotten anything you told me—like pointing out that the Rules don't say a thing about faith. They basically say: Try not to kill or hurt anyone. It's the same with being chosen as a Guardian: It was never about what we believed. It was what we *did*. The reward for that was just fine. So I chose to keep on doing rather than ascending."

"But you decided to keep on doing it differently." No more celibate warrior. "You changed that."

"I did. I bought this house, a little land. I took a day now and then to travel. I started stopping for coffee, chatting with the old men, buying ice cream."

And began taking a few other steps, she realized now. Like working with Special Investigations. He hadn't always—and not every Guardian did. But it required him to keep in touch with other Guardians. That contact would lead to relationships with people who *did* understand him. Not romantic ones, but working relationships. Maybe friendships.

She hoped he wanted to cultivate this one again. "So it's better."

"Yes." His expression darkened. Not looking back at himself with humor now, but simply remembering. "A hell of a lot better."

"I wish I'd known. I'd have looked for you. But maybe you wouldn't have stopped for me, either."

"I'd have stopped for you," he said, taking her breath. "Now give me your next question."

He'd made this one so easy for her. "Will you come over here and kiss me?"

"Yes." But he didn't move, and his fingers clenched on the edge of the countertop, as if holding himself back. "You need to ask me a few more things first, though. Such as, How did I like Bangladesh?"

Oh. Yes, that was important. Bangladesh, and the other regions in her territory. They could easily travel back and forth several times a week by using the portals through Caelum to cut down the flying time. And they didn't have to spend it all in bed. He could fight at her side while she patrolled her territory, and she'd do the same here with him. Partners, of a sort . . . and she'd love to hunt with him.

"How did you like it?"

"It was the worst trip I've taken," he said, squeezing her heart almost to nothing. "There I was, hot, odors all around me—from the food, the flowers, the people—and color everywhere. I spent three days walking through the jungle, the cities, flying across the plains. I couldn't appreciate a damn bit of it. Because I'd done a good job of putting you out of my head, but there . . . I only wondered whether you'd walked the same roads before. I wondered what you thought when you saw something, how your perception would be different from mine. I wondered what you'd say. And so I spent the whole trip wishing you were with me."

Her heart filled again, too fast. She blinked away the stinging in her eyes. "When you come again, I'll tell you what I see."

"Good. Now ask if I'll do much more than kiss you tonight."

He'd better. "Will you?"

"No," he said, but disappointment couldn't touch her, not when his eyes glowed so intensely green. He *wanted* to. That mattered more. "Because as it stands now, that list of mine begins and ends with you. I don't mind keeping it that way."

Only her. Astonishment roiled into fierce possession. Only *hers.*

And it was stupid, so stupid—but she was glad of it. She'd been the only one to mean something to him. She wished he'd been happier in his life, that he hadn't been lonely, but if this was how they'd ended up . . . Radha wasn't sorry that it had been her.

"So I'll kiss you, but I don't want to rush to the bed. I want you to be sure of me first. *Absolutely* sure," he emphasized when she opened her mouth. "That takes more than a few hours, and I'd prefer to wait than to see you hurt, if you realize you made a mistake. And on my end . . . I want to savor you. I want to find out what you like a little bit at a time, learn every inch of you. Even if that means a year passes before I'm inside you again."

A year of waiting? Oh, no. She wouldn't survive the frustration. "I'll die. You'll kill me."

His *grin* killed her. "It'll be fun."

Yes, it would be. Because she'd tease the hell out of him in return, and she loved doing that. She loved the way he took it.

"Now ask me if I'll see that you're satisfied tonight, and every night while we're building up to it," he said. "Unless I'm misreading you—and after you leave, you don't plan to come back, and you don't want me to visit you there."

Satisfied. Her anticipation mounted. "You're not misreading me."

"Good." Despite the relief in his reply, his tension increased. "Now I've got a question. What are you here for? Are you hiding? Tell me how to help you."

He still thought she was in trouble? And he wanted to fix it for her. God, that was so hot. Confidence, strength, and protection, in one sexy package.

"I'm not hiding. I saw you in Caelum last week, and I was worried about you."

"You were?" Clearly taken aback, he shook his head. "Why?"

"Because you looked like you thought the world was ending."

His surprise rolled into a laugh. "Ah. It feels like that sometimes."

"But you don't really think it will?"

"Not as long as I'm standing."

Not arrogance, just an intention to fight to the end and come out on top. God, that was sexy, too. And it was exactly what she planned to do.

He studied her face, as if gauging her through this new perspective. "You know I'm all right."

"Yes."

And getting better. A *lot* better, as soon as he kissed her. If he didn't soon, she'd take matters into her own hands.

"So you're done here. You could leave," he said.

"Yes."

"But you haven't." His fingers clenched on the counter's edge again, hard enough to crack the tile. "Radha, when I kiss you—I'm assuming you want me to. I'll assume that's true until you tell me it's not. You understand that? I can't hold back with you. I'm only doing it now because I have to be sure. I have to be absolutely sure."

So he wouldn't hurt her again.

"I'm sure," she said.

He *didn't* hold back. But he came slowly, so slowly, holding her gaze with every step. Her heart thundered as he bent his head toward hers again.

"I'm only surprised that *you* held back," he murmured.

So was she. Breathless, she said, "I didn't want to take advantage of you again. I want you to be sure, too. But as soon as you kiss me, all bets are off."

"All right, then."

He framed her face with his hands, his callused palms cupping her cheeks. Her breath shuddered. His lips opened over hers, hot, immediately searching. *Finally.* Joy swept aside the need, sweet and light, and she laughed against his mouth. Marc. She felt his smile, the curve of his lips, then he licked lightly into her mouth and desire came crashing back, stronger, hotter. Moaning, she rose onto her toes, trying to get closer.

No waiting. She needed him now. *Now.*

Her fingers fisted in his hair. The table skidded back as she pushed off it, leaping onto him. Her legs wrapped around solid muscle at his waist. So long and lean. So hard everywhere. Clinging to him, mouths fused, she rubbed against his aroused length.

His groan fueled her need. She deepened the kiss and tasted him, vanilla and wet heat. Rough hands dropped to her thighs, his fingers spreading over bare skin.

She tore her mouth from his, panting. "Higher."

His hair disheveled by her fingers, eyes shining with need, he carried her to the table again. "Slower."

Foolish man. He could try.

He set her on the table, the surface cool against the backs of her thighs. Deliberately, Radha lay back, spreading herself out before him.

She grinned wickedly. "Did you like the ice cream?"

Without giving him the chance to reply, she formed the illusion: a scoop of vanilla at the juncture of her thighs, melting from the heat of her flesh. Marc, kneeling between her legs, holding her open and gently lapping. She made him taste it, sweet and cold.

His body stiffened, gaze fixed on the scene before him. Slowly, his eyes lifted to meet hers. His voice was low and rough. "That's how I'll satisfy you this time."

God, yes. Her back arched, offering her entire body to him, his to feast from.

"But you've got it wrong." He stepped between her legs, through the Marc kneeling in her illusion. "When my tongue's on you, I could never be so dainty."

And he wasn't. Not when his mouth found hers again. Not when he slowly kissed his way down her body, learning every inch and coming back for another taste. Not when he knelt, unleashed his hunger, burning her alive.

But she wasn't satisfied, not just by that. And not by sucking her fingers into her mouth, casting tactile illusions that made him stiffen and groan while he fed from her. Not until he was solid against her tongue, shuddering as he shouted her name—without a single illusion between them, just pleasure that was perfect and real. Not until he said dazedly, "I'll never last a year."

Then was she satisfied. But only for now.

CHAPTER 5

The coroner would have probably been too easy.

Special Investigations hadn't been able to send Marc everything he'd asked for by the time he'd arranged to meet Dr. Richard Brand at the county morgue, but they'd come through with a substantial background. The info on Brand had been squeaky-clean—not even a speeding ticket to his name, or an indication of a payout from Bronner in his financials. For a man of sixty, that perfect record was a hell of an accomplishment, and enough to raise Marc's suspicions a little more. Demons with fake identities often kept their backgrounds spotless.

At four o'clock in the morning, no one was around to question how Marc and Radha traveled from Riverbend to the county seat without a car. Silver-haired and robust with health, Brand met them at the morgue's receiving doors. His mind was shielded.

For a moment, Marc considered blasting through those mental blocks to see if a demon lay beneath. He held out his hand instead.

Beside him, Radha tensed and stepped forward, leaving behind an image of the suited Special Agent Bhattacharyya. Demon or not,

Brand wouldn't see the crossbow she called in, her slick movement, or the bolt she held an inch from the man's temple when his hand extended to Marc's. Ready to fire, if Brand attacked.

He clasped Marc's hand, shook. Warm skin, not hot like a demon's, not cold like a vampire's.

Human.

Damn it. Marc glanced at Radha, and with a sigh, she backed down and returned to the position that her illusory double stood in.

Through wire-rimmed lenses, Brand studied Marc's face. "You're not cold enough to be a vampire. What are you?"

If the man already knew about vampires, no harm in telling him the rest. Especially since Marc might have reason to work with him again in the future.

"A Guardian," he said, and when Brand looked to Radha, she formed her wings and added, "Me, too."

"Guardian," Brand repeated softly, his gaze tracing the arch of her wings before she vanished them again. "My grandfather always said you were out there. I wasn't sure whether to believe him."

"Your grandfather?" Marc asked.

"Abram Bronner." The man must have seen Marc's surprise. "He didn't tell you."

Some of the lines on the man's face weren't just age, Marc realized, but grief and exhaustion. "He said you took a payout."

"Ah, well." Turning, Brand preceded them inside and down a short corridor, hard-soled shoes slapping against the concrete floor. "He probably said that to protect the family, so that no vampire could use us against him if they decided to challenge his leadership. We always protected him in return—a Brand tradition, with one of us always in position to help keep the community hidden. My grand-daughter would have been next, to her dismay. After tales of Guard-ians, she was more interested in becoming one of you . . . and especially when she heard that one came to town a few months ago. That was you? My grandfather said you killed the demon."

He'd slain *a* demon shortly afterward. He wasn't convinced it was the demon who'd murdered Jason Ward.

"I was here for a bit," Marc said. "I took a look into Jason's coffin, made certain he had been a vampire."

Brand shook his head. "I'll admit, the one time I ever really became angry at Jess was when I found out she'd been telling the Ward girl that her brother had been transformed. Teasing her with it, I think, knowing the girl wouldn't believe her."

Jess . . . ? Marc put it together. "Jessica—she's in high school and drives a Cherokee? She's your granddaughter?"

"Miklia's friend?" Radha's surprise echoed his.

"That's her," Brand said. "And I was angry at first, but after Jason was killed, I kept the truth from the Wards. By then, though, Miklia knew what he was . . . there was no one else for her to go to but Jess. And Jess was shocked by it, too, needed some reassurance of her own."

And now his granddaughter was more interested in becoming a Guardian. That explained the training, then, and the books they'd been reading at Perk's Palace—and how Miklia had become friends with the girls she'd once called the Brainless Bitches. Jessica must have shared the truth with Ines and Lynn, too.

"Not that it matters now," Brand continued. "They've both lost any connection to the community—Miklia to her brother, and Jess to . . ." The lines in the old man's face deepened. "You saw the remains? You're sure it was him?"

"We found his ring."

At Marc's mention of it, Radha called Bronner's ring and his partner's jewelry into her palm from her cache. She carefully wiped them free of ash before showing them to Brand.

With watery eyes, the man nodded. "That's his. So let's try to find out who did this."

He led them into a small examination room. Concrete floors, a long metal table, instruments, and recorders. Paperwork covered a small desk. Brand must have already finished his examination. All that remained was the smell of blood, death, and disinfectant.

"Were you able to identify the woman?"

Brand nodded. "Marnie Weaver. She's a local. My grandfather paid her to come in twice a week, and she has been for the past twenty years. Nice girl—woman now. I've known her since she was just a young one. She never asked questions, but I don't know. Maybe she'd figured it all out."

"Were you able to get a fix on the time of death?"

"Not the time you're looking for. Sunrise this morning was at seven-oh-four. Considering how cold my grandfather always kept the house, I'd put it anywhere between six and eight."

Damn it. That time couldn't tell him definitively whether a vampire or human had been responsible. But he realized Brand had more to tell him.

The old man sank into a chair, heaved a sigh. "A neighbor saw her car pulling up to the house this morning, though. At seven thirty."

After the sun had risen. Marc glanced at Radha, saw the dismay in her eyes. A human, then. Someone that he and Radha couldn't physically catch or kill—someone they couldn't even *touch* if the person didn't want to be touched. Not without breaking the Rules. Exposing that person, however . . . that they could do. As soon as they knew who the hell it was.

Unfortunately, Marc thought he *did* know.

"I know what that means." Brand looked from Marc to Radha. "It wasn't a vampire hoping to take over the community. Tell me that you'll catch this demon bastard."

A demon couldn't have done it, either. "If a demon killed this woman, he's already be dead," Marc said. Rosalia and Deacon would have slain him by now—but they'd also have let Marc know they'd been here. "Do you have any idea who else might have known about the vampire community?"

"Anyone else . . . you mean, *people*?"

"A human, yes."

Brand sat speechless for a moment, shaking his head. "No. Everyone who knows, they're related to the vampires by blood. They have just as much reason to protect any vampires here."

"All right," Marc said. If the man didn't want to see, he wouldn't—especially if that meant looking at his own blood. "You've helped me. Thank you."

Brand nodded. "I hope you're wrong about it not being a demon."

Marc hoped he was, too.

The last time Radha had visited a morgue, she'd been with a novice Guardian-in-training. She'd managed to fill a room with zombies and frighten the poor boy half to death before he'd realized they were illusions. If she told Marc later, he'd probably laugh.

Not now, though. That weary expression came over him again, the burdens of the world. They exited through the receiving door, into the dark, icy parking lot. Without a word, he formed his wings and launched up—but didn't go far. He landed on the roof of the nearby courthouse, standing at the edge to look down at the empty street below. Radha landed next to him.

"Tell me I'm wrong," he said.

He didn't have to explain. She took his hand, loving the strong, warm clasp of his fingers. "Using a stake to kill a vampire is the mark of a demon trying to set a scene . . . or the act of someone who doesn't know what the hell they're doing. It's difficult, inefficient."

"They learned quickly, though. All the others, killed while they were sleeping, then dragged into the sun." Jaw clenched, as if he still wanted to deny it, Marc shook his head. "Miklia was late to school yesterday morning. You remember Sam mentioning that?"

"Yes."

"Late because they were killing vampires, killing a woman. And not a one of them walked out of the school looking like they killed anyone that morning, even accidentally. Did they?"

No. And that was disturbing. They'd shown no remorse, no guilt, or any other emotion. With the vampires, Radha could understand it, a little. She didn't feel remorse or guilt for slaying demons. They were evil, pure and simple.

The girls must have believed the same thing about vampires—even though those vampires had been one of their brothers, their grandfathers.

Somewhere, they'd gotten the truth twisted around. Maybe a book they'd read, something they'd overheard, a movie or television show they'd seen. Maybe they'd heard of a vampire like the one who'd killed Radha, and that convinced them. Maybe when they discovered that the Guardians' mission was to slay demons and to protect humans, they mixed it all up, thought vampires were the demons, or that the vampires were possessed. Something.

Whatever it was, they'd taken it too far.

She gently squeezed his hand. "We both know how belief can be warped, so that people think they're doing something good—when in reality, they're just destroying other good people." Guardians and vampires were basically the same as they'd been before their transformations. Their personalities didn't change; only their abilities did. "But to kill a woman, and not feel any remorse—that means they feel justified destroying anything standing in their way. And it'll happen again."

"I know," Marc said. "And if it had just been the vampires—hell, it's not *right*—but I'd have just set them straight about vampires, make them understand who they killed . . . and then make them live with what they'd done."

"Maybe not punishment enough, but still punishment." And if the other option was turning the girls over to the vampire community, and letting them dispense justice or punishment . . .

That wasn't even an option. Maybe in some circumstances. Not this one.

"Yes," he agreed. "But for what they did to Marnie Weaver, that's not our decision to make."

No, it wasn't. That was for the human courts to decide, and he knew this territory and the law of the land better than she did. "What will you do?"

"Most likely, I won't have to do anything. There will be evidence. Someone will have seen the Cherokee. The girls will have left a fingerprint. There's no chance that four teenagers got in and out of there without leaving some kind of trace. So I'll wait. I'll head back to Riverbend and keep an eye on them, make certain they don't slay any more vampires. And if it seems like the sheriff isn't getting anywhere in the investigation, I'll point him that way. Maybe send him those text transcripts when SI puts them together."

"That's probably the best way." Radha rose up onto her toes, softly kissed his mouth. "This is one of the harder ones. It's not just the vampires, not just a woman—those four kids threw their lives away, too."

He nodded, focusing on her lips. Maybe thinking of the kiss she'd just given him so easily. "You have to go back?"

"Not right away. Rosalia and Mariko are covering the news for me. Nothing has popped up yet."

And that was the most efficient way of hunting most demons. They stumbled across some demons, so regular patrols around a territory were necessary, but almost all of the other demons Radha found came from a mention of something odd in the papers, a detail that didn't make sense, or a half-heard rumor flying around a city. It was all a lot easier now with computers, and with Special Investigations digging up leads from all around the world. Still, Radha had recently spent two months in London on another mission—and though other Guardians had covered her territory, she wasn't ready to leave it again for more than a day or two at a time. Anything else felt like ignoring her responsibilities.

So, maybe another day here . . . and then he could come to her in another day or two, when everything in Riverbend had been settled.

She looked up at him. "We'll work this out, won't we?"

His eyes sparked with green light. His kiss was hot and thorough. The perfect answer.

Until his phone rang. Marc groaned, held her for another long, scorching second before pulling away. Radha grinned, appreciating his reluctance to break away almost as much as the kiss.

"Hopefully SI with those transcripts," he muttered, glancing at the screen. He frowned. "Local."

"Someone you gave a card to?"

Humans, vampires. How many people had he talked with? But if someone called at five in the morning, it was most likely a vampire.

"Probably." He brought the phone to his ear. "Revoire."

Radha had no trouble hearing the other end of a telephone conversation from this distance, but to begin, there was only a brief silence. Then a young female voice: "Agent Revoire?"

"Speaking. May I help you?"

"My friend Sam said you talked to him yesterday. About Jason."

Marc's brow furrowed. "Miklia?"

"Yes," she said, before continuing with obvious uncertainty. "I wondered . . . if I could talk to you. About . . . a few things. If you could talk to me and my friends."

His face stilled, a quietly dangerous expression hardening his eyes. "About what you did yesterday morning?"

Another silence was followed by a long, indrawn breath. "Kind of. No. My friend said . . . said you might be a Guardian."

Had Brand already told Jessica, and she'd passed it on? Maybe.

She saw the same question in Marc's eyes, but his voice didn't betray it to Miklia. "I'll talk to you. What do you want to know?"

"Not on the phone. Not where someone might overhear."

"Where would you be comfortable? The library?"

"No. It's . . . it's closed."

Radha met Marc's gaze. The girl broke into a vampire's house, but worried about a closed library?

"The football field," Miklia said. "No one's here right now. And it's open."

Wide open, a public space, free of witnesses—and apparently, the girls were already there. Radha's instincts were telling her that something was off.

"When?" Marc asked.

"Can you be here in ten minutes?"

"Yes."

"We'll be here. Thank you." The girl rang off.

Radha shook her head. "You're in their way. And you can't touch them, defend yourself. Not without breaking the Rules."

Marc grinned. "And they'll stake me?"

All right. Put that way, her worry was ridiculous. He wouldn't let them get close enough to stake him—and humans simply couldn't match a Guardian's speed. He could run across that football field faster than any of those girls could blink.

His grin faded. "This might be the only chance to set them straight. If not for that, I wouldn't bother. I'd just wait for the sheriff to catch up to them. But once he does, no one will tell them the truth about vampires and Guardians. It will all be cast aside as nonsense."

True. "I'm going with you."

"Of course you are—though I'd prefer they don't see you. If they brought a gun instead of a stake, and they get lucky enough to knock me out with a head shot, I'd like someone to pull me out of there."

Because a bullet anywhere else would hurt like hell, might slow him down, but it wouldn't kill a Guardian. A bullet to the brain wouldn't kill him, either—but lying unconscious on a football field probably wasn't how Marc wanted to start the day.

"So I watch over you?" She liked that.

"If you have to. But I think it's more likely that we'll just need a few of your illusions to back me up."

Either to drive a point home to the girls or to scare them straight. Radha grinned. "That sounds fun."

"I hoped you'd say that." His own smile faded quickly. He tilted his head back, closed his eyes. "A demon could have impersonated her voice."

"And that's what you're still hoping for?" Radha had to admit that she was, too. "That he's trying to lure you there?"

"Yes. Or that maybe of all the girls, just one of them is. But if one of them *is* a demon, he shouldn't have chosen to face me on a football field. He should have chosen the protection of the library, of concrete and stone."

Because of his Gift. And when he turned his face toward her again, Radha almost didn't recognize the change that came over him. That quiet, dangerous look—but intensified. Marc, the Guardian warrior. Hardened with experience, determined to win.

So damn sexy. And, thank the heavens—no longer celibate.

She'd make sure he was even *less* celibate when they were done with the demon and she got her hands all over him again. Forming her wings, Radha leaped off the building's edge.

"Let's hurry, then."

Marc obviously didn't intend to mess around. As they flew in over the field, he lashed out with a psychic probe strong enough to pierce even Radha's shields—but unless one of them was a demon, none of the girls waiting in the middle of the field would feel it.

"All human," he said softly. "And no one else is here."

Damn.

But, human or not, Radha wasn't messing around, either, and she wasn't taking any chances. Marc could speak to these girls, he could do this his way . . . but he wouldn't be where they thought he was. Even Marc might not realize that she'd concealed his body and created a perfect double of him, an illusion that immediately mirrored his voice and movements—except that it landed five feet closer to them than he truly did.

Radha settled gently onto the ankle-deep layer of crunchy snow covering the field. This illusion required her to watch Marc continually, so that she could perfectly mimic his actual movements. By standing off to the side and even with Marc's double, she had a wide enough view to see both him and the girls, standing shoulder to shoulder at the midfield line.

Or what would have been the midfield line in real football, Radha supposed. She didn't know what they called it in American football.

The little blonde closest to her was Miklia, she remembered. The slim, dark-haired girl had been driving the Jeep—so she was Jessica, the coroner's granddaughter. The two other girls were Lynn and Ines, but Radha wasn't certain which one was the tall, dark blond teenager and which one was the redhead with the faint orange tan.

None of them carried weapons, unless they'd managed to stuff some beneath their puffy coats or under their knitted caps. They definitely didn't have any room to hide something in their tight jeans.

Marc didn't vanish his wings. With mouths half open, the girls stared at them—or at the double's wings, in reality. *That's right,* Radha thought. *Be impressed, you little murderers.* She added a subtle glow to the white feathers and his skin, then let a hint of a complex, spicy scent drift toward them. Different, exotic.

And that was laying it on thick, but these girls needed to understand right away that they had no real understanding of anything a Guardian was or did. And that when Marc told them, they needed to listen.

He waited, giving them the opening. If they dared to take it. Tall and strong, arms crossed over his broad chest and legs braced apart, he clearly intimidated them.

And he was clearly so *hot.*

Swallowing hard, Miklia reached for Jessica's hand, seeking support. Kind of sweet. Too bad they were deluded murderers. "You're a Guardian?"

"Yes."

"And you know . . . you know what we've been doing?"

"Yes." Marc's expression turned dark and forbidding. "I know you killed your brother. Why?"

Miklia's face fell. Disappointment and dismay leaked through her psychic shields. "You don't think we should have?"

"Guardians only slay demons. Not vampires, not unless they deserve it. Did your brother hurt anyone?"

Her jaw set; her lips formed a stubborn line. "He wasn't my brother anymore."

"Yes, he was. The body changes, but the soul doesn't." His gaze moved to meet Jessica's. "Abram Bronner, too. The same man. The same *good* man."

Jessica's chin lifted. "Can you prove it to us?"

"Yes."

She blinked. They all looked startled for a moment. Then Jessica collected herself, glanced at the redhead next to her. "Ines, you and Lynn need to be watching on each side of the field now, making sure no one is coming."

Ines looked at Marc again, her gaze lifting to the apex of his wings. "But—"

"We talked about this, Nessie," Jessica snapped, cutting off her protest. Clearly the leader. "You got to see him up close. Now you have a responsibility to uphold—or will you fail us and leave us all exposed, like you almost did when you left your book open for everyone to see?"

Oh, guilt trip, because someone might have seen a book open. This was a hard-core little group.

Ines's lower lip trembled. "No one did."

No one except for Gregory Jackson. But Radha noticed that Marc didn't point that out—probably to protect the kid. These girls would probably go after him if they knew he'd seen a few titles and drawings.

"Only because someone is looking out for us," Jessica claimed. "The book said a door would open, and it did, didn't it? We're on the right path, but only if you take the needed steps—and right now, those steps are not standing here. So, go. And you, Lynn. Now."

No more arguments. The girls took off in opposite directions, heading for the stands. So they *had* worked it out in advance—probably using the highest bleachers on each side as a lookout point.

Jessica looked to Marc again. "So where's your so-called proof?"

"You have it," he said. "It's your memory of everything they've ever done. Has any of it been evil? Name one thing."

They apparently couldn't. Angrily, they simply stared back at him.

"What have they *done*? Tell me why they deserved to die. Just one thing."

"They hide their evil." Miklia found her answer and immediately warmed up to it. Fists clenched, she tossed out, "They lie!"

"They lie," Jessica echoed. "Just as demons do. Isn't *that* true?"

"Vampires aren't demons."

"And demons sow doubts. Don't they?"

Oh, Radha saw where this was going. Marc wanted them to doubt their actions. Therefore, he was obviously a demon. Marc must have seen the direction they were taking, too. With a sigh, he shook his head.

"And they can take any form! Isn't *that* right? But you can't hurt us. So we're not afraid of you!"

"I'm almost sorry for that," Marc said, and he glanced at Radha. Debating whether to try something else, she knew, or just leave.

Leaving seemed like the most sensible option. These girls weren't going to be talked or scared into anything—and certainly not into accepting any truth but the one they already believed. Nothing she or Marc did would change that.

The sensible option wasn't any fun, but that was sometimes the life of a Guardian.

Jessica crossed her arms over her chest. "Do you really have *any-thing* to tell us?"

Was there anything they'd listen to? As if tired, Marc rubbed the back of his neck. Yes, completely done with this whole scene. Radha was, too.

"Just try not to hurt anyone," he said. "That includes vampires. That's all I can tell you."

"That's *all*?" As if stricken, Miklia fell to her knees. "Then you can't be a Guardian. A Guardian would have supported us, no matter what."

So much for the power of glowing wings and a mysterious spicy scent. She met Marc's eyes, gestured upward, and concealed her voice from the girls. "Ready to go?"

He nodded, but a movement in the bleachers across the field tore Radha's gaze away from him. Not long enough to affect the illusion she'd created, but—

What is that redheaded girl doing with a crossbow?

Ripping pain slammed through Radha's wing and shoulder from behind. She cried out, stumbling forward from the impact.

"Radha!" Almost instantly, Marc crossed the distance between them and swept her up before she fell. He knelt, cradling her against him, his big body shielding hers. Face white, his gaze dropped to her shoulder. "God damn them. Are you all right?"

Through gritted teeth, she forced out, "Fine."

A bloodied arrowhead and shaft jutted through the front of her right shoulder. It hurt—a lot—but that was what happened when a Guardian was stupid enough not to keep her eye on a deluded human: she got a surprise crossbow bolt.

It didn't matter. She'd had worse. Still, it would hurt more before it got better. "Tear it out," she told him.

Jaw clenching, he nodded, broke off the jutting arrowhead. Behind Marc, Jessica and Miklia stared at them, mouths hanging open. Her illusions had shattered, Radha realized. Another unfortunate consequence of a surprise crossbow bolt through the shoulder.

Jessica came out of her shocked stupor. "There's two!" she shouted. She fell to her knees beside Miklia.

"Bl . . . blue." Miklia was staring at Radha, stuttering from astonishment. "And wings."

"Shut up! And hurry!" Jessica shouted at her, ripping off her gloves and digging through the snow. "Ines! Come on, shoot!"

"It'll hurt." Marc reached for the feathered shaft still sticking out the back of her shoulder. "I'm sorry."

So was she. But it was the fastest way—she'd begin healing as soon as it came out. "Do it quickly."

He yanked. Radha screamed.

The ground shivered. Eyes glowing, the power of his Gift slipping through his shields, Marc looked over Radha's head to the bleachers behind her. Lynn was still back there, Radha realized—the girl had shot the crossbow at her. Aiming for the illusion of Marc, but an invisible Radha had been in the way.

Aiming for Marc. And Ines was still in the other bleachers—

A wet, horrifying *thunk*. Marc jolted forward. His arms went limp. Radha tumbled from his grip, onto the snow. A crossbow bolt was embedded in his upper back. He hadn't been struck through the brain, but through the spine.

Almost as bad. He couldn't walk. She couldn't fly.

"Grab them, Miklia!" Jessica shouted—and dragged a sword up from beneath the snow. "If you hold on to them, the Rules say they can't get away!"

They couldn't. And these girls knew exactly how to slay them. They'd planned it perfectly. Her own sword in hand, Miklia scrambled toward them, her determined gaze narrowed on the back of Marc's neck. No wooden stakes now, because to kill a demon—or a Guardian—they needed to cut through the heart or chop off the head.

Marc's power shook the ground. Unable to move, but still able to use his Gift. Yet if he hurt these girls with it—even inadvertently, while taking Radha and himself away from here—he'd break the Rules. He'd break them protecting her.

"No need," Radha whispered to him.

Rising to her knees, she circled his shoulders with her uninjured arm, easily supporting his deadweight. Miklia and Jessica were almost on them. Not fast enough. Radha could form a hundred illusions before they took another step.

She usually didn't like to remember past hurts, but Marc had a bolt sticking out of his back—and her illusions were always best when based on something real.

Discovering a demon's collection, bodies gathered from graveyards and put on display for his sick pleasure.

Radha and Marc burst apart in an explosion of putrid gases, maggots spilling out of rotting flesh. With a shriek, Miklia skidded to a halt, began gagging. Jessica didn't waver.

Almost falling beneath a demon's sword.

Too quickly to avoid, a blade sliced through the air, through Jessica's wrist. Blood spurted, melting the snow. Eyes widening in terror, she stared at the exposed flesh and bone. Then disbelief vanished, and she began to scream.

Her sword dropped from her real—and still attached—hand.

In the bleachers, Ines was reloading her crossbow, but Radha had a brand-new wound to share. *Surprise crossbow bolt through the shoulder.* The girl cried out, dropping her weapon. A moment later, Lynn did the same.

For thirty seconds, she let them scream and cry—and wanted to cry herself when she tore the bolt from Marc's back. She gathered him close, then vanished the illusions.

Always fun, except for when it was horrifying.

"Go," she told them. "Run now, straight to the sheriff, and confess what you've done. If you don't, I'll hunt you down, and I'll give you nightmares that a demon couldn't dream of."

They only stared at her, sobbing. *Enough.* She rose up, thirty feet tall, eyes blazing down on them with the fires of Hell. Lightning streaked the sky behind the whirlwind of her hair. The ground shook beneath her steps.

Her voice thundered. *"GO!"*

They ran.

CHAPTER 6

Radha hadn't been able to fly, but her one uninjured arm was more than strong enough to lift him, and her legs could run as fast as her wings could fly. Marc couldn't say that he was proud to have been carried off the playing field and into the empty high school gym, but the tenderness with which she'd held him as they recovered from their wounds more than made up for it.

Her injury had healed within a half hour, but she remained snuggled up next to him on a blue wrestling mat. As soon as Marc was able to, he slid his arm around her. He could have gotten up then. He liked this better—because Radha was there, and because he had plenty of time to think.

"We were almost killed by four human girls," he said.

"Is that the way you look at it?" She lifted her head from the pillow of his shoulder and peered down at him. "It wasn't even close. I could still run and carry you. You had your Gift. What were you planning to do with it? A dirt wave to ride us out of there?"

Not quite. "Just a wall to protect us, thick enough that they couldn't knock it down."

"Oh. That would have been simple."

He was a simple man. "I'd have used it if your illusions failed."

She gave him her best *Don't say stupid things* look. "Marc."

He grinned. "I have to consider the seemingly impossible. After all, we were almost killed by four human girls . . . who knew exactly how to kill us and had a near-perfect plan to carry it out. What are the chances of that?"

Her expression pensive, she pillowed her head on his shoulder again. "Not very good," she said. "It's odd, isn't it?"

Yes. And Guardians didn't ignore strange things like that.

They also didn't ignore that no human girl could bash in a reinforced basement door . . . or that one said to another, *The book said a door would open, and it did, didn't it?*

"Which book do you suppose they were talking about?" Marc wondered.

By noon, not everyone in Riverbend had heard about the shocking confession from four high school girls yet, but enough had that the astonishment and disbelief rippled through the town. By noon, Gregory Jackson was behind the counter of his mother's coffee shop, watching an American football game. Across the street at the library, children's story hour had just begun.

Radha had to give Marc another look when he held the library door open for her—but she supposed that a library was probably the most appropriate place for an invisible friend. No one noticed his strange behavior, anyway . . . not even the old bat at the circulation desk.

Which was why, in the end, Guardians were always going to win out over demons: Guardians kept their eyes open.

In the corner, a semicircle of three- and four-year-olds sat enraptured while a woman read to them about giving a mouse a cookie. A few adults browsed the fiction shelves. A teenage boy sat at a computer, casting wary glances now and then at the circulation desk.

None of them noticed when Marc called in his sword—no one except Mrs. Carroll, the crotchety old librarian.

But only because Radha let her see it.

Her eyes widened behind horn-rimmed spectacles. Her voice lifted, shrill with alarm. "Who are you? What are you—"

The blast of Marc's psychic probe cut her off, and beneath the cracks in the librarian's shields, Radha felt the scaly touch of a demon's mind.

The demon fell silent, glowering at Marc with narrowed eyes and pursed lips.

"It was perfect," Marc said. "You're everything a demon almost never appears to be: old, frail, in a position of service—a position that requires you to help people. The perfect disguise to hide from a Guardian, or to hide from Basriel when he was taking over this territory. But hiding just wasn't enough, was it? You decided to start meddling. And who better to meddle with than teenage girls, who could do any killing for you? Especially if they were trained to kill Basriel—or later, to kill a Guardian that they believed was a demon."

The librarian glanced at the children before looking back at Marc. "You won't do anything in here."

"Yes, I would. Because if you'll notice, no one is pointing at my sword yet. I could slay you now, and no one would see a thing."

"I don't believe you."

"Of course you don't." Marc nodded. "Radha?"

With the slightest adjustment of her illusion, she appeared visible to the demon—crossbow in hand, only a few steps from the circulation desk.

"Now you'll notice that no one is pointing at the naked blue woman," Marc said.

Naked? Not even. When she wanted to be naked, there'd be no mistaking it. But she'd have to show him later.

The demon stood, calling in a long, curving sword to each hand. No one reacted. As if emboldened by the lack of response, crimson scales suddenly erupted over its skin. Black horns curled back from the librarian's wrinkled forehead, and the demon shape-shifted—

growing taller than Marc, its body heavy with muscle. Its eyes began
to glow crimson.

"Come on, then," the demon challenged them.

Marc shook his head. "I just want to know about the book you
used to poison Miklia and her friends. Did you write it yourself?"

"It's a work in progress." The demon smiled, exposing long, dangerous fangs. "So were they. And after I kill you both, I'll just write
another one, and find another human."

Radha sighed. Why did demons always sound the same? *Blah
blah kill you all blah.* Neither Radha nor Marc was worried about the
influence that book might have on someone who picked it up, because
it had probably been written specifically to exploit the girls' individual vulnerabilities—but it might have information that would
expose the local vampire community.

She guessed, "So you wrote something like instructions or a
revelation, then left it for them to find. Or maybe you dropped it
out of your cache, and it seemed to appear by magic to them. Did
they think a Guardian was doing it? Watching over them, guiding
them?"

The demon's lips drew back in a sneer. "They all *loved* the Guardians. Pathetic."

The insult was probably as close to a confirmation as they'd get.
Good enough. They'd search the library afterward, just in case, but
if the demon kept the book in his cache, it would be destroyed when
Marc slayed him.

Not in here, though.

"Pathetic, but they almost took us out," Marc said. "I have to
appreciate that. And since you didn't do any killing, I'm prepared to
let you go. But you have to promise to leave now, today—to fly out
of town and never return."

The demon laughed. "Lies."

"No. I'm prepared to offer a bargain. If you walk out this door
now and fly away, we'll let you leave, no fighting or blood drawn.

Neither of us will fly after you. You just have to agree to go without fighting or drawing blood."

"Why?" The demon's wary gaze ran from Marc to Radha. "There are two of you. Though mistaken, you must believe you'll defeat me."

"I just want you out of this town," Marc said. "You've done enough damage; I won't add to it now by destroying half the library while we fight. I'll hunt you down another day."

"And you will back this up with a bargain?" The demon all but licked his lips. Anyone who broke a bargain would find their soul trapped in Hell for eternity—and so that meant Marc couldn't lie. It was a free pass out of Riverbend. "I leave, then. None of us draws blood while I go out. I fly away, and you don't fly after me. Is that the agreement?"

Marc nodded. "Yes."

"Then it is done. Fools. I know your scents now, but you will not know mine. I will kill you so quickly that you will still be screaming while your head rolls on the ground."

Would the bastard ever stop talking and just leave? Demons were even worse than fanatics. Irritated, Radha asked, "Kind of like this?"

Whimpering, a double of the demon's head rolled across the library floor, bumping along over its black curving horns.

The demon bared its teeth at her. "I'll hunt *you* down first."

"Back off, demon." Marc's expression hardened. "If you don't leave in a few seconds, you'll be breaking your bargain."

And the demon wouldn't risk whatever diseased thing passed for its soul, either—not when it meant eternal torture in Hell. Swords held at ready, it came around the desk, backing toward the door on cloven feet.

"I'll keep you hidden from human sight until you're out of mine," Radha said. "So fly away, demon."

Its huge, membranous wings formed as it passed through the door. Marc followed it out, vanishing his sword.

As soon as it stepped onto the sidewalk, the demon smiled. "I didn't draw blood on my way out. I'm out now. I could kill you."

"You'd be a fool to try," Marc said. "Because this is all an illusion, and I'm really standing behind you."

The demon whirled. Radha grinned while Marc shook with silent laughter. No one stood behind the bastard. Still, it wasn't sure. Carefully, it extended a sword, poking the air.

"He said he'd let you fly away," Radha reminded it. "So, go."

It hissed. "This isn't over, Guardians."

"'Bye," Radha said. "Before I remember that *his* bargain doesn't stop *me* from slaying you."

With another snarl, it flapped its giant wings. Radha watched it climb. When she glanced back at Marc, he'd already left her side, heading toward a small strip of bare earth at the end of the street. She followed him, tracing the southbound flight of the demon.

"We should have slain him in the street."

"That's not as fun." Marc glanced at her, smiling. "And it would never have left the library if we hadn't said it could fly away."

She knew. Still, she worried. Marc's Gift allowed him to haul dirt, he'd said . . . and the demon had already flown high and far. "Do you wait for him to land?"

Marc didn't immediately answer. His eyes had narrowed on the demon in the distance, and the power of his Gift became a low, gathering hum against Radha's shields. Strong, overwhelming all of her senses—she could almost *smell* the fresh dirt. Reflexively, she looked down.

His feet were bare, toes digging into the frozen soil.

"Radha," he said, "he's about to fly over an empty field, do you see?"

Flat, covered with snow. "Yes."

"Create an illusion that duplicates that entire area. The field, the sky, everything in between. Anybody who looks in that direction has to see the same thing they would now. Ready?"

The field, the sky, everything in between. Was he serious?

Her heart pounding, she created the illusion. "Yes."

The gathering hum of his Gift suddenly wound higher, a controlled thrust of incredible power against her shields. The entire field erupted upward in a long column, as if pushed from below by a giant hand into a rectangular tower of dirt and stone—directly beneath the demon. The field at the top of the tower hinged like an enormous jaw. Unable to avoid it, the demon stopped flying, sword drawn, as the earthen mouth opened around its body. Hundreds of tons of soil and stone snapped together.

Maybe *thousands* of tons.

"Marc." She breathed his name, awed. She'd never seen anything like his Gift. "Marc."

"Keep the illusion up," he said softly.

The tower receded again, carrying the crushed demon back to earth. The field returned to its proper altitude, but the thrust of his Gift continued, hardening now against her shields, no longer smelling of soil but of molten stone.

Then hotter, and his Gift pressed like a burning, heavy weight against her tongue. "What are you doing?"

"Burying the demon."

Far enough that it affected the sensation of his Gift? Past the Earth's crust? But she shouldn't have been surprised, she realized. She'd believed his Gift had fit him, the young farmer that he'd once been; she just hadn't known how well. But he was solid, so strong— and he burned within, too.

"How deep?"

"Deep. It's not Hell, but it's hot, and—he's vaporized now. There's nothing left to keep burying." He glanced at her, and his eyes were glowing. "Keep holding the illusion on the field."

This time the thrust of his Gift held a delicate edge, was more than just pure power. The field lifted again, but not in a solid tower. Columned temples formed from dark soil and stone. Elegant domes rose, covered in snow. Thin spires speared into the sky.

A smaller version of Caelum, replicated—and just as beautiful in dirt and snow as it was in marble. She hadn't realized how much she needed to see the Guardians' city whole again. Sweet, painful emotion filled her chest, and she reached for his hand.

"Thank you."

"I hoped you'd like it." A hint of laughter entered his voice. "Now look away, because I have to bring it down again."

No, that didn't matter. It wouldn't bother her or remind her of how much it had hurt to see Caelum in ruins. The important thing wasn't that Caelum had crumbled—but that it could be rebuilt again. Like a friendship. Maybe like love.

She looked up at him as the touch of his Gift receded. His arm circled her waist, and he drew her against his hard chest.

"Are you still invisible?" he asked.

"Yes."

"Am I?"

"No."

"So that's why everyone who drives by is looking at me like that." Radha laughed. Barefoot, and holding an invisible woman. "Yes."

"Was it fun, at least?"

"Oh, yes."

And this was definitely like love. Not that she was rushing into anything. No, she'd just put it off for a hundred and forty years—and somehow, she hadn't lost him in that time.

"All those idiots who ascended," she said softly, "I'm glad you weren't one of them."

His eyes glowed. "I had a bit of Heaven once. It wouldn't have been half as good without you there."

"Especially if you're really being probed on a spaceship," she said, and while he laughed she leaped up into his arms, wrapping her legs around him. Her lips found his, tasted, before breaking away again. "You look respectable now. No one will know that I'm about to rip off your clothes, back you up against that shop wall, and ride you until we both have our own little Ascension."

His body instantly hardened. His big hands swept up the length of her thighs. "Not for a month."

Radha would never be satisfied with that. And neither, she determined, would Marc be. She slipped the tip of her finger into her mouth, lightly sucked, and sent the sensation spiraling down. He shook with pleasure, closed his eyes.

"A week," he said, and Radha grinned, perfectly satisfied.

Then he lowered his mouth to hers and began to satisfy her again.